WWW.SIRENPUBLISHING.COM
EROTICA ROMANCE

SEX RATING: SCORCHING

This book is for sale to adults ONLY as defined by the laws of the country in which you made your purchase. Please store your files wisely where they cannot be accessed by under-aged readers.

SIREN SEX RATING

SENSUAL: Sensual romance with love scenes comparative to most romance novels published today

STEAMY: Heavy sexual tension; graphic details; may contain coarse language

SIZZLING: Erotic, graphic sex; explicit sexual language; may offend delicate readers

SCORCHING: Erotica; contains many sexual encounters; may contain unconventional sex; will offend delicate readers

SEXTREME: Excessiveness; many instances of unconventional sex; may be hardcore

Books by Lara Santiago

THE TIBURON DUET

JUST A KISS
JUST ONE EMBRACE

THE WIVES TALES

THE MINER'S WIFE
THE EXECUTIVE'S WIFE
THE LAWMAN'S WIFE

Single Title

THE BLONDE BOMB TECH

Coming Soon

THE PROSECUTOR'S PARAMOUR
The Wives Tales Prequel

THE MERCENARY'S WIFE
The Wives Tales 4

Published by Siren Publishing

The Wives Tales

Print Collection

Erotic Futuristic

In the year 2076, the Tiberius Group invades U.S. society, implementing a new plan for the good of its citizens giving woman new rules.

The Miner fights for his bride, the Executive pays a fortune to wed while the Lawman pays a pittance to marry. Three women auctioned off in separate venues to genetically bred strangers are uniquely destined to discover love in unusual places, offering their tale of seduction.

"With intriguing plots, sassy heroines, scrumptious heroes, and scorch-your-fingertips sex, Lara Santiago's Wives Tales books should be on every reader's must-have list." —**Leslie Kelly, Award Winning Author**

REVIEWS for Lara Santiago's
The Miner's Wife

5 Stars: WINNER: Ecataromance 2006 Reviewers' Choice Award. "*The Miner's Wife* is a story that will capture your attention and keep it. With an intriguing plot, engaging characters and explosive sex, this story has it all. Hannah's background is almost unbelievable. The quick and powerful rise of the new Tiberius Group has surprised everyone, especially the women. Their antiquated views of women and their place in society are in direct opposition to what she's worked so hard for all of her life. When she meets Brutal, she expects him to treat her in the same manner that her father and her previous husband did. But he eventually surprises her, showing her gentleness, caring and support throughout the story which she hadn't received from the men who were supposed to care for her. Brutal is a bio-genetically engineered man, who must have sex in order to recharge his batteries. I loved this! Brutal is definitely all man, strong, sexy and a hard worker. Not only does he need sex, he gets a better charge from his partner's satisfaction, and boy, does he satisfy! Hannah and Brutal are highly combustible, enjoying their sexual escapades and explorations. But what I really liked about Brutal was his caring attitude toward Hannah. He allows her the opportunity to work and show her intelligence and believed in her when no one else would. The pace of this story is just right, telling about their backgrounds then quickly moving to their relationship. With a little danger from Brutal's nemesis and a surprise from Hannah's past, you won't find one minute of boredom is this story. Add this one to your must read list and keep on the lookout for the other Wives Tales!" —**Trang,** *Ecataromance*

5 Angels: "Lara Santiago has created a wonderful story mixed with futuristic elements, uncertainty of ones emotions, and a splash of danger from an evil miner. Hannah is a feisty, charismatic woman that is passionate and has a personality that readers will love. Brutal, although he can be very deadly, offers readers a possessive and protective man that is honorable regardless of the arrangement between Hannah and him. The chemistry between Brutal and Hannah is explosive, mind-blowing, and quite tantalizing to say the least. As the plot intensifies, readers will be pleased with a couple of surprises along the way. These surprises will only make the readers love Brutal more and cheer for Hannah to have what she wants. *The Miner's Wife* is a wonderful story about finding love when and where you aren't looking for it!" —**Jessica, *Fallen Angel Reviews***

5 Hot Tattoos: "*The Miner's Wife* by Lara Santiago is a great book. I love the premise and plot. I could not put the book down. There is action, suspense, and romance all combined to make a reader's heart race. The well developed characters grow as the story progresses. Brutal looks like a gruff rough miner but he has a heart of gold. His tenderness and understanding towards Hannah started my heart to fluttering. Hannah is a modern independent woman forced under the new world order's thumb. The determination and strength she possesses helps her succeed in her changing world. The racy love scenes between Hannah and Brutal leave little to the imagination. An instant attraction bonds these two lovers and propels them into a sensual world of desire and passion. I would gladly live on another planet for a man like Brutal. Ms. Santiago has created a vivid futuristic story for the romantic. I can not wait for her next work." —**Ophelia, *Erotic-Escapades***

4.5 Blue Ribbons: "*The Miner's Wife* will take you into a future where women are reduced to mere possessions in a male society. Hannah's plight will have you empathizing with her even as you realize how much Brutal truly needs her, and not just for his sexual desires either. They're both wonderful characters who are wronged by the very people who should have cared for them. This story is powerfully moving and truly a delight to read. I can't wait to read the other two books in The Wives Tales series." —**Chrissy Dionne, *Romance Junkies***

4.5 Hearts: "This book is a never-ending adventure, and readers will find themselves wrapped up in the drama that Brutal and Hannah create. Brutal lives up to his name with a dark and sensual air that readers will love. Hannah is a free spirit who finds that maybe all men aren't alike. The love scenes are so hot, the pages almost burn with the heat. This is the first book I have read by Lara Santiago and Siren Publishing. I can certainly say that I will be on the lookout for more of this author's work in the future." —**Angel,** *The Romance Studio*

4.5 Kisses: "Lara Santiago has a refreshing and delightful writing style. Not only is *The Miner's Wife* a very creative story but her characters are mature and well developed. I really appreciated that while Hannah did not embrace what happened to her, she didn't place blame on Brutal, which allowed them to have a sweet, fun, and healthy relationship. The humor is perfectly timed, as is the action and adventure. Not only are the love scenes hot but they are also sweet and full of emotion. I highly recommend *The Miner's Wife* and look forward to reading the other books in The Wives Tales series!" —**Kerin,** *Two Lips Reviews*

4.5 Stars: "*The Miner's Wife* is a science fiction story about a future controlled by a corporation and the archaic laws that they enforce concerning women. It is a novel idea for a story even though I think I would probably be one of the first women to form a rebellion against the nitwits. There was considerable thought up into the universe that Ms. Santiago has come up with. There is a plausible explanation for the new laws and how they affect the female population. Ms. Santiago's characters are believable and very likable or despicable depending on the character. The love scenes for the most part are very, very hot. Brutal turns out to be a very gentle and caring lover when Hannah allows him to be. I am interested in reading the rest of the series to see if the women really do take to these new laws [or] if they rise up and stomp some bureaucrat's ass." —**Oleta M. Blaylock,** *Just Erotic Romance Reviews*

4.5 Unicorns: "Taking us into a world where women are no more than property and sexual tension relievers, this author pens an interesting story of a couple brought together under less than ideal circumstances. Hannah [is] a woman after my own heart even if she no longer has rights in her country, because she still shows spunk when she's not fainting. Her miner isn't half bad either because from the onset, he is willing to protect the woman he initially sees as an energy source and outlet for his needs. After making the best of their situation, these two become ideal partners in and out of the bed. With its action, passion and touching moments, readers will enjoy this [first book in] The Wives Tales Trilogy." —**Rachelle,** *Enchanted in Romance*

"I fell in love with Brutal Blackthorn in *The Miner's Wife*. He was a big ole sweet man who tried to be tough, but once he fell in love with Hannah, she was his whole world and I liked that. It made me all warm and fuzzy inside that a hero as tough as Brutal would become putty in Hannah's hands. As for Hannah, for having gone through what she did, she was an extremely strong, intelligent woman. She was in control of Brutal without him even knowing it, and I loved that! *The Miner's Wife* is the first book I have read written by Lara Santiago and it will not be the last. The storyline kept me spellbound and the romantic interludes of the characters were extremely erotic. In fact, I couldn't put this book down until I read the last word. Lucky for me, there are two more books in Ms. Santiago's Wives Tales Series, *The Executive's Wife* and *The Lawman's Wife*, that I look forward to reading! If you are a fan of futuristic books, or even if you aren't, *The Miner's Wife* is just a good, all-around read that is totally satisfying!" —**Talia Ricci,** *Joyfully Reviewed*

REVIEWS for Lara Santiago's
The Executive's Wife

5 Stars: "Once again Lara Santiago has written an intriguing and engaging story in *The Executive's Wife*. Having waited ever so patiently for this follow up to *The Miner's Wife*, I can honestly say it was worth it. Sophie and Matt have an explosive chemistry which is immediately apparent. Initially, they are concerned with the employer/employee relationship but once the Tiberius Group institutes its changes, all bets are off. Matt will use any means at his disposal to get the one woman he wants. Sophie's character may seem a little unruffled at first, but it is soon obvious that she's got a will of steel and will do anything in her power to help those that she loves. The premise of this story follows the previous in that Matt is bio-genetically engineered but there are subtle differences. The adversity that they immediately face in their marriage adds an intensity and urgency to their relationship which is revealed in their frequent lovemaking. In addition to all of that, this well paced story also has a lot of suspense and even a few surprising twists in the plot. *The Executive's Wife* is a must read for fans of Ms. Santiago as well as the Wives Tales." —**Trang,** *Ecataromance*

4.5 Stars/Hot: "The Wives Tales 2: *The Executive's Wife* was refreshing and scary at the same time. I'm sure someone in the world would love nothing more than to see women's rights taken away and Lara Santiago presented what would happen in detail. The fact that Sophie got the man she always wanted was good fortune, but life did not work out so well for her sister. I'm dying to read [Hannah's] story, but I was more than satisfied with The Wives Tales 2: *The Executive's Wife*. Sophie and Matt were dynamic characters that kept me turning the pages. I wanted to see more of them and the love they shared. Their sex life was stimulating and well earned. Matt's father was obnoxious as well as determined. The man just would not give up on his dream for his son. It was more like an obsession. I had to give him credit for his gumption. Moreover, he made the story more interesting. After reading *The Executive's Wife*, I am greedy for more. While I wait for the next installment, I plan to read the first Wives Tale [*The Miner's Wife*]." — **Suni Farrar,** *Just Erotic Romance Reviews*

4.5 Kisses: "Lara Santiago is a very talented author and the men in her books are absolutely to die for. Matt is honest, straightforward, sexy, protective and a loving alpha male that no woman could resist (or would want to). He doesn't hide from his feelings which is very refreshing and even shows his vulnerability to the woman he loves. Sophie is funny, kind, and a wonderful mate for Matthew. The heady combination of these two characters makes the intensely erotic love scenes even hotter. I recommend reading *The Executive's Wife* and look forward reading more pieces written by Lara Santiago!" —**Kerin,** *Two Lips Reviews*

"Ever since reading *The Miner's Wife*, I have been waiting for the release of *The Executive's Wife* by Lara Santiago. It was all I wanted it to be and more. Full of highly erotic and emotionally hot sex, I fell in love with Matthew almost immediately. Talk about a true hero in helping a damsel in distress; I love how Matt took care to keep Sophie safe but allowed her wings to fly, even if just in the privacy of their home. I thought Sophie intelligent and unafraid and I found myself more than once cheering her decisions. *The Executive's Wife* ties in and relates to *The Miner's Wife* beautifully. I love how Lara Santiago has written this series and I can't wait for the third installment." —**Talia Ricci,** *Joyfully Reviewed*

REVIEWS for Lara Santiago's
The Lawman's Wife

5 Stars/Hot: "*The Lawman's Wife*, book three of The Wives Tales, was well worth the wait. Ms. Santiago knows how to capture her readers and keep them entertained until the very last word and demanding more. Grace's character suffered a horrible sexual encounter when she was a teenager that left her emotional scared by sex. I enjoyed the way Grace was able to overcome the challenges that she had and was able to be a wonderful mother. There were times when Grace appeared to be naïve, but as I continued to read I noticed that she was doing everything to protect her child from harm -even appearing to be meek to the man she thought was her husband of convenience, Danny Cox. Jon was also a strong character overcoming his genetic enhancement received as a teenager, instead of turning into a sexual vampire he focused on keeping his sexual needs at bay with the help of medication. The sexual chemistry between Grace and Jon was sizzling from the moment they met in the elevator. Jon was aware of Grace's sexual history and didn't want to alarm her with his desire, but [imagine] his surprise when Grace turned into the sexual aggressor in their relationship. Just Smoking!!!! The action in the book was on point and well written. Nothing appeared to be out of place with this story. Bravo Ms. Santiago, for another job well done!" —**LT Blue,** *Just Erotic Romance Reviews*

5 Kisses: "Jon is a wonderful man, with a kind and caring heart. It doesn't hurt that he's also drop-dead gorgeous and sexy to boot! The manner in which he cares for Grace and Emma is sweet and will fill your heart with emotion. Grace has been through so much and her unwavering commitment to her daughter is beautiful while her own search for peace will pull at your heartstrings. The chemistry between Jon and Grace is undeniable and their love scenes are scorching. This latest installment of The Wives Tales is definitely the most intense and adds a good balance to the series. I definitely recommend reading *The Lawman's Wife* and feel that the entire The Wives Tales series should be on everyone's must-read list!" —**Kerin**, *Two Lips Reviews*

4.5 Stars: "As the third book in the Wives Tales, *The Lawman's Wife* definitely delivers. Ms. Santiago paints a picture of oppression and desperation for Grace and other women. Even with her painful past, Grace manages to be a sweet woman and wonderful mother and when Jonathan rescues her – both times – he is the only man who has ever showed her any gentleness. In addition, he's the only man to ever excite her. Jonathan believes he's only rescuing Grace because of sympathy but in fact, his feelings run much deeper. Their struggle to beat the clock to become man and wife, build a relationship and try to keep their little family together despite a sexual predator makes for one fantastic finish to this trilogy. This fast paced story is one that will draw you in and have you wishing for more." —**Trang**, *Ecataromance*

4.5 Blue Ribbons: "*The Lawman's Wife* is the final book in Lara Santiago's The Wives Tales series. Despite all the strides women have made toward independence I found this story shockingly thought provoking. I can imagine something like this happening at some point in the future. Grace is a character whom I truly admire. She does everything in her power to protect herself and her daughter and faces her fears head on. Jonathan is a genuinely honorable man. He's worried about his job's impact on their lives and seriously considers finding her another husband, one whose job doesn't keep him from home for months at a time. *The Lawman's Wife* is a book sure to cause a riot of emotions in readers and leave them with a warm feeling at the end." —**Chrissy Dionne**, *Romance Junkies*

"Although circumstances are bleak, the hot desire between Jon and Grace warms them, lights their lives, and leads them to a place of love and passion. [Brutal and Hannah] from *The Miner's Wife* are part of the story, and with *The Lawman's Wife*, Lara Santiago tells of a time fraught with strife and ugliness that might be, but, with people like Jon and Grace, will not last forever. I recommend it." —**Maggie Anderson,** *Romance Reviews Today*

"*The Lawman's Wife* is book 3 of Lara Santiago's The Wives Tales. Set in the future, it is the story of Jonathan and Grace, two strangers who met and comforted each other on a stuck elevator and who now have no choice but to consummate their relationship or risk losing things they hold dear. I was pleased to be reintroduced to Brutal, Jonathan's brother in law from *The Miner's Wife*. Jonathan and Grace had secrets but I was comforted by the fact that they loved each other, the good with the bad. *The Lawman's Wife* was an exceptional read. I can't wait to read it again!"—**Talia Ricci,** *Joyfully Reviewed*

ABOUT THE AUTHOR

Lara Santiago always loved to write. However, her pragmatic, analytical side got the upper hand at an early age and informed her she should be getting a 'real' job and not pursuing a creative writing career.

She joined the Air Force and spent her four years of service in Blytheville, Arkansas working nights in Supply issuing aircraft parts to guys working on the flight line. Her husband discovered her there and married her to continue getting his aircraft parts quicker than all the others.

Lara soon earned a degree in the field of Logistics—a word she thinks is very sexy. No logisticians will ever be the bad guy in any of her novels.

After the military, Lara spent many practical years working at a 'real' job, allowing her analytical side total free rein. Then one day, the characters banging incessantly inside her brain simply couldn't be silenced any longer. She bought a laptop with the sole purpose of writing a book to allow her creative side to express itself and to let all those characters out. Her motto…so many characters…so little time.

To those interested, Lara's practical, analytical side is now stuffed in a dark hole and only allowed out once or twice a month to pay bills.

When she isn't hunched over her faithful laptop, now with half the letters chipped off in her zeal to write as fast as possible, Lara enjoys reading, catching up on all her recorded television shows, and watching movies. Oh, and occasionally, she cooks for her family, too.

She hopes her readers enjoy her stories and looks forward to hearing from them—but only if they refrain from insisting she make anyone in Logistics a bad guy. ☺

www.larasantiago.com

Dedications

For *The Miner's Wife*

To my family for their unlimited support and understanding.

And to my Dad, the librarian who always surrounded himself with books and taught me it was the best way to live.

My first book is for you, Daddy. I miss you lots.

For *The Lawman's Wife*

I'd like to dedicate this book to my mom.

She is the perfect model from which all moms should be created. She's the template on which I based by own theories of motherhood: sacrifice, support, and most important of all…a great sense of humor.

Thanks, Mom, for always being there for me. Thanks for always being glad to hear from me. Thanks for understanding I'd rather write romances than mysteries.

Love you.

Lara Santiago

THE WIVES TALES

Lara Santiago

The Miner's Wife
The Executive's Wife
The Lawman's Wife

EROTICA ROMANCE

Siren Publishing, Inc.
www.SirenPublishing.com

A SIREN PUBLISHING BOOK
First Printing, 2007
Copyright © 2007 by Siren Publishing, Inc.

IMPRINT: Erotica Romance

ISBN: 1-933563-28-1

THE WIVES TALES
THE MINER'S WIFE
THE EXECUTIVE'S WIFE
THE LAWMAN'S WIFE
Copyright © 2007 by Lara Santiago

Cover art by Jinger Heaston
All cover art and logo copyright © 2006 by Siren Publishing, Inc.

ALL RIGHTS RESERVED: This literary work may not be reproduced or transmitted in any form or by any means, including electronic or photographic reproduction, in whole or in part, without express written permission.

All characters and events in this book are fictitious. Any resemblance to actual persons living or dead is strictly coincidental.

Printed in the U.S.A.

PUBLISHER
Siren Publishing, Inc.
www.SirenPublishing.com

SIREN PUBLISHING

Lara Santiago

THE MINER'S WIFE

The Wives Tales

Cover Art ©2005 SIREN

The Miner's Wife

In the year 2076, the Tiberius Group invades all aspects of society, taking over and implementing a new plan for the good of all U.S. citizens, especially the females. Hannah Brent is sent via cryo-freeze tube on a cargo spaceship to a moon orbiting Mars. There, she is auctioned off to a Thorium-Z miner.

Thomas 'Brutal' Blackthorn only needs a wife temporarily for sexual release purposes until he finishes mining his claim. Then he'll be rich enough to marry the wealthy heiress waiting for him on earth. He didn't expect the fiery Hannah to conquer his heart.

Brutal turns out to be the first man in Hannah's life to have any respect for her or her desires. He allows her to follow her dream even at his own expense. Will she ever want to leave him, since theirs is only a temporary arrangement?

The Miner's Wife
The Wives Tales 1

By Lara Santiago
Copyright © 2006

Prologue

"I want to see the fresh meat," the tall man said to the loadmaster of the recently docked space transport ship.

"So does everyone else. The auction's in four hours. Come back then," the irate loadmaster said and started to turn away. *Damn miners*, he thought, *always so eager to get a glimpse of the merchandise. Or fondle it, more likely.*

"I'll pay." The tall man quickly flashed a disposable credit device with a sizable amount displayed.

The loadmaster's shoulders drooped slightly. He ran a forearm over his eyes, smearing the dirt and sweat from his brow onto an already grimy sleeve. The tall man didn't move. He wore an expression of arrogance the loadmaster hated, but money was money.

He sighed and looked again at the credit device with longing before speaking, "I have to check the other cargo bay. I'll be gone for ten minutes."

The tall man smiled, as if he had known the whole time that the loadmaster would give in to his bribe, and promptly tossed him the credit device.

"Don't be here when I get back or I'll call the authorities," he warned, catching and pocketing the credit device.

"Of course."

"And no touching the merchandise."

"Right," the tall man said. He then turned and approached the first cryogenic unit containing a brunette female with a very curvaceous figure clad only in lacy underwear.

The units were open, but the stock hadn't been revived yet. The loadmaster paused only momentarily to consider the bother of being ten or more minutes late getting the cargo off the spacecraft for the auction. Ah, well, it was worth it, he reminded himself, fingering the credit device in his pocket.

"Damn arrogant miners," the loadmaster said and shook his head, muttering to himself as he stepped into the next cargo bay.

* * * *

The tall man looked over his shoulder at the retreating loadmaster. He smiled and then purposely ran his forefinger down the chilled cheek of the brunette in the first cryogenic unit. *No touching the merchandise, my ass*, he thought and smiled at his own defiance.

He considered the brunette serenely posed in the cryo-unit. She was pretty and had a nicely stacked figure, but he didn't care for her face. Too pouty. The man moved to the next unit, which held a very petite, young Asian woman. No. Far too childlike. He made his way down the row of cryogenic units, ticking off each woman in turn until he got to the one second from the last. She was young, but not too young. More importantly, for his particular tastes, she was a natural blonde, a rarity in this industry. She was also very angelic looking. Fragile almost. She was perfect. The tall man would only bid on this innocent looking creature whenever they brought her out during the auction. That was, if he decided to take a mail order bride at all.

Of all the transport ships he had checked out, this was the first time a woman came even close to fulfilling what he wanted...or desired. His selection was based on not much more than gut feel, but this girl just had a certain look he found vastly appealing. Her honey-colored hair was neither curly thick nor completely straight but somewhere in between waving down just past her shoulders. Her eyes were closed, but he made a bet with himself they were light in color. Her oval face sported lightly tanned skin and freckles on her pert little nose, but her mouth, which was her most delectable feature, stole the show on her lovely face.

Those full lips made him take a step closer. He wanted to kiss her, but instead, he leaned in closer to whisper in her ear, "I'm going to make you scream for me." And he fully intended to do just that, *if* he decided to bid.

The tall man smiled, well satisfied the money he spent to preview the women available this trip had been worth it, especially since he'd finally found a worthy contender for the role of his temporary spouse. He did not want to bid on one woman and then have a better one come along later. He hated surprises like that and was glad he had taken the risk of a bribe.

Whistling to himself for a job well executed, he walked down the path to the exit in plenty of time before the loadmaster saw him and called the authorities.

He glanced at a table next to the hatch door as he was about to disembark from the cargo transport. A paper document sticking out of a half-opened burlap and leather bag caught his eye. Paper documents were rarely used. Probably fake.

The tall man glimpsed the sender's address as he strode by, and it stopped him cold. He snagged the letter from the sack and read the addressee section. He tore it open and read the short missive, heedless of the loadmaster's imminent arrival. His heart nearly stopped in his chest.

Unbelievable! He looked around surreptitiously and tucked the letter in his jacket pocket before leaving the ship.

The letter changed absolutely everything.

Chapter 1

"I can't believe I have to marry some strange Thorium-Z miner to stay out of jail," Hannah mumbled to herself as she sniffed, trying not to let the other women in the transport craft see her tears. They would only make fun of her, just like they had on the whole damn journey. She experienced peace from her wretched circumstances only while she slept in the cryo-unit. But the wild dreams on this journey during her cryogenic slumber disturbed her. The most vivid one was of a deep masculine voice with a repeated phrase still echoing in her mind, '*I'm going to make you scream for me.*'

It had become almost a chant in her idle mind since waking up on the ship. It troubled her because of the hint of dark sexual desire it drove in her. She didn't expect sensual yearning to be any part of her immediate future.

The vivid nightmares of her last month on Earth, which resulted in her new status, colored her memory. Hannah shivered, remembering what she was doing here. She was about to be auctioned off to some grungy miner, and it wasn't her fault either. She wanted to scream this until someone listened, but so far, no one had. Basically, she was about to pay the ultimate price for being a woman.

Hannah wished she had the capacity in her soul to just slit her wrists and be done with it. But she didn't. She of the glass-is-half-full theology would always believe there was hope for her—until her very last breath. Some days, she hated being such an optimist.

Today was one of those days.

Then a voice to Hannah's right shouted at them, breaking her morbid reverie.

"All right now, ladies. Line up by the hatch door in an orderly fashion. Once yer outside the ship, head for the door at the end of the hallway. It'll take ya to the back of the auction building."

"Moo," Hannah said under her breath. The women here were no better than livestock brought in for the slaughter.

Hannah Brent didn't kid herself that anyone cared about her trials. Everyone on this transport had a financial sob story, but she was the only one who hadn't run up a mountain of bills she couldn't pay. Not for clothing, jewelry, shoes, or anything. Her husband had gambled and lost a fortune in a single night.

The next morning, the police had knocked at her sister's door where she had been staying, with a warrant for Hannah to appear as collateral in her husband's trial. Foolishly, she thought collateral meant witness. After she had dressed quickly, the officers escorted her to the police station to greet her idiot husband…now *ex*-husband. The louse.

She looked down at the white knit cotton blouse and matching skirt she wore, wishing, and not for the first time, she had chosen differently. If she had known she was going to be incarcerated, she would have picked a more practical color, something other than white. She felt it was a tad ironic to be a forced mail order bride dressed all in white.

An hour after the police had collected her, she was ensconced in an interrogation room at the police station. Ten minutes after that, a Tiberius medical body scan showed she and her husband hadn't consummated their marriage.

Her husband had hatefully informed them she was frigid and refused to sleep with him, which was a lie. But she had not been allowed to speak. When she tried to, they taped her mouth shut. The bastards! So they let her ex-husband have an annulment if he would agree to sign her over as payment for his gambling debts.

"No problem," he'd said excitedly, whipping out a pen for the paperwork.

Hannah had screamed, "No!" through the tape secured across her lips, but to no avail.

She had been summarily sold into mail order bride slavery, ironically enough, to pay her idiot ex-husband's gambling debts, thus keeping *him* out of jail. After he'd been given the formal annulment, he had practically skipped out of the jail building a free man. They hadn't removed the tape from her for hours because she had screamed herself hoarse in rebellion and tried to strike anyone within a five-foot radius who dared to try to touch her.

She had been forced to trade one bad husband she hadn't chosen for another she didn't want, simply because she was female. The Tiberius Group had recently forced some new laws into existence. They had a whole bunch of fresh new 'rules' for women now. And they all sucked.

Hannah poised and readied herself to become the unwilling mail order bride of some miner—a stranger who resided on excavation station number seven on an environment-controlled asteroid, which circled Mars, a zillion miles from Earth and her family. It was all because of her ex-husband…and her vile biological father. It was unreasonable, but no one cared about her problems. She was utterly alone.

"We'll bring you in one at a time. After the auction price has been paid, you'll be given over to your new fiancé. Together, you'll go to the minister who will perform the ceremony." The loadmaster continued ticking off the procedures for this, her endless personal days in hell.

I don't need no stinking husband, Hannah thought and closed her eyes. The first one had been such a loser; she didn't want to ever marry again. After what her father had done to her mother while Hannah was growing up, she'd never wanted to get married in the first place. She had wanted to teach. But her dreams were now derailed in favor of a new world order, courtesy of the Tiberius Group. They were powerfully evil men who wielded an insane amount of power. They had devised a new, radical social living style for the country—and most especially this new method applied to its females.

"Once the ceremony is over, you'll be bound to the Thorium-Z miner for a minimum of six months, but not to exceed two years." The loadmaster droned on while consulting his digital clipboard now and again for what Hannah guessed was clarity in this barbaric system.

Hannah wondered what a Thorium-Z miner might look like. The vivid picture of a mid-nineteenth century miner forty-niner in California popped into her fertile mind. She'd seen it in a history book once. They looked dirty, smelly, and wholly unappealing to Hannah.

"Yeah, yeah, we know the drill. Let's go and get this over with," a tall red head whined. "I'm hungry and I know I don't get fed until after the ceremony."

"Keep your panties on, Celeste. Dusty had to go out and tell 'em all we're one girl short," the young loadmaster named Buck said.

Hannah inwardly shuddered again. For all her problems, at least she'd survived the trip here. The other mail order brides who'd taunted her back on Earth were much subdued after one of the cryogenic units had failed. Neither loadmaster, Dusty the older one nor Buck the younger one, had been able to revive the girl in the first pod. Her name had been Allison. She had been a brunette beauty and one of the unattached women. Hannah was also unattached. That meant no specific miner had requested her.

The snooty women in the other cargo bay were all about to marry the miners they had corresponded with, exchanged photos with, and who had selected them specially. They were part of the *premium* cargo.

No one had selected Hannah especially, and she quelled the urge to break into tears again at the rejection she felt for that slight, which was stupid. Like she cared what a bunch of Thorium-Z miners thought of her. She wasn't going to cry because she didn't win a popularity contest here, but on some level, it hurt to know she was thought of as a lesser person even in this disgusting place.

"Maybe some of them miners will fight over us, seein' as how we're the last cargo for a while," gushed a rough-looking bleached blonde who looked like she'd endured a difficult life up to now. The expression 'rode hard and put away wet' slid unkindly into Hannah's mind.

"Well, Dusty's tellin' 'em that, too," Buck said with a slight smile. "There might just be a fight or two today."

"Get in there and tell Dusty to hurry up. I'm staaarving."

"Quit yer bitchin', Celeste. You've been here often enough, you should know the routine," Buck said, shaking his head and seemingly dismissing her. He sauntered over and grabbed a dilapidated leather satchel off a table in the room outside of the hallway where they waited.

The other bad news for the soon-to-be-disappointed miner not getting married today was that no more transport ships with mail order bride cargo were coming anytime soon. The Tiberius Group had halted all further transports until they could review the mail order bride procedures and ensure they conformed to the new laws. Plus, they probably wanted to negotiate a cut for themselves in this legalized flesh-peddling industry, she thought irately.

For Hannah, it didn't matter in the least. The same fate would have befallen her on Earth. Either way, she was being bought for someone else's pleasure.

A grungy miner's wicked pleasure.

Fear snaked its way down Hannah's spine again. She would be here no less than six months at the mercy of whichever miner ended up with her. Her incarceration length depended on how high the bidding went for her. The higher the bid, the longer she stayed. Thankfully, the maximum time was two years. Hannah decided that to be thought of as undesirable in this venue was perhaps not a bad thing after all.

"Pick a number," Buck said, startling her. He held out the open dirty leather satchel for her selection. Hannah reached in the bag with as much enthusiasm as if grabbing for a poisonous snake. She should be so lucky.

Hannah felt around in the bag and encountered what felt like wooden discs, certainly not real wood, but she retrieved one, and the loadmaster moved on. It had a number etched in the center. Lucky number seven. Unfortunately, she didn't feel so lucky today.

Buck then shuffled the irate women into numerical order in front of the door to the building where the auction would take place. The rest of them waited in the hallway connected to the ship they had arrived on. It was sort of like waiting on the jet ways at airports back on Earth to enter or exit airplanes.

However, instead of being on her way to take a fun trip or being greeted by loved ones upon her return, she was getting a grungy Thorium-Z miner for a husband.

Dusty returned from the building and started a low, earnest conversation with Buck.

Hannah heard Dusty say in an irate tone, "I didn't tell 'em yet. I figure the news will go over better if I have a girl standin' with me." Then they started whispering, and she couldn't hear any more.

After several minutes, the two loadmasters seemed to come to a decision, and Dusty ushered the first mail order bride for consideration into the building.

Hannah looked down at the wooden disc in her hand, testing the sharpness of the soft edge. Dull as dirt, she registered with a sigh. Even if it were razor sharp, she'd never use it to take her own life.

"Would you look at that!" came a boisterous voice through the slit of the door to the building. "I'm bidding everything I have on you, sweet thing."

Hannah moved a step ahead towards the door to the auction building. Brides from number two through the end of the line all automatically took a step forward to fill in the space from the first woman's departure into the auction house, as if they were all in a dream. Five more until she was put on the block to be bid on. How humiliating. How could this be happening to her? Girl number two was then called in as the next lot, and the four women ahead of Hannah moved forward, leaving a space in front of her.

However, she found she couldn't make herself take the step forward. This was wrong. Suddenly, Hannah didn't feel very well. Fear would do that, she supposed. She let her mind wander to what her 'new' husband might look like but could only conjure the picture of the ugly miner from two centuries ago. What if the new man in her life was smelly and ugly? What if he wanted to put his grimy, calloused miner's hands on her body? The next flash in her mind was a vile, sordid vision of the conjugal rights her new husband would demand from her.

"Move it!" said the girl standing behind Hannah in line. But she couldn't move it. She couldn't move at all. She couldn't think. She couldn't see. She reached out to grab the wall to steady herself but missed it, her body suddenly weightless. She felt herself slide towards the floor. Black dots consumed her vision. And then she only saw blackness.

Chapter 2

"The auction is about to begin," said a twangy voice trying to sound formal, which was a complete waste of effort in a mining town barroom, Brutal thought.

"Bring out the all the girls," said a rowdy voice from the back of the room. Thomas 'Brutal' Blackthorn agreed with Mr. Rowdy. He was ready to start the bidding. It was already going to take all damn day just to get a woman…he meant a 'wife.'

Dusty, the auctioneer for today, glanced around the room once, heaved a deep sigh, and promptly left the stage as if in a huff. He returned a few minutes later with a petite Asian woman dressed like the sordid porno version of a schoolgirl complete with pigtails and knee stockings. Together they walked across the expanse of the small stage as hoots of appreciation and hollering ensued. She was led to the space next to the podium for auction. Brutal thought she looked bored. Not surprising. The women here knew how the auction worked.

Most brides sold themselves into this life because of an addiction to expensive shoes, fine clothes, and unaffordable jewelry. Most just wanted to do their time quickly and return to their credit cards back on Earth. They would take the cash they earned from marrying miners for a short time and then come right back for more. No better than prostitutes for current fashion.

Brutal wouldn't prostitute himself for anything as shallow as fashion, but he understood the reason why. It was perhaps similar to the motivation for his living on this harsh planet in a backbreaking job—the dream of a better life on Earth. However, he worked hard to better himself and wanted so much more out of life than simply fashionable attire.

Brutal had experienced a couple of other auctions when he first arrived here four months ago. He foolishly decided at the time that he wouldn't need more than a month or two to reach his mining goal and secure enough cash to live the good life. He was mistaken.

The landowners he rented his mine from had been less than forthcoming about the rate at which ore could be retrieved here when he signed the contract to excavate. But he was up to the task as long as he had an outlet for his pent-up testosterone. He needed a woman, thus the reason he was giving up a day at his mine to obtain a regular sex partner…he meant a 'wife.' He needed sex. And he needed it soon.

Today, said his horny libido forcefully.

The original expeditionary party who founded the society on this asteroid almost two decades ago had decided quickly to outlaw whorehouses and drinking establishments right off the bat. They wanted a civilized operation, and to that end, built in lots of social rules early on. No drugs, no gambling, no drunkenness, no loose women or prostitutes.

The word 'no' was pretty much the standard answer for everything here.

The founding expedition members knew the value of the Thorium-Z as a replacement for fossil fuels, which was in abundance on this moon circling Mars. But they didn't want to own a rowdy, corrupt town in space. So if a miner had a woman living with him here, he had to be married to her. A few miners brought wives with them, but the majority opted for temporary wives. Probably not what the owners had in mind originally, but things changed over time.

The miners who had come to work way before Brutal got here found a few loopholes in the laws laid down—the most important being that a marriage didn't have to be permanent. They decided that marriages could be annulled, or couples could be divorced after their service was no longer required, or if the bride's previously established 'time' was up. The minimum sentence…he meant marriage…for a mail order bride here was six months, the maximum two years.

"Okay, listen up, you miners. I need to make an announcement before we begin these here proceedings. This is important, so pay attention," the senior loadmaster for the transport craft said irately. "Now, all the men who had attached wives will still get their selected women, unless you don't want her anymore. See me if that's the case."

"Get on with it, Dusty. I'm horny," said the rowdy voice from the back of the room. Laughter burst from most of the other occupants along with other grunts of approval.

"Well, keep it in your pants. There's a slight problem with the unattached females on this run."

"I know what it is," said the same rowdy voice. "They're horny, too, so get on with it." The room burst with loud laughter once again.

"One of the unattached females…didn't make the trip," Dusty said to the laughter dying down. "We weren't able to revive her from cryo-freeze. That means there is one less female up for auction today."

Brutal flinched inwardly. He needed to take a woman home today. It was imperative. At this juncture, he'd be unable to continue if…no, he wouldn't even consider the option of *not* going home with a woman…he meant a 'wife.'

"So someone's going back home with a chunk of wood between his legs today then," Mr. Rowdy said in disgust.

"When is the next transport, Dusty?" another voice inquired.

"Well, that's something else I need to tell ya about. The thing is, there ain't no scheduled bride transports, at least not at this time." Loud groans and grumbling ran through the crowd of men.

"Now, wait a minute. It don't mean they won't send one later on, but there's gonna be some changes 'cause a new group's in charge back home." Dusty went on to explain briefly the Tiberius Group's takeover and the new plight of women at home.

Interesting turn of events, Brutal thought as the auction finally began. He wondered what other changes were going on back in the U.S. since his arrival here.

As the parade of mail order brides were brought out, auctioned off, and dwindled quickly, Brutal felt the first stirrings of true panic. Twenty-five men had appeared today to bid on the available twenty-four mail order brides in the auction. The first twenty-three had been bid for quickly and contracts were already being drawn up.

Brutal and one other man remained to bid on the final woman available. The bidding thus far had been higher than usual for these events because of the supply and demand issue. Brutal was about to bid against his arch nemesis, Erik Vander. Erik had the distinction of being the only other man at this mining colony who was taller and heavier than Brutal.

"All righty then," Dusty said. "Here's the final woman up for auction today. Now, she ain't much to look at right now, on account of her fainting earlier and one of the other girls throwing water all over her to wake her up, but she cleans up nice. You can take my word for it."

"Get on with it," Erik's chilling voice cut through the din of conversation from the others watching the drama.

"Since all the attached women have been claimed, there's only one girl left for the two of you remaining. Do either of you want to back out?"

The room was completely silent until Erik said clearly, "Hell, no!"

Brutal merely glared at Dusty, certain the negative response was evident in his eyes, but he shook his head slowly to remove all doubt.

"Buck!" Dusty yelled over his shoulder. "Bring her out."

The final mail order bride shuffled out to the podium, her face pointed to the floor. Her shoulders slumped in what could only be described as utter mortification.

She was quite a bedraggled-looking little creature with wet, stringy blonde hair hanging over her eyes. Her arms were crossed over her chest. Brutal figured she was hiding the size of her breasts under the sodden, see-through blouse and skirt she wore. *Too bad*, he thought, but then anticipation rose quickly in him at the pervasive visual of her in his bed without her garments. She looked like she'd just emerged from a pool of water. He would have loved to see that.

Someone must have thrown five gallons of water on her. Brutal glanced around the room and saw the smirking face of one of the previously bid-on females. He also wished he had witnessed the catfight resulting in the soaked girl dripping before them now.

"Make her uncross her arms," Erik said, breaking Brutal's trance. "I want to see her tits."

"Eat shit and die," came the muttered curse from the girl, which was heard by everyone in the pin-drop silence of the room.

"Now, missy, don't insult the man who might just be your lord and master for the next two years," Dusty admonished her before turning to the room again.

Brutal hid a smile. He loved feisty women. Erik, he knew, liked women who were downtrodden. This would be his fifth temporary wife, if he succeeded, which he wouldn't because Brutal wasn't going to allow that to happen. He was already planning the best way to peel off the sopping wet white blouse and skirt clinging to her trembling body. Then he would help her warm up.

"Now, we have a provision for this unusual circumstance, believe it or not. We can flip a coin, or you two can fight until one of you is incapacitated. That means unconscious or dead," Dusty explained.

"Fight," both men said in unison, and each began peeling off his outer constricting clothing.

"Ask the girl which one she wants," shouted the rowdy voice from the back of the room.

"It don't matter which one she wants," Dusty said in an exasperated tone. At the same time, the blonde girl uttered a resounding, "Neither!"

"Rule number one," Dusty said, ignoring the ensuing outburst, "either of you two may, at any time, surrender your interest in the female. Rule number two, the two of you will fight for the right to marry this female until one of you is unconscious or engages rule number one as explained. Do you both understand?"

Brutal and Erik both nodded.

"First, I deserve to see what I'm fighting for," Erik said and strode two steps over to the female, grabbing both of her arms and pulling them away to view her breasts through the translucent shirt. She kicked him in the shin. Erik quickly tightened his grip on her forearms. He then twisted them up, making her cry out and fall to her knees.

"Just the way I like to see my woman," Erik smiled callously, "on her knees, crying."

"Enough." Dusty stepped between them. "Do that again, Erik, and you lose."

Erik grunted once and released her, retreating with sardonic amusement on his cruel face.

Brutal wondered if this very last mail order bride would root for him to win now that Erik had shown her his good side. She remained kneeling on the floor with her head down and didn't look up.

"I'd like to know the name of the woman I'm fighting for," Brutal said in an even tone. Her head moved slightly, but she didn't look at him.

"My name is Hannah Brent," she finally said, raising her eyes to meet his momentarily before she looked back at the floor.

Brutal stepped over to her and squatted down. "If you want Erik, I'll step out of the fight right now," he said and watched her head snap up as she glared at him.

"Stomp his ass, and I swear I won't give you any trouble," she whispered in a trembling voice.

"As you wish. I hope you're worth the effort, Hannah." Brutal inhaled deeply of her scent before he stood to face Erik.

So Brutal readied himself to fight Erik, the biggest, meanest miner on the off-world planet, for the right to marry a woman temporarily. He'd fought bigger, meaner men in his colorful past and beaten them easily. It was no competition. Brutal felt confident this battle was already a victory for him, even though both men were spurred on by lust.

Brutal even more so now because he had gotten close enough to inhale her delectable fragrance while crouched next to her. And she smelled incredible, not perfumed up like the others. Possibly due to the unexpected shower she had received, but he caught her natural scent and the light fragrance of her hair.

Need sex today, his libido commented, also responding to her scent.

Brutal wanted her. Soon. Now. He hoped he could wait until he got her back to his mine to take her for the first time. Conjugal rights were the primary reason he was marrying. Just like every other miner here.

"I'm going to knock you on your ass," Erik mocked.

Brutal didn't bother to respond. He pondered his best strategy to ensure he stayed on his feet before crushing Erik as quickly as possible. He and Erik circled the room twice before they just rammed into each other.

Brutal was at a disadvantage in weight and height but had the edge in natural fighting ability. He'd been a very good fighter in his younger days. In addition, he had been bio-genetically engineered to always win. He never once doubted his ability—or the inevitably of the outcome.

Erik was big, and he fought dirty, too, but Brutal knew the outcome would be in his favor. And he was right. They traded punches for a few minutes as Brutal toyed with him and pretended to be giving the fight his all, but he wanted this fight over with quickly. She waited for him. He dodged a punch to his face, ducking down before bouncing right back to tag Erik in the stomach once with a solid jab. Then three vicious punches in quick succession to Erik's face sent him staggering into a table before Erik put a hand up on the wall to steady himself.

Brutal followed with lightening speed and pinned him to the wall. He then simply pinched a nerve in Erik's neck, rendering him unconscious in seconds. Erik slumped to the floor in a heap. Brutal stepped away, brushing imaginary dust off his clothing. He was now ready to collect his prize.

"And the winner is Brutal," Dusty exclaimed formally.

Brutal looked up and into the horrified eyes of the woman he had just won the right to marry in a mostly fair fight.

"Your name is…Brutal?" she said in a voice laced with fear and promptly dropped to the floor in a dead faint—again.

Chapter 3

"Is there something wrong with you?" Hannah heard as she roused from her second collapse since being revived on the cryogenic ship. She opened her eyes to the face of the man about to be her new husband. He stood over her, his arms crossed in an angry stance–a man who'd just pummeled a guy three inches taller and fifty pounds heavier.

And his name is Brutal, said a very anxious internal voice.

She focused her eyes on his face, looking for a hint of serenity in his attitude and seeing none, found he wasn't hard to look at either. The harsh tanned planes of his face appealed to her on a dark and dangerous sexual level. He was a foot taller than she was with a wide chest and rippling muscles pretty much everywhere. His deep brown eyes simmered with intensity as he watched her. He was no grungy miner forty-niner, thankfully. His slightly wavy dark hair was in need of a trim, and the circle of whiskers around his mouth and chin intrigued her. Would it tickle when he kissed her? Would he kiss her?

Watching the two contenders for her hand in temporary marriage, she'd been frightened to death Erik would win. Part of her second fainting trip to the floor had been from pure, unrelenting relief.

Looking at Brutal now, Hannah suppressed a shiver and wondered why she'd been relieved. She watched with rapt fascination as her future husband laid his opponent, Erik the Evil, on the ground after a fairly short battle. Brutal was then declared the winner. He stepped away from Erik's slumped body and gave her a positively searing, possessive look from head to toe.

He might as well have screamed, "Mine, mine, mine."

Hannah was about to officially become his fiancée. Five minutes or so later, she'd be his temporary wife. He could do with her as he pleased for at least a year, as had been previously decided by the two loadmasters before the fight had begun.

She felt his gaze burn down her body from across the room. She shrank down a little. If he were to abuse her, she would never be able to stop him. Short-lived relief had been replaced with panic. Then she'd blacked out, again. How embarrassing. At least the catty, mean girl hadn't been allowed to soak her awake this time.

"Yes, there *is* something wrong with me," Hannah murmured. "I'm being forced to marry someone to pay for a gambling debt I didn't incur."

Hannah looked to Brutal for some measure of compassion but didn't get any. He just shook his head and stepped away from her supine form on the floor. He strode over to the table where Buck waited with paperwork for him to sign, paperwork sealing her to him.

"Now, missy," Dusty began patiently as he helped Hannah to sit up, "we been over this a hundred times already this trip. It don't matter what happened up to now or how you came to be here. The fact is, you're here, and you gotta marry this man or else."

"But look how big he is. If he wants to hurt me, I won't be able to stop him," she whispered, hearing the whine in her own voice.

"Well, now, Brutal *is* a fighter. That's a well-known fact, but I'm sure you'll work something out."

"His name is Brutal. What does that tell you?"

"It's just a name, missy. Personally, I think you're better off with him than with Erik."

"Why?"

"'Cause you woulda been Erik's fifth wife in three years if he'd won," Dusty said in a confidential tone.

"Great. I got the rock instead of the hard place. I feel so much better now," Hannah muttered contritely, allowing Dusty to help her to her feet. Brutal had a document in his hands as he approached them. Dusty gave her a don't-be-stupid look and walked away.

"You better not leave her alone, Brutal. I'd hate to charm my way into her pants and have you forced to kill her for infidelity, as the new rules for women on Earth stipulate," Erik said salaciously from behind her. She jumped towards her husband-to-be at the sound of Erik's sardonic voice.

Brutal put both of his arms possessively around her, tucking her close. *My, he is warm,* Hannah thought, feeling his fevered skin even through her clothing. In five minutes, she'd be completely dry if she were to stay wrapped in his arms.

"She's my future wife. She'll be with me always," Brutal replied matter-of-factly, shrugging.

"She'd better be. This isn't over, Brutal. Maybe I'll just come to your mine for a conjugal visit and take what I want," Erik purred, giving Hannah a leering once over. Hannah couldn't help but let a quiver run unstopped down her body. Brutal answered with a comforting squeeze.

"You can try," Brutal said, smiling in challenge, "but I'll just kick your ass again."

Hannah glared at Erik. "I won't let you touch me, you bastard."

"No, *I* won't let him touch you. What's mine is mine. Next time, Erik, I won't just render you unconscious," Brutal threatened as he squeezed her once before she could take a deep breath to say more. She glanced up at Brutal, sending him a harsh questioning frown at his firm hold around her waist. He merely raised his eyebrows and drilled a 'behave yourself' look in return. He wanted her acquiescence. Yeah, yeah, he was the new lord and master and the only one allowed to beat up evil men.

"At least for a year," she whispered more to herself as she prepared to participate in the ceremony marrying her to yet another stranger, the second one in as many months. At least this one was not the ugly, smelly miner from her previous vision. Brutal smelled great, and he was attractive in a big, muscular, dark, scary sort of way.

The couple ahead of them was Celeste and a balding, short miner named Iggy. After the ceremony, the groom, in his haste to lay claim to his wife, hadn't waited for any privacy to consummate the marriage. He'd marched Celeste over to the nearest table and bent her over it, flipping her skirt up and then taking her voraciously from behind as a circle had formed around them to watch. The impromptu sex halted only for a short time as everyone obligatorily watched the next marriage take place...Hannah and Brutal's.

Hannah was horrified at the sight and looked away, her cheeks warming in embarrassment before she stepped up for her vows.

Marriage vows. What a joke.

Brutal grabbed her to him securely, probably thinking she was about to hit the floor again. His warm body infused her with strength, surprisingly enough. They stepped up to the official minister together, arm in arm.

Hannah would have been even more upset about the copulating couple if Celeste had been even remotely distressed about it. But she wasn't. She seemed to have expected it, as if she was bored with the whole affair and was simply waiting for her next meal. If Celeste had been carrying a nail file, Hannah had no doubt she would have used it to shape her claws throughout the very public sexual display.

* * * *

"You are now man and wife," the officiating marriage broker said. "Would you like to kiss your bride—or otherwise seal the bargain?"

Brutal couldn't help but look over at the grunting Iggy, who had resumed immediately after the marriage broker said, "—wife."

He took in Hannah's round-eyed, appalled look, which was directed at the public copulation. He hoped she didn't faint again. Her eyes moved over to focus on another vacant table across the room. She glanced at his face, her thought as clear as if she had spoken it aloud.

Brutal shook his head. Before she could pass out again, he quickly leaned in, grabbed the back of her head one handed, and kissed her mouth long enough to realize she tasted as good as she smelled. As horny as he was, he was still not an animal. He could wait. He'd never wanted to share women before and wasn't about to start now. He wouldn't get any thrill out of the miners here watching him fuck her in public. He broke the kiss, swallowed his lust, and headed for his vehicle to take her to his mine dwelling.

Brutal would have to protect his investment and live at the mine. Originally, he had thought he might put her up in the hotel at this space station and visit as needed, but he couldn't leave her here now with Erik on the rampage. He'd spent more than he expected on a wife. Instead of six months together, she had to sign on for a year. Now, *that* gave him a thrill. Having Hannah, available in his bed, for an entire year.

Once his intent to leave registered, several miners were vocally disappointed not to have a two-ring show going, but Brutal didn't care. He would be dick deep in a female in less than an hour. Just the thought of that made blood rush to his groin. He felt himself thicken into fuck mode.

Time to go home to bed, my sweet Hannah, he thought. His lust roared through his fevered body. Brutal grabbed her arm to haul her out of the building faster before he gave in to his lust and changed his mind about the vacant table.

Hannah hesitated and resisted slightly at his touch.

"Move now, or do you want to reconsider the open table across the room?" Brutal practically growled. She lowered her eyes and stopped fighting him. He led her easily to his motorbike.

* * * *

Brutal took her to his mine on a high-powered motorized four-wheeler. It moved pretty fast, and he had enjoyed her clutching to him on the trip home. Upon his arrival several months ago, he set up his primary residence there and made it fairly comfortable. He was sure it wasn't her Barbie-dream home, but she was here for only one reason anyway.

The unexpected close quarters combat with Erik had drained him physically. He needed rejuvenation. She was lucky he didn't like an audience, as the unoccupied table had looked good to his long-deprived and very vocal libido.

Brutal wasn't going to apologize for what he wanted to do with her, but he knew he was different. He couldn't wait to hear her come. Loved that sound from a woman, especially the first time they were together. A woman's pleasure was a powerful rejuvenation tool for the genetically engineered.

They entered his land, which was gated and fenced for property boundaries. The gate automatically opened for his vehicle. He drove down a gravel lane towards the mine opening a hundred yards ahead. Once through the opening, the strings of lights attached to the walls and ceiling blinked on. He had a motion detector set for the lights. It was handy for security when visitors showed up, too.

The lit cave ran another hundred and fifty yards at a slight downward angle until it ended at two air-locked doors. Brutal parked the four-wheeler at the smaller door, shut off the engine, got off the vehicle, and quickly grabbed a leather bag from the back basket.

Hannah stepped off the four-wheeler and followed him. He put his hand on a scanner next to the door and his face in a retinal detector above it. The big metal door made a few noises and then opened slowly.

"First things first. Take your clothes off. Your mouth inflames me every time I look at it. During our marital kiss, I almost lost complete control. A day fucking you will rejuvenate me. I've gone too long without." He started unbuttoning the blue shirt under his leather jacket.

Her dismayed gaze stunned him. Didn't she understand how this worked? Didn't she know she would enjoy it, too? Didn't she know how desperate he was?

"Don't worry, my temporary wife. If you don't enjoy the experience, I will only get half the rejuvenation charge."

"Meaning you'll spend two days raping me instead of one. Big deal." She crossed her arms and turned her back on him. He strode over to her and turned her around.

"It doesn't work that way. I'd watch my tongue if I were you. I don't rape. That's why I married you. Besides, I stomped Erik's ass like you asked me to. I thought that bought me no trouble from you."

"Fine. Whatever. Just get it over with. I won't fight you," she said in a deflated tone.

"Perfect. Take your clothes off. Now."

Hannah gave him a sour look and slowly began to unbutton her blouse.

Brutal's temper was pricked, but then he remembered reading the papers he signed to become engaged to her. Her first husband was listed by the company as having sold her into the mail order bride company to pay off some gambling debts. Brutal questioned her ex-husband's lack of judgment in getting rid of a gorgeous girl like Hannah.

Brutal couldn't imagine selling a woman who looked like pure sexual delight, which she did, but whatever. Her ex was a fool to have let her go for any reason. For a man to relinquish a woman like

Hannah…well, he would have expected a much larger bride price, one in which he would not have been able to afford. Brutal was not a fool.

By her surly attitude, he guessed she hadn't had a good experience with her ex-husband in the conjugal rights department. Perhaps her ex had mistreated her. Perhaps he hadn't been a good lover. Perhaps she'd never experienced an orgasm with him. Or ever? No, that was just too much to hope for.

Perhaps he should get on with showing her that he was capable of providing pleasure for her as well. She was in for a treat because Brutal knew he was an excellent lover. Because he was bio-genetically engineered, sex was an important tool for him, to charge up the batteries, so to speak. He had been programmed for such when he was engineered back at the lab on Earth where he'd been raised. It was why sexual activity was fuel for him, but only if shared one on one. The more he cared about his partner, the bigger the charge.

Brutal took great pains to make sure his lovers experienced ecstasy as well because he got such a vibrant charge out of it for himself. A total power rush of rejuvenating energy enveloped him upon hearing a woman he touched scream in delight from being thoroughly satisfied.

Very unlike the women Brutal had paid to fuck in his past. Paid prostitutes were a very poor substitute for gratification. The paid women were doing a volume business and didn't ever want to take the time to enjoy it. 'Get in, get out, next!' was how they operated. He'd only lowered himself to that level when he'd gone too long without. He drove himself to the brink of death to avoid it.

Acquiring a mail order bride had been an inspired idea. They both got something out of the arrangement. She would get money to start over. He would get laid regularly, adding to his work strength, power, and stamina in the mine, thereby completing his goal sooner.

Even with Hannah's excessive price, he would recoup the bride price in extra strength within a month. The rest was just bonus. His original six-month plan, which had then shifted to a five-year plan, had now turned into a two-year plan with this temporary marriage. And in the end, they wouldn't be stuck with each other for a lifetime.

Hannah had stopped unbuttoning her blouse and turned her back to him, presumably to complete the task, but her fingers had stilled. She hung her head in defeat, or perhaps to bear up to have sex with a stranger.

Brutal didn't know anything except that her time was up. His barbarian brain was taking over more and more of his rational mind.

Now.

Take her right now.

Just bend her over the table and take her, his lust-filled mind screamed.

He took a deep breath and came up behind her, ignoring the ardent voice in his head. Instead, he slowly put his mouth on the sensitive spot at the base of her neck. She jumped slightly.

"Need some help?" he murmured, kissing a path up and down her neck. Hannah didn't stop him when his hands slipped up the front of her blouse. He finished helping her unbutton it. He couldn't wait any longer. *Take. Woman. Now.* Lust reverberated in his brain. *Bend her over the table. Flip up her skirt and introduce yourself.*

It was already going to test his patience not to pretend she was a paid-for female and just take her over and over until sated.

For their first time, he would bring her with him over the edge of oblivion. He could almost feel the wash of rejuvenation it would bring. Much better that she climax just before or during the experience than for him to come first. His fingers skimmed up her torso as he nipped and tongued her shoulders and neck as he pulled the shirt from her as slowly as he could.

Brutal felt her relax against him as her arms fell to her sides. His fingertips had reached the underside of her lace-enclosed breasts. He took a hearty nip on the cord of her neck as he palmed her breasts and pinched both peaks.

Her sharp intake of breath at the sudden sensation filled him with need. His cock reared, and he pressed it against her soft buttocks. He pushed her towards the table edge with his thighs. Before her legs connected with the furniture, she turned clumsily around in his arms to face him. Her hands landed on his shoulders, almost pushing at him. Her face turned up and her eyes showed a plea she didn't voice.

"What?" His voice sounded more harsh than he intended. *Take her! Take her now*, his mind drilled. *Bend her backward over the table!*

"Please—for the first time…" She stopped talking and just stared at him. Did she think he could read her mind? Even if he weren't in a berserker sex-loaded frame of mind, he still would not be able to read her thoughts.

"What?" he repeated practically in a blood-lusted shout, taking a step closer so their bodies touched. *Exquisite. Soft. Female in proximity. Take her. Take her now!*

"For the first time, will you…do it…as you face me…and not from behind?" she blurted out, then closed her eyes.

"Why?" Brutal paused. Even his barbarian brain wondered why and paused, too.

Her eyes peeked open. "Because I don't want the first time to be like…like the woman at the bar. You know, on the table."

"You might find that you like it—on the table, bent over in capitulation," Brutal teased her and smiled as she responded.

"I don't think so," she said with all seriousness.

He nodded. "Fine. For this first time, and only this first time—no fucking the new wife from behind against a table." Surprisingly, his new little wife was shy and apparently inexperienced in alternate sexual positions, considering that she had already been married. Her ex-husband must have been terrible in bed.

Brutal would teach her later on how good it could feel for her from behind. He was certain she would enjoy it once he demonstrated to her what he could do with his hands as he plowed into her while she braced herself over a table. And it wouldn't be like the freak show at the auction house either.

Perhaps he'd show her tomorrow.

Hannah peeled her soft white shirt away, and he saw her lace-covered breasts begging to be played with and sucked on and…

Perhaps later today he'd introduce her to the table.

For the here and now, however, Brutal grabbed her to him and pressed his substantial erection into her belly, and then he planted his hungry mouth on her timid one. He hugged her tighter to his frame. Hannah slipped her arms tentatively around his neck.

Brutal ground his erection against her soft body. This was going to feel so incredible, he thought. He grabbed her up by each of her thighs and opened her to him as she held on. He rubbed himself against her parted legs through the clothing they still wore. She seemed skittish and broke the kiss to look questioningly into his eyes.

"I won't hurt you, Hannah. You'll enjoy this. I swear it," he told her earnestly as he gazed into her eyes, willing her to believe him. She merely watched him warily. He'd just have to prove it to her. He leaned closer and kissed her mouth chastely once to prove he could be gentle, at least for a second or two longer. He wanted her to trust him. She nodded and leaned in to him to kiss him in return. This time, her tongue entered his mouth tentatively, seeking his. He paused, the blood rushing through him in a primal pulse.

Take her. Take her now! He ignored his raging libido in favor of a slow seduction.

Brutal carried her around the partition to the bedroom area of his small dwelling. The lights were dim in this corner, but he could still see what he wanted.

He had a huge bed, since he was a huge man. He put her down and undressed her as slowly as he could–not very–he hoped she knew how to mend cloth. Then he quickly undressed himself.

Leather wouldn't tear, so he had to disrobe himself the old-fashioned way. He picked her up and put her naked body on the bed then lay down next to her. If he climbed on top, it would be over too soon.

Brutal kissed her and let his hands roam over her body. He felt one of her arms across his shoulders. She began playing with the hair at the nape of his neck.

After a few minutes, he kissed a wet path down her throat and ended with his mouth on her breast. He stroked his hand down her body and rested his sizeable fingers between her legs. He stopped suckling her nipple long enough to whisper huskily, "Touch me, Hannah."

"What?"

"Put your hand on me."

"My hand is on you," she whispered.

"Grab my cock."

Chapter 4

Hannah wavered at his crude request, but he was insistent. When she hesitated, he grabbed her closest hand and placed it unerringly on his throbbing member. She tentatively wrapped her hand around his hot, impressive shaft while wondering how he would ever fit inside her. Then she lost that thought when his fingers began strumming her below in an unfamiliar yet delightfully rhythmic way.

A warm, delicious feeling enveloped Hannah. Brutal's mouth landed on her breast again, sucking her nipple so insistently, she moaned reflexively and tightened her hand around him. He moaned seductively in response, and she felt his enormous sexual organ move in her hand.

It gave her a certain feeling of power in her powerless world. So she clenched her hand around him again, and then again. In return, he growled deep in his throat and stroked her harder and faster with his fingers, sucking on her nipple more intently until she was sure she would die from breathless sensation.

Brutal had scratchy facial hair trimmed in an oval around his mouth and chin. His mouth was currently wrapped around the better part of the center of her breast. It was very hypnotic to watch.

Was she allowed to watch?

A warm sensation flooded down between her legs set to the rhythm of his mouth pulling on her very sensitive peak. She looked down at the decadent display, watching him strum her. His hand worked between her legs, his head moving to her other breast, his mouth drawing on her nipple, and her world tilted.

Hannah opened her mouth to take in more air. As the exquisite feeling of her first-ever climax came over her, she screamed.

How could she not?

Then she sucked in more air and screamed again as the sensation carried her to a dreamlike state. Her new husband made a satisfied noise against her breast. He released his mouth from her nipple after several minutes and stared intently into her eyes. He leaned up and kissed her cheek.

"Was that your first orgasm?" he whispered in her ear. "It felt like it to me."

Hannah opened her eyes but couldn't catch her breath. She managed a slight nod. He smiled with a look of wicked pleasure. As they stared at each other, she in awestruck wonder, he in satisfaction of a job well done, he removed his hand from between her legs. His fingers were covered in the wetness she'd expelled during her screaming orgasm. He willed her to stare at him as he then stuck those moist fingers into his mouth and sucked the essence from them. She watched wide-eyed as he licked each finger slowly and deliberately, smiling again in wicked pleasure at her.

"Mmmm," he moaned and shifted, breaking their gaze so he could kiss a path down her belly. "I'm going to need some more of that."

Hannah knew what he intended to do and could only watch in her boneless and thoroughly satisfied state. He lifted her legs, bending them at the knee. He watched her again as he ran his whisker-covered chin down her inner thigh. She knew what he was going to do next, too. She didn't know if she would live through the experience. She hoped she would.

Brutal teased her, kissing that very sensitive bud lightly and then running his chin up her other thigh. She watched as he settled his mouth against the apex between her legs and reached his long arms up her torso to pluck at her pebbled nipples. He licked her several strokes as if to lap up the creamy moisture from her release. His tongue swirled over her clit. She was about to climax…again.

Everything Hannah thought she knew about sex had just been erased. Her view now radically changed in only a few minutes here tonight, by a virtual stranger. She hadn't known women were supposed to enjoy sex, too. She knew it only as a duty.

Hannah looked down to see the top of his head moving between her legs. She could feel his lips firmly wrapped around and sucking on the most sensitive piece of flesh she possessed. The sensation was superb.

She heard him moaning as though enjoying a fine meal, and then stars exploded behind her eyes. She inhaled, moaning in pleasure, and screamed again.

How could she not?

Hannah's legs reflexively clenched together as if to trap his head, which was attached to his very splendid mouth, which was doing brilliant things to the lower half of her body. It took Hannah much longer to recover from the second climax. She lay on her back in a stranger's bed with her legs spread wide. The aforementioned stranger's head was locked between her thighs. She was in a completely sated, boneless state having just experienced two of the most body-rocking, exquisite sensations in her existence. She wondered how in the world she ended up here.

Hannah whimpered in pleasure. She sensed more than saw his movement. He shifted his body towards her. It was his turn, and he had earned it. He deserved an award because he was right. He'd sworn to her she would enjoy it. And she had.

Twice.

Hannah looked up in time to see him grab his immense member and place it at the now very drenched opening of her body. It was time to pay the piper, and he had earned her cooperation. She should probably do something besides just lie here and wait for him, but she couldn't move. What he had done to her made her weak and soft and satisfied.

Hannah knew what would happen next. She'd gone to a health class. Brutal ought to have her as much as he wanted for as long as he wanted. The thought of what waited ahead made her quiver in anticipation. Yes, he ought to have her for making her feel so incredibly good. Her new husband slipped the tip of his penis inside her. She could feel her pulsating vaginal muscles automatically try to accommodate his substantial girth. She hoped he was not about to be disappointed. He should feel as fabulous as she did right now. She watched as he closed his eyes, grabbed both of her thighs with his hands, and rammed himself inside her to the hilt.

Hannah could only scream again at the sensation she felt.

* * * *

As Brutal plowed inside her tightness for the first stroke, he heard her scream again, but it didn't register immediately what had happened. He moaned at how utterly wonderful she felt.

But she screamed as he breached her maidenhead, his cock sliding fully inside to the hilt. She sucked in a breath as a low keening sound came next, but not quite in pleasure this time.

It took three solid to-the-hilt strokes before that vital information made it through to his lust-saturated brain. He finally stilled in utter shock, completely embedded in his new temporary wife who had just turned out to be a virgin.

God's wrath, what had he done?

Mindless with want after her second orgasm because she screamed in seemingly newfound bliss both times, he had felt that fresh, wonderful, invigorating sound all the way to his core.

The first sound of pleasure torn from her lips reverberated to his soul. He knew it had been her first climax by the utter electrical charge he got in his gut as her back arched in passion. It was like a pre-orgasm for him. She'd screamed her second climax, too. Another lift for him, and she tasted good, too. He'd smiled in smug satisfaction of a man who had pleasured a woman not expecting to be gratified.

Brutal couldn't wait to plunge inside and feel her clamping on him. He entered her with only the head of his cock at first to see how snug her entrance was. God's wrath, she was tight, but she was slick from her earlier pleasure, too.

Take her. Take her now. His impatient libido had waited long enough for satisfaction.

Brutal paused to center himself to fully take pleasure in the sensation of ecstasy he was on the brink of enjoying. He'd taken a deep breath and driven home his first thrust, aiming to press all the way to her womb with his first sure stroke. He'd then wanted to repeat the motion until sparks showered out of the end of his dick inside her sweet, wet passage while her vaginal muscles clamped repeatedly on his shaft in combined satisfaction.

Instead, he'd savagely taken her virginity, plowing into her like a berserker, never once considering it would be her first time.

How could that be? She'd been married, for God's sake. Brutal had seen the papers. His eyes popped open to see her tear-filled ones. He was trembling, on the brink of a massive release, but he stilled his movement and lowered his body to hers. Her arms came around his neck as she pressed her face against his shoulder.

"I'm so sorry," she sobbed.

"Why didn't you tell me?" he asked quietly, trying to hold himself from impaling her mindlessly.

"I didn't get a chance," she whispered.

"I wish you'd taken the time, Hannah."

"I didn't know how to tell you," she said in her quiet voice, caressing his senses with her innocence.

"God's wrath, woman, I wish you'd found a way." He pressed his forehead to hers as his cock throbbed inside her. He moaned deeply, trying to find some control.

Virgin or not, he needed to come. *Soon. Now. Finish this!*

"What was I supposed to say?" she sobbed. "My ex-husband thought me so repulsive, he failed to make an effort to have sex with me even once. He found the nearest gambling hall instead to quench his passion."

"I'm sorry. If I'd known, I wouldn't have..."

"What? You wouldn't have bothered either?" And she unleashed a torrential flood of tears. He felt those tears on his throat.

"No, I would definitely have bothered. I just would have entered in such a way as not to hurt you. I could have—oh, God—I need to..." He couldn't finish his sentence because he needed to finish fucking her. His cock throbbed inside her again, straining in need for completion of the act. He groaned and tried to pull out, but couldn't and settled himself to gain control.

"You don't have to stop, Brutal," he heard her quiet voice. Then she sniffled a couple of times to calm down. She remained quiet for a moment and then whispered, "Please, it's okay. You aren't hurting me. It just feels...different. You fill me up."

His embedded cock actually throbbed a thank you as he nodded in kind. "I'll go slowly."

"Okay...if you want." She kissed his throat tenderly, and he felt her tongue slip out and lick him. He throbbed within her again, on the utter brink.

"If I could have what I want, I'd pound into you so hard, you'd submerge to the floor through the mattress on this bed," he growled.

"Okay," she said, then tilted his face down to hers and kissed his mouth chastely. Her tongue flicked out and slid along his lips. She actually licked him twice more before he opened his mouth and devoured her.

Brutal moved inside her exquisite tightness. After three strokes going as slow as he could, he picked up speed. She moaned again. He kissed a path to her throat and back to her lips again. He kissed her mouth as he felt her hips arch toward his, connecting and meeting him as he thrust inside her. *Superb.*

Brutal finally and exquisitely thundered his release, growling against her lips. He felt her clamping on him, milking his seed out of him. A rush of power washed over him, the likes of which he'd never felt. He wouldn't need a whole day with her to recharge. One or two more times ought to do it.

Once he came down from his orgasmic high, the doubt seeped in. He had never been so turned on, so completely satisfied, or so wretchedly guilt-ridden for having enjoyed himself so much. If he'd ever had a more satisfying experience, he didn't remember it. Or it had just been replaced by an incredible new memory.

Brutal regained his senses pretty quickly. He was still embedded deeply inside her, his mind working ten thousand miles an hour. A virgin who'd never had an orgasm before. An unexpected gift Brutal would never have expected. Nor would he ever forget.

Chapter 5

"Are you hurt?" Hannah heard Brutal say as his still rapid breath caressed her neck. "Did I hurt you?"

"No, of course not," she responded quickly. She could hardly focus on speech. She felt good. No, she felt great, better than she had in months. Who would have thought sexual activity would make her so utterly and deliciously content?

"God's wrath, woman, you're certainly full of surprises."

"So are you. Who would have thought sex would be such a good idea?"

Brutal chuckled lightly. "I would have."

"Feeling all charged up, are we?" she teased.

"I feel very satisfied, but let's discuss you. I thought because you'd been married that...you know...I didn't know..."

"Let it go. I don't want to explain the humiliation of my last marriage to you." Hannah lost her after-sex glow quickly in memory of the past several weeks, which put her here, in a stranger's bed for his pleasure. Okay, for hers, too.

"Fine, but in my opinion, he was an idiot. You are definitely worth it. The fight. The price. All of it." Brutal lifted himself off her, slid out of her body, and rolled to his side.

"Great. I'm glad you feel like you got your money's worth," she said sarcastically and turned away from him.

"Don't be that way, Hannah."

"I said I wouldn't be a problem. I never said I would be the happy little homemaker. I'm not going to be the contented little wife, you know."

"I expect you'll be whatever I want you to be," Brutal said harshly. Apparently, the afterglow was gone for him as well.

"Oh, yeah, that lord and master speech again?"

"What's up your ass?" he asked.

"I shouldn't be here. I didn't do anything to deserve this," she lamented.

"This? Complete and utter sexual gratification at the hands of a master? No, you didn't deserve it at all, but I did."

"Don't kid yourself about what is going on here!" Hannah railed at him. Total and utter satisfaction aside, she was still virtually a prisoner, and she didn't deserve this existence.

"If this is your definition of not giving me any trouble, we need to crack open a dictionary," he said harshly.

"You read my file. You know why I'm here. It's not fair."

"Fair or not, I needed a regular sex partner. A temporary mail order bride seemed like a good idea to me. I'm reconsidering my options right now, Hannah."

"Well, too bad. You're stuck with me now, Brutal." She turned back over and sneered at him even though she didn't think he deserved it. She was just mad about her own circumstances.

"And your mouth should be doing something besides yammering. Do you want to kiss me, or should I think of something else to occupy those luscious lips you possess?" His eyes drilled hypnotically into hers.

Hannah took a deep breath and lowered her eyes. As angry as she was, Brutal hadn't done anything wrong. Not really. He didn't deserve her wrath. She took another deep breath and slid closer to him. She looked up into his chocolate brown eyes. She refused to apologize but hoped her lips conveyed her regret when she kissed him with all the sincerity she could muster.

Brutal responded in turn by taking her on yet another satisfying, sexually climactic journey, then another, and then more journeys all night long.

* * * *

The next day, Brutal made her breakfast. He was fully charged up and ready to spend the day carving out his future in the mine. He watched Hannah covertly as they ate in companionable silence. She had on a short robe and her hair was pulled up into a ponytail, making her look even younger this morning. Even more beautiful, if it was possible.

He was still very curious about her past, but not enough to invite her wrath by asking her about it. He got up from the table, planning on packing up what they would need. But then she removed the breakfast dishes to the sink. She returned with a dishrag and suddenly bent over the dining table to wipe it down, the silky robe tightening across her ass when she reached to the far side. The material framed her lush derrière perfectly, and his mouth went dry.

Brutal found himself suddenly in need of her once again. One could never be too charged up, and besides they had time. He approached her silently, then pinned her easily against the table with his hips. She didn't stop him or resist in any way. His arms came around her, stilling her movements. He removed the rag from her hand and tossed it to the sink before placing his hands next to hers on the table, effectively trapping her against it.

"Remember yesterday when we talked about capitulation with regard to this table?" He placed his mouth on her exposed neck.

"Vaguely. I have slept a little since then," she replied in an amused tone. But then she also leaned and twisted her neck forward to give his mouth easier access. Then her body melted back seductively into his, causing his dick to immediately rear to life against her butt. He moved a leg in between hers, spreading them further apart. He ran his hands up her arms, which were still locked at the elbows resting on the table.

"Let me refresh your memory." Brutal slid a hand inside her robe to stroke a bare breast. When he pinched the tip, she drew a sharp intake of breath and arched her back into him. He peeled her robe back over her shoulders to expose her breasts completely but left her arms trapped in the material. He kissed his way to her shoulder and palmed her bare breasts, stroking her with utter care, listening as the tempo of her breathing increased.

He stopped playing with her chest only long enough to pull his t-shirt over his head and unzip his pants, freeing his now fully erect cock. He placed his hands on her outer thighs and pulled the hem of her robe up to expose her luscious ass. He raised his hand to the center of her naked back, pushing her gently forward and into the optimal position for what he had in mind. His other hand came around the front of one of her legs to play with her clit. He wanted to assure himself she was ready to play this morning. She was dripping already. He moaned at the realization she was as aroused as he was. He continued to finger her as she trembled in response.

"Hot and wet. Very nice. I see you *are* ready to surrender to me today."

Hannah didn't say anything. She merely moaned. He didn't make her wait. He wrapped his arm over one of her shoulders so he could capture and play with her breast. He moved his hand from between her legs long enough to grab his cock and direct it between her oh-so-ready lower lips already drenched in readiness for him.

He pierced her slowly at first in deference to all the times he'd taken her the night before, but she was not inclined to wait patiently and rocked back to take his whole length at once.

The sensation of being fully embedded in such a tight, wet place sent a bolt of lust up his spine. The next two rapid strokes in unconscious reaction were perhaps uncalled for, but she only groaned and matched him stroke for stroke. He latched his mouth to the back of her neck, plucked at her nipple and fingered her clit as he pounded into her from behind. The resistance of the table only added to the pleasure enveloping him.

"Oh, Brutal," she cried out suddenly. He felt her inner muscles clamp down hard in release on his thrusting cock. He lasted only a few more strokes before growling his own climax. Gasping harshly, he relaxed and bent over, pinning Hannah to the table.

"So that's what capitulation feels like," she panted. "You were right. I do like it."

Brutal laughed and kissed her shoulder. "Keep in mind I'm going to remember this moment the next time you bend over in front of me."

"So noted."

Afterwards, he led her to the shower. He washed and massaged her from head to toe. And then he took her, for good measure—from behind as she bent at the waist. He loved to hear the scream of her climaxes.

Brutal figured with Hannah as his sexual refueling station, he could easily work for eighteen hours at a stretch. It would make long days for her deep down in the mineshaft, but he couldn't leave her alone. He didn't trust her not to run, and more importantly, he didn't trust Erik not to make good on his threat to rape her at the first available opportunity.

Brutal dressed in his standard insulated blue button-up shirt and black leather pants. He had a leather jacket to wear, too. He had bought a few sets of similarly insulated clothing for Hannah before the auction. He selected a matching shirt and slacks in a medium size for the bride he brought home. Luckily, the clothing fit her very well, perhaps because he'd been thinking of her when he bought them.

Hannah didn't do too much physical work on her first day down in the mine, but she didn't complain or whine either. She just wandered around and studied the mine and its rocky formations, generally puttering around as he worked all day.

She distracted him once or twice when she bent over and presented him with a delectable view of her backside, giving him several salacious ideas.

The first time he cleared his throat repeatedly until she finally turned around in question. She then smiled and immediately straightened up with an almost apologetic smile and shrugged her shoulders. If it wasn't so cold down here, he might consider some sexual escapades. It was well below freezing, not the place for extended exposure of naked skin.

Frostbite on your privates would be a real bitch.

After nine hours, Brutal stopped wielding his ax and told her it was time for lunch. He had packed something for them both earlier. Later on, he'd show her what he expected as her contribution to their daily living.

"You'll want to bring a bed roll down here and sleep while I work tomorrow," he said offhandedly as they sat down to eat.

"Why?"

"Because I intend to work eighteen-hour days."

"That's insane."

"Maybe so, but it is a fact of your new life, a husband who works hard. I'll outline your chores once we get back tonight. You'll have to do most of them while I sleep."

"My chores? I thought I fulfilled my one and only chore on my back or bent over," she said caustically.

"You get to share cooking and cleaning duties, too," he said matter-of-factly.

"But what if I work down here, too?" She took a bite of sandwich.

"That would be helpful, but I don't think you can handle the capacity I can. This is backbreaking work for regular people. I can do it easily because I was bred for it."

"Bred for it?"

"Bio-genetically engineered." Brutal watched to see if she were bigoted about the genetically enhanced.

"Is that why you're so good in bed? Were you bred for that, too?" she asked, her eyes wide.

He smiled at her awe-filled voice and responded with pride, "Yep."

"Hmm. Interesting. I've never met anyone who was engineered." She sounded intrigued, not disgusted in the least.

"That you know of anyway."

"I'm sure I would have remembered."

"Not everyone shares the information. As a matter of fact, I've never shared it willingly."

"Why not?" she asked with innocent sincerity. Hannah certainly didn't have the same attitude as his ex-fiancée, Charlotte, in this matter, Brutal thought and then quickly willed that notion away.

"Some people are not as accepting of genetic engineering in humans as others. Some feel it goes against God and nature. Most people who find out are wary of someone like me."

"I think it's like every other designation of people. There are going to be good people and bad people. I think you're good."

"Thanks, I guess. Eat up, Hannah. I still have lots to do here tonight," he said, changing the subject.

"Right. So, do you have documentation and testing samples from where you're digging?"

"How do you know about that?"

"I had some college classes in geology."

"Good to know."

"I can help you, Brutal. I could do a mine evaluation for you and locate the best places to find Thorium-Z here."

"Already done, but thanks for taking an interest."

"Still, I'd like to look. It will, at the very least, keep me occupied and out of your hair while we're down here."

"Well then, when we get back, I'll show you where I keep my charts and test results. Maybe you won't distract me so much."

* * * *

Several hours later, once they had arrived back at the dwelling, Hannah took all his charts and information on the mine and read for the rest of the evening. Completely immersed in the documentation, she took several pages of notes while Brutal cooked dinner for them. This pattern remained the same for the next several nights as well.

"You actually have to work while you're living here, you know," Brutal said as he gave her a large bowl of stew on the fifth night in a row, "and you have to cook, too."

"Unfair. I worked in the mine today." She took a bite of dinner, closing her eyes in sumptuous approval of the meal. Brutal was a fabulous cook.

"You looked around and watched me work," he huffed.

"I was studying the igneous rock formations."

"Really?" He sounded completely unimpressed. He sat and dug into a large bowl of the stew as well.

"Yes, and now that I've had a chance to study all your documentation thoroughly, I have a suggestion."

"What's that? You pick up an ax and help mine so it goes faster?"

"No, I think we should start mining closer to the surface. I think there's a greater chance of finding more of the ore you seek."

"And what makes you think so?"

"You need to mine where the mantle of the planet meets the outer layer of crust. It's only about three kilometers down the shaft. You can tell because the color of the stone changes. Statistically, that is where the richest deposits of Thorium-Z are located. Typically."

"How do you know? You're a physical fitness trainer." At her surprised glance, he said, "Yeah, I read your personal file. So what?"

"Physical fitness was only what I minored in. My major was geological studies as they pertained to Type-C planets containing similar compositions as the sun. We're on a Type-C planet, by the way," she said, crossing her arms with superiority.

"Really?" he said, his voice laced with disbelief, and perhaps a touch of sarcasm. The cad.

"I swear."

"So what? Everyone on this planet knows that."

"Oh, yeah. *All* the women who traveled to this godforsaken rock had scientific backgrounds and knew the composition of the planet they were about to visit? I don't think so," she responded with her own sarcasm.

"But you don't have a degree in this field of study, correct?"

"No, but—"

"Stop," he interrupted her. "You don't have a degree, so why should I trust you?"

"Because I'm right. Why is it so hard to believe I've had formal geology training?"

"I would have had to pay ten times your asking price if you were a degree-carrying geologist."

"I was three classes away from completing my degree before the Tiberius Group took over. They told me it was better for me to go off and get married to someone my *father* chose for me. Want me to tell you again how great that was for me?"

"No, thanks. The earful you gave me and Dusty just before we got married was enough."

"We aren't married," she groused and promptly pushed back from the table, stood up, and turned away from him.

"Oh, yes, we are, and I have the papers to prove it. So, are you changing the subject to our marriage for a reason because I could use a sexual fix tonight." He moved closer to her in that cat-like, silent manner he had, startling her when he brushed the hair from her shoulder and planted a kiss there.

"I'm not changing the subject." Her tone was still petulant, although a tendril of want spiraled its way down her spine with sultry memories from all the sexual satisfactions she had experienced in the past several days.

Damn her traitorous body.

Hannah felt the heat from his body caress her as his lips danced from her shoulder to behind her ear. He felt hot to her touch, like he always ran a fever. Maybe this was because he'd been genetically engineered and all. Whew.

Sexy, she thought then shook it off. She was making a point. Unwilling to be sidetracked from her original train of thought, she stepped away and started speaking quickly, "Why can't we just look at a cross shaft closer to our living quarters?"

"Why? Because it's a waste of time. Maybe you just want to spend more time with me than just a year. Are you already addicted to my lovemaking, Hannah?" He moved closer to her. Hannah had no doubts about his ability to seduce her.

Brutal was, in fact, stupendous in bed. *Stop! He's making you change the subject again*, her rational mind intruded.

"It isn't a waste of time. I know what I'm talking about. And for the record, the longer it takes you to earn the money you seek, the longer I'm stuck here. I'd rather be with my family back on Earth, thank you very much." Hannah was almost convinced. She missed her family, but being with Brutal wasn't exactly a hardship.

"You are not a geologist."

"But I almost was, and more importantly, I'm right. Can't we just take a day and check it out?"

"No. I refuse to waste time."

"But—"

"No buts, except for yours, which I'm about to seduce."

"If I have sex with you, then could we look at a cross shaft closer to the mouth of this mine?" she asked, trying to keep the desperation out of her tone.

"You can't use sex as a tool to get what you want."

"Why not? You do."

"Yeah, but I paid for the privilege."

"Oh, I'm paying for the privilege, too, believe me!" she stated caustically.

"Don't press me, Hannah. I'm not in the mood for a woe-is-me lecture tonight."

"Please, couldn't you just trust me once?" she pleaded as she turned into his arms. "One time, Brutal. Couldn't you just give me one time, please?"

"I could trust you once. I just don't want to waste my time in the mine. It's lots of work. I don't want to get behind, at least any more behind than I already am from taking a day to get married and a one-day honeymoon."

"I swear to you, Brutal, it isn't a waste of time. I promise," she said earnestly. Brutal watched her closely as if to gauge her seriousness.

"There is a cross shaft already cut somewhere between the third and fourth kilometer marker down the shaft. Tomorrow on the way down, we can stop and look at it. Will that satisfy your curiosity?"

"Yes, that would be perfect. And you'll see. I'm right."

"Are you? Perhaps if you had sex with me, I'd be more fully convinced."

She smiled with enthusiasm and launched herself onto him, wrapping her legs around his hips. He caught her around the thighs with a grunt just as she fastened her all-too-willing mouth to his. She sucked on his lips a couple of times before thrusting her tongue into his mouth. This earned her another grunt of approval. He tightened his arm around her back to hold her while he kissed her in return.

She was so focused on his delicious mouth and tongue making love to hers she didn't realize he'd carried her into the bedroom until he tried to put her down. She whined and clung to him as her feet hit the floor beneath her.

He tore his mouth from hers long enough to say, "Don't you even want to get undressed?"

She planted her mouth on his and one-handedly tried to unbutton his pants. She couldn't do it because the tremendous hard-on he was sporting blocked her effort. It was a wonder he didn't lose consciousness as his baseball bat sized erection filled with fluid to satisfy her every time.

Brutal pulled away, breathing hard as he undressed quickly, but he never broke their searing eye contact. She also stripped at warp speed, popping a button off her shirt in her eagerness.

She backed up a step and felt the edge of the bed against the back of her legs. She sat and scooted backwards, motioning him to follow. He climbed on all fours over her, collapsing on top once her head hit the pillows. His mouth landed on hers again as he kissed her with a wild, needy ferocity she reveled in.

Moments later, she felt his long, thick shaft enter her with that same wild, needy ferocity that his kiss still distracted her with. Soon, his stroking tongue against hers matched the rhythm of his hips pounding pleasure into her body. She came and moaned into his mouth at the same time he released with a grunt and an extra, powerful thrust. She tried to remember which one of them was supposed to be convinced about something, but she couldn't think about anything beyond this moment as she basked in the aftermath of her gloriously satisfied body.

Chapter 6

The next morning, on their customary one-hour morning trip to his regular site, traveling at a whopping twenty-five miles an hour, Brutal stopped at the cross shaft after about fifteen minutes.

"Here it is," he said, shutting off the tram they were riding on.

"Perfect. Did you cut this cross section?"

"No, it was cut by the last miner to work this claim."

"I wonder why he didn't continue here. This is the optimum spot on your entire property."

"He died suddenly."

"Oh," she said quietly. "Why didn't you continue here then?"

"This was an initial cross section he cut at first. He didn't find anything, so he cut way down to where I am now. It took him five years. He died before he ever saw much Thorium-Z, only enough to keep him going day to day."

"Did he leave the mine to you? Is that why you came here?"

"No, the other miner didn't own the claim outright, just as I don't. A corporation on Earth owns it. I bought the right to mine this stake for three years with a two-year additional option if I end up finding anything. The corporation gets twenty percent of everything I dig up."

"Why did you pick this particular mine?"

"I did some research and paid an independent geologist who would only tell me that, of all the claims available on this planet, this particular one would yield the most Thorium-Z."

"A geologist to the rescue."

He laughed mirthlessly. "Not so far," he said and brusquely led her inside the short cross shaft. It was only seven feet tall, so Brutal had to watch his head as they moved through the passage. It was only cut about fifty feet before it ended in a flat wall of jagged rock.

Hannah looked around along the way, stopping to chip out places every so often.

"You should be mining here, Brutal," she finally said. "You won't find a more optimal place to dig."

"Well, great, I'll think about it. In the meantime, let's get going. I have a long day ahead of me."

"That's it? You'll think about it? But—"

"No buts. Let's go. I said I'd think about it."

Brutal was not at all convinced. Hannah spent the entire day trying to talk him into beginning an excavation at the cross section until he wished he hadn't said he'd think about it.

Back at the dwelling that night, Hannah marched immediately over to his desk and started rummaging through the documents there in an effort to convince him.

"If you'll just let me show you—"

"Hannah, it doesn't matter—" Brutal started to say until he saw her pull out a private drawer with something inside he didn't want her to see.

Of course, she saw it anyway.

Hannah picked up a bunch of documents, and along with it, a certain letter, which fell out of the pile at her feet. Before Brutal could stop her, she scooped it up and stared at the return address. He snatched it out of her hand and slapped it back in the drawer. Then he locked the drawer, trying to ignore the look of hurt now registered on her face.

"Okay, I'll look at your documentation," he said in a completely hopeless effort to avoid a conversation about the letter.

"Who is she?"

"What do you mean?" He knew full well what she meant, damn it. He should have hidden the letter more securely. He could kick himself.

"Who is that letter from? I saw her name, Brutal. Charlotte Stanfield. Oh, and down in the drawer, I noticed another one with Mrs. Thomas Blackthorn and a smiley face inside a heart."

"So?"

"I was led to believe *I'm* Mrs. Thomas Blackthorn at this moment in time. Don't I have a right to know what other women you're corresponding with?" Hannah asked in a not quite jokingly tone.

"No. If we were in a permanent arrangement, then there wouldn't be any other correspondence from other women."

"I see," she said frostily.

"I doubt it," he murmured, wishing now he'd had the foresight to burn the letters from Charlotte.

"I'm going to bed," Hannah said in a quivery voice.

"I'll join you."

"No, thank you. Maybe your letter will keep you company tonight. I'm not in the mood." She turned away from him and disappeared into the sleeping area.

One minute later, he heard her sobbing quietly. Brutal shook his head, wondering how his life had become so complicated so quickly. A week ago, he'd been in complete control of his emotions, if not his libido. Having a woman around changed things. The simple dynamic of his dwelling was now fraught with drama over some letters he should have destroyed. It was his own damn fault!

Hannah didn't need to be jealous about Charlotte Stanfield. But then again, it ultimately protected him from having Hannah get too attached to him. That would be bad, wouldn't it? Better for Hannah to think he had someone waiting for him when her year as his mail order bride was over.

Brutal thought back to when he saw Hannah for the first time, peacefully sleeping in the cryo-chamber cylinder hours before the auction. He had known she would be important to him the minute he'd laid eyes on her. Did she remember hearing him while she slept? He'd done more than just run a finger down her cheek. Did she remember what he'd whispered in her ear?

'I'll make you scream for me,' he'd told her a few times. And he had made her scream. A delicious, innocent screamer currently occupied his bed. Too bad he was ousted for the moment.

The day he'd married her, Brutal had panicked when Hannah hadn't shown up until the last lot for auction. He had worried she was the one who hadn't revived. He didn't know what happened to the brunette, but he did remember her.

Mostly, he remembered the letter he snatched from the postal bag on the way out of the air lock. It was from *her*.

Charlotte Stanfield.

The woman he had left behind on Earth. The woman who was

supposed to have joined him long before several celibate months had elapsed to be his permanent wife. But it turned out Charlotte had her own agenda, which didn't include him anymore. It probably never had, but she did like to play games with other people's lives.

Once she'd declared her undying love for him, she'd then quickly gotten rid of him by convincing him to sell his soul to this godforsaken mine where she would soon follow, and they could be married. Then she had teased him each mail call with letters explaining one excuse after another about why she just couldn't leave Earth to be with him quite yet. With each mail call, he had hoped Charlotte would just show up, but she hadn't.

The missive she had sent directly before the one he'd found on the cryo ship had said she couldn't possibly join him for another year as her dear sister was getting married and she needed to help with the elaborate wedding plans, but she promised to write faithfully. Like her fucking letters would appease his deprived cock for a year.

Brutal couldn't wait for her another year. He wouldn't, because he needed sex. He had already waited longer than any man with his condition would ever expect for her to come to him. So he had conceived of the get-a-mail-order-bride plan. He would acquire a temporary wife for a year, make his fortune, and be free of said mail order bride in time to head back for Earth a rich man to again woo the wealthy, respectable Charlotte Stanfield. At least until the said mail order bride had turned out to be spunky, gorgeous Hannah.

Brutal had read Charlotte's latest missive on the cryo-ship hurriedly before entering the auction. All his plans altered irrevocably with that letter. He was so glad he'd snagged it. Otherwise, he wouldn't have received it until after the auction. What if he hadn't married Hannah? What if he'd foolishly let Erik have her? He might have eliminated himself from the group of bride-seeking miners.

The additional news of no future scheduled mail order bride ships would have forced him into a difficult corner. If he hadn't fought for Hannah, he would have forfeited all of the considerable backbreaking effort already put into his mine. He'd have been forced to Earth for his genetically engineered sexual needs, which was at times, a big pain in his ass. Technically, he could last for around six months even though the lusty brain in his cock was fairly irate after one. Without Hannah, he would have lost everything invested here.

But fate had intervened, making their match inevitable.

Brutal hadn't been as desperate to marry until he'd read the letter from Charlotte informing him she had found someone else and was no longer making plans to join him. He wouldn't allow his feelings to be hurt. Charlotte hadn't meant as much to him once her true attitude regarding genetic freaks was exposed.

Hannah didn't think he was a freak. Her attitude bordered on awestruck over his engineered body. He had already convinced himself she was falling for him. He didn't know if that was good or bad. Quickly, he decided it would be bad if she got attached before the year was over. He only got to keep her for the one year and wondered why that suddenly seemed like not nearly long enough.

From the direction of his bedroom area, he registered silence. Hannah had stopped crying, but then he heard her sniff a few more times. He should go comfort her, probably.

What in the hell was he doing with a temporary wife anyway?

The obvious answer came when a wickedly satisfying sexual memory of his first time with her danced across his barbarian brain. Oh, yeah, he remembered now. He'd been horny. And she'd given him so much more than expected in this temporary marriage bargain.

Brutal wasn't used to sharing emotions with others. On some level, he knew having a wife, even a temporary one, would test new boundaries for him. He was also intrigued to learn what it would be like to share space with another. He found it agreeable on many levels.

Day to day, it was nice to have someone around to converse with, and especially to have sex with on command.

Brutal realized perhaps he was the one getting attached to Hannah, and he shouldn't. She had a sweet smile, which hid an intelligent mind. She was interested in his mining efforts. How many of the other women auctioned off gave a shit about mine output and how they could increase capacity? None.

He decided that for someone who wasn't falling for her, he already missed her, and he needed to stop it. Hannah wanted to go home to her family at the first opportunity. He didn't blame her. She had been sorely abused by the new system of social graces on Earth. She deserved his cooperation after the year was over, not a declaration of love.

Now that her father was dead, only her brother would be able to sell her into her next marriage. The thought of another man listening to her scream her release made him gut sick. Brutal wondered, and not for the first time, what it would be like to spend the rest of his life with Hannah.

It was unfair to compare her to Charlotte, the woman back on Earth he'd sacrificed everything to come here for. He had come to earn Charlotte Stanfield's hard-to-win regard by working and becoming rich. Now that she had dumped him for someone else, Brutal wondered why he was still so determined to be successful on this planet.

In one simple word…Hannah. She made it worthwhile. She made him want to earn *her* respect and esteem. There was nothing left for him on Earth now. No one was waiting for him to come back. No family who longed for his return, ready to open their arms and embrace him. Hannah was technically his only family.

Brutal selfishly decided to keep Hannah as long as he could. He was finding it difficult to picture his future without her. Perhaps he should contact her brother and find out what kind of permanent bride price he would be asking for…*God's wrath!*

What was he thinking?

Hannah didn't want him. She was only here because she had no choice but to be here. No one had helped her, and no one, including her brother, had tried to save her from the mail order bride servitude.

Besides, they had a deal. An arrangement that was to last for a year. He wouldn't stop her from leaving when her year was up. And he *would* let her go when it was time.

Brutal couldn't help the pain he felt around his heart at the thought of no more Hannah. He would be losing someone extraordinary, and more than that—someone special to him.

Brutal would be losing the only woman in existence who had ever given him her virginity. The purest and most personal gift imaginable. He would never forget it for as long as he lived. It was absurd for a man like him to feel this way. Living with a woman had turned him soft and domesticated. He should go fuck her and get his macho, barbarian attitude back, but his heart wasn't in it.

Brutal didn't hear her crying any longer. Or any sound at all. He strolled to the sleeping area and watched her sleep. He could still see tears trailing down her cheeks and wondered why he was being such a bastard.

What did it matter if they spent even a day or two at the cross shaft to satisfy her curiosity? Not much. He would do it. He would do it for her because she deserved one request. But he wasn't going to tell her about Charlotte. He didn't want Hannah to see how livid he still was about Charlotte's betrayal. He'd been a fool to believe a woman like rich, pampered Charlotte could ever love him.

Chapter 7

Hannah knew she was dreaming when she saw her sister. The vast space between them was never far out of her conscious mind, or her dream mind, as it turned out. At least dreaming about Sophie enabled her to pretend she was home again.

For just a little while.

After seeing Sophie's face, her dream turned dark. Hannah relived the day when everything changed, the day the Tiberius Group made their bold move and women suddenly had different rules to obey. It had been surprisingly easy for them.

The U.S. had been following a trend of increasing social conservatism for the past several decades. More women were going the marriage and children route, and upon finishing high school, the majority of women not even opting to go to college.

Hannah wasn't one of them. She didn't want to get married because of what her father had done to her mother.

"Women should get married, stay at home, have children, and leave the work force to the men," the Tiberius Group said.

"That's why unemployment is so high," they'd said.

"All the problems of the U.S. would be solved if only women would admit their place was at home," they'd said.

The Tiberius Group had then infiltrated all aspects of government, law enforcement, institutes of higher learning, and the majority of all Fortune 500 companies, for a start.

Hannah had been denied entrance to her senior-level college physical fitness class at the university where she'd been studying. She was only three classes shy of completing her bachelor's degree when she had been instructed to wait at home for further information.

"Women don't need to get college degrees," the representative from the Tiberius Group told Hannah several days later. They were seated in her college dorm room because she was no longer allowed outside without the accompaniment of a male relative. Unfortunately, her brother Jonathan was out of the country.

"What am I supposed to do?" Hannah asked the Neanderthal seated before her.

The Tiberius representative gave her a tolerant look as if she were five and didn't understand how the world worked. "All you need to do is wait here in your home for your father to come and find a husband for you."

"I don't want a husband," she told him, "and I don't have a father. Never have."

"We have located your father for you," he said brightly. "He'll be here by tomorrow morning, and all will be well for you."

Hannah thought her nearest male relative would be Jonathan, her younger brother. But no, the Tiberius group had scraped the bottom of someone's shoe and found her biological father at a bait-and-tackle shop in California.

"As a matter of fact, yesterday your father found a wonderful husband for your sister Sophie."

"Sophie has a husband?" Hannah hadn't been able to get a hold of Sophie after being denied access to her class and then imprisoned in her dorm room.

"Yes, she is a very lucky woman. Her husband paid a lot of money for her at the corporate auction," the representative said meaningfully, as if being prize sow in a pig auction was grounds for jubilation. Hannah didn't think so.

"Who's her husband?" Hannah asked fearfully. She knew Sophie was secretly in love with someone already, someone she wasn't supposed to be in love with, as a matter of fact. The top executive at her place of work held her spellbound. He was so secret and unavailable that Sophie hadn't even told Hannah his name.

"A man your father found suitable, Hannah. That is all you need to concern yourself with, and he'll find someone suitable for you as well," the condescending Tiberius representative said.

Hannah had been worried about her own circumstances by the time

Sophie had been auctioned off to the highest bidder in a private corporate auction.

But her sister was a permanent bride, bought and paid for by a senior-level executive at the company where Sophie had been employed as an executive business analyst—until the Tiberius group came.

"I still don't want a husband, and if you still insist I must have one, then I want my brother to pick him out for me," Hannah said for all the good it did her.

"I'm sorry, Hannah. Your father takes precedence."

"Why?"

"A father knows what's best for his children, especially daughters," the representative said with superiority.

"My father deserted my mother with two toddlers while she was six months pregnant, but not before he helped himself to all the money she saved from working her ass off for fifteen years," Hannah informed the representative in a near shout. "My father has no idea what's best for anyone except himself, and especially not for the daughters he hasn't even seen in over twenty years."

The representative gave her that insipid, tolerant look again. In his eyes, she was still child-like in her lack of understanding.

The mandatory donation to the new National DNA database made it easier for them to locate her father. And hadn't the two daughters he abandoned before they could even talk enriched his life undeservedly? Her father was the worst kind of opportunist, as he had shown their mother decades ago. Hannah wasn't sorry he was now dead.

The representative didn't comment on her father. Instead, he pulled out a phone and started talking to someone, dismissing her as if she were no more important than an annoying fly buzzing around his head.

Once off the phone, he turned to her as though she hadn't ever said a word. "Women simply need a man to take care of them. It is the way the world should work and will work," he actually said this to her with a straight face.

"Don't do this," Hannah said, knowing full well the zealot in front of her would never change his mind.

"It's the natural order of things," he said in parting.

The bastards.

Hannah learned later when her father had shown up on her doorstep that he'd gotten a record-setting amount from Sophie's new husband, minus the auctioneer's fee, from the highest bidder in a corporate auction held at Sophie's former place of employment. How humiliating *that* must have been for her sister! Men who had been her peers and employees were able to bid on her as if she were a piece of meat.

Her father, Dennis Hoskins, had then shown up the next day. He packed up Hannah, and they had gone directly to Sin City, Las Vegas, the gambling Mecca of the world. Her last name Brent was her mother's maiden name. Her father spent the first several hours with her whining about this, perturbed that she didn't carry his name. She felt he didn't deserve any recognition.

Her father took the money from Sophie's wedding dowry and blew it in less than two weeks playing big man around Vegas. It could have given him a comfortable lifestyle for at least five years or more if he had been prudent, but the word conservative wasn't in his vocabulary. It only included phrases like "It's a sure thing," and "I'm on a hot streak," and Hannah's personal favorite, "I just can't lose on this bet."

He almost doubled his money the first few days there after a three-day gambling marathon. Hannah was backhanded when she suggested he stop after winning so much money. Then soon after, she made the audacious and completely inappropriate request for him to stop gambling. He lost the very next roll of the dice at the craps table, and then seriously started losing his ill-gotten gains. That turned out to be her fault, as well. Her father decided she wasn't a good luck charm any longer when he started losing and relegated her to the hotel room for the remainder of their time there.

Hannah, trapped in her hotel room daily, had eventually called her sister on the sly as she had seen Dennis come back with less and less money each day. She had resorted to stealing money from him while he slept at night. It was the only reason they had any money for food once her father had gone through the entire stake from his eldest daughter's new husband.

When her sister had invited them back to her home in Kansas City, it had been a Godsend because they barely had enough money for food, let alone the transportation there. Sophie arranged for the tickets to be available at the airport. Hannah had told her not to send cash.

Then they had an unfortunate, and as it turned out, fatefully long layover a couple of hours away from Sophie's house. In the last leg of their journey, her gambling-addicted father had cashed in their airfare tickets that Sophie's very generous husband had graciously provided them. Unfortunately, her father wasn't good at waiting. He decided all of a sudden that he felt lucky and had used the absolute last few dollars they had to gamble big on a long shot at the dog track. She watched helplessly as Dennis Hoskins took the entire amount and bet on a dog that had the same name as his first childhood pet.

"A sure thing," he'd said.

"He couldn't lose," he'd said.

"It was fate," he'd said.

"And the winner is…" Not her father's bet. It didn't pay off.

"What a shocker," she'd said and had been summarily backhanded again for her sassy mouth.

So her worthless father married Hannah off to a man who *had* won the race, which was how she ended up with her first husband, Reggie something. He was looking to travel with a wife and father-in-law as cover to escape some bookies he owed a lot of money to. He had just won big at the dog track and didn't want to pay back the money he owed yet, at least not until he had an even bigger stash. Even when addicted gamblers won, it was never enough, Hannah observed in the short time she had spent with her father in Las Vegas.

Her father had convinced Reggie that, for a nominal dowry fee, he would let Reggie marry Hannah if he would also fund their trip to Sophie's house. He further convinced Reggie that, once at Sophie's, they could easily skim more money from his other daughter's rich husband. Reggie thought it was a smashing idea, especially after he thought he'd seen one of the bookie's thugs roaming around the track.

So they went to marry Hannah off to Reggie something.

When Hannah crossed her arms and refused to say, "I do" to a total stranger, she'd been smacked in the face yet again. It hadn't mattered anyway because the racetrack justice of the peace quickly informed them her consent wasn't needed, only her *father's*.

Then they'd gone like beggars to her sister's house, trailing a stranger her father had forced her to marry. Sophie, meanwhile, unaware that Hannah's wedding had taken place, had planned a big dinner party to introduce Hannah to a man her husband thought highly of from work, a man Hannah suspected she would have easily married to escape her father, given the chance.

Paul, the man Sophie's husband had picked out for her, was a very sweet man. He was a mid-level accountant at the company where Sophie's husband worked. Unfortunately, Hannah had already been married off only hours before and was currently unavailable for Paul, the accountant.

Her father and 'husband' hadn't even waited to finish dinner that they had arrived late for in favor of going out on the town to celebrate the 'nuptials.' Sophie and her husband were nice enough not to embarrass her further by suggesting perhaps Hannah should be included in any nuptial celebration as the two gamblers ran out of Sophie's house.

Hannah was grateful to be alone. If she had a place to go, she would have run away that night. In retrospect, she should have run anyway, but she was broke and essentially alone. Women traveling alone garnered too much attention. In fact, they weren't really allowed to travel alone without permission from the men who owned them. She simply would have been tracked down and hauled back.

Hannah refused to ask Sophie for any more money. It smacked too much like something her father would do. She spoke only briefly to her sister that night, her wedding night, before hiding in the guest room and crying herself into emotional exhaustion. She then slipped into bed, unaccompanied—on her honeymoon.

The next morning, Hannah had woken, still alone, to lawmen knocking on the door of Sophie's house. Once at the police station, she learned her father was dead, which surprised her, but not as much as when they told her she was sold off into mail order bride hell. They immediately put her into handcuffs because her louse of a husband, a stranger she had only been married to for less than twenty-four hours, had managed to run up a substantial gambling debt overnight.

The gaming thugs who were owed had just killed her father outright for failure to pay, but her husband had a wife with which to barter his life. She became his get-out-of-jail free card. Reggie told the Tiberius government police, after a body scan showed she was still untouched by him sexually, that she was a frigid bitch who refused to submit to his carnal whims.

Which was a lie. The bastard. Hannah tried to tell them her story and version of events. "What happened was..." she'd started to explain, only to be shushed and her mouth taped.

Then she had been shuffled out to a truck, placed on a cargo ship, and put into a cryogenic freeze for a month, only to arrive in time to snag Brutal Blackthorn as a temporary husband.

And he was the very best husband she could have ever hoped for in this place, or any place, truth to be told. He cooked, he cleaned, and he took care of most of the heavy work, including the mining. And he was reasonable, to a point.

He still didn't want to talk about her geological conclusions regarding the mine where he slaved each day. But then, why would he?

Hannah was just supposed to be some temporary piece of ass that only came to this planet because of credit card debt. Everyone on the spacecraft and on the planet here had been right. It didn't matter whether it was fair or not. It was just life. It wasn't Brutal's fault she was here, far, far away from Earth and missing her family.

If Hannah were truly honest with herself, she would admit she was actually jealous. *That's right. Jealous with a big, green, capital J.* Brutal only wanted Hannah for a year because he already had someone waiting for him back on Earth. Charlotte.

A selected female. A premium-cargo-type of female. Hoity-toity Charlotte Stanfield. Fucking bitch selected female. Selected by Brutal to be his permanent wife. Not Hannah. She hoped Charlotte, Brutal's next wife, would appreciate him.

Oh, yeah, that hurt.

Hannah wanted Brutal to be happy with his choice of permanent wife. He deserved to be happy. She could have done so much worse if Erik had gotten her. A shudder ran through her at the thought of losing her virginity to a cruel man like Erik. She'd probably be dead by now.

But in the end, the reason Brutal was working so hard here on this planet was for...another woman...Charlotte of the expensive stationary.

Hannah woke up suddenly from her nightmares. She couldn't help the tears once again flowing down her cheeks. This time, though, it was at the thought of not being allowed to stay with Brutal permanently. She looked over at the other side of the bed. He was sound asleep on his back. He didn't even snore. And he was so very attractive, not in the classic sense of beauty as defined by the society she used to live in, but in her eyes, he was kind, and he had treated her well. She hated to admit she was falling in love with him, a man she couldn't keep.

She slid closer to his warmth, snuggling up in case her nightmares came back. She vowed to enjoy her limited time with him. She would be the model temporary wife. No more tantrums.

Chapter 8

"Why are you so stubborn and bull headed? You aren't giving me a fair shot!" Hannah railed when Brutal dared suggest they concede defeat at the cross section after only a few hours.

"I told you this was a waste of time in the first place. I gave you four hours. Now, I need to go down to where there is actually some ore to mine," Brutal retorted.

Last night, he'd been willing to give her a day or two, but the more time they spent not finding anything here, the more antsy he became to get back to his regular site.

"But—"

"No, we're done." Brutal dropped his pick ax and turned his back on her. He had merely stopped to let her see for herself that the crosscut cave was a monumental waste of time. Only Hannah wasn't convinced. In fact, she saw possibilities everywhere. She yammered non-stop for the first hour about the cross section having the perfect conditions for a large deposit of Thorium-Z.

"What would it take to convince you to mine here for three days?"

"Three days! Nothing short of a gun to my head will convince me. Now, let's get going. I can still get twelve hours down at the other site." He took a step towards the mouth of the cross section.

"Brutal, please," Hannah said in a small, anguished voice.

Something in that tormented tone stopped him dead. She was serious. Hannah wanted to do a full excavation of the cross section. It would take a minimum of three days to fully explore it. Five days would be more realistic if he believed, as she did, that it contained a big deposit…and yet, he didn't.

Brutal turned back to face her. "Would you be willing to sign on for an additional year with me?" He didn't know what possessed him to ask her for an additional year at that particular moment. Probably because he figured she'd never go for it, and he could stop this argument before it got ugly. Or because the lusty little brain below his belt had piped up.

"What?"

Her eyes widened as he spoke, "You heard me, Hannah."

"You want me to sign on for an extra year of sexual bondage to you in exchange for three days in this cave?" Her tone had turned incredulous, but he could tell she was considering it. Surely she'd never agree to his demand, he thought skeptically.

"I can be reasonable. Shall we say a week? Seven days to fully explore this cross section." Brutal moved closer. "And in return, you sign on for an extra year with me of…sexual bondage. What do you say?"

"I…I…" she stammered as he stepped into her personal space, towering over her in the dim light of the cave.

"Have I finally rendered you speechless?" he mocked.

"No, but—"

"Put your money where your mouth is, Hannah. Do you believe this cross section is the mother lode or not?"

"Yes, but—"

"We can go to town right now and draw up the papers and be excavating where you stand as early as tomorrow morning," he purred. His libido kicked in again right then, and a streak of lust hammered through him. He had wanted her last night before she ran off to bed pouting, but he had decided the wiser course of action would be to leave her alone for a night.

It had been difficult.

"Why do you want me for an extra year? Isn't Charlotte waiting for you back on Earth?"

"That's none of your affair," he said coldly.

"I'm your wife—"

"Only for sexual bondage purposes—" he began.

"Is Charlotte going to wait for two years?"

"—and you're changing the subject. You don't need to worry about Charlotte," Brutal finished clearly.

Charlotte was no longer his concern. Hannah was. Brutal had been so preoccupied with Hannah this past week, he hadn't even thought about

Charlotte. Losing her and enduring her betrayal hadn't been as traumatic as it would have been if he hadn't acquired Hannah during the auction, Brutal realized.

Hannah was so completely opposite of Charlotte, it was like comparing night to day. Brutal had decided that he much preferred nights with Hannah to days with Charlotte.

"All right then, I agree to your ridiculous demand," Hannah stated emphatically, breaking his reverie.

"What?"

"You heard me. Let's go into town and sign new papers."

"Why is this so damned important to you?" he asked her, shaking his head.

"Because I'm right, and I'll prove it to you. And I'm adding my own stipulation on to the new papers."

"What stipulation?"

"When I'm right, you release me no matter how much bondage time I've served. When we discover the vein of pure Thorium-Z, you'll be able to mine it quickly. You'll be able to earn a thousand times what you normally would sifting through the crap at your regular site," she said forcefully.

Brutal actually felt a punch in his gut at the thought of losing her before a full year of sexual gratification with her was up. Or was it more than that? His libido wavered at the demand she made, a weakness he patently refused to acknowledge.

"Fine, but let's just keep this bargain between the two of us," Brutal said. If she were correct about the large vein here, he didn't want word to leak out.

"Why? Afraid you'll lose your piece of ass now that you have me all broken in?"

"You overestimate your significance to me." No, she didn't. "I just don't want any hint of a big vein to leak out to the other miners."

"Why? This is your stake for as long as you're here. No one can mine the claim but you, right?"

"Unless I'm dead. I don't want to be fighting off the scum who live here until I've pulled out every gram of ore from this godforsaken mine."

"Do you swear to abide by it?"

"Do you?"

Hannah held out her slim hand to him. "Let's shake on it."

"I've got a better idea." Brutal grabbed her hand and pulled her the final step to press into his body. He then fastened his mouth on hers to seal the unlikely deal they'd just made.

* * * *

Hannah couldn't believe she'd just gambled a year of her life. Maybe she was more her father's daughter than she was willing to admit. And why would Brutal agree? Why would he want her for more than a year anyway with a woman waiting for him? Her mind reeled at the possibilities and opportunities before her as she shared a decadent kiss with her husband to seal an unholy bargain.

His tongue stabbed into her mouth yet again eliciting a tingling buzz of sensation below. The rough and velvety texture tangled with hers, stroking and swirling around leisurely as if they had all the time in the world to taste each other. Brutal's lip-licking, sensuous, French kisses made her want to faint in ecstasy. His arms tightened around her back as his mouth continued its determined course. She wanted to pull him to the cave floor regardless of the freezing temperature.

In the end, Brutal was the one who finished the kiss. He buried his face in her hair, breathing hard.

"I'll need some supplies," Hannah said after a few moments of her own heavy breathing, still trying to recover from his passionate assault on her lips. It was below thirty degrees in the cave, but Brutal's body was like a furnace. If ever she needed warmth, she just stepped closer to him.

"Let's go to town then," he said, still holding her close. "I need some things anyway."

"Thank you, Brutal," she said sincerely. For all his arrogant warrior ways, he was the first man to actually give her a chance to prove she was capable at her chosen profession, the profession she'd likely never get a chance to experience otherwise.

"When we get to town, stay close to me. Don't trust anyone," he cautioned, patently ignoring her gratitude.

"Of course," she responded, stepping away from his warmth.

Brutal led the way as they went out to the tram, rode back to the large airlock, and closed off the mine. Once through, they hopped on his four-wheeled vehicle and went back to the mining town under the dome of the space station.

Hannah certainly had a different attitude from the last time she came into this place from the cargo ship. She was looking forward to going there to buy supplies for her endeavor. Brutal burst her balloon a little when he informed her he would purchase the goods in town for her. She was a piece of property, and she didn't have any money anyway. He asked her what she needed, and she ticked off five essentials and a couple of luxuries.

Brutal parked in front of the only supply store in the mining encampment. Hannah was reminded of the towns she'd seen in history books of the California gold rush. The moon on which this mining operation existed was Terre formed to support human life. Huge processors had been set up to supply the oxygen and nitrogen atmosphere the miners could exist in.

Thorium-Z was used as the fuel source to power the processors. It was clean burning, and little was needed to power the atmospheric processors. Hannah knew this from reading all of Brutal's documents, but the encampment looked like an 1850's gold mining camp. Thorium-Z was mined like gold in the days long past. It was backbreaking work for most men. Perhaps that was why she'd been so sure her husband would look like a grungy miner forty-niner. Instead, he looked like pure sex bottled in leather.

They entered the supply store together, Hannah staying right on Brutal's heels. She looked around for Erik, the only rational fear she harbored, but didn't see him. Hopefully, he was back at his own mine pouting alone. Hannah shivered for no reason.

While Brutal bartered and argued with the shopkeeper for all the supplies he wanted, Hannah wandered around and looked at the things available in the store. She saw more girly stuff than she would have imagined. There were dresses, shoes, perfume, hats, and even a small library of books from which to chose, but nothing Hannah held dear. She wanted mining supplies.

"Do you want to get Brutal's mail while they're busy arguing?"

asked a soft female voice, startling her.

Hannah turned around and saw a woman behind the counter at the opposite end of where the men were locked in a heated verbal battle over the price of mining tools.

"Sure, why not?" Hannah moved further away from the men to stand before the tiny, dark-haired woman. Her nameplate said "Carla."

"This came today on the transport." Carla handed Hannah a letter with a familiar looking handwriting. "It's funny not to be having an auction today. I guess only mail and mining supplies will be the cargo from now on until the Tiberius Group decides about the mail order bride business."

"I guess," Hannah responded but had stopped listening. She held in her hands another letter from Charlotte Stanfield. It was postmarked a week ago, the day she'd gotten married to Brutal. An ominous sign, Hannah thought, staring unblinkingly at the expensive stationary. Her heart actually ached while pounding out a dismal dance in her chest.

"Does it hurt?" the dark-haired woman asked Hannah in a near whisper.

"Yes," Hannah responded in a wounded tone, not thinking. It hurt like hell to be falling in love with a man who had another woman waiting for him back on Earth. "I mean…What?"

Hannah looked up into the expressive eyes of the shopkeeper's wife. She had a wide-eyed look, which she then directed down the long counter at the two men still in animated negotiations.

"Brutal's so big. I wondered if it hurt—you know, to have sex with him." Carla then fairly leered at Brutal. Speaking quietly, she added, "All the women here want to know."

Hannah couldn't believe it. Carla, the shopkeeper's wife, had a lust-filled crush on Brutal. Apparently, lots of women did. Wasn't Hannah just the luckiest temporary wife on the planet? All the mail order brides here wanted to fuck her husband. Great.

"The answer is no. Brutal would never hurt me," Hannah said, but then reversed her private opinion, feeling the weight of the letter in her hands. She wanted to read the contents almost more than she wanted to prove she was right about the cross section of the mine.

"All the women here wished he would bid on them, but he never bid on anyone until you," Carla said wistfully, continuing her leering perusal of Brutal, who was completely oblivious to her sultry regard.

"Is that right?" Hannah said off-handedly, wondering how she could sneak this home to read it before handing it over.

"Yes, lots of them were mad, too," Carla whispered, still watching Brutal with lust evident on her thin face. Hannah expected drool to drip out of her gaping mouth.

"You don't say," Hannah remarked, turning her back to the men and their escalating argument. She slipped her finger under the seal of the letter, took a breath, and then broke it in half.

Oops, she thought. *I accidentally opened the letter.*

Carla, the shopkeeper's wife, had her eyes fully on Brutal, so Hannah felt safe in flipping up the envelope flap and then accidentally pulling out the single sheet of stationary.

'*My darling Thomas,*' it began.

Thomas? Oh, yeah, his real name. Hannah decided she preferred Brutal. She continued reading the missive quickly, trying to listen with one ear to the men at the end of the counter while keeping one eye on Carla to keep from getting caught.

'*You must come back to Earth at once, darling. Daddy wants me to marry a horrible, degenerate man. I've been able to put him off for now, but you must contact me. Please, Thomas, you must come for me. I need you now.*
With all my love and devotion, Charlotte.'

Hannah winced at the pain in her middle. Pain like she had just been sucker punched in the gut took her breath. She slipped the letter back into the envelope and held the flap so the shopkeeper's wife wouldn't see that she'd violated the confines of the mail.

Hannah tucked the letter inside her jacket and wondered how she would ever be able to give an opened letter to Brutal, especially when he was so adamantly opposed to her knowing anything about his love, Charlotte. She was no longer patiently waiting for him back on Earth.

She wanted him to come back home *now*…desperately. She needed him.

Hannah took a moment to pout, and then the rebellious part of her brain took over. She wanted her chance. *So, too bad, Charlotte*, she thought. *You'll have to keep Daddy at bay for a little while longer, you pampered little princess.* Brutal was hers for another year, or at least until she could prove the mine was the mother lode.

Hannah wanted her opportunity. Seven days. That was all she needed. Surely Charlotte could wait for seven damn days. Then she and Brutal would both be free to return to Earth. It only hurt her stomach for a moment or two at the thought of giving Brutal up for his next impatient wife. Okay, so it hurt for longer than a moment or two. It hurt like a bitch.

A fucking, impatient bitch named Charlotte.

Chapter 9

Once they returned from the supply store, Hannah took her jacket off and hung it up, pretending to be casual. She also pretended the letter she was hiding, which had fairly burned a hole in her pocket all the way back to the mine, didn't matter.

But it did. It made her want to cling to Brutal and never let go. An interesting concept had festered in the wake of the shopkeeper's wife sharing the salacious information regarding all the other mail order brides coveting that which was hers and hers alone. Brutal.

Well, he was hers only until he found out about Charlotte's heartfelt plea for his return. Hannah didn't want to go down the path of depression just yet. One more week. She deserved one week after all she'd endured.

She watched as Brutal secured their purchases on the mine tram for the next day. She glanced with interest as he moved easily with the supplies slung over one shoulder. She loved watching him move. Seeing him swing that double-sided pick ax everyday as his muscles worked bunching and contracting was delicious enough to make her glad she was a woman for once. He told her they would rest up tonight for an early start in the morning. Meanwhile, she was contemplating several seduction scenes buzzing around in her over-aroused mind. The longer she thought about them, the more convinced she became she couldn't continue until she tested all the possibilities.

Brutal shrugged off his leather jacket while she watched him. She knew her mouth was hanging open in appreciation of him. Was there ever a man who had ever looked so good in leather? No, she thought not.

"Why are you looking at me like that?"

"Like what?"

"I don't know. Like you've never seen me before." His hands rested on his hips, and he nodded his head forward in question. His tone still sounded a little annoyed at the argument he'd had with the shopkeeper over the supplies, she suspected. Time to soothe the savage beast who was her husband, at least for the time being.

Hannah strolled forward and didn't stop until she stood directly before him. Her head tilted completely back. She didn't break eye contact as he stared at her questioningly.

"I was wondering," she paused a moment to build her courage, "if you would let me take control if we went to bed right now?"

His eyes darkened. Did he understand her intent?

The heavy-lidded perusal he laced her with said he did. She put her hands on his hips and pulled him forward until their lower halves touched. The intensity of his chocolate-eyed regard made her insides melt and want to surrender to him. She smiled at the huge bulge she felt rising against her stomach. She had his attention, all right, but would he let her ride him like she longed to do?

"You want to be on top?" The tone of his voice had lowered an octave. She licked her lips in anticipation of his mouth on her body. Maybe the position wasn't so important after all. Maybe she simply craved his touch.

"Yes."

"And you think I'm going to turn you down?"

"I'm not sure." His heat-filled stare left no doubt they were about to have carnal knowledge of each other in the next charged moment, but the dominate position was still up in the air. Now that he was pressed up against her where she could immerse herself in his scent and warmth, the position of being on top became less important than just wanting to be satisfied. The position didn't matter at all two seconds later as she took another deep breath of him. His warmth fairly tanned her skin. Just getting naked with him became paramount.

"Lead the way," he invited huskily. "And for the record, you don't have to ask permission ever again. I'm yours whenever you want me, however you want me, in any position you desire."

A rush of breath she hadn't realized she was holding pushed out of her lungs. She grabbed his hand and led him to the bedroom.

Once there, he stood stoically while she undressed him, one piece at a time until he was gloriously naked and his proud sex jutted out waiting for her next command. Hannah undressed herself quickly while he watched, practically licking his lips. She waited for his amusement, but it never came. She directed him to the bed and requested him to lie on his back. He complied, placing his hands behind his head as if to watch curiously for what she would do next. She stood at the foot of the bed for only a moment before crawling up to cover his body with hers.

Before she lost her nerve, she straddled his hips, the ridge of his erection resting on her very slick entrance. She leaned forward to kiss his muscular chest while she slid her warm, wet opening up and down his massive sex. She trembled suddenly in need as her clit stroked across the tip of his penis. Her heart pounded madly against her ribcage in desire. She stroked herself across him a few more times and heard herself moan. Brutal unlaced his hands from behind his head and slid his fingertips into her hair. He pulled her forward to kiss him. She pushed closer into his lips, dipping her tongue into his mouth aggressively as the shift in her body put the very tip of his sex in position to enter her drenched passage.

She wrenched herself from his mouth and plunged down, impaling herself on his massive, thick, and ready shaft. The sensation of his penis overfilling her anxious wet heat sent a rush of air out of her lungs followed immediately by her sharp intake of breath as her body tried to accommodate his substantial girth.

She placed her hands on his chest for balance and then rose up and slammed herself down on him again. And again. The pressure within was exquisite. When she chanced to open her eyes, it was to see Brutal's shining ones watching her. His heat-filled regard made her wild. She held his steady gaze as she rode him. When she leaned forward slightly, she was able to scratch the itching demand made by her anxious clit.

She groaned upon finding satisfaction in rubbing herself against him until the orgasm took her by surprise. Brutal watched her climax and she saw it reflected in his eyes. A satisfied smile crossed his face at her release. His hands went to her hips in the next moment as undulating waves of pleasure wracked her internally. He held her hips in place as he surged up for several strokes, his gaze still smolderingly and passionately directed at her. She got to see his climax as well. His eyelids dipped twice as he growled when he came slamming upwards into her completely satisfied and still clenching passage.

Brutal reached up and pulled her into a bear hug, his long arms wrapped around her as if he'd never let her go. She wished for it to be true. She could be happy forever in his warm, strong arms.

* * * *

Brutal was exhausted at the end of the first day in the cross section. He knew Hannah was, too, but she fairly glowed with anticipation of living her dream of being a geologist.

As they lumbered painfully into the living quarters, Brutal decided he didn't even want food. First, he wanted a shower, and then he wanted sleep. But Hannah was all juiced up. She grabbed his face with two hands and kissed him like she hadn't seen him for a week. He knew where this was going to lead and smiled inwardly. Hannah was full of surprises, as it turned out.

After they had returned from getting the supplies the day before, Hannah had been in an odd mood. She had barely spoken to him on the trip home. He'd been thinking about the heated argument with the crook that sold supplies in town. Brutal knew the shopkeeper overcharged him, but unfortunately, he was the only game in town for mining supplies.

Once he'd bought everything they needed, Brutal turned to make sure Hannah was close by. He was waiting for Erik to jump out and grab her at any moment. She stood pensively at the end of the counter with the shopkeeper's wife. Had they been talking?

Carla watched him like a cat eyeing cream. He made a note to ask what she had talked to Hannah about, but then completely forgot when they arrived back at their quarters, and Hannah had immediately wanted to have sex. Brutal hadn't expected it. Having Hannah initiate the amazing sexual encounter the night before was all the sweeter for him. He'd been trying to get her to try other sexual positions, and she had chosen one of her own. She climbed on top of him and rode him until they were sweaty, sated, and more than completely satisfied.

It also had rejuvenated him to full capacity for today.

Now, at the end of their first day, even as tired as she had to be, Hannah had that same look in her eye. It was the one from last night, which meant she was in the mood yet again. Playing geologist was apparently a potent aphrodisiac for her and certainly no hardship for him.

"Let's go take a shower, Brutal. We're filthy," she said between lustful kisses across his mouth.

"Right now? Don't you want to eat something first?"

"No."

"Lead the way, my anxious wife."

Hannah stripped him with the ferocity of a wild animal. Once they were both naked, she led them to the shower. First, she rubbed her body with soap while he watched, and then she rubbed her body all over him. She soaped him head to toe, spending copious amounts of time making sure his cock and balls were completely clean, too. After water sluiced over both of them, removing the suds, Brutal found he was as rock hard as the first day he'd taken her. Like he had been celibate for six months and not just a day.

Brutal would never, in a thousand millenniums, forget the gleam in her eyes as she pressed kisses down his throat. She didn't retreat either. She continued kissing a path down his chest, her hands resting on his hips.

When she kissed him just above his belly button, she also slipped down on her knees in front of him. He made an inhuman noise somewhere between a growl of disbelief and a howl of jubilation when he felt her lips around the tip of his penis. He looked down to see her slip his cock into her luscious mouth, forcing him to brace his arms against the shower walls for balance. All the while, hot water blasted his back.

Brutal knew she had never done it before, but that didn't make it any less erotic to watch. And he watched her. She was careful. Deliberate. She put him all the way in as far as he would fit and then withdrew, sucking until he thought he would lose his mind in pleasure.

He could always last for hours before shooting his load, but one innocent, little temporary wife was about to turn him into a minuteman missile. Brutal felt her suck him back into her mouth again. He realized he had closed his eyes to keep from letting loose.

"Hannah?" he managed to say. He put a hand on her head to pull her off. But God's wrath, he didn't want her to stop. She was going to get a really big surprise in a second.

"Hannah!" He was about to burst. She stopped and slid her mouth off him slowly and looked up at him, smiling. He smiled back, like a lovesick puppy, he was certain. She pursed her lips and kissed the end of his rock-hard cock.

"It's okay, Brutal. I know what I'm doing. I saw a movie once," she said with utter confidence and put his substantial erection right back in her mouth. And sucked him.

Once he was as deeply embedded as possible, he felt her hands slip around to his ass and grab hold. He felt her fingernails digging in, pulling him closer and further into her mouth until he couldn't take the seductive power of it any longer. Back and forth she sucked, harder and harder with each thrust, taking him deeply into her mouth. Her tongue darted all around his sensitive, plum-sized head as the suction from her mouth increased.

Steam swirled around him, hot water pounded his back, and Hannah was sucking his cock like a pro. He wanted to watch her, but he knew he couldn't. If he looked down at her luscious, wide mouth on his shaft, her wet hair ticking his thighs, it would be over. But God's wrath, it would feel so great to just let go.

His head dipped forward. His eyes opened, directed by his voracious libido. She pulled him inside her mouth, and that was his last coherent thought.

Brutal understood what true nirvana was when he released his wad, howling while she swallowed every drop from him. Not that this was the first time he'd ever had a blowjob. Not even the first time a woman had swallowed his cum, but it was so unexpected from her, a virgin geologist on her first try.

It was absolutely the best he had ever experienced.

Brutal fell to his knees in front of her, clutched her to him, and resisted the urge to tell her he was falling in love with her. No need to give her a weapon like that.

Instead, when he stopped trembling and got enough of his strength back, he pulled her to her feet and soaped her from head to toe, massaging every place on her body in reciprocation.

He placed her hands against the wall of the shower and turned her away from him. He slipped his hands around to her breasts to play. She bent slightly, backing her butt into his already stiff again cock. He slipped a hand from her breast down her belly and fingered her until she screamed her release. She was so wet. Creamy moisture dripped from between her legs, and he decided he needed a drink of her.

He pulled her away from the tile and positioned her exactly where he'd been when she'd taken his cock in her mouth. He adjusted the shower so warm water kneaded her back, and he kneeled before her. Her eyes widened as he grabbed her by the ass and buried his face in her curls, groaning his pleasure at her utterly intoxicating taste.

Brutal licked her creamy center until she vibrated in need, and then he took her clit between his lips and sucked on her until she climaxed again. At some point, she had twined her fingers into his hair. He kissed a path up her belly to suck on a nipple. He held her steady when her legs gave out from under her. The water started to cool, so he rinsed her off and carried her to their bedroom.

Once in bed, she climbed on top of him and promptly fell asleep draped all over him as though she were afraid he might get away in the night. Not likely. Brutal clutched her to him, stroking her hair and body and wondering what he'd done to deserve Hannah. He was a lucky bastard.

In the days to follow, Brutal discovered that a charged-up, motivated Hannah was a sight to see. Every night for the first five nights after spending a grueling day in her cross section of the cave, she had done exactly the same thing.

Hannah rushed him to bed every night until he didn't know if he were more exhausted from mining or from *her* insatiable sexual demands. He recharged every night, and the frequent rejuvenation process almost made him tired. Almost.

After the sixth night with nothing to show from her mine, she began to show her concern. They didn't make love that night. The morning of the seventh day, Hannah said little before they left, and he didn't provoke her.

Brutal wasn't going to be a sore winner, but he was going to collect on the debt. He planned to take her to town and get it in writing on the morning of day eight. It was a dirty trick, but he didn't want to let her go. He planned to woo her. He wanted to marry her, permanently. He didn't expect her to agree unless he spent the extra year persuading her. And he intended to do just that. Whatever it took.

* * * *

For all the hard work they did over the seven days in the cross shaft, the Thorium-Z weight count they'd managed to get out by the beginning of day seven amounted to about eighty grams, which translated to about what they needed to output in an hour to merely keep up with the day-to-day expenses.

Brutal's regular mine had been yielding a minimum of one hundred pounds a month, and most months he got a hundred and twenty pounds. And he was being so nice about it. Never once all week did he hurl insults at the low production. Never once did he say a cross word about her theories. Never had Hannah worked so hard for so little in return.

In hour seventeen of day seven with no hope in sight of the huge deposit she felt in her bones was here, Hannah decided not to give up. She would simply beg Brutal for one more day. They were close. They had to be. She wasn't wrong. She simply couldn't be.

"I know this mine has been stubborn, Brutal, but I still believe in it."

"Well, you have fifty-seven more minutes to prove it," he said. Hannah listened closely, but he didn't sound like he was gloating. Yet. He would be in fifty-seven minutes. How could she convince him to give it another few days?

"I think we might need just a little more time—" she started out.

"No," he cut her off. "I gave you a week. I'm already going to have to kill myself to make up for losing a week's worth of output from the other site."

"Please, Brutal…"

"Don't 'please Brutal' me, Hannah. I admire your tenacity, but this mine isn't going to yield anything, no matter how hard you wish for it to be true."

"I'm not wishing it. I went to school for this. I worked hard to learn it. I can feel it in my gut, Brutal. One more day."

"No."

"I'll sign on for another year," Hannah offered. It stopped him. He put down the pick ax he'd been wielding and fixed a disbelieving gaze on her.

"What makes you think I want another year with you?" he asked matter-of-factly. His stare burned to her soul. He was giving her that big, bad wolf glower he got sometimes. It was blatantly sexual and never failed to have an impact on her. She wanted him.

"Why did you want the second year you're about to get?" she countered with a yeah-I-want-you glare of her own.

"I like making you scream," he said with a sardonic chuckle.

So did she.

But back to the topic at hand, she wanted—no, she *needed*—one more day. Before she could open her mouth, he said, "No."

"You are *so* stubborn," Hannah said, realizing she had lost, and she owed him a second year. She turned her back on him.

"And you're a poor loser," Hannah heard him mutter.

* * * *

"No, I'm not," Hannah said passionately, turning back to him. "I'm right. I know I am. Can't you feel it, Brutal? We are *so* close."

He *had* felt a certain expectant vibe in the air from her conviction and passion that she was on the trail of a big find, but it hadn't panned out, and time was up.

A deal was a deal.

Brutal knew she would have expected him to let her go if they had found the mother lode of Thorium-Z.

"No, I don't feel anything but how tired I'm going to be trying to make up for a week of wasted work. Besides, you still have forty-four minutes by my calculation. Are you giving up?" he teased.

"No, I'll never give up," she said solemnly and resumed chipping away the center of the flat surface with a small pick ax.

Brutal let her work out her anger hammering away at the mine until they'd gone past the eighteen-hour mark by half an hour.

Then he called it.

"All right, it's over. Stop."

"No."

"Hannah, you gave it your best shot. I've never seen anyone work as hard to accomplish anything, but you have to know when to quit."

"But if I quit, then I'm a failure," she said and burst into tears.

"That's not true," he said quietly with as much sincerity as he could offer while she sobbed. Brutal had admired her endless spirit all week. She fought hard for what she believed in.

"Yes, it is." She slumped to the ground and cried a river. He let her get her frustrations out for a few minutes before approaching her. He squatted down, and she threw her arms around him. He felt her hot tears on his throat.

Brutal picked her up and carried her still sobbing to the tram and back home again. He put her in the shower with him and tenderly shampooed her hair and scrubbed her body. Hannah allowed him to wash her without comment, but she did snuffle a little.

Afterwards, he made them something to eat as she sat in her robe and stared into space. At least she had stopped crying. Her tears bothered him more than he was willing to admit. He knew what despair felt like, having endured it himself regularly in his life, and he hated to see her beaten down like this.

Often the world was not fair, and perhaps Hannah needed to learn this lesson. Or perhaps she didn't. Perhaps she knew exactly how the life-is-not-fair lesson worked.

Brutal led her to bed, expecting her to keep to her own side of the large space, but she surprised him. As soon as he got beneath the sheets and settled on his back, Hannah slipped over to him and climbed on top of his body. His hands went to her back to massage the muscles there. Her head rested on his shoulder, and one of her hands trail up to his face. He was about to say something comforting when she moved her face to his and began kissing him ferociously.

"Love me, Brutal," she said between urgent kisses.

I do, he thought as he gathered her in his arms, but he still couldn't find it in himself to say the words out loud to her. He had said them to Charlotte, only to have them flung back in his face later on. It was harder to make the same mistake again.

"You're beautiful, Hannah. I'm so lucky to have you," he murmured, kissing her hair. Soon she slid her luscious body over his seductively, making him as hard as the rock he mined.

"You're wrong, Brutal. I'm the lucky one."

Without warning, she lifted up and impaled herself on his ready shaft until he was balls deep, stretching her womb. She pulled back up part way and slammed down on him again. Soon, she was aggressively pounding up and down as if to wrench an orgasm from him. He didn't want to come alone, but when he tried to touch her, she refused to allow it. Was she further punishing herself?

Hannah pinned his hands above his head to make her point, never slowing the rapid pace of her body, allowing his to pierce hers repeatedly. Once satisfied that he wouldn't try to pleasure her, she slid her hands to his shoulders and dug her fingernails into his skin.

Brutal watched her. The determination on her face was rigid. She wanted to fuck him, so he let her. It was perhaps a way to gain some measure of control on her part after being beaten by the mine.

Brutal allowed all the sensations he was experiencing to envelop him. Her damp hair tickled his chest. Her short fingernails pierced the skin on his shoulders. Her slick, vaginal passage sucking on his cock as she crashed her tight entrance above him over and over made for an exhilarating experience.

She was so tight as he filled her that he couldn't hold off much longer. He heard her rasping breaths, and then a tiny scream erupted from her and she stiffened, arching slightly as she wrenched an orgasm out of herself. He felt her clench up and down as she continued her assault. He couldn't wait.

I love you, Hannah, he screamed in his mind.

A tidal wave of sensation surrounded his groin and he spewed inside of her as he growled his utter satisfaction. After several moments of bliss, Brutal tried to breathe normally again. He chanced a look at Hannah. She had a slight smile playing across her lips as if she'd conquered something important.

Whether she knew it or not, she *had* conquered something important. His heart.

Chapter 10

The next morning, Hannah couldn't help but try once more. The night before, she had been angry and had poured her frustrations out by aggressively fucking Brutal. He hadn't complained, of course, but it had been cathartic for her. He had been sweet enough to let her do with him what she wanted. He'd already told her she didn't ever need to ask permission, but last night had been different for her. She loved him so much, but didn't know how to tell him, or if she even should since she didn't get to keep him. This thought set her attitude for this morning at very petulant.

She just couldn't face going back to Brutal's regular dig site when she still believed fervently that her cave was better.

"Brutal—" she began cautiously.

"No," he responded without looking up from his breakfast.

"I didn't even say anything yet."

"I don't have to be psychic to know you are about to beg me to go to your cave once more."

"I don't want to give up." She tried to keep the whine out of her tone.

"You don't have to give up, Hannah."

"I don't?"

"No, but it doesn't mean I'm going back to dig there anymore. I need to mine at my regular site."

"Then you're going alone. I can't stand to watch you waste your time when I know a veritable gold mine is in that cave," Hannah flung out the ultimatum she had only thought of moments ago. She was prepared to fight until he agreed.

"Do I have to carry you? I *will* throw you over my shoulder barbarian style and haul your ass down the mine."

"Why? You don't need me down there." She pouted.

"I want to keep my eye on you."

"Just leave me here. I don't want to see you. It's not like you can fuck me down there anyway. I'll just stay here."

"You are the most stubborn woman."

"Gee, I wonder where I learned that from."

"You are going, and that's final." Brutal jerked on his leather jacket and reached for hers.

"No, I'm not."

"Hannah, so help me God!" Brutal grabbed up her jacket to fling at her, and the opened letter from Charlotte dislodged from her inner pocket and fluttered to the floor between them. The one she had opened last week at the supply store. The one she hadn't gotten around to hiding in a better place. Damn it.

The expensive stationary was recognizable, of course, even as it landed face down. There was a heart scrawled on the back flap surrounding the broken seal of wax on the letter.

"What was that letter doing in your jacket, Hannah?" Brutal asked in a cold, chilling voice. Her jacket now crumpled between his hands, forgotten.

"Oh, did I forget to mention I picked up a letter for you when we were in town last week?" She managed to keep the quiver out of her voice. "Silly me."

Brutal stood like a statue, a war of expressions fighting for recognition on his chiseled face. He twisted her jacket, bunching it between his fingers, still staring at the letter on the floor.

She had debated this whole past week about whether to give him the damn letter at all. Hannah just didn't want him thinking about Charlotte as she worked like a slave in the cross section of the mine. She knew it was childish, but she had wanted Brutal all to herself.

Hannah especially didn't want him to take one look at the pleading letter and divorce her. He couldn't leave her, could he? They had to spend at least a year together, right? Or was that just wishful thinking on her part?

Oh, who was she kidding? All he had to do was sell her to someone else or lie and tell the officials she had done something shameful, like failing to spread her legs to his satisfaction.

"You neglected to mention you were reading my mail behind my back." He stared down at the obviously broken wax seal of the letter. A tic had formed in his cheek as his jaw clenched. He glanced at her jacket twisted in his hands as if seeing it for the first time. He hung it back up on the coat rack.

"I'm not sorry," she said.

"Aren't you?" he remarked, but he didn't seem too surprised.

"It's a letter from Charlotte, as you can clearly see. I opened it, and I read it, too. She is begging you to come back and marry her," Hannah said defiantly. *In for a penny, in for a pound*, she thought wildly.

"I see. And you did this because...?" He still wasn't looking at her. His hands now rested on his hips judgmentally.

"Because—all right, fine. I was jealous of her. I admit it. Are you happy now? I finally ended up married to someone not horrible. I just wanted to know how much you meant to her. I wanted to know what kind of woman you would kill yourself in this environment for, seeing as how it isn't me." Hannah ended her tirade on a sob.

"I told you, she's none of your business."

"But—"

"No buts. Why couldn't you leave it alone?" Brutal grabbed the letter without looking at her and stalked out. He looked angrier than she had ever seen before, like he might enjoy killing her with his bare hands. She shuddered at her own foolish thoughts. Brutal wouldn't hurt her no matter how much she deserved it.

And this time, she probably did.

He paused at the door. "I won't be back until late. Lock the door. I'll knock tonight," he said before he slammed the portal door shut.

"I'm sorry," Hannah called out to the closed door. He hadn't heard her. She slumped to the floor and allowed herself a good, pitiful cry. It would never be the same between them. She had just bought herself two years of purgatory.

Purgatory with the man she loved, who loved someone else.

Life was so unfair.

* * * *

Brutal stomped out of his quarters and over to the door leading to the mine. He opened the letter and read what Hannah had known for a week.

"…with all my love and devotion, my ass," he muttered to himself as he made his way through the air lock to the mine and over to the tram.

He traveled for five minutes before it occurred to him that Hannah didn't know his true feelings regarding Charlotte. It finally occurred to him he'd never said anything that would make her think the relationship between him and Charlotte was over.

At first, it had been a comfortable defense for him so he could dismiss her in two years, but now he didn't want Hannah to leave. He loved her infuriating ways. He admired her undeniable thirst to force a mine to yield what she wanted because she insisted she was right.

He enjoyed every minute of every day they had spent together. He wanted her desperately. And he loved her, as he'd never loved any other woman before.

Brutal took a couple of minutes to consider things from Hannah's point of view. She said she was jealous of Charlotte. He had never given her any reason to doubt that Charlotte was the reason he was here killing himself. She was emotional about the failure at her mine. It occurred to him she hid the letter because she wanted her chance to prove she was right about her theory without having Charlotte to think about.

Brutal actually smiled at her still begging this morning for another day. He was planning to surprise her and give her one more day. He had planned to ride down silently on the tram as if it were any other day, and not even say anything until they got to the cross section. She would have been so happy.

Intercepting his mail was unconscionable. He read the letter from Charlotte again. Charlotte had never intended to marry him. She had only used him as a ploy to goad her father.

Brutal had been wholly unsuitable as husband material, but she had assured him her father would concede and allow his courtship, if Brutal were to acquire a substantial sum of money, the initial reason he was here busting his ass.

The letter he had received the day he married Hannah had been from Charlotte informing him she had found someone even more unsuitable. She was releasing herself from their agreement, a pact, she informed him heartlessly, she had never planned on keeping anyway due to his background. Besides, there was a bartender who really made Daddy furious, so she was moving on and told him to do the same.

'I know you love me with all your heart, Thomas, but I could never love or seriously consider marrying a genetic freak like you. Of course, I never planned to join you at the mine. I thought you would come to understand this eventually. Yet, each week you sent another missive asking me to come to that godforsaken mining planet. You may stop waiting for me. I have a certain standard of living to maintain, which you will never be able to fulfill. You need to try to move on,' she'd written in her last, hateful missive, the one Hannah had seen in his desk. That letter had led him to an unexpected bargain with Hannah and the right to her body for another year. He smiled at the realization he now had two years to convince her to care for him.

Brutal *had* moved on—very easily—to sweet, stubborn Hannah. Thankfully, this letter didn't mention anything about her last eye-opening letter.

My, how Charlotte had changed her tune when things didn't go her spoiled, bratty way. Now, it was time to ponder Hannah's response. She had been jealous? Did she care for him? Perhaps he needed to find out.

Just then, Brutal arrived at the cross section cave. Hannah's mine, as he called it now. He stopped the tram, taking a deep, cleansing breath and letting it out again. He looked at the hole Hannah had insisted for over a week was the mother lode. She was so certain it had a huge vein of ore in it. It was only fifteen minutes by tram down the shaft. It would simply be too good to be true for a substantial vein to be located so close to the mouth of the mine opening, wouldn't it?

He thought of the night before. He reminded himself he'd planned to give this hellhole one more day to produce. The argument this morning, which led him leave her alone, was fast fading. Hannah was jealous of Charlotte. Did that mean she was falling for him? He sighed, chuckling to himself at her stubborn attitude this morning, and shut off the engine on the tram.

One more day, for Hannah.

Brutal entered the shallow cross shaft and looked at the wall Hannah had been focused on the day before. He picked up the ax and swung with all his might at the very center of the surface. He hit dead center and a shower of stone sent grit backbiting into his exposed skin.

It was very unusual for the rock to shatter in such a manner. Brutal looked up at the depression in the stone. He squinted at the hole.

What the hell!

In the very center of his first pick strike for the day; he saw a lighter color of stone emerge. *Thorium-Z!* Brutal picked up the ax and started swinging like a berserker. He chipped all around the lighter stone. After only half an hour, he had uncovered a five-foot diameter hole of solid Thorium-Z.

The largest find to date.

She had been right! Brutal hollered out loud. Although part of him wanted to rush and get her, bring her back and apologize over and over for not believing in her theory, he needed to accomplish something more. If he spent just a few more hours here, he would be able to bring a big chunk back for her to see.

A big, Thorium-Z colored surprise.

Hannah was going to be so excited. Brutal couldn't wait to see her face.

* * * *

Hannah heard Brutal knock at the door after being gone only an hour. Had he forgotten something? Was he back to throw her over his shoulder and carry her down the mine barbarian style as he had threatened earlier?

A lick of excitement careened down her body at the thought of being slung over one burly, muscular shoulder. She should take every opportunity with him. Would they have time for a quickie? Would he still be angry with her? Should she be scared to open the door to him? Hannah headed towards the airlock with trepidation, then shook her head. Brutal would never hurt her. If she knew nothing else, she was certain of that fact.

Hannah was convinced he wouldn't start now. She turned the lock and swung the door open.

"Did you miss me...?" Hannah started out, but the words died on her lips as she stared at the large form filling the doorway.

Oh, God, no. Erik.

Chapter 11

"I'm going to fuck you until you bleed," Erik Vander said as he stormed through the portal door to their quarters. His big hand shot out, catching her completely unaware as he punched her in the chest. The blow knocked her on her ass. She struggled to suck air back into her lungs from his wicked, unexpected blow.

"Get out!" she wheezed with all the bravado she could muster.

"Oh, I don't think so, my precious whore." He slammed the door shut. It bounced, hitting the frame so hard it vibrated back open about an inch.

"Brutal, help!" she screamed, wishing for a miracle she knew wouldn't come.

"He can't hear you, bitch. I heard the tram. It's just you and me and an overdue fuck party." He advanced towards her as Hannah scrambled to her feet. She skirted around the dining room table as if it would stop him.

"You're wrong. He'll be back any minute."

"I say you're lying, you cunt," he spat out and lunged over the table at her. "Besides, it won't take me long to get my fill of you."

"Oh, so you're quick on the draw, huh? That's too bad. Brutal can go for hours," Hannah taunted him, perhaps imprudently. She was on her own with Erik the Evil for as long as she could last. Probably not long, but she wasn't going down without a fight.

Hannah dodged his grasping hands as he dove over the dining table at her. The plate from breakfast went crashing to the floor. She danced away and made a beeline for the portal door. If she could just get to the mine entrance door, she could open it and lock it from the other side. The door had a coded keypad.

"You're mine!" he screeched. Erik tackled her face down before she got within five feet of the door. His tremendous bulk flattened her and knocked the breath out of her again. Damn it!

He grabbed her by her hair and hauled her up as she tried in vain to suck air into her lungs. She twisted and elbowed him in the solar plexus with all her might. He grunted but was otherwise unaffected by her blow, so she kneed him in the balls. That made him let go of her hair at least, but he was now between her and the door.

Hannah turned, searching for a weapon of some sort. Brutal probably just used his bare hands, so she didn't think he had any weapons. *Kitchen. Knife.* She ran without thinking.

She made it as far as the dining area when Eric slammed into her, pinning her to the table. She had been kidding herself. She only lasted as long as she had thus far because she had been a physical fitness minor in college. She knew a few moves, like the infamous groin kick, but without help, she was done.

In about five minutes, she probably wouldn't care. She already hurt everywhere. Erik had no compunction whatsoever about hitting a woman. He bent her over the table where Brutal had fed her last night and this morning. He had cooked again after her miserable final day of failure at the mine.

Hannah wished she could turn back time. She wished she hadn't been so hardheaded about her theory and gone with Brutal today. He *did* need to work, and she had thrown the equivalence of a tantrum. Not well done of her. And now, an additional pitfall to her pride, she knew Brutal wouldn't be back for many hours.

Erik grabbed her neck and pressed her face against the table. He pulled her stretchy pants down to her knees. The cold air on her ass gave her incentive to fight harder. She used her feet, now hampered by her clothes, and tried to kick at his legs. He easily dodged her, and it seemed to inflame him even more.

Then she heard a zipper. She closed her eyes. After he violated her, she would be the one blamed for the infidelity. She opened the door to him. There would be no leniency for her.

Even if Brutal didn't want her dead, the marriage officials would demand she pay for more of 'her' sins. She didn't even know if her life could be spared. Would Brutal want her dead?

"Brutal will be here any minute. He'll kill you!" she panted out one last futile effort to at least stall him longer.

"No, he won't. You and I both know he won't be back for hours. I've been watching. Once I'm done with you, he'll be forced to kill you for cheating on him. I've read up on the new laws posted in town by the Tiberius Group."

"Oh, you can read?" Hannah asked. He grabbed her hair and slammed her face down on the table. Ooh, yeah, that was going to leave a mark. Like it mattered.

"They call this rape, you bastard, even in the new world order that hates women. And Brutal would never kill me."

"You opened the door when I knocked, bitch. Then you came on to me. I tried to stop you, but I am only a weak man. I couldn't help myself." She felt his fetid breath on her cheek and an alarming bulge against the back of her thigh.

"If you do this, I will not stop until you are dead," she said coldly.

"Then maybe I'll just save Brutal the trouble and kill you myself when I'm through with you. It shouldn't take too long to get my fill." She sensed him fumbling around behind her. A single tear slipped down her cheek. Hannah closed her eyes and braced herself.

I'm so sorry, Brutal. I love you, Hannah sent out a mental thought full of her anguished regret.

"Get off my wife!" The very best four words she'd ever heard strung together in her life thundered behind her from the door.

Brutal was back! Thank God. A miracle.

Erik stepped back grinning and made the mistake of releasing her. Hannah turned, noted the evil grin, and punched him solidly in the groin with her adrenalin-powered fist. He fell to his knees. She quickly pulled up her pants one-handed and gave him a sidekick to the head while he was distracted holding his battered nuts from her first punch.

Erik reached for her, a grimace on his face, but she easily jumped out of his range. Hannah scrambled over to Brutal and hid behind him. She ran her hands over her husband's back, not really believing he was there. He had just saved her.

"So, do we fight for her again, Brutal?" Erik asked, trying to laugh even though the area between his legs surely must ache.

Brutal pulled a gun from a holster Hannah had never seen him wear before. Where did that come from?

"No, this time I'm going to shoot you, then I'll call the mine owner's authority and tell them you broke into my private quarters," Brutal said quietly.

"Only a coward shoots an unarmed man," Erik sneered.

"Oh, I'll make sure you have a weapon by the time the authorities get here, Erik. Thanks for your concern," Brutal sneered back.

"Listen, just between us men, she wanted it. She's a slut. She'll do anyone."

"You fucking liar!" Hannah started to come around from her secure place at Brutal's back to kick Erik in the nuts again. Brutal held out his arm, stopping her from advancing.

"Are you truly going to kill me over a mail order whore?"

"It's as good a reason as any to kill you," Brutal said, sounding much too calm to suit Hannah.

"Before you shoot me, I have some news which concerns you."

"News? I doubt it." Brutal took aim.

Erik started talking fast. "A transport ship came in today. I heard some big lawman from Earth was asking about you around town."

"So?"

"So maybe I have some information to give him."

"You don't have any information," Brutal scoffed.

"I do. It's regarding you and a certain bribe to the loadmaster on the mail order bride craft the day you got married. You know, the one where one of the whores didn't make it? You kill me and he'll arrest you."

"If you had information, you'd have already spilled your guts."

"Not if I can have what I wanted in the first place," he spat. "I want to taste her, Brutal. Let me have her just once, and we'll call it our little secret."

"Get out, Erik. I'm tired of you. Next time, I'll kill you on sight," Brutal promised. "Don't come back."

"You're making a mistake."

"I doubt it. Now, get out."

Erik limped through the door, and Brutal locked it behind him.

Hannah had stopped listening to the conversation when she heard

Erik say a transport ship had come in. She pondered the possibility of whether Charlotte had sent any more letters to Brutal. Her eyes watered up as if all was lost.

Hannah put her face in her hands and cried. It was so unfair to be in love with a man who wasn't hers to keep.

"Don't cry, Hannah." Brutal put his arms loosely around her as she sobbed.

"I'm so sorry." Hannah threw her arms around his neck and buried her face in his throat. "I'm sorry about the letter, and the mine, and everything."

"I know," he whispered. "It's okay. I'm also to blame."

"No, you're not. It was all me," she sobbed.

"I shouldn't have left you alone. I swear it won't happen again. That was why I came back."

"No, it was all my fault. I let my guard down and opened the door. I didn't even look. I thought it was you coming back to drag me down there with you. I'll shut up now. I promise to go with you and mine wherever you say." *Anything to keep you here with me and not off to marry Charlotte*, she thought.

Perhaps it was a good thing they hadn't found the mother lode after all. Otherwise, Hannah would be gone. Brutal could get rid of her to be with the woman he wanted.

"Really?" He sounded skeptical.

"I swear," she said, raising a hand and two fingers in salute.

"All right then, let's go."

* * * *

Brutal could barely contain his grin as they traversed down the shaft on the long ride to his former mine. When he got to her mine, he stopped. He couldn't wait to see Hannah's face when she saw the find.

"What are you doing?" She had a funny sound to her voice. It was that hopeful voice again, the one he realized he missed from this past week of furious mining in the cross shaft.

"We left some tools here. We need to get them before we head down," he said matter-of-factly. He was about to burst with giddy excitement. What was wrong with him anyway? It was because she'd worked so hard and come so close to never realizing her dream. He knew how that worked.

"Oh." The dejected tone was back. *But not for long*, he thought.

Brutal and Hannah stepped off the tram to enter the cross shaft mine. Before they stepped inside, Brutal grabbed her up into a ferocious bear hug.

"You worked so hard in here," he said with regret in his tone.

"It doesn't matter, Brutal. I appreciate the opportunity. No one else would have given me the chance you did."

She then wrapped her legs around his waist and planted her lips on his in a ferocious kiss. He made sure to face her away from the wall of Thorium-Z he had uncovered earlier.

The range on his meter told him it was more than fifty feet deep, because that was the max reading on his Thorium-Z-meter. Brutal carried her inside, kissing her as if it would be the last time.

Maybe it would be. After she saw the find, things would be different. She'd be able to pay off her debt in five minutes and be on the next transport back to Earth.

"Hannah? I want to show you something," he said between ferocious lip locks with her. She wasn't paying any attention to the mine around them.

"Is it big, wide, and satisfying?" she asked, laughing.

"I believe you'll think so." He positioned her so she could see the wall of ore he'd uncovered before leaving to fetch her. He placed her on her feet. She stared up into his face so trustingly.

"Turn around, Hannah."

She laughed and shook her head. "No way, I'm not freezing my butt off so you can get your rocks off down here."

Brutal laughed in return. "Maybe we could do a little mining in here and work up a sweat."

Hannah sobered up. "That is so sweet of you, Brutal, but I won't waste any more of your time."

"Turn around, Hannah," he said again and nodded to the wall behind her. She finally turned to look, then glanced back at him and smiled. He got to see the recognition register on her face. He wasn't disappointed.

Hannah's eyes popped wide open, as did her mouth. Then she did a double take, and a small sound erupted from her throat, a sound of disbelief. She turned back to him, eyes wide and full of tears.

"How did you…?"

"You did it," he said with pride. "I tried to pass the place and couldn't do it. You were so sure, and you'd worked so hard. I was going to let you have another half day when we left this morning, but—"

"But I was being a brat. Oh, Brutal!" She turned to face the wall of Thorium-Z. "Have you ever seen anything so beautiful!"

He looked at her face and said truthfully, "Yes, I have. Your face when I make you scream for me."

Hannah turned and gave him an odd look. "I dreamed someone said that to me on the flight here."

"I whispered that in your ear when you were still in your cryo-tube."

"You saw me before the auction?" she asked. "I figured Erik was lying."

He shook his head and smiled at her. "I waited for you. I was only going to bid on you, whatever it took."

"Really? What else did you do to me while I was sleeping?"

"Nothing. That was why I asked for your name. I was hoping to endear myself to you."

Hannah didn't respond. She smiled, shaking her head in amusement. She turned to look at the find again. Brutal stepped up behind her, pressing himself up against her backside before whispering in her ear, "Get to work. You know you want to."

They spent the next twelve and a half hours mining and accumulated more Thorium-Z than Brutal had seen in total since he had started mining on the planet. They had already agreed to store the find deeper in the cave and keep it a secret until they were ready to sell the entire load.

Brutal became more melancholy as the Thorium-Z mounted, knowing Hannah had earned her freedom after about the first two hours. He wondered if she'd stay long enough to finish mining all of what was here or if she would be on the first transport out. If one had arrived earlier today, it meant he could have as little as three more days with her before she was able to go.

Brutal didn't want her to leave. He was almost willing to admit he loved her. She would probably laugh at him and leave anyway, so he remained silent.

"Aren't you tired?" Brutal asked her a few hours later.

"Yes, but it's a good tired," she responded sprightly and kept working.

"I'm hungry. Let's go home, woman," he groused.

"I know you're right, but I just can't seem to stop."

"I'll make you dinner," he offered, trying to entice her.

"So does that mean, you'll make dinner for me, or I am dinner?" Hannah teased him.

"Either works for me, but I'm done here for today, Madam Taskmaster."

"Wimp. All right, we can leave, but we're coming back early in the morning. Agreed?"

"Whatever you want, Hannah." He hoped she wouldn't realize she was actually free to go once they sold the output for today. They got on the tram, not speaking during the entire fifteen-minute trip back to the air lock. They looked like coal miners.

Brutal couldn't wait until he got her into the shower. He couldn't wait to make love to her tonight. She would be high on life for being vindicated at her mine. She'd want to celebrate all night long.

Lust streaked across his weary body and perked him up at the thought of their night ahead. He opened the air lock and stepped through, turning to take her hand but missed it when the punch from a big, meaty fist caught him off guard and sent him flying.

Chapter 12

Brutal was surprised by the sucker punch. He'd been watching Hannah's grimy, rejoicing face. The fist to his jaw, an occurrence so rare that Brutal almost didn't know what to do, laid him on the ground. So he came out with a vengeance. He pulled his gun and took aim.

Luckily, he was able to catch himself in time before he fired. Otherwise, he would have hit Hannah. She screamed and threw herself into the intruder's arms. It took him a moment to realize it wasn't in pain or in protection of him. She sounded pleased. It would have devastated him if she'd screamed the same way she did when she climaxed. Thankfully, it was a different kind of scream. It sounded happy.

Brutal watched as the intruder pulled a gun on him in return. Hannah threw her arms around the strange man's neck and wrapped her legs around his waist. A stab of jealousy hit him with an impact more forceful than the punch he'd just endured.

He sat on his butt in his own damn home, gun in hand, now unable to return fire because Hannah was wrapped like a monkey around the stranger. The primate in question then looked over her shoulder, smile in place, until she saw him on the ground.

Then she frowned. Finally. What the hell was going on here?

"No, Brutal, don't!" Hannah unwrapped herself from the man, dropping to her feet in front of him. The man had on a helmet with the visor raised. Brutal could only see his eyes, eyes seething with hatred. At him. Why? Brutal took the opportunity to stand up and face this new threat.

"Hannah, step back." The intruder muscled his way in front of her.

"Brutal, it's my brother," Hannah said. "Put your gun down."

Neither man lowered his weapon.

The intruder removed his helmet one handed, letting it fall to the ground, and displayed a grim face. He placed his arm around Hannah again. The other was firmly gripped on his weapon still pointed in Brutal's direction. The tall stranger looked down at her dirty face before fixing his glare on Brutal again. "You forced my sister to work in your mine with you. Are you some sort of sadistic slave driver?"

"No, I'm her husband," Brutal quipped.

"What else is she required to do for you?" her brother asked, his tone menacing. Brutal could see him tighten his grip further on the gun he held.

"Nothing I'm going to share with you."

"I'm taking her with me," Hannah's brother stated emphatically.

"She's my wife. You don't have the authority to take her away from me." Brutal's weapon hand twitched.

"Be nice, boys." Hannah turned to her brother. "Where have you been, Jonathan? Did you talk to Sophie? How did you find me?"

"I was out of the country on business. I was only allowed to speak to Sophie on the phone, and I had to chase halfway across the galaxy to find you. Are you hurt? Did he hurt you?" The intruder gave Brutal a glare. Man to man. Still, he didn't lower his gun.

"No, he saved me. Put your gun down, Jon."

"No," and her brother took aim.

"Call him off, Hannah." Brutal repositioned his own gun on her brother's head.

"Jonathan Alexander Brent! Take your gun off my husband. Now!"

"Hannah..." Her brother's voice conveyed impatience, making Brutal soften for a moment. It was the tone he'd often used with her himself.

"Impasse," Brutal said.

"What?" Jonathan Brent's eyes narrowed, but Hannah also looked with question.

"We are at an impasse. Neither of us wants to lower our weapon, and yet both of us have to. Are you willing to risk Hannah's life in a gun battle?" Brutal asked his opponent.

"No, are you?"

"No, but I'm a better shot. I could kill you even if Hannah were still wrapped around you. Can you say the same?"

"Yes, I can."

"Both of you, stop it!" Hannah released herself from her brother's grasp even as he tried to keep from relinquishing her. Brutal relaxed for a moment.

"Hannah, are you crazy? This man can't be trusted!" her brother ground out.

"How do you know?" When he didn't respond, Hannah stepped in front of her brother with her back to him and finally looked at Brutal. She reached out, putting her hand on her brother's gun arm and attempting to lower it.

"Hannah, step back," Brutal said.

"No, I won't let you kill each other. You both mean too much to me."

Brutal took one look at her eyes tearing up and lowered his weapon to the side with a long-suffering sigh. Her brother did the same. But they still glared at each other.

"Let's go inside," Hannah suggested and pushed her brother to the door of their quarters. It still looked like an interloper had broken in and tried to rape her earlier in the day. The dining room was a mess, and the living area wasn't much better.

"Did you two have a disagreement earlier?" Jonathan stepped over a plate.

"No," Hannah said but didn't elaborate further.

* * * *

A few hours later, after she and Brutal had showered separately, and Hannah had made something to eat, the three sat in the living area to talk.

"How did you find me?" she asked her brother.

"It wasn't easy. I had to come on another pretense. There was a death on the cryogenic spacecraft that brought you here. I'm investigating the death for a private party."

"Is it her family?" she asked with sympathy.

"No, for the corporate insurance. Someone is out the money she would have brought for the match," her brother responded in a matter-of-fact tone.

"Naturally," Hannah said with disgust. What had she been thinking?

"What in the holy hell happened to you, Hannah? Good God Almighty, when the Tiberius Group took over, I was caught out of the country on a job," her brother started out.

Hannah knew he didn't actually expect her to answer because he was venting. "I didn't even know Dad was alive. I expected to come back to have two sisters to marry off. Instead, both were already married. One wasn't even on the planet anymore, and the other warned me away from her house. I only spoke a few words to Sophie.

"Her new husband was peeved about something our dad did with regard to money or gambling. I didn't get the whole story. She said he'd been in league with your husband, so I expected the worst when I got here."

"Wrong husband," Hannah murmured.

"What?" Jonathan scrunched his eyebrows in puzzlement.

"Her first husband sold her into the mail order bride business to absolve his gambling debt. I paid the debt," Brutal interjected on her behalf.

"Could you leave us alone to chat for a couple of minutes, maybe?" Jonathan asked Brutal, giving him a surly glare.

Hannah knew Brutal didn't want to leave them alone, but he surprised her by agreeing.

"I'll be outside," he said and left them in the quarters alone.

"I have money, Hannah. I can pay the debt for you."

"Jonathan..."

"How fast can you pack and be ready to go?" he demanded.

"I'm indebted to him, Jon. It's more than just money. And besides, I don't think money will be an issue."

"Then what's the issue?"

"I love him."

"No, you don't. It's not possible. How long have you known him? All of three weeks?" her brother scoffed.

"He didn't do anything wrong. He's been decent about everything."

"Unh-huh? So he didn't force himself on you? I find that very hard to believe."

"Well, it's true." Hannah felt a blush of warmth in her face at having to explain anything to her brother about her sexual activities with Brutal.

"And who gave you the shiner on your face? I can tell it's from today. Did he hit you?" He put his hand on the butt of his holstered gun again.

"No, he didn't. He saved me from someone."

"He should have kept you from getting a shiner from 'someone' in the first place. Hannah, you aren't thinking straight. You're going with me."

"No, I want to stay…" Hannah paused, thinking about Charlotte. With the Thorium-Z find, they could both be free. Brutal could marry his love Charlotte, and she could settle down with a man her brother selected for her back on Earth. The thought made her frown.

"But?" Jon asked pointedly.

"But I'm only his temporary wife. He has someone waiting for him back on Earth."

"Of course, he does." Her brother rolled his eyes. "Hannah, I need to get back. The transport leaves in two days. You and I are going to be on it. I'll have your marriage to Thomas Blackthorn annulled."

"How? I mean, it's not like I'm a virgin anymore."

Her brother's facial expression shifted immediately into a mask of retribution-seeking fury. She imagined he wished he hadn't heard the word virgin or the part about 'not any more' with regard to his sister.

"I'm supposed to bring him in for questioning, Hannah. He is the number one suspect in the death of that girl on the cryo-ship. If he's convicted, then you'll be free. The marriage can be annulled."

"That's crazy. He didn't do it," Hannah said sincerely.

"I have a witness who saw your husband enter the cargo hold before you were revived. I have another witness who said your husband bribed his way onto that same hold of the ship several hours before the auction. He was left alone with all the women for an undetermined length of time."

"So what? I already knew that."

"After he left, they couldn't revive her. She was dead, Hannah. It could have been you."

"He didn't do it. He wouldn't. I know him," she said dismissively.

"You don't know him," Jon said forcefully. "Besides, it doesn't matter now. There is going to be a warrant issued for his arrest if he doesn't come willingly. He's going with us."

"Now?" Hannah said wide-eyed. She didn't think forcing Brutal into town against his will was a very good idea.

"Yes, call him. We're all going into town together. Help me take him in quietly."

"Help take me *where* quietly?" Brutal's voice sounded from the door. How long had he been listening? He probably had bionic hearing wired in that big, brawny, genetically engineered body of his. Hannah was sure she had a guilty look on her face when she turned to him.

"Brutal, there's going to be a warrant issued for your arrest in the death of that girl from the spacecraft!"

"Hannah, shush!" Jonathan pulled his gun again. Hannah rushed to Brutal's side before her brother could grab her, refusing to believe he was involved.

"What am I being accused of?" Brutal took Hannah in his arms, turning her away from the threat of Jonathan's gun.

"Wrongful death and willful destruction of property." Jon then reached behind him and pulled a set of handcuffs off his belt as he maintained the gun on Brutal, who still held his protective stance covering her.

"Unless you're planning on wearing those bracelets yourself, Lawman, you might as well put them back on your belt. They aren't going on me."

* * * *

In town at the mining authority official headquarters, and also part-time bar, a group of miners had assembled for the inquiry. The crew from the spacecraft that had brought Hannah was also in attendance.

Dusty and Buck were there as well as one of the loadmasters she hadn't met. Hannah looked around the bar as memories of the last time she was in this room assailed her. She held fast to Brutal, both of her arms wrapped securely around one brawny arm. If this were to be her last day with him, she was spending it soaking up his warmth and scent. She didn't know what her brother might do to separate them once the inquiry was over. Then there was the Thorium-Z tucked away waiting to be sold, which gave reasonable doubt as to a further relationship with him in her near future.

Brutal didn't seem to mind her being sucked up close to him, thankfully. Jon, on the other hand, wore a perpetual scowl every time he glanced in their direction whether they touched or not. So she touched while she still could.

In a seeming huff to get away from their embrace, Jonathan strolled over to speak privately to Dusty and Buck once the three of them approached the area reserved for this particular inquiry. He gave Brutal a meaningless look of warning before stepping away to speak to the loadmasters.

Erik the Evil was also present and evidently gloating for some unknown reason. He kept looking at Hannah, licking his lips and leering. Brutal looked ready to shoot him.

Jon obviously hadn't let Brutal wear his gun into town but had finally agreed to at least bring it along. It was currently strapped to her brother's hip. Otherwise, she had no doubt they'd both still be back at the mine arguing about it.

Her head fell onto Brutal's solid upper arm just below shoulder level. She heaved a sigh, wishing for things she wasn't ever going to get. Every breath she took was filled with Brutal's mouth-watering and intoxicating masculine scent. She took several deep breaths to secure it in her memory, although it was just an excuse to smell him. It wasn't likely she'd ever forget. She wanted Brutal with all her heart and soul, but she hoped when the time came, she'd be able to let him go.

She would likely be required to do so once this stupid inquiry was over. They would cash in on the Thorium-Z find at the mine, he would release her to her brother, and eventually he'd go back to Earth, too, a wealthy man able to marry rich princess Charlotte of the expensive stationary.

Not wanting to dwell on Brutal's next wife, she happened to glance at the table across the room where Celeste and Iggy had staged their public copulation as Hannah had said, "I do," to Brutal a short three weeks ago. It seemed like a lot longer than three weeks since she had learned that sex was, in fact, very good. Especially in the masterful hands of her gorgeous, genetically engineered husband. Hannah smiled at the memory.

"You certainly have a much different look on your face than the last time you saw that table," Brutal whispered, barely audible.

She laughed out loud before she could stop it and twisted to look up into his amused face. An unspoken bond between them transpired, and she fondly remembered their tryst on the dining room table, even though she'd pretended to bend over in capitulation. In fact, the very thought of that particular 'surrender' made her cheeks warm in fond memory.

Then just as quickly she frowned, realizing for the first time she might never have the opportunity to experience making love to him again. It made her heart hurt.

He nodded as a melancholy look covered his face as well. He winked at her reassuringly as if he understood her errant, unspoken thoughts. How was she ever going to allow another man to touch her as he so expertly had?

She didn't voice her thought but wanted to say, "I suspect you've ruined me for all other men, Brutal. I hope you're satisfied."

Just then the assembled participants of the inquiry panel were called over to address the issue of the day. Hannah remained at Brutal's side.

* * * *

Hannah walked in step with him over to the group assembled for the inquiry into the death of the brunette beauty who had died mysteriously three weeks before. While having Hannah pressed up to him was not unappealing, Brutal didn't want her brother to kill him. On the other hand, he should enjoy what time he had left with her. Her brother would just have to get over it for now.

Jonathan and the assembled parties gathered around in the room where Brutal and Hannah had been married only a few short weeks ago.

"We found your DNA on her, Brutal," Dusty said apologetically, beginning the inquiry. "When her body was processed back on Earth was when it was discovered."

"Kill him," Erik said.

"Shut up!" Hannah interjected immediately. Brutal had to hold her down. She was a feisty little thing when riled. He was glad she was on his side.

"I'll admit I bribed my way on to the ship to take a look, but I only ran my finger down her cheek," he said. "I didn't do anything to cause her death."

"That's in line with what the evidence showed," Dusty said. "But you were the only one to go in prior to the auction."

"How do I know that? Any number of miners could have paraded in both before and after I left," Brutal said in his own defense.

"Nobody else witnessed any others entering or leaving the area," Dusty said with regret. Brutal suspected he didn't want to blame the man who had given him the bribe in the first place.

"What killed her?" Brutal asked.

"Someone messed with the unit. One of the coolant tubes was detached on purpose. Someone didn't want her to wake up," Buck said.

"What motive could I possibly have? I ended up having to fight for the last available female, the only one I wanted," Brutal said the last part under his breath, but one look at Hannah, and he knew she had heard him. She smiled and squeezed his arm even tighter, if that was possible.

"Was his DNA on the tube?" Hannah asked.

"No," Dusty said. "It would burn the skin off his fingers if he touched the bare tube."

"Well, then you can look elsewhere," she said emphatically. "His fingers are fine."

"Arrest him and take him back to Earth. You can prosecute him to the fullest extent of the law there," Erik said, moving into the circle. "He's your only viable suspect. Justice demands you do this immediately."

"Why are you even allowed to voice an opinion in this matter?" Hannah asked, sending a positively malevolent glare his way.

"Because I have a huge interest in the outcome of this inquiry. You should have read the fine print of the marriage documents more closely, Brutal," Erik said in satisfaction. "We had to fight for this whore weeks ago, but if within thirty days you are parted for any reason and you lose your rights to her, well then, I win that fight by default." He turned to Hannah with a lust-filled stare. "Once Brutal is arrested, you'll become my property, and I'll have you on your knees sucking me off before he's even dragged from this room, bitch."

Brutal didn't know if what he said was true or not, but he decided he didn't care to find out. In one fluid move, he stripped Hannah from him and grabbed Jonathan Brent's gun from his holster. Less than one second after that, he had Erik pressed against the nearest wall. Jonathan's gun was securely fastened underneath his chin, the safety already snapped off. His finger pressed dangerously on the hair trigger of the weapon.

"But if I just blow your brains out right now, Erik, it solves that problem along with so many others I've let you get away with to date."

"Mr. Blackthorn, I would sincerely appreciate it if you'd please lower my weapon from him," Brutal heard Jonathan say. Then he heard the click of another safety snicking off, followed by the poke of a gun barrel against the back of his head. It was probably his own damn gun.

"Sorry, I can't do that—Mr. Brent," he added sarcastically. And he wouldn't. He should have killed Erik back in his mine dwelling, but he hadn't wanted Hannah to witness him murder someone. Now it seemed unavoidable.

"Do you sincerely believe I will allow any harm to befall my own sister?" Jon's tone dripped with disdain. Brutal watched as Erik registered Hannah and Jonathan's relationship with the widening of his already horrified eyes. It was never a good idea to get on the bad side of a Lawman for any reason. But sexually insulting a close relative, especially a sister, was at the very top of the list, second only to insulting a Lawman's mother.

"Well, I know if I pull this trigger, you won't have to be troubled. First and foremost, I want to ensure my wife's safety if I'm unjustly taken into custody."

"Unfortunately, there are all these troubling witnesses to the crime. Or are you saying you really did kill the woman in the cryo-unit and you have nothing to lose at this point?"

"You know I'm not. I had nothing to do with her death. I can't allow myself to be arrested in error. I won't risk it."

"Brutal?" Hannah's frightened voice wrapped around him, making him pause. "You don't have to kill him. I don't want to lose you because of a vile piece of wasted humanity like him. I know you didn't kill that girl, and we'll just prove it right now."

"How?"

"Well, whoever did it would have used gloves, and there would be a burn mark from the tube, right?"

"That's right, whoever did it *had* to use gloves," Dusty said distractedly. "The tube was minus 100 degrees centigrade. The gloves used probably *would* have a burn mark on them."

"Well, then let's talk to all the miners present on the day of the last auction and look at their gloves," Buck said.

"The guilty party won't willingly submit to his gloves being looked at unless he's stupid," Dusty said disgustedly.

"Why don't you just look at the film footage?" Jonathan Brent asked.

"What film footage?" Erik Vander asked in a shocked tone. Brutal felt Erik's body stiffen as if in surprise. "There are no cameras in the load areas."

"How do you know?" Brutal asked suspiciously and kneed him in the thigh. "If there is film, I want see the footage, too. It will prove me innocent."

"Dang me. I forgot all about the new camera installed," Dusty said excitedly. "I'll get the ship captain to pull the film."

Erik Vander suddenly moved and tried to fight, but Brutal held him fast against the wall. "There are no cameras in the loading dock. I know because I checked the area with a bug sweeper myself when I was there..." Erik caught himself and clamped his mouth shut.

"When were you there?" Brutal asked in a lethal tone and lowered the gun, dropping it to the floor at his feet so he could grab Erik with both fists and hurt him with his bare hands.

Erik didn't answer but sent a damn-I-guess-I'm-caught look to Brutal. Brutal responded by pulling him off the wall and landing three very satisfying punches to his face. Erik slid to the ground in an unconscious heap. He turned to see Jonathan with his gun still raised and pointed at his head.

"Feel better?" Jon asked and deliberately lowered the pistol and re-holstered it.

"Actually, I do. Now, you can go pull the film and see for yourself I'm innocent, since I'm sure you still don't trust me."

Hannah threw herself into his arms, wrapping around him with her face pressed securely into his neck. Apparently, she was already satisfied of his innocence.

Over her shoulder, Brutal watched her brother's body tense up at their close embrace. He may have won the battle, but the war was far from over. It was clear Jonathan Brent did not want him for a brother-in-law. With Hannah's record-breaking Thorium-Z find, he didn't really have a hold on her any longer. He'd promised to let her go back to her family if she was right. She'd been about as right as she could be regarding her cross shaft mine.

Dusty came back a few minutes later with the film footage from that day. Erik's bug sweeper had missed the camera. It clearly showed him detaching the hoses.

Jonathan had him cuffed before he regained consciousness. As they stood him up, Hannah asked, "Why did you kill her?"

"I wasn't trying to kill her. I only wanted to use her once before the auction. The last time she was here, she felt she was too good for me," he sneered. "She wasn't."

After all the paperwork was filled out and Erik was securely in the brig awaiting the journey back to Earth, Jonathan invited Hannah and Brutal to dinner. They decided to eat in the hotel restaurant where he was staying until the flight departed.

"Why don't you go up to my room, Hannah, and get freshened up? I brought some of your clothes. They are hanging in the closet. Brutal and I will wait for you in the bar."

"I'll be right back," Hannah said, her expression wary.

Brutal watched her turn to go, but then she just as quickly turned back and threw her arms around his neck. He in turn crushed her to his chest and ground his mouth on hers. She opened for him so he could kiss her like he wanted to. He stroked his tongue against her sweet soft one methodically like it would be the last time he would ever get to taste her, because it might be the last time. After she went upstairs, he would explain to her brother about the marriage contract between them and the additional agreement he had established in a weak moment, thinking it would buy him another year with her.

Meanwhile, Brutal sensed her brother's annoyance and blew it off.

After a very sensual lip lock, which lasted several long, satisfying moments, he breathed deeply of her unique scent before he released her. She slid down his body until her feet were underneath her. He wanted to say the words to her he swore he would never say to another woman, 'I love you, Hannah.' It should have been easy, but he found he couldn't do it. He smiled at her instead.

"Be right back," she said, smiling in return. He nodded and turned to Jonathan when she was gone.

"I don't care what your arrangement with her is," Jonathan said sternly. "She's going with me back to Earth when I leave. Are we clear on this, or do I need to persuade you of this fact?"

"You had best keep her safe once she's back on Earth with you then."

Jon looked surprised that Brutal gave in without a fight.

"I will release her into your custody. Tell Hannah I'll give her thirty-five percent of the stake we found. Don't force her to marry..." Brutal trailed off his sentence. Her brother would find a suitable man for her, even though the very thought made him seethe with a fury he'd never endured before.

"Not staying for dinner?"

"No. Have a safe journey." Brutal retreated to his mine alone, leaving Hannah in her brother's capable care. He exited the hotel quickly before she came back. There was no need for a tearful good-bye, especially not from him.

* * * *

Hannah risked life and limb to visit Brutal at his mine. She had to sneak out of her room at the hotel in town. Then she'd rented a four-wheeled conveyance, telling the man it was for her brother.

It was strange coming back to the mine as a guest. Her flight was scheduled for later in the day, but she wanted to see Brutal alone one last time. She stepped off her ride and headed for the door. He answered it before she even knocked.

"Hannah, what are you doing here? Are you alone?" He peeked around her shoulder to see for himself if anyone was behind her.

She shook her head. "No, it's just me. I wanted to say good bye, Brutal, without my brother hovering around watching us with a perpetual frown on his face."

Brutal's hands went to his hips as if he were supremely perturbed with her. "Well, I'll have to take you back then. Even with Erik put away, it isn't safe for you to be out here all alone."

"You sound like my brother."

"Does he know you're here?" he asked incredulously.

"Not exactly," she admitted quietly.

"God's wrath, Hannah." His voice sounded gruff like he was angry, but he didn't seem that angry. "Guess I'll have to take you back right now then, won't I?"

"No, wait. Did you miss me, even just a little bit?" she asked him hopefully.

"It was only two nights."

"So, did you?"

"I missed you all right. My bed is lonely without you thrashing about at night," he said brusquely.

"I never thrashed about once."

"I just hid the bruises from you."

"Brutal, I have to know before I leave…" She stared up into his dark eyes. *I have to know if you love me*, she wanted to say.

"What do you need to know?" His luscious chocolate brown eyes caressed her face.

She chickened out at the last minute and asked instead, "Do you forgive me for what I did with your letters from Charlotte?"

"I do," he said, sounding very sincere. "Now, I have a question for you. You said you loved me the other day. Was that true?" All of a sudden, he pulled her into his arms, squeezed her, and then kissed the top of her head.

"When did I say that?"

"I believe it was when Erik was behaving badly, right before I spoke up and distracted him so you could punch him in the nuts."

"I said that out loud?" She hadn't realized she'd spoken those words burning with regularity in her mind. At the time, she'd been slightly distracted.

"Perhaps it was merely the circumstance of the moment."

"Oh, yeah, I remember now. My brother taught me how to fight dirty." She smiled in satisfaction.

"Good for him, although your brother probably wants me dead, too."

"Undoubtedly."

"Is it true?"

"That he wants you dead? Perhaps, but I won't let him hurt you," she said coyly.

"No, that you love me. Is that true?"

"I don't want to keep you from what you wish."

"You still owe me a year, Hannah."

"I do not. You're rich because of me. And what about Charlotte?" Hannah raised her head and sought out his gaze.

"I told you not to worry about her. Anyway, it doesn't matter. I'm ready to fulfill the bargain. You can leave. You earned it."

"But..."

"But what? You're free to go, Hannah. So go."

"I need to know if you love Charlotte. I really need to know, Brutal. Please tell me the truth."

"I don't know why my manly pride is so obstinate where Charlotte Stanfield is concerned, but here's the truth. The day I married you, I got a letter from her releasing herself from our engagement. She informed me she never intended to marry a bio-engineered freak like me anyway. She was just trying to rile her daddy. So I washed my hands of her, married you, and knew I'd never think about her again."

"What a bitch," Hannah said.

"Well, anyway," he chuckled at first and then turned serious. "I obviously didn't hold you to the extra year because you found the richest Thorium-Z mine in the history of this planet. So you don't even have to stay for the original contract. I just want you to be happy. I already released you to your brother. I gave him thirty-five percent of the projected stake to hold for you."

"That's it?"

"What? You want a bigger cut?"

"No, I don't care about the Thorium-Z. How can you just release me like I mean nothing to you?"

Brutal tried to form the words she wanted to hear. He wanted to say them, but he just couldn't bring himself to do it. Perhaps he needed to hear them from her when Erik didn't have her bent over a table. Or perhaps he was just a fool. Let her go. She deserved a better life than one forced on her by circumstances beyond her control.

"Yeah, I can. Good luck, Hannah. And thank you."

"But—"

"No buts, Hannah. I'm not even going to seduce yours."

"Why not? I love you, Brutal. If Charlotte doesn't stand in my way, then I want a life with you. Can you honestly say I mean nothing to you? Nothing at all?"

"I thought you wanted your life on Earth back. I thought you wanted to choose your own husband."

"Why would I want that? I have a husband. Listen, Brutal, I wanted to be right about the mine, and I was. So you will, of course, have to listen to me gloat about it from now on. I mean, who else would? I truly don't want to go anywhere without you. I wish…"

"What do you wish?"

Hannah closed her eyes. She was about to bare her soul and didn't want to see a look of pity on his face if she were mistaken. "I wish we were married permanently. Forever. I do love you. Don't you care for me just a little?"

"I don't know, Hannah. That means I'd get to be your lord and master for all eternity. I might get tired of you after a couple hundred years or so."

Her eyes popped open to his smile.

"I love you. Will you marry me forever, Hannah?" he asked.

"I will. Do you want to seal the bargain by taking me over the next table you see?"

"Maybe, as long as your brother isn't in the same room."

"Coward."

"Is that how you're going to treat your lord and master?"

"Only for the first couple of hundred years."

"Then we have a bargain, Madam Taskmaster," Brutal said before he devoured her mouth to seal their final deal.

THE MINER'S WIFE

The Wives Tales 1

THE END

WWW.LARASANTIAGO.COM

SIREN PUBLISHING

Lara Santiago

THE EXECUTIVE'S WIFE

THE WIVES TALES

The Executive's Wife

In the year 2076, the Tiberius Group invades all aspects of society, taking over and implementing a new plan for the good of all U.S. citizens, especially the females.

Sophie Brent loses her job at Westland Industries and is put up for auction in a corporate venue of former peers. She's the record high bid and soon-to-be-bride of the worst lecher in the company, until her boss outbids all and saves her.

Matt Westland spends a fortune to marry his former employee, Sophie. He has wanted her since a delicious incident under the mistletoe at Christmas. Secretly in love with him, Sophie is an all-too-willing partner in Matt's passionate seduction, and the two fall madly in love.

Unfortunately, Matt's power-hungry father will stop at nothing to get rid of Sophie and find a more politically connected wife to ensure that his son becomes the next president of the United States.

The Executive's Wife

The Wives Tales 2

By Lara Santiago

Copyright © 2006

Prologue

Christmastime, Earth
In the year 2075

The wicked incident, which changed her life forever, happened just before Christmas. It was Sophie Brent's last day of work before she embarked on a long awaited holiday vacation with her family. Her very last act for this particular calendar year at work was the mandatory Westland Industries Christmas celebration.

It was her first such event, having only worked for the company for six months. The spectacular event materialized with much pomp and circumstance in the grand ballroom, which took up the entire eighth floor. What a luxury, she thought. An entire floor devoted just to in-house celebrations.

The party was in full swing by the time she made her way down from the Logistics department. Sophie was a very bottom rung junior executive. She stepped off the elevator and into the chaotic din of holiday revelers dancing, eating, drinking and generally having a drunken good time. It was hard not to be swept up in the magic of the holiday spirit. No expense had been spared to create a Christmas paradise transforming the entire floor into another world.

Westland Industries was a premiere import export business headquartered in the heartland of the U. S. and had connections everywhere in the world. They had access to every type of exotic goods from every continent around the world. It seemed to Sophie as though everything available with a Christmas theme was displayed here tonight.

No one seemed to notice her entry, and that was just fine with her. She was probably the last to grace the party with her presence. She looked around for her supervisor. She needed to be seen by him and make enough of an impression that her presence would be noted, as this was a mandatory function.

She was also on the lookout for Orin Prichard, the senior sales VP and resident letch. He was someone she needed to avoid tonight. Sober, he was a handful. Drunk, she imagined it would be harder to give his blatant advances the big brush off. And she certainly didn't want to get caught alone with him. He'd tried to corner her against his desk on her very auspicious first day, but luckily, someone had saved her.

Someone wonderful. Someone yummy.

There was no need to dwell on that unattainable dream now. Mr. Yummy was not hers, nor would he ever be. She sighed wistfully, studying the extravagant decorations and lively atmosphere enjoyed by the very well-dressed crowd in attendance. Sophie strolled through the magical expensive themed version of winter wonderland, marveling and absorbing the sheer ambience of the room encompassing her.

The party designers had transformed the space into a giant white tundra with lots of white background and ice sculpture for the backdrop, then distracted the entire visual with detailed groupings of bright colored holiday scenes strewn about the room as if in orderly chaotic fashion. Everyone in the company was expected to dress to the nines for this annual overindulgent celebration.

Sophie was no exception, and to that end, she wore the only cocktail dress she owned, a sexy black halter number that her sister Hannah had talked her into buying from a clearance rack at a fancy department store the summer before. She brushed imaginary lint off her skirt, not caring that it was technically last year's fashion.

The texture of the soft black velvet made her feel very sophisticated and boosted her confidence a notch, as if mere rich fabric could transform her from the poor little girl from the wrong side of the tracks into a desirable debutante worthy of a man's regard.

Lord, she'd been reading too many fanciful romance novels of late. But she didn't care because it was the holidays and she should be able to indulge herself. She could dream about being more desirable to men, if she wanted.

Or to one man in particular.

Perhaps if she got tipsy enough, she might even get the guts and pretend to be a seductress. As a seductress, she could approach and speak to the object of her deep-seated fantasies. Heaving a deep sigh, she headed for the punch bowl for a booster shot of courage. She'd over heard a conversation a while back that the punch bowl was always spiked at this annual event. All the better.

After the first delicious glass, she found herself ladling out two more cups in rapid succession, consuming them one right after the other. The warm glow generated by the alcohol made her feel lighter, happier, and practically giddy. She grabbed a fourth cup and pretended to circulate around the party to admire the decorations, but in reality, she watched for *him*.

As if choreographed in advance, the object of her sincere desire and repeated star of all her erotic fantasies entered the party from the bank of executive suite elevators. Matthew Westland, CEO and owner of Westland Industries, AKA Mr. Yummy, was now in attendance.

She stared at him surreptitiously as she gravitated back to the punch bowl. Snagging another cup of courage, she headed in his general direction to get a better look. Matthew circulated through the party, greeting his employees one after another, never once catching her eye or seeing her stare at him probably like a lovesick teenager. Why would he? He could have anyone he wanted. He surely did. There were rumors of customary late night trysts in his office with rich debutantes.

Sophie wished to be a debutante just once, so she could gain access to his private domain and find out for herself what went on behind closed doors with Matthew Westland. She concluded in her semi-drunken state that wicked decadent wonderful things took place at the hands of Mr. Yummy. She made a vow as she swallowed her last bit of her punch. She vowed to discover his most private secrets…someday.

Sophie lowered her glass with her wishful, decadent reverie still fresh and looked directly into the soulful gaze of the object of her desire. He was surrounded by a group of senior level executives. He watched her staring no doubt salaciously at him over the rim of yet another empty glass. The warmth of the smile he expressed in return, along with the sizeable amount of liquor in her system, prevented her from turning her gaze away and pretending indifference, as she would normally have done.

Indifference was replaced easily by her grinning, probably like a drunken Cheshire cat. She allowed her eyes to travel from the top of his head all the way down to the expensive shoes he wore, stopping for an extra second or two at the space below his belt. She'd heard rumors about *that,* too.

He stared back at her as if she were the only other person in the room. She watched him excuse himself and make his way towards her, and she snapped back to reality. Her smiled faded momentarily. She stood there like a marble figurine with stage fright and waited for him to come to her.

The golden highlights in his brown hair caught the dancing lights of Christmas surrounding them and made her itch to bury her fingers in his wavy locks. His sapphire blue eyes distracted her momentarily with a look intense enough to hypnotize, until he flashed her a million dollar smile. Damn, he was fine. She grinned again in return.

She knew she didn't really have a chance with him, and not only because he was the boss and she truly needed her job, but also because they had disparate backgrounds. However, she just wanted to dream a little. It was Christmas after all, and with all the alcohol in her system, she decided she was due. She smiled and waited anxiously for him to get closer. The utterly magnificent scent of him hit her first, like a lustful punch to her libido.

"Merry Christmas," he said, stepping dangerously into her personal space. His hand grazed her shoulder in friendly greeting. Her heartbeat skipped once at the sensation of his touch on her bare skin. Her eyes traveled up to the gorgeous face of the man she'd been drooling over for months.

"Merry Christmas yourself," she laughed then of course lost her balance stumbling heavily into his tall, muscular frame. Her four-inch, 'fuck-me' heels were new and drinking apparently didn't help her walk in them.

Matt caught her up in a one armed rescue. Nice build, she thought as she placed her hand on his chest then ran it up and down slightly to feel a pectoral underneath his suit. His arm remained in place around her waist as if to continue to steady her and she almost stopped breathing.

"Are you having a good time tonight?" he asked, seemingly unconcerned about her flagrant flirting or her hand on his very delicious person.

"Of course, it's a party," she told him. She laughed for no reason, unable to stop herself. She was drunk enough to be uninhibited, but sober enough to know she shouldn't be this close to Matthew Westland. Later she'd have plenty of time to curse the one percent of her mind warning her about the stupidity she displayed. But for the here and now, the other ninety-nine percent of her inebriated brain thought she sounded very witty. Mr. Yummy didn't seem to notice.

He exuded the aura of the quintessential successful executive. He was rich, powerful, and magnetic. And he smelled decadently good, too. Sophie leaned in and took a deep breath near the front of his shirt, inhaling his scent. She closed her eyes in shameless appreciation and made her own yummy noise, then smiled into his amused face realizing she'd just sniffed her boss. She laughed joyfully, too far gone on liquor to care about impropriety.

At her amusement, a slightly predatory gaze came onto his handsome face. She felt her lips part, as if making a wish. She studied his luscious mouth with eager fascination. If he leaned down to kiss her right now, she wouldn't stop him. Hell, she'd probably require surgical intervention to pry her lips from his.

"Matt!" a voice called from the loud party. He glanced over his shoulder to nod at the VP of Marketing, breaking the trance-like stare between them. When he focused his gaze back at her again, the spell was broken. Sophie sobered up a little and took a step away, realizing she couldn't be trusted with Matthew Westland, not even in a room full of people.

"I hope you have a very Merry Christmas, Sophie." He stepped away. The look of disappointment on his face touched her. She loved hearing him say her name.

"Merry Christmas to you, too, Mr. Westland."

"Call me Matthew." He flashed a grin before she left his pheromone range.

"Merry Christmas, Matthew," she whispered.

She needed to get far, far away, before her black velvet dress, which now surely smoldered, burst into flames. She exited the loud party to hide and wait for her pre-arranged taxi in the parking garage. She snagged one last very full glass of spiked punch for her journey as a consolation prize.

She slipped away, hopefully unnoticed, retrieved her purse from her office, and made her way to the bottom floor. All the way down in the elevator, she mentally banged her head against a wall for her audacious behavior in between gulps of punch. God, this stuff was great. She resisted the urge to hit the up button in the elevator and go back for more. But she couldn't because *he* was there, and she'd only want more of *him,* too.

The doors to the elevator opened with a cheerful "ding" to an empty vestibule in the basement. The tile floor, when she stepped past the doors, echoed with the clacking sound of her 'fuck-me,' four-inch, black velvet pumps. The ones she'd spent entirely too much money on to match her last year's clearance designer dress.

Sophie sighed and drained her red plastic cup of spiked punch. It sent a fresh warm feeling down her throat, blazing a final path of holiday spirit all the way to her stomach. She should have eaten more— correction—she should have eaten something. Her oversized cup was now empty, but the buzz of alcohol filled her up nicely. She exited the elevator vestibule to the connecting hallway leading to the parking garage.

A huge sign hung on the wall, pointing to the right of the T-shaped hallway directing the elevator occupants helpfully to the parking area. She dropped her cup in the trashcan and turned to the right at the T to head for the garage. She wasn't quite walking straight, which made her giggle all the way to the parking garage door.

She shivered, realizing it was freezing in the hallway. Damn. She'd forgotten her jacket. Glancing at her watch, which blurred slightly when she tried to keep her wrist steady, she decided she didn't have enough time to retrieve it from her office. She'd pick up another at her apartment when she collected her luggage for her trip later tonight.

Sophie heard the ding of the elevator behind her as she stood watching the blustery wind outside fretfully blow a scrap of newspaper around the street. She'd freeze her ass off once she stepped outside, but better frozen than to chance running into her boss again. If she went on a search to retrieve her jacket and ran into him again, she might get more than she bargained for...and so might he.

"Sophie?" A deep voice full of surprise came from behind her. Matthew Westland, AKA Mr. Yummy, spoke a single word and his sultry voice made her panties dampen.

She turned, not believing her boss stood there. He didn't say anything else. His gaze raked her from head to toe, as if he couldn't believe she was standing there in damp undies, either. Unimaginable need engulfed her as another hot rush of moisture shot into her underwear at his intense regard, with the unmistakable Pavlov's dog response to hearing a bell.

He pocketed what she presumed were his keys when she heard the jingle. He pierced her with an interested gaze before he glanced above her head and smiled that beautiful million-dollar smile. She looked up, and for the first time, saw what amused him. She also smiled. He dropped his head, pierced her with a seductive gaze, and closed the distance between them in a few long strides of his powerful, muscular legs.

Someone had placed mistletoe above the door. Maybe he'd done it, using the holiday tradition as an excuse to do something wild and wicked to a virtual stranger, or a lovesick employee, along a deserted hallway in the name of mistletoe.

Matthew didn't say another word. He just lowered his head and kissed her as she'd never been kissed in her life. His hand palmed the back of her head. His lips danced across hers at first before she felt the tip of his tongue on her all-too-willing lips.

Sophie, so shocked at the whole experience unfolding like a fantasy from her most recent sleep-deprived dreams, opened her mouth for him.

She didn't stop him, as she should have. Not only didn't she stop him, she participated with much enthusiasm. The spiked punch was no longer the only factor in her decision-making. She just wanted a small taste. She wanted enough of a taste to place in her memory for the future. He tasted like pure sultry sin with a touch of peppermint. She slid her hands from his chest on a slow path up and around his neck and plunged her fingers into his silky hair

His arm tightened around her waist as her tongue shyly sought his out, brushing it gingerly with her own. She heard him make a noise in his throat. A sexy noise. Sophie took half of a step back to rest against the solid metal door. She pulled him along with her so they wouldn't break the seal of the kiss. The exquisite feeling and languorous warmth of his tongue exploring her mouth made a ferocious sensation travel straight down her body. A hungry sensation. Her legs opened wider as if pulled apart by the sheer force of his will.

As if they had an agenda of their own, one of her ankles slipped around the back of one of his calves, rubbing up and down once or twice before settling. This action opened her thighs further and allowed for Matthew's very impressive,stiffening cock to fit closely against her lower stomach. And still she didn't stop.

The arm around her waist, which had been pulling her tighter into his firm body, slipped down to aid her leg in its journey around the back of his calf. His hand caressed one sensitive cheek of her butt before rounding over her hip and hooking under her outer thigh. He pushed into her, and at his thrust, she felt the bite of the metal against her back.

This action made her want more, more, more.

Her hazy attention was drawn back up to her mouth. Matthew kissed her deeply, yet slowly, as if he had all the time in the world to take her on a sensuous, mistletoe-ignited trip.

His tongue wrapped around hers with deliberate strokes. She felt every lick of him now, matching the rhythm of the subtle pressure she now felt below from his rolling hips. Somehow he lifted her body up, and suddenly she felt his cock against her clit. Her very slippery clit ached with need.

Indescribable sensations ran up and down her responsive body. The very thought she could evoke a reaction like this from him made her tremble. Not to mention his effect on *her* rioting emotions. She felt the inner muscles between her legs twitch in response to his hard-planed body, overwhelming her from head to toe.

God, she wanted him. Right here. Right now.

She'd watched Matthew Westland with a perverse fascination since her first day at Westland Industries. He was a gorgeous, intelligent, personable single man by all accounts. A man she couldn't have. Her boss. The man she was now grinding her pelvis against in a common hallway leading to the garage where anyone could stumble across them.

And this passing thought also didn't stop her.

Fearing that, on some level, once they stopped she would never again feel this way, made her reckless. She'd never have the opportunity she was taking advantage with Christmas wishes wrapped up in holiday tradition under mistletoe.

She wanted to savor every moment of it. She wanted to remember each and every smell, taste, and touch of him. So she relaxed and melted into the moment, allowing the wicked sensations to march across her body. Hearing his breathing increase in tempo as his hips ground into her to match the rhythm set only made her that much more excited. Were they about to have sex right here, right now?

Was sex allowed under the mistletoe, she wondered fleetingly? She hoped so because she wasn't going to stop.

His hand had slipped closer to her center, lifting her thigh higher. She went up on the tip of one toe to allow a better connection for his driving cock to rub her clit and scratch the ferocious itch between her legs. Had anything ever felt so good?

Her other ankle still firmly wrapped around his leg pulled him closer. His hand moved with determination from her thigh up her torso to palm her breast. She was braless. He plucked her hardened nipple through her velvet halter. She felt his hand slip between the strap of her dress and her bare skin. Indescribable warm electric sensation enveloped that lucky breast. His warm fingers brushed across her sensitized bare nipple, pausing to squeeze the pebbled tip he discovered. She moaned as the tingle of his touch rose inside her.

Ohmigod, she wanted him so much. Was she dreaming? Was she drunk? Who cared?

The friction of his cock ground expertly across her clit through her bunched skirt and nearly visible undies. If he didn't have a wet spot on the front of his pants yet, he was about to. An unexpected and extraordinary sensation burst through her, centering on her lower body and then spiraling upward to encompass her entirely, especially between her legs, vibrating her whole being.

Sophie sucked in a deep breath, broke the seal of their lips, and cried out loud at the monumental climax she experienced. Matthew's cock stroked across her sensitive clit once more and she screamed. She only wished his impressive cock had been impaled inside of her.

The sound of her panting climax echoed down the otherwise empty hallway. Then repeated gasps tore from her lips, when he kissed her face repeatedly, latching onto her hungry mouth again. Another gasp came when he trailed a path of kisses across her jaw to a sensitive spot below her ear.

Her pulse throbbed out of control. He kissed the column of her neck, her collarbone. He pulled the halter aside and fastened his mouth on top of one breast. He didn't quite reach her nipple, but then she felt his tongue lick a path between the dress and her skin. The velvet of his tongue dipped beneath the cloth. It found and stroked the aching tip.

Her dress wouldn't move far enough out of his way for him to suck on her, so he then put his mouth on her through the dress. A little shriek erupted from her as his teeth nipped at her nipple through the velvet. Meanwhile, his pelvis pressed against her rhythmically, with his rock hard cock still in motion against her still throbbing clit.

She pulsated in utter delight. Her whole body was a mass of warm sensation. She tried to catch her breath. His hands stroked her, his mouth sucked at her nipple through the velvet of her halter. She was wrapped in his arms and his magnetic presence. His mouth lifted slightly. He kissed a path to the hollow of her throat. She felt one of his hands lower to the front of his slacks. She waited for him to kiss a path back up to her mouth. She wondered if he would take her against the metal door. Yes. She wondered if she would let him. Yes. She wondered if it was wise to screw the boss even in the name of Mistletoe.

Um...okay, yes.

She batted down the glimmer of rational thinking, which started to slide into her mind, but a horrifying sound interrupted her sensual languor to replace it.

Ding.

The elevator down the hall sounded its joyful arrival. A rifle shot piercing her heart would have been less startling. The exuberant sound of loud laughing party revelers doused Sophie's warm, blissful, orgasmic experience. They were about to intrude on a holiday tradition involving mistletoe to discover Sophie and Matthew wrapped around each other sharing not only a kiss under the mistletoe, but wicked sexual pleasures. She was seconds away from discovering the long-awaited and secretly dreamed-of penetration by Mr. Yummy...

But instead, Sophie panicked.

Moments from being caught in a seductive clutch with the man who paid her salary, she'd summoned strength from the core of fear pounding through her and tore away from him. She stopped only long enough to grab up her purse forgotten in a heap next to her. She heard him grunt as she ran from him to the garage door leading away from temptation.

She flew out the door to safety, freedom, freezing breezy wind, and heartbreaking guilty loneliness.

Chapter 1

Springtime, four months later
In the year 2076
Three weeks after the Tiberius Group has taken power over the U.S.

Sophie Brent wanted to die. No ifs, ands, or buts about it. Death was the preferred evil of the two bad choices she faced today.

The auctioneer started the bidding at five thousand dollars. Sophie was led to center stage in the corporate amphitheater of Westland Industries so the prospective bidders could get a better look at the *merchandise* they were here to buy.

"Six thousand dollars," the auctioneer called out, pointing to someone in the audience.

The blazing spotlights directed at the stage from somewhere above blinded her and made the spectators impossible to see. It was probably a good thing she didn't know exactly who was bidding. It wasn't like she was being auctioned off as a date for an evening to benefit a charity.

This was forever, or at least until death parted her from the highest bidder.

"Seventy-five hundred," said the auctioneer to another faceless member of the audience.

Unfortunately, the one bidder she *could* see was Orin Prichard. He sat in the front row, dead center. Sophie could see *him* clearly. She also saw him lick his moist, disgusting lips every time he raised the bid.

"Fifteen thousand," Orin said out loud even though all he had to do was raise his weenie little paddle.

Orin, a middle-aged paunch-bellied alcoholic with graying hair shaped into an unflattering comb over, was also a full time womanizing skirt chaser. And most time successful vice president of sales in the

Westland Industries, a company where *he* still held a job. He'd divorced his second wife shortly before the Tiberius Group came to power, making new monumental changes in the lives of the female citizens residing in the country.

Regrettably, Orin was a single man for today's auction of corporate females in Westland Industries, the formerly progressive company where women used to hold executive positions. The Tiberius Group put an end to female executives.

"Sixteen thousand," said a faceless voice Sophie didn't recognize from two rows back. Whoever it was, she desperately chose him over Orin.

"Sixteen thousand and one dollar," Orin said with confidence, as he puckered his lips in a jutting kiss and winked at her.

Yep, Sophie wanted to die.

"Sixteen thousand, five hundred dollars," the auctioneer called out to recognize a new bidder from the center of the audience where she still couldn't see.

The bidding petered out at eighteen thousand, but Orin didn't have the high bid. It was a faceless man two rows back, and Sophie hoped he wasn't a worse choice than Orin.

"Eighteen thousand dollars, going once. Eighteen thousand dollars, going twice," the auctioneer sang out and took a breath for the final call out.

Sophie held her breath.

But then Orin smiled deviously up at her fidgeting on stage and winked again as he said, "Fifty thousand dollars," and thus sealed her fate.

Sophie swallowed hard. Tear welled up in her eyes. No one would top his bid. Whispers of awe swept through the room. It was the largest offer to date for a woman to become a man's wife in the newly formatted society. In fact, it was twenty-five thousand dollars over the highest recorded offer ever. And that had been for a society princess last week.

Sophie was just a junior executive, or rather she had been until the Tiberius Group had convinced the country that women should stay at home to be housewives and raise children. Then they'd written it into law. Then they'd forbidden women to work. It was the first step of many new outrageous laws enacted.

Sophie glanced down at Orin. His smug face told her all she needed to know about how he planned to treat her once they were wed. He arrogantly stood up before the auctioneer even rapped his gavel. He adjusted his pants and tapped a finger on his zipper, smiling at her salaciously. Sick bastard. She'd sooner bite his tiny dick off in one snap than service him. But the thought of having her mouth anywhere near his crotch sent a wave of revulsion to the pit of her stomach. She pressed her lips together and fought to keep her breakfast down.

Orin had chased Sophie around his desk on her first day with the company. He'd explained jokingly that she'd go far if she spent some quality time on her knees in his office. It was what he referred to as the fast track to corporate success for a woman. She'd been so incensed she almost paused long enough to let him touch her.

At a foot taller and outweighing her by at least a hundred pounds, he tried to persuade her by crowding her against his desk. She was about to knee him in his balls, but Matthew Westland, the owner and CEO of Westland Industries, had saved Orin's jewels by entering the office right then. He caught Orin in his natural, wicked, reptilian environment.

Sophie asked Mr. Westland right then and there if his definition of fast track was the same as Orin's. He assured her it was not and threatened to castrate Orin if he ever heard a whisper of rumor regarding his behavior. Sophie's heart melted for Matthew in that moment.

Orin, on the other hand, had glared at Sophie from that day forward whenever he saw her. If she became his wife today…he'd certainly make up for lost time. Her 'if' statement wasn't even an option. A bid for fifty thousand dollars became a 'when' sentence waiting to happen.

Sophie had been so very grateful to Matthew Westland for rescuing her on her first day. Her melted heart turned into a healthy crush, but she kept her feelings to herself.

Well, mostly she had. He was the tall gorgeous boss, after all, and she was a junior executive and never the twain shall meet. With the small exception of a scandalous drunken interlude she shared with him in a certain hallway under some mistletoe.

Her last and best sexual memory.

Now her mind went to her two bad choices for today, death or marriage to Orin Prichard.

"Fifty thousand dollars, going once," the auctioneer said excitedly, since he had a record bid. "Going twice," he said quickly.

Sophie wished he'd slow down. The auctioneer sucked in a quick breath and raised his gavel to pound as he sealed her fate.

"One hundred thousand dollars," said a loud, deep, familiar voice from the very back of the amphitheater. Sophie let out a huge audible sigh of relief as Orin turned angrily towards the back of the room.

Sophie couldn't see her savior but recognized his powerful voice. The last time she'd heard it was in the hallway leading to the parking garage during the company Christmas party. Right after he'd brought about her most powerful orgasm.

Mistletoe hanging in the hallway had started 'the wicked incident' as she'd later referred to it. Her panting climax, combined with the inopportune timing of party revelers, had ended it.

She flashed to the memory of peeling her satisfied body away from Matthew Westland, the owner and CEO of Westland Industries. Upon reflection, she remembered he hadn't actually said anything, he'd just moaned. She'd fled the corporate offices, straightening her clothing, while moving on rubbery legs away from the chief executive officer of the company where she worked, too fearful to look back and see if he'd followed her.

With his hundred thousand dollar bid, he'd just bought the right to finish things up with her. She couldn't help the zing of thrill, which ran down her spine…or the sultry, moist feel of her panties.

* * * *

Matthew Westland bid a staggering sum to procure a wife. His father, former senator John James Westland, was going to absolutely shit a brick when he heard the news.

That wasn't the primary reason Matt had done it, but it was a nice side benefit. He offered double the floor bid so he could get the wife he wanted.

Sophie Brent.

Beautiful. Intelligent. And not the cock tease he'd momentarily accused her of being that salaciously infamous night of the Christmas party. Orin called her that under his breath regularly. Matt was ashamed that the thought glanced through his mind at the time.

He'd been about to unzip, free his ready cock, and go for it against the wall, thinking nothing more than how good it would feel to slip in and take her. He'd wanted her from the first time they met. But she was his employee, one of his best, and he wasn't the kind of man who crossed that line.

Sophie tore herself away from him the night of the Westland Christmas party moments before he would have been caught red-handed banging an employee. Against a door, no less. She'd saved him.

He'd cursed himself for releasing her enough to get away. He'd cursed himself for almost getting caught. Mostly he'd cursed himself for the fact she'd never approached him afterwards. He wanted to apologize, but she went to great lengths to avoid him after Christmas. He left her alone, adding to his own misery and longing for her every day afterwards.

She probably thought he was exactly like Orin. He was lucky she'd just avoided him these past four months and hadn't pressed charges. Corporate sexual harassment charges were very hard to prove even before the Tiberius Group take-over. Now it was impossible because women weren't allowed to work.

"One hundred thousand dollars going once," the auctioneer said in a quivery voice. Matt walked to the podium to collect his bride. She squinted into the audience. Apparently, she couldn't see him, but she wasn't chewing on her lush lips any longer in apprehension. Did she remember his passionately growling tone of voice from the Christmas party and forgive him, or was it just that anybody would be better than Orin Prichard?

"One hundred thousand dollars going twice," the auctioneer said with more confidence.

Matt got close enough to focus in on Orin's belligerent face, which followed his progress down the center aisle to the stage. He wondered briefly where Prichard had come up with the fifty thousand dollars he'd bid. Prichard was a gambler, among other things. Must have had a rare winning streak, Matt thought dismissively.

Oh, well. Too bad, so sad. Orin didn't deserve her, and Matt had waited a long while to approach one Sophie Brent with the intention of making her his bride.

After Matt had gotten to know her within the parameters of their work environment, he found she was intriguing not only to his libido, but to his business acumen, as well.

The fact that she was beautiful beyond words was merely a bonus.

Sophie Brent looked like a temptress born from a vivid sexual fantasy. Her striking shoulder length wavy blonde hair, surrounding smoky gray eyes that fairly smoldered with raw passion in everything she did, framed a drop-dead gorgeous smile, which lit up her face when she laughed. Matt knew from working with her she was also very intelligent and had very unique ideas regarding her approach to solving his logistics problems.

He'd been trying to figure out a way to have a relationship with her and still keep her as an employee. When he got the heads up about what the Tiberius Group planned, he'd gotten distracted by the world at large. It would've been much easier to marry her, if they'd already had a relationship before the take over.

Once she'd been dismissed from Westland Industries for her gender, he hadn't been allowed to contact her. She'd only been brought back to this corporate forum at the behest of whatever male relative was selling her off. He'd been relieved to see her name on the list of former female executives coming back to be sold off like so much cattle at today's auction.

The Tiberius Group had received an anonymous memo with the brilliant idea to keep things simple by putting unmarried women on the auction block at whatever work place they'd haunted prior to the reorganization. It became known as the Working Woman's Auction Memo. It was a hated memo that applied to all women in the country. But it had served his purposes very well in his wish to obtain Sophie as his wife.

This morning his horoscope told him to "Seize the Day." So he had.

"Sold to Mr. Matthew Westland for one hundred thousand dollars," the auctioneer stated loud and clear, thus sealing his future.

There was a loud buzz of conversation in the room, which Matt ignored. His eyes focused only on his future bride. His mind was alert to all the sexual delights he had planned for later today...on their honeymoon.

* * * *

Sophie didn't want to die anymore. She was saved. Orin turned around to glare at her. One strand of hair had escaped the confines of the swirl plastered to his bald head and hung limply down the side of his face. The look he gave her after being defeated by Mr. Westland radiated pure waves of unrelenting rage.

Yeah, how dare she allow herself to be bid on by someone with more money, the nerve of her? The lock of greasy hair hanging unattractively to his chin made Sophie even more grateful he wasn't about to be her—what was it the crazy new world order referred to this as?—her *lord and master.*

Orin looked the exact same way as he had on her first day of work. His nostrils flared in righteous indignation at having been thwarted by Matthew...again.

Sophie had needed her job because she helped support her mom and sister. She'd been fortunate Mr. Westland had agreed that Orin should be castrated instead of rewarded. She might have faced termination for failure to get along with her peers in any other company.

She and Mr. Westland exited Orin's office, but she'd scurried away from his magnetic presence before she did something inappropriate, like throw her arms around him, latch her mouth to his luscious face, and refuse to let go. No, she'd saved that for a few months later at the Christmas party. A vibrant thrill ran through her at the memory of his hard-planed body trapping her against the metal door to the garage.

The auctioneer cleared his throat impatiently and motioned her off the stage urgently, as if she should hurry because he'd just made a bunch of money on her. She instead sauntered to the steps, earning his frown. She resisted the urge to stick her tongue out at him as she passed behind him on stage.

"If you would step over here, sir, we can officiate the contract," the Tiberius representative said to Sophie's future husband at the foot of stairs off the stage.

The contract of marriage these days had a whole different meaning. Promising to love and honor *et cetera* went by the wayside to be replaced by who got what percentage of funds spent for the bride being auctioned off.

Sophie's worthless scum of a father, a sperm donor at best, got to have a whopping ninety percent. Eight percent went to the auctioneer, and finally two percent went into the coffers of the Tiberius group. A cut they told everyone they earned by officiating the contract and ceremony joining the couple in matrimony. Plus the forty-eight hour body scan done to ensure consummation of every union. They certainly didn't want people getting married to escape Tiberius persecution.

Men being forced to have sex with whomever they married supposedly made them more cautious about their ultimate choices. But Sophie only understood the rules favored men, and they could do as they pleased regardless of their initial choices. An uncontrollable and unwanted urge to weep came over her and she fought to stay serene.

The official Tiberius marriage broker stepped up and motioned impatiently for Sophie to come off the stage. It was time to meet the groom. As if he read her mind, Matthew Westland looked up at her, still paused on stage, and smiled lightly.

From behind her, Sophie heard the auctioneer say, "We'll start the bidding for the next bride at five thousand and see where it takes us." She paused at the head of the steps and gazed at her groom.

"Hello," he said warmly and held out his hand.

Sophie remained quiet, fighting tears threatening to spill over burning eyes as she descended the few steps. If she so much as uttered one word, she'd burst into loud, uncontrollable sobbing. Her desolate mood stemmed from the narrow escape with the deviant in the front row along with the general horror of the auction. Unqualified and here-to-date unknown relief now raced through her, making her very emotional. A single tear slipped out and ran down her face before she could wipe it away.

"Why the tears? Is there someone else you would prefer to marry?" he asked in a low voice, taking her arm.

Sophie reached up and wiped away moisture and shook her head.

"It's the whole auction situation I find disturbing." She then added quietly, "And if I ever find out who authored the Working Woman's Auction Memo, which put me up for sale in my own damn company, I'm going kick his balls up his ass."

Matt's eyes widened briefly, but didn't acknowledge her response. He simply led her to a room behind the stage where the funds would be paid and the ceremony performed. Sophie could smell his expensive cologne as they stood together, the scent of which sent her right back to last December and the wall she'd been pressed against when he'd kissed her that first time…and then…more.

Sophie watched him out of the corner of her eye. Her whole body vibrated with the memory of the last time they were together. He saved her, again. Maybe he remembered the kiss at Christmas. Maybe he felt something for her.

"Thank you for saving me."

His sudden sardonic smile startled her as he whispered, "I didn't actually do it for you."

"Then why would you marry a veritable stranger? I can read the papers. I know you have…well, other choices."

"You aren't exactly a stranger," he said, leaning in close, whispering in her now sensitive ear. "I know exactly how you taste, how you smell, and especially how you feel in my arms when you scream in climax. It's an intriguing combination. One I found I couldn't pass up."

Sophie closed her eyes and felt her face go hot in memory of that supremely gratifying sensation, which had stabbed through her at his assistance long ago, as if she were experiencing it all over again. "I didn't think you remembered. You never…" Her head bowed and she found she couldn't finish the sentence.

"Neither did you," he stated coolly as she felt his arm circle her shoulders.

"You were my boss," she snapped with accusation in her tone, still unable to look him in the eyes.

"Yeah, that was my excuse, too. But it isn't an issue any longer." He squeezed her shoulder once and pulled her closer. "Is it? Are you ready to marry me, Sophie?"

This time she looked in his beautiful blue eyes before answering.

"Yes. I would be…grateful to marry you."

"I don't want gratitude."

"What then?" She sounded breathless to her own ears.

He laughed before he said, "Well for starters, I'd like to finish what we began in the parking garage hallway. That particular experience, while gratifying in many ways, has always seemed a bit incomplete to me."

The combination of his warm, sexy body pressed up close, his sultry voice caressing her senses, and his decadent I-want-to-fuck-you-this-second cologne wafting all around made another rush of moisture accumulate between her legs in readiness. Sophie's heart beat so thunderously in her chest, she couldn't speak. She took short breaths to calm herself, but with it came Matthew's sexy scent, the fragrance of which made her insides quiver in long awaited need.

He leaned in suddenly, right into her personal space. "And then I'd like to do it some more. And then some more after that."

"Oh…" Sophie managed to say as a rush of air whooshed out of her lungs. He remembered, all right. Her sex rampantly thrummed for his further attention. And now she owed him in more ways than just the one.

What would he do with her if he had a bed at his disposal instead of a metal door in a parking garage? The better question, what would he do with her *first* since he obviously wanted to finish what they started? Sex was what they had started so long ago. She was ready to get started on *that* right now. Once they were alone, would he finally impale her with his oft-whispered about amazing cock, all the way to her collarbone? Whew, she hoped so. Another gush of wetness shot between her legs and her sex clenched with desire, wishing desperately that his cock was already imbedded inside her to squeeze in pleasure.

Sophie gazed into Matthew's volcanically and very sexually charged eyes and put a smile on her face which she hoped would convey her eagerness to participate in whatever plan he had ready.

She found herself very excited at the prospect of paying up again and again…and again, if he wanted.

Chapter 2

Matt wanted Sophie. It was as simple as that. He'd wanted her from the first time he'd seen her in Orin's office when the letch had cornered her backwards over his desk. She'd avoided both him and Orin after her auspicious first day, but Matt watched her from afar. He wanted to fire Orin, but sexual harassment cases were impossible to prove and almost as extinct as the principles of the Twentieth Century justice system where it originated. It would have been a waste of time to bring charges.

Smart, beautiful Sophie was also spunky, but she hid it. He'd been half in love with her before the Christmas party, but afterwards, he endured regular wet dreams at night after the holidays he'd wanted her so much. No other woman seemed quite right afterwards. Certainly not the boring society women his father had paraded before him these past few months in an attempt to marry him off to a family with political power. If Sophie's father had been in politics, it would have been so easy to get his father on board. Pity. Matt had to maneuver several people and sneak around to get what he wanted. And that was one Sophie Brent as his bride.

"Sign here," the Tiberius group representative said efficiently, pointing to a signature line on the marriage documents. "And here."

Matt signed over the substantial bid amount via electronic payment. Sophie managed to look embarrassed and relieved at the same time as the transaction was approved.

"When do I get my money?" asked a man from behind him. Matt turned to observe the man who looked completely down on his luck. He looked vaguely familiar, but Matt couldn't place him. Sophie knew him though. She shuddered in response as the man came into their close circle. Matt decided he must be the male relative selling Sophie off in matrimony.

"The funds will be available by close of business," the Tiberius representative said to the familiar stranger. The relative had a grizzled face surrounded by greasy unkempt gray hair and his clothes smelled slightly of fish.

"Well, now, aren't you glad I put you in this auction after all, girly?" the stranger asked Sophie. "I think you made out just fine. Yes, I do."

"Do not speak to me," she grated out. "Just take your money and go."

"Now, is that any way to speak to your father?" he asked her in a harsh tone.

"I don't have a father," Sophie replied.

"Now, *that* just ain't nice, girly" Sophie's father grabbed her arm with a snarl in his voice. Matt immediately grabbed the old man's fingers and removed them from Sophie's arm, crunching them tight.

Sophie's father had the same color of eyes that she did. He looked at Matt with surprise and said coldly, "You aren't her husband yet."

"You're right. Would you like to give back the money and try the auction again?" Matt asked him, releasing his fingers.

Sophie's father fisted his hand and sneered, "That ain't gonna be necessary. Guess I'll just move on to finding my other daughter a husband." He smirked at Sophie and turned his back to leave the room.

"Wait!" Sophie grabbed her father's shoulder and stopped him. "Don't marry Hannah off so fast. She's not experienced with men and…"

"She's a woman in need of a husband," her father said, cutting Sophie off. "And I'll do what needs to be done."

"No, please…Hannah is…well, uncomfortable around men. Please don't marry her off to someone who will abuse her. She needs someone quiet, with a respectful nature towards woman. Oh, and someone not too tall. She's afraid of tall men—"

"A father knows what's best for his daughters. Even that new Tiberius Group says so," he interrupted her again. Matt heard Sophie take a deep breath. She was about to explode on the man she didn't think of as her father.

"Why don't you bring Hannah back here?" Matt asked. Sophie and her father both turned towards him. "Perhaps I could help you select a suitable husband here in town. Then your daughters could reside in the same city."

"Very generous of you, Westland. I'll think about it," Sophie's father said quietly, his forefinger and thumb stroking his whiskered chin as if pondering Matt's offer. More likely, he was counting on getting another hundred thousand dollars.

Matt didn't think he could find anyone who'd pay that much, but he could find someone who would be right for a younger sister who was 'uncomfortable' around men. He could certainly find a short man who wouldn't abuse her. Besides, the gratitude now radiating in Sophie's eyes was payment enough for him to follow through.

"Shall we say two weeks from today? You can bring Hannah and be our guests for a wedding celebration at our home." He reached into his inner jacket pocket and pulled a business card, which included his private home address. He handed it to Sophie's father.

"Two weeks? Sure. That'd be just fine. Meanwhile, I'm on my way to try my luck in Sin City, Las Vegas."

"What about Hannah?" Sophie asked.

"She'll be going with me, for luck," he said and turned his back on her, walking away as if he didn't care one iota for his daughter's welfare. Matt hadn't realized Sophie's own father had put her up for auction. He'd noticed the name Dennis Hoskins on the paperwork and until now had assumed it must be an uncle or nearest male relative, as required by the Tiberius Group.

"Mr. Westland, you and your bride-to-be can go on to the ceremony room. It's been set up down the hallway in the corporate conference room," the Tiberius representative said.

"Shall we?" Matt held out his arm to her. She gave her father's retreating back one last glance and then nodded at Matt.

Matt led her to the ceremony room. He wanted the ritual behind them as quickly as possible. And if he could then get her out of the building without being seen, he might just pull off his big secret plan with his senator father none the wiser.

At least until it was too late.

The ceremony was quick, as Matt had requested. When the officiator had pronounced them husband and wife, he'd kissed her lightly on the corner of her luscious mouth. Anything more would have caused a serious block of wood to form between his legs. He wanted her, but she was his wife on paper only. He needed to make her his wife in the important sense…in the flesh to be exact.

"Thank you," Sophie said as they departed the room back into the amphitheater, where some other poor soul had just been sold for fifteen thousand dollars.

"For what?" he asked distractedly. They needed to get out of here.

"For Hannah," she said quietly.

"More gratitude?"

"Maybe." She smiled at him shyly, but Matt knew she wasn't always shy. She could be very friendly given the right circumstances. Like mistletoe and a drink or two, or six.

"I can't wait to get you alone," he said, trying not to sound like a pervert.

Sophie gave him a wide-eyed look of blatant passion in return, which sent a sexual zing down to his balls and tightened them in preparation for their honeymoon. She was about to say something else, but a door burst open at the back of the amphitheater.

Former senator John James Westland had arrived and Matt's escape was thwarted.

* * * *

Sophie's head was spinning. Matthew had been pushing her towards a side door exit near the stage when someone entered the back of the large room, creating a loud scene.

"Where is he?" a man barked, striding down the center aisle with a purpose. In his wake were several reporters and cameramen. Sophie thought he looked familiar but couldn't quite place him for a moment. Then she heard one of the reporters ask the commanding man a question.

"Senator Westland, are you aware your son just spent a record amount on the woman he married today?"

"We'll see about that," the senator thundered, spotting them across the seats.

"Matthew!" Senator Westland bellowed and made beeline for them.

"Damn it," Matt said, giving Sophie a defeated look. "Listen to me, Sophie. We're married. Nothing he says can change it, okay?"

"Matthew, what have you done?" the former senator stepped up close to the two of them, giving Matt an evil stare.

"I got married," he said simply, locking gazes with his father.

Matthew's father then looked down his blue blood nose at Sophie as if she were something he'd just scraped off the bottom of his shoe. "And who is she?" he asked as if it didn't matter, because she wouldn't measure up to his standards regardless of her lineage.

"I'm Sophie Westland," she said, extending her hand with a bright smile in place. "Nice to meet you...Dad."

The former senator did not shake her hand or speak to her, but she saw the glimmer of a smile on Matthew's face. After the bad day she'd already had, she wasn't in the mood to be talked down to by a pompous ass. Even if he was her new father-in-law.

"Whom do we need to speak with in order to annul this travesty?"

"I'm thirty four years old. I can pick my own wife," Matthew said.

"It's apparent to me you cannot. How do you expect to run for office without the support of a government official? It is imperative you marry someone in your own...class." He paused before uttering the last word to give Sophie a distasteful glance.

"You know what? You are a vulgar, hateful man." Sophie couldn't stop herself from speaking. "You don't even know me. Stop talking about me like I'm not even here. It's rude!" She felt the sudden pressure of Matthew's hands on her shoulders.

"You do not even understand your place," the ex-senator said, glaring at her. "What did you do to trick my son into marriage?"

Sophie shrugged. "A few blowjobs under his desk." Something about hateful people brought out her bad side. She'd always been able to shock the vilest of people if she felt they deserved it. The senator was her definition of worthy.

"You little piece of white trash—"

"Stop." Matthew cut him off. "Leave her out of this. You're angry with me. Talk to me."

"You are throwing away your chance at the presidency."

"I never said I would run for office. That's your world. I'm still not interested. I have a business to run."

"Your *business* is barely viable this past quarter."

"Well, I lost several key employees recently." Matthew glanced at Sophie. Had she been one of his key employees?

"You mean women," Matthew's father spat out.

"Yeah, half my executive staff isn't allowed to work for me any longer."

"They're better off."

"I know *I* am," Sophie popped up. "Now, I can get off my knees and onto my back."

Matthew hid a smile behind his closed fist, pretending to cough. She'd had a very colorful roommate in college and learned much with regard to speaking candidly to deserving snobs.

Matthew's father gave Sophie an evil look and turned back to Matthew smugly, "Andrea needs you. I know you two broke up, but you need to go see her right this instant."

"Why?"

"Who's Andrea?" Sophie asked.

"Matt's former fiancée." His father smirked. "Unlike you, she's a lady."

"Lady or not, I take exception to my husband trotting off to visit his former fiancée five minutes after he's married me. Go away."

"You should learn to hold your tongue and further temper your abrasive attitude. You do not dictate anything, young lady. You would do well to learn your place."

"I know my place." Sophie slipped an arm through Matthew's with familiarity, hugging up close to him and smiling sweetly. "It's with Matthew, my husband."

"Perhaps I should tell her what kind of man you really are, Matthew. As your new wife, she *should* know the truth about you." He gave Sophie a smug look. She wondered what he meant when Matthew's face morphed into a rigid, angry mask.

* * * *

Matt separated himself from Sophie and marched his father several steps away. Sophie didn't need to hear about his ex-fiancée colored with his father's praise. She also didn't need to learn about what kind of man he really was.

"Keep your mouth shut. I mean it. If you tell her, then I tell the world. It won't serve your purposes either, if others know about…my past." Matt glanced at Sophie then looked back at his father. "How did you know I was here?"

"I have my ways." His father smiled imperiously.

Matt wondered which of his remaining employees had ratted him out. Not many knew he intended to be here today. Orin Prichard's name flashed in his mind.

"What do you want?"

"I want you to ask Andrea to be your wife."

"No, thanks."

"She and the governor will most assuredly press charges to get this unfortunate marriage annulled."

"On what grounds?" Matt had no doubt his father was up to something but didn't want to know the details. He wanted to get on with his honeymoon.

His father took a deep breath and let it out slowly with a look suggesting that Matt should acquiesce without question. "Andrea has admitted to her father that you two had consensual sexual relations at Thanksgiving, and again at Christmastime. She's no longer pure. You need to marry her because she takes precedence."

"Listen to me carefully. I'm never going to marry her, not for any reason." Matt couldn't believe the lengths his father would go to in order to pretend he could get him to run for office. "Besides, it's too late. I'm already married!"

"Then get an annulment right this instant and go beg Andrea to be your wife."

"That's not going to happen. Andrea was no longer pure well before any 'relations' I had with her at Thanksgiving or Christmastime."

"She says otherwise. If you dispute it, a court will decide for you. Until then, you won't be able to consummate today's farce of a marriage."

"The hell I can't. Good-bye."

"Does this mean the honeymoon is over already?" Sophie asked from behind Matt.

"No." Matt put his arm around her shoulder. "Come on, Sophie."

"You were with someone else at Christmastime?" Sophie asked him. He didn't miss the hurt in her tone of voice.

Damn his father anyway. If they'd had only finished the marriage ceremony one minute sooner, they would've made a clean get away.

"It's not what you think. I'll tell you about it later, Sophie. Let's go."

"I'd think about it if I were you." Matt's father gave Sophie a smug, I-know-something-you-don't-know stare.

"Why?" she asked

"If you go off with him, you'll still lose him as a husband in a court battle against Andrea. And it won't even matter if you get knocked up."

"Why?" Sophie's eyebrows scrunched in question. "I'm already married to him. My legal marriage takes precedence over whatever Little Miss Pampered Princess wants."

Matt knew that money talked, and Andrea's father was richer than God with more clout than the current president. Still, Matt didn't want Andrea. He wanted Sophie.

"The woman with the status of governor's daughter will always win over white trash in court, especially the newly enacted Magistrate's Court." Senator Westland straightened as if about to give an impromptu stump speech. "Matt will be forced to marry you off to someone else when you lose. Is that what you want?"

"So rich Andrea the princess loses him, but I marry him in good faith, and I'm the one out the door?" Sophie crossed her arms as a sudden frown creased her face. "Surely you don't expect me to believe that. I have a college degree. Oh, yeah, and a brain."

The senator took a menacing step towards her. "Brains won't help you in this world, little girl."

"Enough." Matt stepped between his spunky new bride and his overbearing father.

"Matthew, please. Get in my limo. We'll go to the house. You can talk to Andrea and sort this whole thing out peacefully."

"No." Matt hugged Sophie closer with the sudden fear that if he didn't hold on tight, he'd lose her.

"Get in the limo or I'll have this marriage annulled right now! I have the power to do so, as you well know." The senator gave Sophie a satisfied smirk. "However, I'd prefer to see you do it all on your own, and very publicly."

Matt pressed his lips together to keep from saying what he truly wanted to. No doubt one quick conversation between his father and a Tiberius official would, at best, have Sophie back up on the stage to be auctioned again. Or at the very least, Orin Prichard, the second highest bidder of the auction, would become Sophie's new husband before the hour was finished.

Matt wouldn't allow that to happen.

Thinking over his dismal options, he decided to get in the limo. He needed to consummate his marriage to Sophie before his father made good on his threat. Senator Westland would, of course, want Matt to trash Sophie in public by divorcing her or just selling her outright.

Unfortunately, Matt knew if he made it to his father's house without sexual intimacy in his marriage to Sophie, the senator wouldn't leave them an opportunity to do so. It was time for Plan B. The one he'd just dreamed up four seconds ago. Not as viable of an option since it depended on Sophie's cooperation, but now it was unavoidable.

"All right, fine. I'll ride in your limo because Sophie deserves it," Matthew said, "but I'm not changing my mind. And even if you find a way to annul this marriage, I'm not going to marry Andrea. That's a promise."

"Asher, go with them and I'll meet you at the house. I need to make a statement to the press."

"Wait a minute. Why does Asher need to come with us?" Matt asked.

"Chaperone," Matt's father smiled deviously. "Wouldn't want you to do anything which would ruin your choices now, would we?"

Chapter 3

"Why do we need a chaperone again?" Sophie asked as they exited the Westland Corporate amphitheater and into the adjoining parking lot.

"I'll explain in the car." Matt gave his father's political aide, Asher, an angry glance as they approached his father's stretch limousine.

"And will you also explain about the fiancée you had at Christmas?" she whispered. "The one you neglected to mention when you had me pinned against the wall in the garage hallway."

Whoa, *that's* what she was upset about? He thought of the possible Christmas sex Andrea was accusing him of, sex that he didn't remember participating in because he'd been so upset at losing Sophie. He only remembered his own foolishness at letting Sophie get away from him that night.

"I didn't have a fiancée at Christmas. I promise. That's my father's delusion."

She stopped halfway to the limo. "Do you swear it?"

He turned to her. "I swear to you, Sophie, I never asked Andrea to marry me. Only you."

She nodded but promptly asked the question he didn't want to answer. "Did you sleep with her? I mean…after we…you know."

Matt wasn't sure if he had or not. He'd gotten pretty drunk directly after the luscious hallway encounter. He figured the truth might set him free in this singular instance.

"The truth is, all I remember is getting rip-roaring drunk after letting you go. I should have followed you, fallen to my knees, and begged for your forgiveness before I pleaded with you to stay with me. I didn't hear the elevator full of people like I assume you did." His eyebrows went up and she blushed. "I don't know if I ended up with Andrea. I hope not. I only remember being with you that night." He raised a finger to brush a tendril of hair that had blown over her cheek, pausing to stroke her face once. He focused his gaze away from his task to her beautiful gray eyes. "I swear."

They remained in an intense staring contest, as she seemed to mull over his response. After a full thirty seconds, she said, "Okay, then." She smiled up at him, grabbed the hand he offered, and they resumed their walk to the limo, hand in hand. Matt was a lucky man.

Senator Westland's limo was the largest in the city. Sophie's eyes rounded as they approached the black stretch vehicle. Matt's father never spared any expense where his image was concerned.

"You should consider doing what your father is asking, Matthew. It would be for the best if you had a more politically connected wife." Asher tucked his synthetic fiber newspaper under his arm to get into the back of the limo ahead of them.

He proceeded to get comfortable on the bench seat across from the limo's well-stocked bar. He was also going to be only an arm's length of the two of them once they got inside. Matt refused to listen to a commercial on what his father expected of him for this journey.

* * * *

"You can ride up front with the driver," Matthew told Asher, sliding in behind Sophie in the back of the luxury limo. She settled on the ultra soft seats and smiled as she stroked the supple leather with careful fingertips. She'd never ridden in a limo before. It probably wasn't genuine leather, but it felt good all the same.

Matthew left the door propped open and gave Asher a dismissive tilt with his head.

"My instructions are clear, Matthew. I ride with you until we get to the mansion." Asher reached over to procure a crystal decanter of what looked like brandy. Sophie guessed this because he poured a liberal amount into a brandy snifter. She had lost track of time, but still wondered if it wasn't just a little too early in the day to be drinking.

"Then move to the far end of the limo. I do not wish to converse with you during the trip," Matthew said in an acidly condescending tone.

"As you wish." Asher carried his snifter and newspaper to the seat right behind the driver but still faced them. The stretch limo was very long and if they were to try to carry on a conversation with Asher, they'd have to raise their voices. The thought made Sophie relax a little. Soon, Asher opened up the daily paper, held it up over his face, and ignored them.

Matthew pushed a button on the armrest and music began to play, further hiding any noise or rustle of paper from Asher.

"Don't react to what I'm about to say to you, okay?" Matthew leaned in and whispered in Sophie's ear. She glanced up to his determined face and nodded. Now what? She darted a look back to Asher. He apparently hadn't heard them or was patently ignoring them. Either way, it worked for her.

"We need to consummate our marriage before we make it to the mansion," he whispered.

To her own credit, Sophie's only reaction was a widening of her eyes to saucer proportion. His implication was clear. He wanted to have sex in the back seat of the limo while some pious associate of his father's looked on.

"And we only have about twenty minutes to accomplish this," he told her.

Sophie turned her wide-eyed stare away from her feet to his face. She mouthed the word 'how' and her eyes shifted to Asher sipping brandy, his head still hidden by the paper he read, seeming to ignore them. Matthew looked over and closed his eyes, sighing.

"Carefully," he mouthed back, then leaned in and whispered, "It won't be the experience I planned, but it's imperative for our future."

"I don't think I can do it," Sophie whispered back.

"We have to."

"No. We don't." Sophie was *not* about to have sex while someone watched. She'd go back to wanting to die again.

"If we don't, my father will find a way to annul this marriage. Once we fulfill the dictates of the Tiberius Group, it will give us leverage."

"Leverage?" Sophie barely listened to him. The implication of having sex in front of someone overshadowed anything else he said. She jumped as his warm hand landed on her bare thigh.

"Please, Sophie, trust me." Matthew slid his warm hand up under her short skirt. "We don't have to completely undress. I just need to come inside of you."

"Come?" She whispered the word, knowing full well what he meant. It was so shocking for the given context, she couldn't believe she'd said it.

"When the Tiberius Group comes to check the validity of our marriage, at the forty-eight hour mark, they will do a body scan on you. The scan must show I've ejaculated inside you at least once during that time period or other options can be put in place," he patiently explained.

"Can't we sneak off after we get to your house? Maybe a closet?" Sophie tried to think of another way. Surely there was one other way to accomplish the inevitable consummation. In their case, all they needed was an empty hallway and a sprig of mistletoe.

"We won't be left alone. And my father has lots of security." Sophie looked into his eyes. His resigned expression told her this was the only option left. The regret in his eyes was plain to see as he silently pleaded with her to accept this extreme plan.

"Asher isn't likely to allow this," she said, allowing the resignation to color her voice.

Had she just agreed to this?

"How is he going to stop us—or rather, me? It'll only take me a few strokes."

"Good to know." Sophie smiled lightly and watched him bite his inner cheek presumably to suppress the grin he was not quite hiding.

The grin faded. He zeroed in on her face with a sincere expression. "Once we assure our future together, I'll make it up to you. I promise."

Sophie winked at him. "That's what they all say," she murmured.

He leaned forward and one whiskered cheek brushed hers. "I'm going to kiss you first. Once I slide you down to the seat cushion…don't fight me, okay?" His barely audible tone caressed her sensitive ear.

"Tell me why and I'll cooperate," she whispered back. The scent of his cologne signaled a salacious memory from Christmas and made her want to start peeling her clothes off…almost.

"Why?" His fingertips were tickling her upper thigh under her skirt.

She almost forgot her own question. Sophie couldn't quite understand why he would go to all this trouble for her. "Why me? Why did you want to marry me and not the rich, connected princess your father picked out?" She still saw herself as the woman his father had seen. She didn't have a single connection to her name. She wasn't rich. Blatant insecurities from a life as a 'nobody' reared up and overcame her. She worked her ass off for her chosen career only to be auctioned off today like a piece of furniture.

Matthew kissed her ear. His whisper filled with tender emotion as he answered, "I'm infatuated with you, Sophie. Don't you know that? I have been since the day we met. I haven't wanted any other woman since you stormed out of Orin Prichard's office on your first day at Westland Industries."

"Oh," she managed on a sigh. His utter sincerity touched her. Matthew Westland was a man used to getting what he wanted, no doubt. But he wanted her, and so she allowed herself to be swept away in the romance of the moment...so to speak.

"Let me kiss you for a minute or two and then I'll take care of the rest. We need to finish before we reach the gate to our property. Time is running out."

Sophie nodded and with the movement a curtain of her hair brushed against his collar.

"I promise I'll never say this to you again, but please don't make a sound." She nodded her understanding yet again and felt a blush creep up to her face. No moaning or screaming out loud like she had under the mistletoe. Otherwise, the other occupant might lower his paper and stop them from completing their tryst.

The only thing worse than getting caught, she decided, was getting caught and failing to succeed in their task to secure their future.

And given the choice, she sincerely wanted a life with Matthew Westland, whatever it took.

Matthew twisted his head and placed his lips on hers, seductively teasing them open with a single lick as his hand moved further up her leg. Nimble fingertips buried themselves quickly under her skirt. His tongue quickly wrapped around hers in erotic plunder. He grabbed her underwear and tugged them down a few inches. She stifled the urge to suck in a sharp breath at his bold actions and concentrated on his lips to forget where she was.

Don't make a sound, don't make a sound, don't make a sound, she chanted to herself.

Matthew had the most luscious mouth. It took all her focus to not react like she wanted to. A moan of appreciation bubbled up in her throat wanting to escape. His fingers niggled their way between her legs and stroked once, the sensation of which sent a sharp longing through her body. She was embarrassed to be wet for him already. She'd moistened up with supreme gratitude upon hearing his deep rich voice say, "one hundred thousand dollars."

Not because she cared about his money. She honestly didn't. No, she realized right away that with his generous bid, she'd get the opportunity to finish up what they'd started under that sprig of mistletoe. She was about to get her Christmas wish after all, albeit four months later than expected.

Moistening up was not hard for her to do when Matthew Westland said anything. Besides, it wasn't as if she hadn't longed for him aching through each and every lonely night since the Christmas party months ago. His magnetic presence enveloped her as powerfully now as it had back then. Sophie focused on the memory of their first sexual encounter instead of the distinct possibility Asher was about to catch them banging quietly in the back seat of a luxury stretch limo, no less.

She'd relished every lip-licking erotic moment with Matthew against that metal door, but afterward in the gray reality of January when the mistletoe had been thrown away, she was horrified at her actions. She experienced her first man-in-the-same-room induced orgasm. But when he'd reached for his pants to give her what she wanted, the ding of the impending elevator sounded through her like a twelve-foot diameter gong. She shoved him off and ran to escape being caught. She should never have let things go so far and yet a part of her also pouted about having been interrupted.

Her cab to the airport had arrived miraculously at the very moment she'd launched out the metal door. She'd jumped in the taxi, locked the door and told the driver she was late for her flight. She'd been breathing hard and she remembered the taste of Matthew Westland still on her lips as the taxi pulled away.

She hadn't looked back, afraid to see that he'd come after her. She was afraid that if he had, she wouldn't have been able to resist him. If he'd so much as crooked his little finger, she would've swum across frigid lake water to kiss him one last time. She knew her fatal weakness, and his name was Matthew Westland.

Her hand brushed the barely damp spot on the halter of her sexy velvet Christmas party dress directly over one lonely aching nipple, as the cab pulled away. A shudder had run through her, a shudder of needful, shameful want. She wanted more, craved more, of Matthew's touch. But at that particular time, she couldn't have it. He was her boss for God's sake.

Matthew Westland was not an avenue she could explore. At least, not until now.

Sophie zoomed back to the present and the luxury stretch limo. The desperate need to consummate her humiliating auction-induced marriage to her former employer was in progress. She was wrapped around her boss—no—Matthew, her new husband, about to have sex as quickly as possible so his father wouldn't marry him off to someone more politically connected. Not the dreamy honeymoon she'd envisioned, but she understood the necessity. Matthew promised to make it up to her. Actually, he already had against a metal door under the mistletoe.

Matthew kissed a path from her lips to her throat as he pulled the crotch of her panties aside. She felt his fingers slip inside of her very moist aching core, ever so slightly brushing past her clitoris, and she stifled the urge to jump through the tinted skylight she noticed in the ceiling of the limo. She was wet and ready for him, and now he knew it, too.

Should she be embarrassed? No time.

Matthew shifted silently on the seat and prepared to mount her. Her legs were spread as wide as they would go across the leather seats now caressing her half-naked butt. She managed to relax and opened her legs wider. She opened her eyes and caught sight of the not-distant-enough newspaper in her view. It only made her tense up again, so she turned her face away and buried it in Matthew's shoulder.

She couldn't believe Asher couldn't hear them. Matthew already had his zipper undone and she hadn't heard it. She felt the ridge of his enormous cock resting on the inside of her thigh. Another thrill ran through her at the knowledge she was about to find out if he was as big as she suspected. Her first feel of him was a memory from back under the mistletoe. Those oft whispered rumors of his impressive size were not at all exaggerated...then or now.

"Ready," he whispered. She turned away from his shoulder to look in his face and nodded her assent. She held his sexy gaze until Matthew lowered the lids of his eyes seductively, and pierced her to the hilt with one very deep and very satisfying thrust. She sucked in silent breath of unbelievable pleasure as he quickly stroked inside her again, and again and again. The immense thickness of him penetrated and stretched her core to the limit with each deep stroke of his cock. Her body accommodated him...barely, but he kept up the pace of his thrusts even as she wondered what his definition of a few strokes was.

Sophie melted into the smooth rhythm of his powerful thrusts, relaxing to allow the pleasure of it to seep into her tingling body. She pushed her hips forward to meet his next thrust and his cock seemed to slide even deeper. Whisper quiet, Matthew drove his cock inside her yet again. The angle of his thrust almost stroked her clit with every other push and the stirrings of a bone shaking climax grew within her.

The combined scent of the leather her half-naked butt rested on with Matthew's unique scent of starched shirt and fuck-me-now cologne tinged with the acrid knowledge of being caught caressed and yet heightened her senses. Thrust. Stroke. Thrust. Stroke. Matthew was about to make her climax. She held back fearful she'd scream like a banshee if the wash of climax took her suddenly. Thrust. Stroke. Thrust.

God, he felt incredible. Better than she ever thought possible. She'd wanted his cock buried inside her desperately back in that empty hallway. With him driving repeatedly into her now, sending bolts of delicious sensation deeply inside her core, she was on the verge of release. Sophie held back even though she wanted to sing, moan, and scream.

Oh, God, did she just make a noise?

Sophie heard the newspaper at the other end of the small space rustle. This was quickly followed by a choked gasp and the sharp thud a brandy glass being dropped hitting the carpeted floorboard of the limo.

"What the fuck?" Asher screeched, trying to stand as his rumpled newspaper fell aside in the center of the limo aisle.

Chapter 4

"Exactly," Matt said aloud, breathing hard as he pumped inside Sophie twice more swiftly until the powerful sensation of exquisite release overtook him. He thrust his cock deeply one last time and released a long awaited ball-tightening climax inside his wife, Sophie. The vise tight grip of her pussy made him want to continue making slow sweet love to her for a few more hours. Unfortunately, they'd been caught *flagrante delicto*. He figured they would be. Matt tried to be upset, but he felt too damn good at the moment. It was amazing he'd been allowed to finish at all given that he'd lasted for many several strokes longer than expected, so he was doubly satisfied with his most recent actions.

"Get off her. What did you just do, Matthew? I can't believe your audacity." Asher's voice was still in shriek mode.

Matt barely heard him. His head swam in pleasure as he tried to come back down to earth from the magnificent climax vibrating through him. Poor Sophie was trapped beneath him. One of his legs had slid off the seat and onto the carpeted floor, but they were still deeply connected. His cock already wanted more and remained hard despite his long-awaited and exquisitely satisfying orgasm only moments ago. Trying to think about benign things to get his cock to cooperate wasn't working. His randy dick throbbed inside Sophie wanting more of her deliciously wet, tight pussy. Now, please.

"Are you okay?" he managed to whisper to Sophie. He felt her nod and pulled back to see her face. The tears trailing down her pink cheeks caught him off guard. He clenched his stomach from the pinch of pain at the thought of her crying. His cock finally cooperated...slightly.

"Oh, God, did I hurt you?"

"No. I just..." she sniffed. She was embarrassed, of course. He was an idiot.

Matt found a reserve of strength and lifted enough to turn his attention to the incredulous look on Asher's face. Asher knelt on the carpeted floor. One knee still rested in the large puddle of his spilled brandy.

"Turn around, you pervert."

"Pervert? Pervert!" he screamed. "I'm the pervert?"

"I said turn around," Matt barked.

Asher shifted to the limo's side bench, facing away from them. Matt could almost see steam rising from his head. He sat with his spine ramrod, straight arms crossed in anger.

Matt slid his finally softening cock out of Sophie. He kissed her mouth once for reassurance and knelt before her to block her view. She sat up, pulled her legs together quickly, all the while straightening her clothing with visibly shaking fingers. He felt like a total shit heel watching her silently wipe the tears from her face and get composed.

Matt zipped his pants back up, turned, and sank wearily into the seat next to her. He put an arm around her back and pulled her across his lap to comfort her. He settled her head on his shoulder and wrapped his arms around her, squeezing her tight. Sophie snuggled up close, her face buried in his throat, her arms securely around his neck. After a moment he felt the shiver of her body as she began weeping quietly in his collar.

"I'm so sorry, Sophie. I should have found another way," he whispered to her.

"It was…probably…the only way. I'm fine, really," she whispered back, her voice catching more than once. Matt rubbed her back as he kissed her face and hair. He'd make it up to her. Nothing could keep them apart now.

* * * *

"We're at the gate," the driver's voice came through the intercom in the back seat of the limo several minutes later.

"We're almost home," Matthew whispered in her ear. "I'll take you to my private wing as soon as we step out of the car, okay? We'll stay the night and tomorrow I'll take you to my house. It isn't as grand as the senator's but it will be all ours."

Sophie couldn't speak without running the risk of sobbing so she nodded into his collar.

"I'll make this up to you." He kissed her forehead tenderly. "I swear it."

Sophie didn't have a response. Her tears were due to her own embarrassment. She was the one who gasped in pleasure, causing Asher to lower his paper. Technically, it was her fault they'd gotten caught.

Besides, what would make up for a voyeuristic experience in the back of a limo? She just hugged Matthew closer. He squeezed her tight in return. They'd certainly had an auspicious beginning to this already odd marriage. A corporate auction, one hundred thousand dollars spent, and then fucked quickly and quietly in a limo with a lazy chaperone sitting ten feet a way. A chaperone who'd caught them in the act.

Had they even been married an hour yet?

The limo came to a slow stop. Sophie opened her eyes and saw the shape of a large house through the tinted glass window. Matthew kissed her lightly on the lips and gave her a concerned look. One she could see was full of guilt. She tried to smile for him. He moved her off his lap and scooted over to the door. He reached for the handle, popped it open, and stepped outside. He looked every inch the rich powerful, successful executive he was.

What on earth was Sophie doing with him?

He bought you, that's what you're doing here, said a fearful voice down deep in her soul. *You better hope he wants to keep you.*

Matthew held out his hand and Sophie gratefully grabbed it as she stuck her trembling legs out of the vehicle. Asher gave her an evil glare as she exited the limo, which only made her smile inside.

"Matthew! There you are. I've been waiting for you, darling." Sophie heard the squeal of a female voice close by as she stepped from the limo. She stood in time to see a brunette beauty attempt a launch at Matthew. Sophie could see her lips forming into smooch mode with the intention of planting her fire engine red lips on his.

Sophie moved between them just as Matthew's free hand came up to fend the brunette off. Jealousy had never been an issue for Sophie. She'd never been a jealous woman, but she never had anyone worthy enough to covet. Now, she did.

"Who is this, Matthew?" the brunette asked and tried to edge her way towards him again.

Sophie crossed her arms. "I'm his wife, so I suggest you keep your hands off."

"But that can't be!"

Matthew's hands caressed Sophie's shoulders softly. "Andrea, I'd like you to meet Sophie Westland, my wife." Sophie leaned back into her husband. "Sophie, this is Andrea Kane."

"You can't be serious. Did you talk to your father, Matthew? I have to tell you—"

"I already talked to my father, and the answer is no, I wouldn't marry you even if I was still available, and you know exactly why."

Matthew slid his hands down Sophie's arms and grabbed one hand. He led her away from the gaping-mouthed debutante. They crossed the expanse of elaborately designed flagstone decoratively placed directly off of the driveway on the way to the huge southern styled porch with huge two-story columns supporting a three story mansion.

As he'd told her before arriving at the senator's mansion, there was an abundance of thick-bodied, scary looking security men stationed just about every ten feet. They passed five men in uniforms before they even entered the house. Two more were stationed just inside the ornate double doors of the entry. Once inside, she saw two more on the upper landing. Then she registered her first look at Matthew's father's house.

Sophie barely noticed the expensive Italian tile gracing the floor of the humongous entryway. Instead, her gaze followed the grand staircase circling the enormous room. The room was easily as large as her high school gymnasium. In the center of the space was a single iron pedestal holding an elaborate fragrant bouquet of flowers, the cost of which certainly exceeded the total price of construction for her high school gym.

Sophie looked around Camelot and wondered how she was ever going to fit into Matthew's life. She wanted to be more than his unworthy wife. Consummated marriage or not, even Sophie wondered what she had ever done to deserve Matthew and this life. Senator Westland was never going to abide her staying married to his son.

"Is there a bathroom close by? I'd like to freshen up a bit." Sophie still gazed around the impressive, palace-like home.

Matthew led her across the tile to a tall ornately carved door on the right opposite the stairway. "Here you go."

"Thanks. I'll just be a few minutes."

"Take your time." Matthew kissed the hand he held before releasing it.

Sophie stepped into a guest bathroom to rival any she'd ever seen in her life. The space was at least half as big as her whole apartment. The room swam in beautiful white and gray swirled marble tile. There were dark green and maroon accents including the luxurious towels hanging on an ornate gold metal towel rack.

Sophie hated to mar the pristine space, but she took the time to tidy herself up after her adventurous first ride in a limo. The mini sponge bath made her feel much better. She touched up her make up and gazed at herself in the mirror. What on earth was she doing here?

Sophie Westland was her new name. There was even a document stating that very thing somewhere in Matthew's briefcase. "Mrs. Matthew Westland," she said out loud. Her words echoed in the otherwise silent bathroom. "My name is Sophie Westland." More echoing ensued, and while she liked the sound of her new name, she wondered if keeping it permanently would be an option.

If she'd still been in high school, she would have practiced writing Mrs. Matthew Westland repeatedly in one of her notebooks. A childish thought, given her current circumstances. Sophie lost track of the time as the reality of her new circumstances intruded in her mind. A smile curved her lips in the mirror. Matthew Westland was her husband. She didn't know how long she stared at her reflection in the mirror over the ornate sink. A part of her knew she was hiding out. She needed courage to face her new life.

After a quick pep talk, she decided it was well past time to make an appearance. She couldn't stay in there forever, although it was very peaceful and appealing. Andrea was somewhere out there with Matthew, probably chasing him around. She put a hand on the doorknob and a smile on her face. Glancing back once, hating to leave her private sanctuary to whatever faced her beyond the ornate wood door, she turned the door handle and exited.

Matthew stood close by the bathroom and smiled when she emerged. Sophie joined him, then stared endlessly at the beautiful surroundings. She heard loud voices from outside as Matthew's father and Asher suddenly entered the foyer. Asher leaned in close, talking a mile a minute as Senator Westland's face got redder and redder. Andrea followed behind the two men, sniffing loudly as big crocodile tears stained her perfect face.

"They did *what* in the back of the limo?" Senator Westland asked in a thunderous tone. Matthew stepped closer and put an arm around her shoulders as the senator sent an evil look her way. It mirrored the one Asher gave her.

Asher certainly hadn't wasted anytime tattling on them to Senator Westland. Sophie wondered how Matthew's father had managed to have a press conference and then make it to the opulent house in such good time. Did bastards like him have brooms to ride like witches?

"We consummated the marriage," Matthew said evenly in response to the senator's question. He promptly turned Sophie towards the wide white and gray marble stairs, which wrapped around the large entryway in a circle and led her to the steps.

Senator Westland's face turned so red it almost looked purple. "You have ruined your political chances immeasurably. Why would you throw your life away like this?"

Matthew stopped and responded, "I got married to a woman I care about. I don't view that as ruining my chances or throwing away my life."

"We'll see about that." Senator Westland ushered a tearful Andrea into a parlor to the right of the auditorium-sized entryway.

Matthew took Sophie's arm and led her up the staircase. She knew she gawked at the beautiful house all along the way but couldn't stop.

"I'm sorry," he said, interrupting her wayward thoughts.

"For what?" There were so many possibilities: the marriage, the limo sex, the ex-girlfriend trying to kiss him, the cranky new father-in-law.

"For everything." He squeezed her hand once as they climbed the last few remaining stairs.

They crested the top of the grand entryway staircase and turned right down a long hallway with seemingly endless doors. Rich wood rubbed to a high sheen lined the walls along the grand hall. Huge colorful paintings hung as if displayed in a museum complete with lights to highlight each work of art. Sophie knew the place must be over fifty years old to have genuine wood products gracing the structure.

She asked herself a recurrent question. What was she doing here? Glancing at Matt, she remembered. She loved him. She'd been in love with him for months, maybe even since the first time she met him in Orin's office. For the first time, she didn't have to hide her feelings. Matthew Westland was her husband until death parted them.

A thrill ran up her spine as it occurred to her that Matthew was leading her to his bedroom. Butterflies danced in her stomach at all the sensual possibilities she might encounter once they arrived at their destination. She took a deep breath and with it came her new husband's delectable scent.

Sophie felt a little like Alice in Wonderland the further he led her down the opulent hallway to her future, "Do I really get to stay with you?"

"You're mine. I'm never letting you go." He squeezed her hand once his tone was resolute.

"Do we have to live here?" Sophie walked past a painting she was certain she'd seen in a museum once.

"No. We're just spending the night. My place is further away and not as set up to repel the media as my father's house."

The media was something Sophie had never had to deal with before.

"Am I going to have to get a food tester for when we visit?" Sophie wasn't stupid. She realized many of Senator Westland's problems could be solved by her unfortunate demise.

"You have nothing to fear from me or my father. He'll come around. Give him time."

"Are you sure you don't want to run for president? I wouldn't want to hold you back."

"Trust me. I don't want to run for public office. That's my father's dream. He lost his big chance due to his own lust and a tell-all book by his former secretary slash longtime mistress. I don't want to fulfill his self proclaimed lost destiny."

"What *do* you want?" Sophie walked hand in hand with Matthew.

"I simply want to run my business. I built it up from almost nothing to what it is today. Now, if I can just manage to keep it intact with all the unfortunate political and social changes I have to live with lately."

"Well, if you need any help at the office, I'll volunteer."

"I'm counting on it. I wish women were allowed to work. If they were, I'd have you chained to a desk in procurement before you could say kiss me." He stopped before the last door on the hall and smiled.

"Kiss me," she said. So, he did.

The kiss he gave her was hot and steamy with lots of hard thrusting tongue. He released her long enough to open the door to usher her inside. She turned as they stepped together into an equally impressive bedroom. It was decorated in an unmistakable masculine format. Dark woods and deep rich colors of blue dominated the room with one very large exception.

The expensive pink set of matching designer luggage piled in the center of the wood lined space was definitely out of place.

"I don't think your father is going to give up as easily as you think. He'll look for another way to get what he wants. Andrea is crying a river downstairs. At what point do we move her stuff out of *your* room?"

"It's *our* room, and the luggage goes immediately." He headed for the pile. He picked up the first offending piece he came to, which looked like a small make-up bag.

"I don't think I belong here, Matthew." This forlorn statement stopped him. He turned back to her with a stern look, clutching the small bag like a football he was about to launch.

"I don't ever want to hear you say that again. You're my wife. On paper and most recently in the flesh." Matt hurled the pink case out the open door as if to punctuate his statement. The sound of its subsequent crash actually lifted her spirits.

"I want to believe. But why do I feel that obstinate forces are against us?" Sophie smiled and approached him, wanting so much to belong to his world.

"Because obstinate forces *are* against us." Matthew took a step in her direction a dimpled grin lit his face. "We'll just ignore them, okay?"

Sophie placed her arms around him and hugged him close. "Okay," she whispered and kissed his chin.

"I'll do everything in my power to deserve you, Sophie."

Matthew lowered his lips to hers and kissed her passionately. His tongue slid around her mouth slowly and methodically. She allowed herself to be hypnotized by it. As they kissed, he danced her backwards towards the bed. His hands ran over her backside, which heated up quickly. The warmth of his fingers massaging her hips now thrust back into him with desire. He stuck a hand under one thigh and hitched her leg up as if in memory of their first experience in the hallway.

All they needed was a metal door...or perhaps a nice big bed would do. Sophie heaved a deep sigh and thrust her tongue in his mouth. He seemed on the verge of making things up to her. But instead they stumbled into the remainder of Andrea's misplaced luggage, almost losing their balance. Matthew grabbed her firmly with one arm secure around her waist, keeping her from tripping to the floor.

Sophie gripped his arms to get her balance. She looked down at the luggage as all her insecurities surrounded her at once and sighed. "Like I said, I don't think this marriage will be as easy to preserve as you think."

"Fucking...pink luggage." He released Sophie so fast she stumbled backwards trying to stay on her feet, wrapping her arms around one of the posts on the four poster bed. He cursed and picked up another designer bag and threw it overhand through the door to bounce against the other small one in the hallway. He picked up two more large pieces of pink luggage, one in each muscular arm and heaved them towards the door.

Sophie had no doubt he wanted to throw them out as he had the other two, but perhaps he didn't want to incur a hernia, as the two he now carried appeared to be heavier. Instead, he strode across the room and shoved the luggage out into the hallway. He turned and did the same with the remaining three pieces of luggage. The final piece, a garment bag, he wadded up before he threw out the door, hopelessly mangled to land on the large heap outside their room.

Matthew banged the door shut and locked it, slamming a dead bolt into place. He turned to Sophie and registered her wide-eyed look. He was acting like a barbarian, a gorgeous hunky sexy barbarian that she wanted with every moistening fiber of her being. She watched as he took a visibly calming breath and approached her slowly. Stealthily.

"You aren't afraid of me are you?" He took another deep breath and she watched as he released his hands from the fisted position.

"Of course not. You don't think I look like a piece of overpriced, pink luggage, do you?"

* * * *

He sighed his relief at her lighthearted statement. "No, I think you look like a tasty treat." Matt took a step closer. He gave her shapely body a once-over look and couldn't help but lick his lips visibly in appreciation.

Had it only been less than an hour since he'd buried his cock in her hot body in the back of a limo? He still owed her at least an orgasm. A big one. Like the powerful one he'd experienced. Damn, he simply looked at her and got granite hard. Every single time.

Today was the first time Matt hadn't forced himself to fight the urge. Finally able to give in to his passion and his ever-ready erection when in her presence, he'd taken her...deliciously and completely and, unfortunately, semi-publicly in the limo. But now she was his and they were all alone behind a locked door.

"Surely you won't throw a tasty treat out of your room, will you?" Her smile was sultry and made Matt want to wrap around her goodness and never emerge.

"Nope, I eat tasty treats. Savoring them on my tongue until they melt." Matt made his way towards her, his dick leading the way. He saw her glance down at the front of his slacks tented with his rampant arousal.

Sophie's face filled with color and yet she smiled seductively. "Think anyone will knock on the door?" she asked as he stepped directly into her personal space.

"Not unless they have a death wish."

Sophie glanced over his shoulder at the door a moment and then shifted her gaze to his, asking with an amused lilt in her voice, "That's a deadbolt, right?"

"Yep." Matt pressed into her as he held her gaze. His hands slipped around her back to hold her tight. "I think it's time I started making things up to you."

"Do you?" Sophie tilted her head back, perhaps in deference to their height difference. He leaned down and pressed his lips to her forehead. He kissed a path down to her lips via one soft cheek.

"I do," he said and moved a hand down to her lush derrière. Her face still tilted upwards towards his, but now she sported an expectant look. He leaned in and pressed his mouth to hers chastely, but she set the speed when she opened for him, murmuring his name in surrender. He tasted her need as she wrapped her soft tongue around his. Her hands circled his waist, pulling him closer. She wanted him all right. If the delicious sting of her fingernails piercing the small of his back were any indication of her eager desire, she was ready.

Matt slid his hands down past her luscious ass to her thighs and lifted her up with ease, pressing her open legs against his yet again rock-hard cock. Once her legs were wrapped around him, he slid a hand up to her back and popped her bra strap through her shirt. He carried her to the massive bed he used when he stayed in his father's house. This would be the first time he'd brought a woman in here. He should wait and take her to his own house to do all the things he wanted to do to her but found he lacked the willpower to leave this room. Not until he heard her moan, or better yet scream, in climax at least once. Maybe twice.

"Sophie, my love, you're so beautiful. I promise to make you delirious," Matt whispered and placed her by the bed. Her only response was a delicious, breathy sigh. She stood on wobbly legs as he undressed her hurriedly. Her head tilted back as he stroked her nipple while taking her bra off. She moaned when he slid her panties down her legs and kissed just below her belly button as she stepped out of them.

Once he had them both naked, he pulled the sheets back and placed her on them before crawling over her. He pressed his body to hers, suppressing a shudder of ecstasy. It was their first flesh-to-flesh encounter. His cock rested at the drenched entrance to her body. Liquid, warm and slick from her pussy, coated the head of his dick. It was all he could do not to slip into that tight, inviting space and thrust until they both screamed in climax, but he held back even as his cock tried to stretch forward. Matt would take pleasure in delighting her first. She deserved some quality sexual foreplay and an orgasm or two without an audience. He stroked his fingertips down her sides before he shifted to expose her body. He wanted to lick and suck on her nipples for starters. His mouth landed on the soft sensitive flesh directly below her ear. Light fragrance from her skin and hair wrapped around his senses, prodding him to taste her flesh there, too.

"Matt...I...oh, you feel so...oh...good. I knew you would." Her husky whisper caressed his libido all the way to his balls as her hand slid across his back and down to his ass. His rabid cock trapped between them pressed against her thigh, throbbing against her soft flesh and almost letting go in bliss.

Matt luxuriated in the feel of her soft body still half underneath his. He barely held back his imminent climax as her hands delicately caressed his back. He kissed a path back to her face before he whispered, "Feel free to make as much noise as you wish."

He'd never wanted a woman as much as he wanted his own wife at this very moment.

Matt kissed her mouth, swirling his tongue in her warm depths before retreating. He trailed wet kisses down her neck on a mission to capture the peak of one breast. He licked her nipple once, eliciting the delectable sound of her quick intake of breath. When he planted his mouth around the tip and sucked on her, she cried out. Her fingertips dug into his back and his cock throbbed against her thigh in near completion.

Matt shifted further off her delectable body before he came on her leg. He ran his hand down to her slick pussy with the intention of seeking immediate entrance with his fingers. As before, when she'd surprised him in the limo, she was already slick, wet, and ready for him. He stroked his thumb across her clit. She bucked her hips upward and her hands dove into his hair. He sucked harder on her nipple in a rhythmic motion set to the same tempo as his thumb stroking her below. He slipped two fingers inside her passage and she rode them. Her breath came in panting gasps now. The sound made him hard enough to puncture a sheet of steel.

Matt moved slightly and his cock came in contact with her thigh again. The sensation of her sweat slicked skin nearly drove him over the brink as he listened to her sexy excited voice while he pleased her.

"Oh, Matt," she cried out. "Oh, my God."

Matt nipped at her tip once and continued curling his fingers inside her as his thumb stroked her clit. His other hand rested on the breast he wasn't sucking on. He plucked at her other nipple until she arched off the bed and loudly climaxed, moaning over and over. "Oh, God, Matt. Oh, God!"

He basked in his ability to pleasure her in a bed instead of in a public hallway. Just as she'd pleasured him in the not-so-private limo they'd arrived in.

Her pussy muscles clenched around his fingers once more in post release. God, she was tight. His cock thumped against her leg in anticipation of entering the space where his fingers rested. He kissed a path from her breast to her mouth. Her hands went to his face as he consumed her for a few minutes before pressing ardent kisses down her throat. He kept kissing downward, pausing briefly at one breast, but had another destination in mind. He kissed his way to her curls, the musky scent of which was driving him insane. He wanted to taste her. Burying his face between her legs, he took a long lick ending at her clitoris and delighted in the small scream she let out.

"Matt..." she panted in that low husky tone.

He didn't respond he just clamped his mouth around her clit and sucked on her until she arched her back and screamed again. He plunged three fingers inside her pussy and felt the sweet, wet heat surround them, at the precise moment the climax rolled through her. He rose to his knees before her open legs, his cock leading the way again, wanting to do nothing more than ram inside until ecstasy took him. But he had a particular position in mind. Would she let him do what he wanted?

"Sophie?"

"Umm. Hmm."

"Turn over. I'd like to try something."

"Anything you want," came her breathy response as she turned over. The sight of her delicious ass just about made him spew his wad, but he held his desire in check. Matt lifted her hips until she was resting on her knees, her derrière almost in line with his ready cock.

He'd never cared for the term doggie-style, but he certainly enjoyed the position. Not to mention the easy access to dangling breasts he could reach for while thrusting deeply and repeatedly. His cock pumped forward in unrestrained desire. Matt hadn't had the opportunity to utilize this position for a long time. He missed it and wanted Sophie to love it.

"Are you ready?" Matt asked, stroking her back with one hand as he stroked his own cock with the other. With her murmur of compliance, he came up close behind her and placed the head of his throbbing cock against her clit and stroked her. She moaned and backed into him, trying to connect as he rubbed their respective sensitive parts together in foreplay.

After teasing his dick for a moment, Matt entered her slick, tight sheath with only the head of his cock and then an additional inch or so. He put his hands on her hips, one palm on each round fanny cheek, his fingers splayed over her hips, intending his first thrust to touch her womb. Surging forward, he slid all the way inside with one sure stroke. Sophie arched her back once he was fully seated to the balls. Her beautiful hair flipped and danced across her lean back. He reached down to grab a handful as he tunneled inside of her pussy once, twice, and again.

Pleasure zipping up his spine in electric jolts from the intimate contact, he reached around to finger her clit, wanting her to come for him while he thrust deeply inside her body from behind. The silky feel of her hair slipping through his fingers prompted him to secure a handful closer to her scalp. The scrumptious scent of their lovemaking drifted up from between their bodies and mingled with her perfume to tease and arouse. Three deep satisfying thrusts later, he had a hold of her head with soft tendrils of her hair wrapped securely through his fisted hand as the fingertips of the other danced across her clit. All the while, he powered his cock from tip to balls slowly in and out with a strength of will he never knew he possessed, then in and out again.

Sophie made a shrill keening noise and stiffened. Her lovely back arched in sudden release and when Matt felt her inner muscles undulating across his dick in climax, he lasted only two final strokes before growling his release in wild pleasure.

Matt bent over, unable to hold his satisfied body upright any longer. His mouth found the space between her shoulder blades to taste her slick skin between kisses. He wasn't the only one panting in pleasure.

Sophie was even more incredible than he'd imagined and certainly worth the long wait he'd endured to have her as his one and only.

His wife…in the blissful flesh.

Chapter 5

Sophie wondered if it would be fatal to feel so good. Matthew, still bent over behind her and intimately attached, kissed her shoulder blades murmuring soothing things while his hands roamed her body, stroking here and there. She'd never felt so decadently fabulous in all her life.

"Matthew?"

"Yes, love."

"That was amazing."

"I'm so glad you liked it." His mouth caressed the center of her back, kissing a path down her spine. She felt his penis slip out of her. She wanted him back inside already.

"Did *you* enjoy it?" She turned her head to look over her shoulder at him.

"No. Let's do it again." He laughed and nipped her shoulder once. "Of course, I enjoyed it. Am I forgiven for the limo ride home?"

"Maybe."

"Maybe?" He stopped his nurturing of her back and flipped her over. Before she took her next breath, he covered her with his body and kissed her mouth passionately and repeatedly never giving her a chance to speak.

"Now, am I forgiven?" He rained kisses across her lips and chin.

"Yes. You are forgiven. But I hope you won't find any interest in voyeurism, because I'm not likely to be talked into it again."

"No problem. I can't believe I didn't have performance anxiety. Now, you see how desperate I was to make you mine in the flesh."

"I hope we get to stay together."

"We will. Forever. You're stuck with me."

A flicker of doubt from Sophie's memory betrayed her. She wondered if her father had told her mother it was forever when they got married. When push came to shove, Sophie's father said whatever he had to in order to achieve his goal. She was naturally distrustful of men in general. She'd lived with hard lessons growing up through her mother's pain.

Her gut said Matthew was the opposite of her father. Or was her over-satisfied libido speaking now? She closed her eyes and wished she could be sure her husband was the man she wanted him to be, and not a replica of her father. The painful memory of finding out her father was a horrible, despicable man entered her mind just then.

The very day Sophie had turned eight years old, she'd skipped downstairs to find her mother, shoulders slumped forward, crying over a letter crushed in her shaking hands. Sophie hadn't made her presence known. On the kitchen table in front of her mother rested a large package she'd apparently recovered from the mail. There were large pictures and official documents spread over the matching homemade placemats.

Sophie had seen the mailman from her bedroom upstairs and come rushing to see if there was anything for her. It was her birthday and maybe her daddy had sent something for her that year. Her best friend Anna had gotten a puppy from her daddy who lived far away.

In the package, Sophie learned much later, was not a present for her, but instead divorce papers from their father. Her sister Hannah had been nearly seven, her brother Jonathan almost six. Sophie got close enough to see the pictures were of their father. He was naked with another woman.

Sophie had snuck out, pretending she hadn't seen anything. By the time she'd entered the room the second time, her mother had hidden the evidence. Sarah Brent had wrapped her arms around her oldest daughter, wished her the happiest of birthdays, and told her how much she loved her, even while she'd surely been mending her own broken heart.

Sophie had never wanted to endure a broken heart over a man. She vowed to never fall in love. But it was too late. She was already falling for Matthew Westland. And had been since the day she'd met him. He hadn't done anything despicable…yet, and perhaps he wouldn't, but she tried to keep an even perspective. Matthew was a man in a world that favored men in all aspects. She should reserve her final judgment for later.

"But you aren't really stuck with me. You could choose to get rid of me if you wanted, and I would be powerless to stop you. Even consummating the marriage only buys me a year of certainty." Sophie spoke the words circling her mind without meaning to voice them.

Matt rose up off of her and stared into her eyes. "I'm not that kind of man. I won't let anything part us, especially not since I've tasted you. No one gets to eat you but me." He smiled mischievously and hugged her close, burying his face in her throat for a sloppy kiss.

He sounded very sincere. She hoped nothing changed him. She hoped Matt's famous father would bow to the inevitable but feared he was much like her own sire. He wouldn't likely be stopped until he got exactly what he wanted.

And it wouldn't matter who got hurt along the way.

"Sophie. What are you thinking?" Matt's concerned voice caught her attention.

She reached up to stroke his handsome face with her fingers. "I'm thinking we'll have to stay united against our ruthless fathers."

"We'll win." Relief softened his features. He kissed her forehead once before pressing light kisses down her face to her lips.

Even with all the embarrassment she'd endured, it had been too easy. They'd have to watch their backs and dodge knives everyday from now on. Sophie wanted to win. The thought of triumph circulated briefly in her mind before she succumbed to Matthew's teasing mouth raining kisses across her parted lips.

* * * *

Matt drifted off to sleep, curled around Sophie after making love to her slowly a second time. He was awakened a short time later from a lusty dream involving Sophie and a large steamy shower, when he heard his cell phone chirping. He sat up searching the darkening room for where he'd dropped his pants. He noted the digital clock displayed a time still early in the evening.

His phone stopped only to start up a second time. Matt crawled over his gorgeous, sleepy wife and retrieved his phone. The caller ID showed one of his father's many numbers.

"What!" Matt growled into the phone angrily.

"Matthew, I'd like to speak to you in my study." His father's cultured, serene voice grated his nerves.

"I have nothing to say to you." Matt glanced over his shoulder watching Sophie sleep. He moved to the bathroom so as not to disturb her in case the call became a loud argument.

"Please, son, just hear me out. Come down to my study so we can discuss this. After you hear what I have to say, then if you want to say married to…your present wife, so be it. I just want to point out a few facts you may not already know."

"I won't change my mind, and her name is Sophie Westland."

"Yes, well. I believe I deserve to be heard, Matthew. Or are you afraid something I say will make you change your mind?"

"I have no doubts about Sophie. If I come down, I won't discuss marriage to Andrea."

"Fine. Just come down to my study. Please."

"Right." Matt hung up and took several deep breaths to calm his rioting anger. He slipped out of the bathroom and approached the bed. He leaned over and kissed Sophie on the mouth. She stirred awake, opened her eyes, and smiled at him.

"Who was on the phone?" she asked.

"My father wants to have a chat with me in his study." Matt leaned against the edge of the bed with one hip.

"Why?" Sophie sat up clutching the sheets to her chest.

"Probably to give me the 'I'm disappointed in you' speech. It won't be the first time." He crossed his arms and sighed. "I also suspect it won't be the last."

"Want me to go with you?"

"No. I'll be right back. You rest up. You'll need your strength later." He kissed her mouth again and searched around the floor for his clothing. He didn't bother to button up his shirt. He didn't plan on being gone long.

* * * *

"What is so damn important to interrupt me from my wedding night?" Matt asked as soon as he opened the double doors to his father's richly appointed study.

Matt registered the disapproval of his father's gaze from twenty feet away. He arrived in his socks with no shoes and his shirt was only buttoned up half way. His slacks were hopelessly wrinkled.

"Matthew, really. Could you have at least dressed properly?"

"I'm dressed properly enough for my own motives. What do you want to talk about?"

"Andrea has something she'd like to say to you."

Matt hadn't seen her until too late. Damn his father anyway. "I have nothing to say to her either," he said and turned to go.

"Matt, please hear me out." Andrea's pleading voice stilled him. She rarely pleaded with anyone. She demanded things. Pleading was a new sound he'd never heard from her, and he sighed once before he stopped and turned back to listen.

"I know you're still angry about the last time we spoke. I'd like to tell you something, if you'll let me."

That was the understatement of the year. Matt truly wanted to leave, but he leveled a gaze at her. Perhaps she needed to get something off her chest. Fine. It wouldn't change anything, but he wasn't such a beast he wouldn't allow her to apologize. Perhaps she needed closure or something. He wasn't angry. He didn't care enough about her to be angry.

"I'll leave you two alone to talk." His father exited the double doors winking at Matt as he passed. Matt resisted the urge to roll his eyes.

"Come and sit with me Matthew." Andrea patted the sofa next to her. Her placating tone put him directly on his guard.

"I'm fine right here." Matt didn't trust her. All it would take was for her to throw herself on him at the precise moment his father jumped back in the room with a camera.

"Are you afraid of me?"

Matt sighed deeply not hiding his anger. "What do you want to say, Andrea? You have five seconds."

"I wanted to apologize, of course. Please don't be cross with me. I know the last time we saw each other was difficult."

"Difficult? No. It was embarrassing for you, maybe, but not difficult. Especially not for me."

"Well, I'd been practically coerced, you see…"

"Coerced, my ass." Matt laughed. "Here's what I remember, Princess. Several months after a fairly unsatisfying drunken episode together, which I don't even remember very clearly, I found you naked and spread eagle in *my* office, on *my* desk, with some far-too-young-for-you junior executive's face buried between your legs. I also heard what you shouted about me. Remember? You said I lacked the ability to satisfy you because I was far too old for your discerning tastes. The only difficult thing for me was replacing the desk you used. I only wish you'd found a different office for your rendezvous and spared me the visual of the two of you."

Her face turned crimson. "I want to tell you something, Matthew…you *are* too old. I never wanted to be with you in the first place. If it weren't for my father pressuring me into your life, I'd never give you the time of day, and furthermore…"

Matt listened to her spew for what seemed like an hour about all his failings and why she ultimately wouldn't marry him even if he were the last man on earth. He wished she could have wound down faster. He was hungry and wanted to shower off the memories of his past.

He glanced at his watch and decided it had been time enough. When Andrea took her next deep breath, he purposefully looked at his watch, tapped the face twice and left her on the study sofa still screeching. He'd been gone for almost half an hour and he missed his wife. Sophie didn't screech when she spoke. He wanted nothing more than to immerse himself in his luscious wife for the rest of his days. Starting right now.

"Matthew. How did everything with Andrea go? Did you two reach an understanding?" His father suddenly shot out of the hallway leading to the kitchen.

"Was that what we were supposed to do? Kiss and make up? You are unbelievable. That's never going to happen." Matt mounted the stairs, taking them two at time until his father's voice stopped him.

"I don't understand why you can't see reason. With Andrea at your side, her father the governor at your back, and my political connections, you would be the most powerful president this country has ever seen."

"Stop flattering me." Matt turned leaning on the balustrade. "Let me make it clear to you. I don't want to be in politics. I never did. Not even when *you* were senator. I always hated it. I will never willingly choose a life in politics."

"Matthew—"

"No. Stop talking. Sophie and I are leaving tomorrow."

"You can't leave yet. The Tiberius Group representative will be here day after tomorrow to check…your wife out."

"Her name is Sophie. Come on try it once. So-phie."

"Once it has been ascertained that woman shared conjugal relations with you, then you'll be free to go." His father ignored him. "Why don't you just stay here for a couple of days? The press will be all over you if you leave now."

"I don't trust you. I'll take my chances with the press. We're leaving tomorrow morning after breakfast. I'll direct the Tiberius representative to my house to conduct the necessary body scan."

"As you wish." His father acquiesced and sauntered back into the study. Matt couldn't help his anxiety at his father giving up so easily. He'd have to be on guard. Especially up until they left tomorrow.

He meandered his way back to his room by way of the kitchen, taking a tray up for their dinner. Once inside his room, he placed the tray on the flat chest at the end of the bed. Sophie sat up suddenly in half sleepy surprise.

The sheet she'd previously had clutched to her to hide herself slipped down to reveal a lovely, rosy-tipped breast. Matt sat next to her at the edge of the bed and leaned in to take a lick of the nipple being presented. Her moan made him stiffen and forget about dinner. He felt her hands slip into his hair and pull him forward on top of her, but then she halted and lifted her head.

"Wait. I smell food."

"I brought a dinner tray up with me. Are you hungry?" he asked before things went too much further.

"Starving. What did you bring?"

"A variety of things. Come on, I guess I can let you out of bed long enough to eat."

Matt handed Sophie an old, navy-colored silk robe of his. They sat down to eat at the small table located directly in front of the large unlit fireplace situated along one wall.

"What did your father want?"

"The usual. Andrea was down there on the pretense of apologizing to me, but it was just another ploy by my father to sway me to consider her for a wife."

She blew out a long sigh. "Were you swayed? I mean, she is rich, connected, and fairly pretty. How come you don't want to marry her?"

"Besides the fact that I'm already happily married to you? Well, let's see. The biggest reason is that I caught her spread eagle on *my* desk at work late one night after hours. The junior executive she was connected to had his face buried very enthusiastically between her legs."

Sophie's eyes widened. "Well, I guess that would do it. Were you angry?"

"Hell yes, I was angry. I had to call in my executive secretary at one in the morning and pay her triple over time to re-type all the papers Andrea oozed love juice all over in her zeal to fuck a guy several years her junior. I don't want to talk about her any more, okay?" Sophie nodded and their meal moved to less incendiary topics of discussion.

During the course of the meal Sophie's oversized robe slipped half way off one shoulder.

"Would you be willing to go topless for dessert?" he asked with a smile.

"Depends on the dessert."

"Fresh strawberries with a side of rich, thick chocolate dipping sauce."

"If it were anything but chocolate, you'd be out of luck." She blushed a pretty pink from waist to temple as she peeled the robe away to reveal the upper half of her gorgeous body. He lifted the lid off of a bowl of strawberries and another off a warmer with melted chocolate. Picking up the berry on top, he dipped it into the chocolate, swirling it around, thickly coating it along with the tips of his fingers, and led it to her mouth.

He watched as she closed her eyes and opened her lush mouth in anticipation of him inserting it in for her bite, but he had another destination. He ran the tip of the berry across one of her bared nipples, smearing chocolate around the tip. Her eyes shot open to his smiling face.

"Matthew! I wanted that chocolate."

"Too bad. You have to share. Here." He placed the strawberry at her lips for a nibble. "You eat your dessert your way, and I'll eat mine, my way." He then clamped his mouth over her chocolate-covered nipple to suck and lick off the creamy, warm treat.

Four strawberries later, she had partially licked-off chocolate on both breasts, on her belly, and on one inner thigh. Matt reached for a fifth strawberry, but she stopped him with her hand in the bowl.

"It's my turn. Take your shirt off," she demanded with a determined look in her eyes.

He removed it quickly, and before it hit the floor, her borrowed robe slipped off completely. She straddled him, naked, and proceeded to stroke a layer of warm chocolate across his collarbone. She immediately followed it with her warm, wet tongue and a happy noise.

"You taste so good, Matthew. I knew when I named you Mr. Yummy, I was right." Then she wiped the berry down his throat and licked him repeatedly until he was completely devoid of chocolate. She popped the strawberry in her mouth and savored it.

"You called me Mr. Yummy behind my back?"

"Only to myself." She reached over to the chocolate bowl and dipped her finger in without a berry this time. She brushed her finger over his lips and followed quickly with her tongue, lapping at his mouth seductively. When the chocolate was gone, he grabbed her hand and sucked the remaining chocolate off her finger.

When an obvious bulge in his pants reared up in between them, she looked at the chocolate bowl again before traveling back to below his belt with a question in her eyes.

Matt cocked his head to the side in mock protest and pretended to be frightened. "Don't even think about that. The chocolate is way too hot."

"It is not, you big baby. You put it on my nipple."

"That was from the top of the bowl. I'm sure the bottom is scalding."

"Is not. Strip down and prepare to be chocolate-coated!"

"Only if you blow on it." Her delighted laughter surrounded him as he stood and stripped slowly. When he was as naked as she was, she dipped her finger in the chocolate and swirled it around until it was thickly coated while he watched in wicked fascination.

She formed her mouth into a tight small "o" and blew on the chocolate as if to cool it down for placement on his dick, which was already standing at attention for her. He bravely endured her brushing cooled sauce all over the tip of his happy cock.

It wasn't too hot, and besides her tongue was hotter. She licked chocolate off the very tip of the head while he watched. Then she spread some more all over and placed her finger in her mouth as she knelt before him, mimicking what she was about to do to his cock.

She opened her mouth wide and devoured him as he tried to stay on his feet. When he'd been thoroughly licked and was completely chocolate-free, she sat him back in the chair and straddled him again. The wet, hot seam beneath her curls was the hottest creamy treat yet as she impaled herself completely. She rode him until he exploded directly after she climaxed screaming his name.

Once in bed later on, Matt curled around his sleeping wife and knew he'd never been as happy as he was in this moment. He tightened his arms around his Sophie's perfect form and knew he'd fight tooth and nail to the death anyone foolish enough to step into the path of their bright future.

* * * *

Breakfast the next morning was a stilted, horrible, polite, conversation-ridden affair. Sophie didn't have much of an appetite but drank some coffee to get her brain started. Morning wasn't her favorite time of day anyway. Staring across an expanse of expensive wood grain at a woman leering at her new husband didn't help her attitude.

"Are you still leaving today?" Matthew's father asked civilly from his end of the table.

"Yes," Matthew answered in a clipped tone.

Andrea started sobbing and had to have one of the many security guards hanging around lead her from the table and out of the room. Matthew ignored her exodus, but the senator gave him a sour, disapproving look. Sophie didn't know what his father hoped to accomplish by leaving Andrea in his household to blubber at every meeting.

"She still loves you." Matthew's father said as if reading her mind. "Are you sure you won't change your mind and reconsider Andrea for your wife?"

Sophie wished to be anywhere else than in this situation here and now. How dare his father ask him that while she sat in the room? What was she, a piece of furniture? Matthew took a deep breath, blew it out, and ignored his father's remarks. Sophie found she wasn't nearly as tolerant.

"Hello. I can hear you. My husband doesn't want to marry your weepy princess. Why don't you marry her yourself if you like her so much?"

Senator Westland looked at her like she was a repugnant bug. He placed a wounded look in his eyes and sent it to Matthew as if to express what a supreme embarrassment Sophie was.

"I have a wife I love. The marriage is consummated. Move on."

"Matthew, I wish you would see reason—"

Matthew stood up so abruptly his dining chair flipped backwards to the floor with a crash. "Let's go, Sophie." He extended his hand to her.

Sophie sprang up as if someone had goosed her and grabbed Matthew's warm fingers. They left behind their unfinished breakfast along with Matthew's father sputtering and shouting in their wake.

Sophie wore her clothing from yesterday as Matthew rushed her up the wide staircase towards his bedroom. She'd been hoping her luggage would be delivered by now. It had been left behind at Matthew's corporate headquarters directly after the hasty wedding ceremony the day before.

She'd washed out her underclothing in the opulent sink in Matthew's bathroom earlier. They were mostly dry this morning. Hopefully, her clothing would catch up with her one of these days.

"Matthew, could we stop at my apartment? I need to get some clothes."

"Sure, but let's get out of here. I sense a plot afoot. We should be wary—"

"Matthew." Andrea sprung out at them as they topped the stairway and rounded the corner of the hallway leading to his room. The mascara on her carefully made up face was running under her red-rimmed eyes.

"Why won't you marry me? Don't you know how much I love you?"

"Get out of the way. We're leaving." Matthew pushed Andrea aside. Sophie trailed along in his wake, hand still laced through his.

"But what about last night?" Andrea wailed. "I thought after we made love in the study, you would reconsider our being together."

"What!" Matt turned around so fast Sophie ran into him.

Andrea took the opportunity of his pause of shock to throw her bony arms around his neck and kiss his face. Matt turned his head and got an open mouthed kiss from Andrea on his cheek.

Sophie reached up and grabbed a handful of Andrea's hair, but she held on for dear life, smearing lipstick on Mathew's face. Sophie pulled once again as hard as she could one handed and yanked Andrea away from a stunned Matthew. Andrea spun away but didn't leave.

"Are you crazy?" Matthew turned wild eyes to Sophie, shaking his head no. "I did not have sex with her in the study last night."

"Why are you lying?" Andrea wailed.

"I'm not lying. Listen, I don't know what you think you're doing, but it won't work. Sophie, let's go. Now."

Matthew grabbed her hand, pulling her towards his room. Sophie looked over her shoulder, but Andrea had already left the hallway. Very curious.

Once they reached the end of the hallway, Matthew tugged her into the room, shut the door behind them, and locked it. He grabbed her to him and leaned into her against the bolted door. Lifting his arms, he rested them near her head, cocooning her in the shelter of his arms. His forehead touched against hers. He took several deep breaths.

"I need to know you believe me."

"I believe you," she said.

"Why? I don't know that *I'd* believe me."

Her lips lifted in a smile. "I didn't smell another woman on you last night when you came back up here with the food. More specifically, I didn't smell Andrea's gag-worthy perfume anywhere on you last night." Sophie took a whiff of him and curled her upper lip. "But even after one short embrace, I can easily detect it now."

Sophie wiped some of Andrea's red lipstick off him. He grimaced and began wiping at his face himself.

"We'll leave this evil house as soon as I wash off her stench, okay?"

"I'll help you." Sophie followed him to the bathroom. She couldn't wait to get out of the senator's house. Matthew was right. Something was going on there. Something sinister. She didn't want to find out what it was or that it could tear them apart. Matthew may have paid for her, but she was the luckiest wife alive and she wanted to stay his wife.

Matthew sported a look of wonder as she stripped his clothing off, one piece at a time. She turned on both showerheads in the large walk-in stall and pulled him inside once the steam swirled in lazy circles around the room.

"I swear I didn't even touch her last night," he said again when she grabbed the soap and lathered it up between her hands.

"I know. Let me wash you off." He watched as if hypnotized as her fingers worked up a rich lather. She started with his face, but soon after began spreading soapy bubbles all over his chest and neck. He stood still-as-a-statue as if waiting for what she would do next.

So she lathered some more soap in her hands and washed his dick and balls until he was hard as the marble in the shower surrounding them. She pushed him under a showerhead and rinsed him off, giving him a devious smile. She allowed the soap to slip out of her hand and on to the tile at their feet.

"Oops," she said and bent over as if she were going to retrieve it. But instead, her mouth 'accidentally' fell on his rock-hard erection. Then she wrapped her hand around the base of his impressive cock and went to her knees to fully express her sympathetic understanding of his innocence. She hoped he knew she believed him with the pressure of the suction she applied.

He allowed her to suck on him for a minute or two and then tried to pull her off, but she suctioned on with one goal in mind. Bring him off. His hands tangled in her hair as his breathing became harsh and erratic. He stopped trying to remove her mouth, but one hand went to the shower stall as if for balance.

The only other noise he made was the guttural sounding climatic one when he came.

Sophie smiled to herself as Matthew pulled himself together still resting his butt against what had to be chilly tile. His eyes closed, he panted and yet grinned like a fool. She'd put that grin on his face and reveled in the power to please him. She knew he hadn't expected it and that made it all the better.

"When I catch my breath," he gasped. "I'm going to wash you off, too, but I'm also going to do wicked things to you until you scream the walls down."

Sophie stood under one of the shower heads, allowing the spray to massage her back. "I'll let you."

"Thank you for believing me." He removed himself from the wall of the shower and took one long step until he was pressed against her chest to groin. "Now, turn around."

It was Sophie's turn to grin. "Is it wicked time already?"

"Turn around." His million-dollar smile was in place, but along with it was a predatory gleam that gave Sophie a thrill at the immediate possibilities.

Sophie turned and placed her hands against the tile. Matthew stepped up behind her and palmed both of her breasts, kneading lightly in massage. He adjusted the spray behind them as his knee came between her legs, signaling her to spread them wider. So she did.

Steam from the shower fogged the space they shared as Matthew released one breast to grab a bar of fragrant lavender scented soap from the ledge. He lathered the skin of her chest, legs and back, trading it between hands to cover her in foam. The infinite tenderness of his massage made her quiver with need.

His cock, which was already hard again, rested at the slit between her legs. She lowered her head to see and shifted her hips so his cock slid across her clit. The rumble of his laughter startled her.

"Patience," he said and kissed her bare wet shoulder. He deposited the soap on the ledge again, put his arms around her and rubbed himself against her, his chest to her back, the soap making them slippery together.

One of his hands slid from her waist to her clit to stroke and rub. The action surprised her, but not as much as having his cock suddenly enter her wet slit from behind.

"Oh," Sophie groaned as pleasure shot through her.

"Don't let go of the wall," Matt whispered in her ear as he thrust slowly in and out of her, his finger dancing across her clit. His other hand brushed across her soapy breasts, flicking her nipples with his nail, the sensation shooting straight to her clit where he still rubbed. His mouth kissed a path along her shoulder where he hadn't put any soap all the way to her neck still bent forward.

"Watch while I play with you," Matt whispered again.

Sophie opened her eyes and trembled in bliss, watching his hand between her legs...the other at her breasts. The slow slide of his immense cock thrust in and out of her body slowly and to the same rhythm of his hands and mouth.

Without warning, he slammed his cock inside of her and bit down lightly on her shoulder as his busy hand between her legs rubbed her to a screaming climax. Her legs sagged at the release, but he held her close until she could stand on her own again. He hadn't stopped pumping his glorious cock inside of her for the duration.

Sophie placed her hands back on the wall of the shower, her legs trembling. "Fuck me, Matthew. I want to feel you come inside me."

He growled, hugged her close and did what she ordered him to do.

Chapter 6

Matt was a lucky son of a bitch. Sophie was the best choice he could have for a partner in the increasingly difficult world in which they now lived.

He'd always been progressive about women's rights, at least until the Tiberius Group had come to power and fucked everything up. He kept his opinions to himself. It was safer to say nothing than to disappear or go to jail on trumped-up charges. He watched it happen to several powerful men across the country, men who had overestimated their importance and underestimated the power of the Tiberius Group.

They'd infiltrated key places and unfolded their plan point-by-point. "Put up or we'll shut you up" was their prevailing motto. They had the powerful political positions locked up. They had the all important finances to take over, and most importantly the muscle to carry it off, for now.

Matt made friends with other like-minded men in his limited social circle before the takeover. However, he didn't trust anyone completely. That would be suicide. He organized a group of unmarried men in his company to spare the former female employees from the public auction house or worse, the Tiberius Institution for orphaned women. He considered this a fate worse than death because if they had children, they'd be separated from them. At least in an auction, either public or private, a woman was allowed the privilege of motherhood.

Matt reassured his single female employees prior to the auction, but he hadn't spoken to all of them. He hadn't gotten a chance to talk to Sophie. He wanted to believe she would choose him if given the chance. He went to great secretive lengths to get what he wanted, hoping Sophie was interested.

And he'd done this all behind the scene, spending vast amounts of funds to subsidize the marriages so his female employees wouldn't suffer any more than they already were, including the procurement of his own wife.

His biggest secret was his involvement in the infamous Working Woman's Auction Memo Sophie adamantly hated. It stated simply that in order to expedite the rampant and numerous single former working women out there with no man to care for them, any woman who had held a job would be auctioned off in the place of business where they had previously worked. Matt was the sole author of it. He should tell Sophie what he'd done, but the only time it came up, they weren't married yet. Given that she wanted to kick the author's balls up his ass, he felt his best course of action was to hide his creative memo-writing abilities for the time being. Some day he'd tell her the truth. He wrote it so he could save her, marry her, and most importantly, keep her in his life.

Orin Prichard hadn't gotten a wife at the Westland Corporate Auction, thankfully, which had been another goal of Matt's. The female employees he'd wanted to protect were now safely attached to decent men. Orin having fifty thousand dollars to bid at the Westland Corporate Auction crossed his mind again. Where had Orin come up with that kind of money?

In the very near future, he planned to initiate a gathering of his former female executives here at the company. Then they could contribute, if they wanted to, from the safety of their homes, as if he had stay-at-home employees. It would work. He'd have his female executives back one way or another. He'd been able to warn each one with the exception of Sophie. She'd been avoiding him like the plague, right up until the day the Tiberius Group forced her to stay home.

Now that his plan was in motion, he'd explain everything to her and finalize the details. In two days, when the Tiberius Group representative came to check the consummation of their marriage, he and Sophie no longer had to worry about his father and Andrea. Thirty-six more hours until the body scan. It couldn't come soon enough for him.

Sophie had scrubbed him down in the shower to rid him of Andrea's stink, as she referred to it. Then she'd done some other wildly imaginative things in the shower to prove she believed completely that he hadn't done the nasty with Andrea. Not every woman would've given him the benefit of the doubt in that volatile situation, let alone a blowjob in the shower to express her undying loyalty.

Having her order him to 'fuck her' afterwards nearly sent him to his knees. Even now he re-lived the incredible sensation of climax.

Matt glanced over at Sophie in the passenger seat of his hybrid Jaguar. He was a very lucky man indeed. Steering around a slow moving vehicle ahead on the road, he was glad he had the forethought to keep a vehicle at his dad's for escapes such as the one this morning.

Petroleum usage cars were heavily restricted. He was allowed to keep his since he'd put a custom energy-saving Thorium-Z-fueled backup operational system in it. His father was part owner of a Thorium-Z mining station on one of the moons of Mars.

It helped to be a former senator's only son, occasionally.

"Where are you going?" she asked when he missed the turn to her apartment and sped towards the downtown part of the city.

"We're going shopping."

"Shopping?"

"Definitely."

"I haven't gone shopping in a long time. I used to go with my sister, Hannah. She and I could always find the best deals." She turned to him. "Do you really know someone nice for her to marry?"

"Yes. His name is Paul Brody. He's a mid-level accountant. Sort of shy, but very non-threatening."

"Yes, I know him," she said. "Thank you."

"Sure. Why is your sister afraid of men?"

"Probably because our father is such a prick. We all grew up in the wake of what he did to our mom. We lived practically hand-to-mouth until we left home for college. It took me six years and a couple of part-time jobs to earn enough to get my degree. Hannah swore she'd never marry or allow a man anywhere near her money once she was on her own."

"You know she won't be allowed to manage her own finances any longer."

"Yeah, I know, but what's worse is she won't be allowed to finish college and earn anything anyway. And she worked so hard, too. She was less than a semester away from graduation. She wanted to teach but…" Sophie didn't finish her sentence. There was no need.

"What did your father do to your Mom, if you don't mind my asking?"

"He married her for her money. She worked for years and accumulated quite a nice chunk of change. She could have retired at the age of forty and lived the good life. But my father found her five years beforehand and pretended to love her.

"He insisted they marry when she got pregnant with me, but she kept him out of her primary accounts. Thirteen months after I was born, Hannah came along. On Hannah's first birthday, my mom was seven months pregnant with my brother, Jonathan. Her doctor told her any more children after Hannah would be a risk to her health, but my father said he really wanted a son.

"Against doctors' orders, she got pregnant a third time. My father convinced her to sign over a part of her accounts to him for safekeeping. He told her he wanted to ensure our welfare, the lying bastard prick."

"I'm guessing he didn't want to ensure anyone's welfare but his own."

"That's right. He cleaned her out the next week. He not only took all her carefully saved money, but as a bonus, he managed to get authorization for several large co-signed loans first.

"After he left on a supposed business trip, my mother was notified as to her new financial status and crushing debt load. He managed to gamble it all away so she couldn't even sue him to get it back."

"He gambles?"

Sophie nodded morosely. "My mom had to go look for a job at eight months pregnant. She went in to premature labor on her second week back at work.

"Luckily, her boss was an old friend of the family and he helped her out. She had three babies under the age of four and she was only worried about us growing up without a father. She always said she got the better end of the deal. 'All your father got was money,' she would say, 'I got three wonderful kids.'"

"I wish I could have met her." Matt remembered he signed Sophie's bereavement paperwork over a month before the take over. When she returned back to work, he wanted to seek her out and comfort her but believed his advances might be met with hostility.

"Me, too. She was remarkable. I wanted to work so she could retire. She died before I could. I wanted to ensure Hannah graduated and got a good start in life, but I failed to do that, too."

"I'm so sorry, Sophie."

"For what?"

"For the general shit women are being put through because of the Tiberius Group. I wish I were in a position to stop it, but I'm not. I'd be put in jail like everyone else who has spoken up. I hope it doesn't make you disappointed in me." Earning her regard was something he wanted from her desperately, especially since his hands were tied by the Tiberius Group in so many other ways.

"I'm not disappointed in you. I know nothing can be done right now. Give it time. It's a flawed system. The world can not run smoothly with men alone in the workforce." She laughed. "Some women will have to work. It's inevitable. I heard they're already making allowances for certain professions."

"Doctors, nurses and most medical technical jobs so far, but they're severely restricted as to going out unaccompanied by their…men. Some secretarial work is being allowed on a case-by-case basis. I've applied to allow several of the secretarial pool at Westland Industries to remain. It's pending, like everything else."

Sophie turned sideways in her seat to watch him. "You don't need to take me shopping, you know."

"What makes you think I'm doing it for you? Maybe I want to watch you do a personal fashion show for me. Then you can strip down and I can help you get dressed again."

"That's so sweet of you."

Matt glanced over at her smiling face and winked. "That's me, sweet as sugar."

"Where's *your* Mom, if you don't mind my asking?"

"She lives in Europe. She has since the split with my father when I was ten or so. She used to come back twice a year to visit me, but I won't let her to come back to the States with the Tiberius Group foolishness. Now, I correspond with her."

"Why didn't she take you with her when you were ten?"

"My father wouldn't allow it. He had big plans for me. He always has, especially after his own fall in politics. Having a mistress with a 'tell all' book is bad, but divorce is death for a politician. Even divorce of one's parents is difficult to overcome in the political ring these days."

"But you still don't want to be president, even with your parents' non-divorced marital situation."

"Nope. I like what I do. I built my company up to what it is today with my brains and my own two hands. I love the fact I'm good at putting people together into successful teams, which then make my business ideas even better. I wish my pool of potential employees hadn't just been cut in half."

"Before the Tiberius Group take over, every woman I knew wanted to work for Westland Industries."

"Why is that?"

"Because it was one of the few places where women still got fair and equal treatment."

He winked at her again. "I'm glad *you* came to work for me."

"Me, too. Especially yesterday."

Matt smiled but didn't respond. He orchestrated yesterday to get exactly what he wanted as he tried to convince himself it was different than what the Tiberius Group had done.

* * * *

The Tiberius representative sent to do the body scan looked harried. He didn't seem to want to spend a long time and hurried the process along with obvious haste. The device he carried looked like the wand they used at airports to do bonus scans of those people who failed the strip-down-and-walk-through-the-box initiation.

He ran the body scan wand two inches away from Sophie's clothing, down her body from chest to knees. Then back up again. It had a peculiar foul smell like burning plastic. It made a beeping sound, and as it passed over where Matt guessed her uterus would be, the beeping became a solid tone. Matthew hoped that was a good noise.

"I've finished my results," he told Matt.

"The test shows you *have* copulated with your wife within the past forty eight hours as required."

"Great. Now that we've complied, I can get Sophie's paperwork for permanent status as my wife."

"Normally that would be true, but there is another matter."

"What other matter?"

The representative looked at Sophie pointedly. "Perhaps your wife would be more comfortable in the kitchen."

"No, she would not..." Sophie stood and Matt had no doubt she'd blast this government toad to kingdom come.

"You may speak freely in front of her," Matt said and sent a placating look to remain quiet.

"I don't advise it." The representative put his magic copulate-o-meter away. Sophie stuck her tongue out at his turned back. Matt gave her a give-me-a-break stare.

"I'm not asking for your advice. Tell me why I can't get my permanent marital paperwork."

"Well, I made a stop at Senator Westland's house before coming here today." He gave Matt another pointed stare as if to say, "Trust me, you really don't want your wife to hear this."

Matt exchanged a knowing glance with Sophie. They both obviously wondered what evil Senator could be up to now.

"I told you specifically I would be at this address today. Why did you need to go to my father's house?"

"There has been a formal complaint lodged against you, Mr. Westland. It seems you've had carnal relations with another female within the past forty-eight hours since your marriage to this woman. It complicates things for you."

"What!"

Mathew couldn't believe it. The complaint didn't have to be true. It would also hold up his permanent paperwork for an indeterminate length of time until a magistrate had the time and inclination to look at it. Damn his father anyway. He should have expected something devious and underhanded. Now he'd have to prove something he knew he didn't do. How could he convince Sophie to believe him yet again?

Sophie's face went white. She shut her eyes and took a long step back away from the two men. The Tiberius representative gave Matt an,

'I told you that you should have sent her into the kitchen' look.

"I most certainly did not have carnal relations with another woman," Matthew said in a quietly seething tone. He turned to Sophie who already shaking, her face turning to a disturbing tomato red color.

"My equipment is not malfunctioning, sir. I did a triple check to verify the status of my handheld device."

"Well, you need to do another triple check, because it isn't working. I only had sex with my wife." Matt directed this comment at Sophie, willing her to believe him.

"I'm afraid with the formal complaint registered by the other woman's father, it will be for the Tiberius Group Magistrates' Division to decide. And you should know, the other woman is the daughter of the governor of the state. She will most likely take precedence over your wife if no viable proof to either side of the complaint is brought forward. You should be prepared to find another husband for her."

"But there is no way they can prove I did something I didn't do."

The Tiberius representative shrugged his shoulders and turned towards the door as if to leave. Sophie made a high-pitched noise and sat down. She put her face in her hands and started sobbing. Matt was afraid if he tried to comfort her he'd be dismissed or maybe punched in the mouth for his trouble.

"I didn't do it, Sophie, I swear I didn't touch her."

"I know...hic...but it won't matter. She's the governor's daughter, so I'm the one who'll be screwed in the end no matter what you did or didn't do."

"What are my options?" Matt asked the Tiberius representative before he could get away.

He shrugged his shoulders again as a response. "You'll have to find a way to prove your innocence. But my testimony won't help your case. I show ejaculate inside the other woman containing your specific DNA. The proof is undeniable. And there is something else."

"What else could there possibly be?"

"The governor's daughter is pregnant. She carries a child which would have been conceived on or very close to the week of Christmas."

Sophie stopped crying and gave Matt a very disturbed look. The implication was clear. Whether he remembered the experience or not, it was very possible Andrea carried his child from his drunken Christmas pout at letting Sophie go.

"The child might not be mine. When can a test on the fetus be done?" Matt asked.

"Oh, they won't allow a test on the child until after it's born. Your fate will be decided by the magistrate long before that, I'm afraid.

"You may be asked to annul the marriage in favor of the other woman carrying the child."

Matt closed his eyes. "I'm the only husband she's ever going to have. What if Sophie's pregnant by the time of the hearing?"

"My scan says she's not pregnant yet. But as I said before, this will certainly be a matter for the Magistrate Core of the Tiberius government to decide. The laws are new and being amended day to day. I can't say for certain how your case would turn out.

"I know, with other cases pending, that timing has a big part in magistrate decisions regarding two women being pregnant by the same man. You know, first come, first served, so to speak." He then chuckled far too long over his stupid, insensitive joke.

Matt couldn't speak. He couldn't see anything except his father's neck between his hands. He shuffled the representative out the door and followed behind him on a path to straighten this out right now. Matt was going to have a little chat with his father.

Sophie ran out of their house after him, calling his name. The Tiberius representative almost had a cow on the front lawn. He pointed an accusatory finger at Sophie and ordered her back inside. She was not allowed to leave the residence unaccompanied. Matt didn't want her to see him strangle his father so he motioned her to go back inside.

"Matthew. Please." He heard her call to him. He turned back, shook his head and motioned her to get back inside by pointing his finger firmly. She'd be angry, but he was stirred to a bloodlust by his father's actions. Sophie didn't need to witness his ruthless side. At least not anymore than she already had.

His father needed to understand how serious he was about not being pushed. He'd have to keep his hands in his pockets as a warning not to pummel them against anyone.

Matt had a few things to share about Andrea's proclivities, and he wasn't hiding them to spare her feelings any longer.

* * * *

"I don't know how you made this happen, but it won't work. I won't get rid of Sophie."

"It will be up to the Tiberius Magistrate Division to decide now. You should get used to hearing the words Mr. President," Senator Westland said smugly.

"Wait until they find out you had me biogenetically bred for politics. Then the people you cater to won't be so happy to put me in office as President. You know, a genetic freak like me."

"You won't tell them, Matthew. It would force you to give up your commerce license as well. And I know how much that foolish business you inherited from your mother's people means to you."

"You don't hate my business because I inherited the start-up company from Mom's family. You hate that you aren't allowed to profit from it. It burns you up that I didn't fail like you originally predicted. I made a success of it, all on my own, without a single contact or penny of help from you."

"Thanks to the genetic head start I gave you. Don't forget that."

"Oh, you won't ever let me forget."

"Does your little slut wife know about your genetic history? Perhaps if I plant a bug in her ear about how you came to be as talented as you are, she might not come so willingly to your always ready cock. Did you ever think of that?"

Matt took a step dangerously close to his father standing next to his desk, fighting the urge to use his fists to make his point. "You already know I'm not engineered with that, and if you make me lose Sophie, so help me God, I'll make you sorry."

"I doubt you have the power to make me any sorrier than I am right now. I am in possession of undeniable evidence that you fornicated with Andrea. I'll show the magistrate if you force me to. Andrea will swear you two had a carnal relationship in the study when I stepped out, the same night of your unfortunate marriage to that other woman." His father moved around and seated himself sedately behind his massive ornately carved and very illegally obtained wooden desk.

Matt took a deep breath to calm himself, and with it came the pungent lemon scented wood cleaner always present in his father's office. "Andrea likes younger men. She doesn't want to marry me. I'm too old for her. I just came over to warn you so you won't embarrass yourself in court."

Senator Westland unfolded his hands from their restful position on his desk and fisted them. "It doesn't matter what Andrea wants. The governor and I will not be stopped. He wants you to marry Andrea, as do I."

"I do not want to marry her. Ever!"

"It won't matter. We have proof. The magistrate will rule in favor of the governor. Save yourself the public humiliation, Matthew, and agree to dissolve your marriage with that woman. Find a nice husband for her, marry Andrea, and I promise to do everything in my power to help keep your business up and running while you are off in Washington."

Matt closed his eyes wondering why he couldn't get his own flesh and blood to listen to him for once. He leaned over the pristine top of his father's desk, placing his hands flat on the edge of the desk blotter. "I can keep my business up and running just fine. I don't need you."

"Marry Andrea and, with the governor as an in-law, you can have both a political career as the president and still have your business once you finish the limited three terms now allowed. You and I will be set for life." Senator Westland sat back in his genuine leather, also illegally obtained, executive's chair, folding his hands over his indulgent rotund belly. "Why won't you bend to your inevitable future, son?"

"Because I never wanted to be like you. I hated you for what you did to Mom. You have a lot of nerve calling Sophie names when you did worse once upon a time. You fucked up your own chances to be President a long time ago. You should have died a horrible political death long ago. Mom protected you because you threatened her using me, but I don't have to do anything you dictate. And I won't."

"You are underestimating me, Matthew. It is a mistake." The senator stood abruptly, his eyes glazed over in a rush of feral anger. "Let me tell you my prediction. After the hearing, you will finally be rid of the white trash female you married. You will either find her another man to marry or perhaps you'll put her in a Tiberius sponsored institution along with all the other women who have no man to find them a husband.

"You will come crawling back to me in order for me to help you attain political backing to make a run for the presidency. Andrea will be the mother of your child already in her oven as we speak, and when all this comes true, I won't even make you beg me for help."

Matt shook his head. Most people didn't know about the senator's volatile temper. Matt knew about it though and he didn't care at the moment if he roused his father into a bloodlust. The senator and the governor could rant and rave all they wanted, but Andrea surely wasn't pregnant with his child. If she were, why was he just finding out about it now? There was no physical way it was possible from the night he married Sophie. He didn't care what undeniable proof they had.

Chapter 7

"When are you going to start talking to me again?" Matt asked Sophie when he returned to their home. She stood pensively in the doorway to the kitchen.

"I never stopped talking to you. You left me alone here to go speak with your father. I just stayed in the kitchen where you left me. I don't think I'm pregnant yet, but I am barefoot," she said, looking down at her feet planted on the edge of the kitchen tile.

"Very funny."

"No. But perhaps a good sense of humor would help us in our situation." Her smile was genuine. "I know you didn't have carnal relations with Andrea on our wedding night. Therefore, anything else they come up with is likely suspect. We just need to think up a way to fight them."

"How am I so lucky that you believe me?"

"Well, I know the kind of father you have. I have one just like him. Ruthless. A man who will stop at nothing to get what he wants, even if he has to cheat. What's not to believe?" Sophie shrugged her shoulders as if it was completely obvious he was telling the truth. "Besides, I remember licking chocolate off of several places on your body on our wedding night once you returned from the study. Do you sincerely believe I would have done that if I had smelled another woman on you?"

"I love you, Sophie."

"Do you? I can't believe you said that to me. Aren't men supposed to wait until their woman says it and then hem and haw a little before admitting any feelings? If you don't watch it, you're going to lose your membership to the He Man Woman Haters Club."

"I was kicked out of that pussy organization years ago, and I still love you."

"Well, I love you, too. I really do. I have for a long time."

"Why, because I pleasured you against a wall in hallway at work, then fucked you for the first time after we married in a stretch limo while someone watched us? I'm wondering what else I can do to win your heart.

"I'm running low on ideas, but perhaps later on I could do you on the front steps of our residence while the neighbors watch and rate us like Olympian contenders?"

Sophie laughed. "Oh, Matthew, you're going to turn my head."

"Well, I'd like to strip you down and do wicked things to you. What are my chances, do you suppose?" He approached her cautiously with a smile. She responded by giving him a visceral look.

"Better than average since you're so talented at it. Don't you want to talk about your visit with your father? What happened?"

Matt felt his face drop, betraying the memory of the genetic history remark his father had made earlier.

Supposedly, he was a better lover, more stamina, *et cetera*, than the average man because of his genetic improvements, but he'd never know. His father had put him in the genetics program very secretly as a child to have implants, well before he'd ever experienced a sexual encounter. And while he'd never had any complaints, he'd heard stories about stamina in various locker rooms. He knew he could go several times in a night if he wanted to. Perhaps he owed that to his genetic improvements. Perhaps not.

It wasn't like he'd had so very many women to make a statistical study. He'd been pretty selective of his bedmates in his adult life since his father's unfortunate experience in the press, which had ultimately ruined the senator's career. But Matt would never know if he was better in bed because of the freaking implants or if he had his own natural abilities. He preferred to believe he was naturally talented.

At least he knew he didn't need sex to fuel himself like some of the other more unfortunate members of his secret biogenetic brotherhood. He felt sorry for those genetically engineered to require sex or suffer in pain until they were able to copulate. He knew there were some evil men lacking souls who took what they wanted by force because of the genetic implants.

It was the reason the program had been shut down years before, and those left with the implants were made pariahs in the process. As a result, now years later, very few men admitted to being genetically-engineered. And when they did admit it, very few listening understood without inserting their bigoted beliefs.

Matt personally hated his secret, even as he harbored self doubt and wondered if he would be where he was today without them.

"Why the angry face?" Sophie cocked her head to the side.

"It's nothing." He forced a smile and took her quickly in his arms so she wouldn't see the worry in his eyes. He kissed the top of her head and wished he could predict the future. He was suddenly very afraid he would lose the battle with his father and Andrea in court.

It was a battle, which was patently inevitable now, and being herded through the system quickly, probably due to the political power players of his father and Andrea's father, the governor.

The court order waited for him upon his return from his father's house. A representative of the magistrate met him at his front door to hand him the packet of lies. The official papers called for him and Sophie to be present in ten days for a hearing at the local Tiberius magistrate to determine who would be his permanent wife.

He was prepared to file a counter motion and deny that Andrea's child was his. Then he could demand a paternity test upon the birth of the child before any permanent wife could be named for him, but he didn't know if it would save him. He sincerely hoped the child she carried was not his.

The bigger worry was that the magistrate would decide that 'just in case' the child was his, he should dissolve his marriage to Sophie and force his marriage to Andrea, until such time as a determination could be made. The best he could hope for was having the permanent paperwork put on hold until the birth of the child. But it would be worse for Sophie in the courts if he waited for the birth.

If he resigned himself to his father's will, he could choose a husband for Sophie himself in advance. If he waited, she would be placed as a ward of the magistrate and her fate would be decided by another auction or placement in the Tiberius institutions. The choices seemed to be either rock or hard place, with regard to Sophie's future.

There would be doubt in the matter of Andrea being pure, since he could enlighten the magistrate about Andrea banging one of his junior executives on Valentine's Day. But that threat wouldn't save him if he'd actually gotten her pregnant at Christmas. He was such an idiot. If there was ever a night when he shouldn't have gotten rip roaring drunk, it was *that* night.

After watching Sophie run away from him in the parking garage hallway, he'd had to hide his almost painful erection from the crowd of partiers as he watched the outside doors close behind her. He hoped the people streaming down the hallway were as drunk as they sounded, coming exuberantly around the corner from the elevators before seeing him. He couldn't chase her and let his employees have any knowledge of what he'd just done with her.

He'd gone and fetched an expensive bottle of scotch out of his office and sucked down half of it, feeling sorry for himself and knowing he wouldn't pursue Sophie after the holidays either. "She's an employee," he'd said out loud after each and every sip.

Matt had a vague recollection of seeing Andrea in his office that night, standing above him, but not much more. He'd woken up alone the next morning in his father's house without a clear recollection of how he got there. His father's limo had been called to drive him. He assumed Andrea had called the driver. Matt never spoke with Sophie again until the day she was auctioned off in the corporate amphitheater.

"What happened with your father?" Sophie asked, breaking his morbid reverie into the past as they retreated into their living room.

"I don't want to talk about it. It makes me too angry. I need to calm down."

She sidled up to him and placed a hand around his waist. "Okay. What can I do to make you relax?"

"Just love me. It's all I need for now."

He felt her hand shift from his waist and slip down to his crotch. Damn. Her fingers stroking him through the material made his cock spring to life in no time.

"Does this relax you? Or should I think up something else?"

"No, you're doing a great job."

He felt her lips touch his throat and he throbbed once in her hand through his slacks. She unzipped him quickly and grabbed hold through the thin layer of his boxers. He took a startled breath. She found the open slit in his boxers and his knees buckled slightly as her soft fingers caressed his cock.

"Now that I have you where I want you, what are my chances of asking for a favor?" she whispered as she continued stroking him bare-handed.

He pressed against her hand wanting to wrap around her and forget about his day. "You can have absolutely anything within my power to give."

"I want to work."

"What?"

"I want to have a job. I thought of a way to help you and do what I want if you'll allow it. Bring some things home to me and I'll work on them and send them back with you. At least I can use the expensive education I worked so long and hard to get. I promise I won't tell anyone."

"Okay. You can work." He was losing his ability to think clearly as her fingers wrapped methodically and rhythmically around his marble-hard cock.

"Really? Somehow I expected more of a fight. Aren't you going to at least give me a lecture on how women need to stay home and make their man happy?" She clenched her hand around him in a vice grip, making him want to throw her down on the sofa and have his wicked way with her for making him so happy.

"Just keep your hand moving, and I'll be perfectly happy. Or if you'd like to fall to your knees and used your very talented mouth, I won't stop you." He chuckled remembering her very talented mouth.

She stroked him, running her thumb over a very sensitive place. He was about to explode in her hand but fought it. He'd always been able to repeat sexual encounters in a short period of time. Sophie made him into a teenaged quickie master.

He leaned heavily into her, unable to speak coherently for a second as her fingers stroked the ultra-sensitive place on his throbbing head.

"Oh, now, I surely couldn't ask you to allow me to give you another blowjob. You must be sick of them by now."

He placed his lips on her neck and kissed his way to her face. "Trust me, I'll never be sick of your mouth on me."

She laughed and sunk to her knees before him and placed her mouth around his cock where her hand had been only moments before.

"Sophie, I was only kidding..." He stopped talking and sucked in a surprised breath when he felt his cock slip between her lips. He sat down on the sofa quickly before his legs buckled. She followed him down, never losing the suction.

God, he was a lucky son of a bitch. It was his final thought before he erupted in utter bliss.

* * * *

The next morning Matt went to work as usual and considered his plan to bring Sophie here tonight. Salacious thoughts of her from the past two days kept him occupied when he should have been concentrating on his business. There was a knock at his office door to further distract him from today's schedule.

"Come in," Matt called out. His regular executive secretary still awaited her work visa and an arrangement with her husband to have him shuttle her to work and escort her inside before driving himself to his own job across town. The Tiberius Group was a pain in Matt's ass but he wasn't alone.

Paul Brody timidly opened the door and entered his office carrying a sheaf of papers and a manila folder. He'd worked for Westland Industries for over ten years in accounting. He was also the very man Matt needed to talk to regarding Sophie's sister Hannah.

Matt motioned for Paul to sit in one of the chairs before his desk. "Paul, good to see you. I've been meaning to call you."

"Thank you, Mr. Westland. What did you need?"

Paul was a very quiet shy nervous sort of man, but he was very intelligent and ever dependable. He lowered his not-too-tall frame cautiously into the chair before Matt's desk his face questioning. He would make a good husband for Sophie's sister Hannah. Shy and not too big for a girl 'uncomfortable' around men. Perfect. At least Matt hoped so.

"I wanted to make a proposition regarding my wife, Sophie."

"Sophie?" The color came up in Paul's face at the mention of her name. "Your wife?"

"Actually, it's regarding Sophie's sister, Hannah."

His eyes widened and his free hand fisted. "What…what do you need from me?"

Paul seemed slightly uncomfortable, but Matt pressed on hoping he wouldn't have to do too much persuading to get Paul to offer for Hannah.

"Hannah needs a husband. I was hoping to talk you into getting married."

"Married?" Paul looked away and studied the corner of Matt's desk. "Oh, I don't know."

"Sophie says Hannah is…well sort of shy with men. The truth is Paul, I thought I'd play matchmaker and set you two up together."

Paul was silent and still avoided Matt's eyes. "I never planned on getting married, Mr. Westland."

"But would you consider it since the world has gone crazy?" Matt watched as Paul chewed over the question. "I'd consider it a personal favor."

"I don't have lots of money to…buy a wife."

"I can arrange something."

"I'll think about it."

"Great. What did you need to see me about?" Matt gestured to the papers in Paul's hands.

"Oh, yes, I found…well something disturbing and odd in the accounts." He fanned the papers in front of Matt. "As you can see, fifty thousand dollars was removed from an offshore account three days ago. That's the disturbing part."

"What's the odd part?"

"It was put back yesterday."

"Put back? The money that was missing was returned? Are you sure it wasn't some mistake and then correction?"

"Yes, sir. The thing is…I wanted to tell you myself because…well the paperwork points to me as the most likely suspect in this matter."

Matt gave Paul a sharp look. If fifty thousand dollars was missing, Paul Brody wasn't the most likely suspect. Orin Prichard coincidentally had the exact amount to bid on Sophie three days ago at the auction. Matt rarely believed in coincidences.

"I'll look into it, Paul. Thanks for bringing it to my attention."

"I'll consider your offer of Sophie's sister. Let me think about it."

"We are having a dinner party in a couple of weeks. You can meet her and decide."

Paul shuffled out looking very nervous. Matt studied the paperwork for an hour before he scooped it all up and headed to Orin's office.

Matt barged inside to Orin's lush, overindulgent office space without knocking. Orin was tipped back in his chair with his feet crossed on his desk speaking into his wireless ear bud phone. Startled when Matt popped the door open, he almost tumbled over backwards.

"What the hell do you want? I'm sick of you bursting into my office without the courtesy of knocking."

Matt looked around and shrugged. "What's the big deal? I know you can't have any women cornered in here since they aren't allowed to work any more. I'm sure they're all resting at home enjoying the break from being chased by you."

"Why are you here, Matthew?" Orin tipped forward, his heels slipping to the floor, and pulled the ear bud from his head, tossing it to the desk amidst the clutter.

Matt flung a sheaf of papers onto his messy desk covering the phone. "It has been brought to my attention that someone embezzled fifty thousand dollars out of Westland Industries offshore accounts the day before the auction. Anything you want to tell me, Orin?"

Orin's comb-over looked on the verge of melting down his face. He quickly slicked it back into place as he'd done a thousand times before. "What are you implying?" More color came up in his already flush face.

"Let's see...how much did you bid to take a wife? Would that be fifty thousand dollars?"

Orin sneered. "Are you accusing me of embezzling, Matthew? I should sue you for libel."

"It isn't libel if it's true! So tell me, Orin, where did a gambler like you get fifty thousand dollars if you didn't steal it from the company?"

"None of your goddamned business!"

"If it's my money, I'd say it's my business."

Orin brightened suddenly. "Maybe I won it."

"It did occur to me, but if you had won that much, it would be in the media. Sums over thirty-five thousand are reported, you know. Or perhaps you don't since that's not how you came up with that much money." It was Matt's turn to sneer. He had Orin by the short hairs.

"Fuck you, Matt."

"No thanks. Why shouldn't I fire you, Orin?"

"Don't bother. I quit!"

"Even better."

"You'll be sorry. I'm the best salesman you have."

"I'll try to go on." Matt rolled his eyes not hiding his sarcasm.

Orin strode out of his office leaving the door ajar in his haste, shoving men out of his way as he departed. Good riddance, Matt thought with satisfaction until an uneasy feeling encompassed him. Orin hadn't actually confessed to taking the money. Matt expected him to be smug about getting away with it for this long. Unexpected reaction.

No matter, at least it was one more worry staunched.

* * * *

Matt took Sophie to Westland Industries after close of business the next night. His smug smile and amplified wink at the guard about what was going on in his office with his wife late at night was apparently enough to keep security from asking any further questions and didn't prompt them to visit his floor at night either. This pattern continued all week.

Each night, Matt ushered Sophie to his office, pretending extracurricular activities instead of what was really going on. Sophie unlawfully working for him. She toiled happily on a special project in the job she used to hold when she was allowed to work for him. She picked up as if she'd never been forced to leave without missing a beat and continued her brilliant progress each night, with no one the wiser.

The preliminary hearing in front of the Tiberius magistrate was also the same day he'd invited Sophie's father and sister to their home. He arranged the dinner party and promised to find Sophie's sister a husband.

Tomorrow would be a big day for them. Matt hoped Sophie was still his wife when her sister and father showed up, expecting him to provide a husband with a large dowry.

Tonight, he watched Sophie working away at his desk like a slave on a plan to help him manage his unruly inventory. He waited for a phone call from Paul Brody, Hannah's intended future husband.

This past week, Sophie had worked tirelessly in his office until after the night cleaning crew was gone. Then she'd make her way down to her own office and the files still remaining there to finish up her self-appointed nightly tasks. Tonight, after a couple of hours, she checked her watch and stood to reach a paper on the corner of his desk.

When she promptly bent over his desk, her lovely ass was in the perfect position for a favored sexual romp. Matt stood without having remembered doing it, but then studied the surface of his desk and the memories of Andrea spread eagle shrieking in passion helped douse any romantic feelings he had for tonight. Besides, he had a phone call appointment. He didn't want to be interrupted in the middle of anything to begin an important conversation. One he didn't want Sophie to overhear.

"Something on your mind?" She looked over her shoulder with a salacious smile on her face. He still stood as if ready to launch into action and Matt knew she'd be only too willing to let him do whatever he wanted. But the memory of finding Andrea here with one of his junior executives ruined it for him. Even with a different desk in place.

He sat back down. "No. Nothing on my mind."

"Are you sure? I can think of some things."

"I'm sorry. I just have certain memories about previous sexual activities, which went on in here. Memories that I hadn't planned on explaining to you."

"Oh." Her eyes widened. "You mean I'm not the first in here and…"

"No, you're the only employee I've ever chased down a hallway or wanted to corner in my office." He paused, not meaning to sound so dramatic when he said, "It's something else."

"What else?" Sophie's frown brought him out of his foolish traipse down bad memory lane.

"I caught Andrea in my office with another man."

"While you were dating her?" Sophie's incredulous look of

compassion registered deep in his consciousness.

"No, I never 'dated' her. She hung around me primarily because her father wanted her to make herself available to me. In fact, she used to be involved with a young executive here named Bart."

"So are they still together or was it a fling?"

Matt huffed. "Don't know, don't care. I just remember that she was screaming about how inadequate I was as she ground herself into the hungry mouth of the twenty-year-old intern she was fucking in 'my' office. This is the woman my father feels is perfect for me."

"And I guess you were a gentleman and didn't disclose her bad behavior, right?"

"Not yet. However, the time may be coming."

He saw her eye the desk with distaste on his behalf.

"Oh…and I replaced the desk, by the way."

"Good. What did you do to the other one?"

"I gleefully set fire to it out on the back dock. I loved that desk, too."

"Good for you. I would've done the same thing. Only I probably would've added some marks with an ax before I lit it up." He returned her smile. "What did she say about you? I can't imagine you being inadequate at anything. I only ask because I don't want to make the same mistake."

"She finds me too old for her tastes."

"Too old? Are you kidding? That's it?" Sophie's brows narrowed in question. "Isn't she your same age?"

"Yes, but she prefers much younger men."

Sophie's eyes squinted even further as if in disbelief. "You're not exactly over the hill yet, Matthew."

"Twenty-two is pretty much over the hill for Andrea. And I'm well past that prime age."

Sophie pondered his statement for a few moments before cocking her head to the side and promptly turning an inquisitive look his way. "What else does your father have on you?" She crossed her arms as if she knew something.

"What do you mean?" He scanned her face to see if she already knew his genetic secret.

"Why is he so smug that he thinks he can get you to bend to his will?

There must be something else?" She arched an eyebrow at him in question.

He shrugged. "It's a secret." Was he sincerely about to open up about his ultra secret genetic enhancements?

"Ooh, I love secrets. I won't tell. I promise. I can keep your secret."

"I don't know. It's a pretty big secret. And I don't know if I'm quite ready to tell you yet. I don't want you to look at me...differently."

"I won't. I promise." Her face showed extreme curiosity regarding his 'secret.' She moved gracefully across the room and sat on the sofa, patting the space next to her in invitation. Her heartfelt curious face made him want to share with her. And he needed to tell her anyway, since it might come up once they were in front of the magistrate pleading to stay together. He should assess her feelings on the genetically-enhanced beforehand.

"All right, brace yourself. No, never mind. I need to tell you why first. You see, my father wanted me to be President and follow in what he felt were his preordained footsteps. He was on the fast track to the presidency when I was about eight years old.

"In his final term as senator, he suffered through a sexual scandal after smugly dismissing his long time mistress and secretary. Bridget had been with him since he'd been in the campus political scene in college."

"Was she a woman scorned?" Sophie asked with wide interested eyes.

"Yes, among other things. She was also a woman who'd given up a lot due to all the promises my father had fed her over the years. She had quietly understood how he needed to marry my mother whose family was wealthy. But ultimately my father underestimated Bridget."

Sophie snorted. "Most men in my experience underestimate women all the time." Her tone was snidely off-handed until she perhaps realized he was included in the category of men. She quickly turned to him and added, "But you don't." She smiled and gestured for him to continue.

"Thanks. Well, as you probably know from all the sordid news coverage, Bridget had kept a series of diaries containing every moment of their time together, which she then released to the media frenzy surrounding the big scandal of the moment.

"My dad weathered the course for a little while during the remaining two years while he was in office, but his party turned their back on him the day he left. He was smart enough to get the information in advance so he could make some preparations with his waning power before he went down all the way. I was included in his plan to get back into the saddle one day."

She leaned forward with interest. "What did he do?"

"When I was ten, after my mom was sent away, he had biogenetically engineered enhancements done on me," Matt watched her eyes widen again, "so I'd be a shoo-in for politics one day and able to realize the dream he lost with his mistress."

"Really?" Her voice sounded full of wonder, not contempt. Good sign.

"You're not disgusted?"

"No. Why would I be? I think it's cool. Besides, you were underage. It wasn't your choice. It was your father's. Now, if you'd felt the need at age thirty to make these improvements, then I might have a different opinion. I guess I view genetic enhancement later in life much like steroid use in athletes. It's cheating."

Matt's eyes widened in surprise at her attitude. "I see." As a rule people could be placed in one of two groups on the subject of genetic enhancement: fearful or jealous. The cheating category would now have to be added to the list.

"Do you have to keep the treatments up?"

"I used to, up until fairly recently as a matter of fact, but not any more."

"I thought it was life long."

"For some it is. It depends on the work done and the age the implants are introduced. If the work is done before puberty, then after twenty years or so it becomes ingrained into the structure of the body or something like that and almost no further maintenance is required.

"I have very minimal enhancements. My father didn't want them easily detected. Now that I don't have to take treatments any longer, if anyone does a body scan it reflects any enhancements as natural to my body and its natural structure."

"What was done to you?"

He tapped the side of his head with a forefinger. "I have added business acumen wired in my brain pathways, and I strategize better than the average guy. Why?"

She smiled deviously. "Well, when I was in college, my roommate told me her older brother had been enhanced, but not until he turned eighteen because their parents forbade it. He wanted to be a super lover, and in order to achieve his goal, he lived at the forbidden facility."

"That was the first enhancement they outlawed because if you get that particular enhancement after puberty, there is a small risk of turning into a sexual vampire."

"Sexual vampire? What is that? And do you have it?"

"No, I don't have it. Quit drooling. It's where sex is required, almost like fuel for the man enhanced. Ninety-nine percent of the guys on that treatment were fine, but that other dangerous one percent, the ones they called sexual vampires, didn't have any compunction about taking what sex they needed by force...genetically enhanced force."

"I think maybe you have a little added sexual something."

"Why?"

"Because you're so big. Admit it. You got the penis enlargement package, didn't you?"

He shook his head slowly back and forth. "Uh-uh, that's all me, babe."

"So you say. But I say it's all mine, at least for now."

"I'll never argue with you about that, now or later."

"Good. How about if we go to my old office so I can test out all your genetic enhancements." She smiled. "Perhaps you'd like to get under *my* desk."

"Are you really okay with me being genetically different? I mean, it's a secret, you understand. If the Tiberius Group finds out, I'll lose my commerce license and my business."

"I know, but it isn't like I've never heard of it before. When I was a kid, it was all the rage. I was just jealous they wouldn't allow girls to participate."

"Do you know someone who's enhanced?" Matt asked, quirking an interested eyebrow.

"No, but I overheard my mother telling someone she wished she could afford to have my little brother enhanced so he'd have a better chance in life, but the treatments were only for the rich or famous."

"Probably a good thing she wasn't able to afford it, as it turned out later. Once the implants are introduced into the body, they can't be removed. Since it was outlawed, those with the implants must keep them secret now."

"Yeah. And besides, my brother's in law enforcement now. He would have been kept out of the government police academy program if he'd been enhanced. And it was always his dream to be a lawman."

The phone on Matt's desk rang, keeping him from commenting. Hopefully, it wouldn't become a problem with regard to his secret genetic enhancements and her lawman brother's sworn duty to report it if he ever found out.

Chapter 8

"Are all parties present for the hearing?" the magistrate's clerk asked in the direction of the assembled group.

Matt stood up to speak, but his father beat him to it. "Yes, we are all here and we have been for quite some time now. We are ready for the process to begin. Is it going to be much longer?" He sounded supremely impatient and blatantly looked at his watch in a superior attitude that had never served him well, but Matt knew he never listened to anyone who told him so.

Andrea sat at the opposite table in the courtroom with her father, dressed in a prim and proper nun-like dress of country blue, her rounding belly already jutting out like his worst, girl-in-trouble teenaged nightmare.

"I'll summon the Magistrate directly." The clerk exited the room for only a moment. When he returned, he heralded the arrival of the Tiberius magistrate in a formality, which immediately annoyed Matt. However, he imagined everything about this day in court was about to annoy him.

Last night, when his phone started ringing, he'd directed Sophie down to her office with a promise to join her as soon as possible, promising they'd sexually christen the desk in her old office.

The call he'd gotten was indeed from Paul Brody, the man he'd selected to be a husband for Sophie's sister, Hannah. He and Paul had spent almost an hour working out several details, including financial payment, in preparation for the dinner party to meet Sophie's sister and the subsequent ceremony planned for the next day afterwards.

Then he'd cleaned up his desk and gone down to meet Sophie in her old office to participate in some creative sexual games on her desk. He'd been in a relaxed mood until entering the hearing room this morning. Matt hoped his increasingly sour mood would improve for tonight's guests after what promised to be a very infuriating court hearing today.

The magistrate for today's debacle was surprisingly young given the significance of the position he held. His tall, rounding body looked even more massive in the dark blue robes he wore, carrying what must have been well over three hundred and fifty pounds on his substantial frame. But his manner was completely businesslike as he gathered official looking papers in front of him. He shifted his dark-rimmed glasses closer to his face before he spoke to the group.

"In the complainant matter before this court today, Governor Tobias Kane has set forth a grievance that accuses one Matthew Westland of morally corrupting the virtue of his daughter, the co-plaintiff, so named as Andrea Kane. The first incident in question allegedly took place during Thanksgiving and the next was during the Christmas holidays, resulting in the basis for the second charge of paternity as she is carrying a child at this date in time from the second offense.

"There is a third charge of adultery, as the co-plaintiff has tested positive for the defendant's DNA in her vaginal canal after the defendant had already married another party. Is this correct, and do I have all the relevant facts in this case, Governor Kane?" the magistrate asked with officially proper decorum oozing forth to the room.

"Yes," the short thin stoic governor said curtly. He then directed a cool angry gaze over to Matt and Sophie standing alone in the defendant's box. Even Matt's father stood over by his pious old crony friend, the governor. Senator Westland's self-satisfied smile spoke volumes as to his publicly held loyalties in this matter regarding his only son.

Luckily for Matt, the media filling all the available seating in the court behind him was not allowed to have cameras or recording equipment in the chamber during the process. But they'd fight a hoard of them on the way out of the building afterwards.

"What do you have to say in your defense, Mr. Westland?" the magistrate asked evenly.

"I do not clearly remember the event at Thanksgiving, but I don't dispute it. I have no memory of corrupting Miss Kane's virtue during the Christmas holidays, and I do not believe the child she carries is mine. I most emphatically deny any relations with her since I got married to my wife.

"Furthermore, Miss Kane never told me herself she was pregnant or carried my child in the past several months. She certainly would have been aware of her status. I believe this to be a ploy by my father, in collusion with the governor, to destroy the happy marriage I now share with my wife Sophie.

"I further maintain these lies are told additionally to embarrass me in the public eye, thereby ruining my reputation as a businessman. To that end, I've filed a countersuit against the three of them for defamation of character against me and my wife."

"I see," the magistrate said and made several scribbled notes on an unseen piece of paper at his elevated bench. "We'll address your countersuit at the end of the current complaint hearing. What atonement are you seeking from Mr. Westland, Governor Kane?"

"I want him to marry my daughter and give his child a name, of course. She is due to deliver in five months. I will not allow the taint of a bastard child to grace my household while Matthew Westland shares his life with another woman."

"You are aware he is already legally married in a Tiberius-sanctioned union, and his permanent paperwork is pending this hearing?"

"But he got my daughter pregnant long before he married *that* woman. And he had relations with Andrea the same night he got married to his precious wife, as they spent the night in the same house, I might add. The Tiberius body scan proves that."

"Yes, I have the report here."

"I don't care what the report says, I did not have sex with Andrea the day I married Sophie," Matt responded angrily, coming to his feet.

"What about the incident at Christmas, Mr. Westland? Do you deny a sexual relationship with Miss Kane four months ago?"

He took a deep breath and focused his eyes piercingly at the magistrate. "My response to that question will likely hurt and offend Miss Kane and her family."

"We are here to ascertain the truth. Speak now or hold your tongue and I'll render my decision without any response from you."

"As you wish. I had a sexual relationship with Andrea Kane long before Christmastime. I used archaic condom protection on the single occasion we had sex to shield us from exchanging body fluids. I was not her first lover then, nor was I her last after the 'alleged' incident during the Christmas holidays, which I do not remember participating in."

"You are a liar!" The governor stood up, his face purple with rage, pointing an accusing finger at Matt.

"Gentleman, sit down!" The magistrate banged a large gavel twice to make his point. "As you may or may not know, this is a preliminary hearing to decide whether or not to proceed with the case further. I find there is probable cause to continue. We will adjourn for today and reconvene five days from now. At that hearing, you both will be tasked to bring your individual undeniable proof of your respective point's of view. I will render a binding decision at that time."

"Your Honor, Mr. Westland should not be rewarded with five more days with his current wife when my daughter suffers the shame of a pregnancy out of wedlock, a pregnancy for which he is responsible. You can take my word for it."

"We are not here to take your word for it, Governor. You brought a complaint to me to decide your fate. Guilt or innocence on the part of the defendant in this case has not been established. Bring your proof in five days and I will ponder the evidence from both sides before rendering my decision, which will be permanently binding."

"What about an appeal?" Senator Westland stood up next to the governor to direct his inappropriate question.

"Appeals have no place in the justice system," the magistrate said with a distasteful look on his face directed at Matt's father. "However, if either party feels in any way slighted by my forthcoming decision, they may have one single appeal to the Superior Magistrate. I'll warn you though, the Superior Magistrate has not overturned any magistrate decisions brought forth to date."

The magistrate banged his gavel and lifted his large, imposing frame out of the squeaky chair to retreat to his private chambers. The audience of media and journalists behind them erupted in to a loud confusion of questions and shouts. The uproar gave Matt a headache, but not as much as the one which had pounded through his brain when he announced and admitted to, with Sophie listening, the single previous sexual encounter he remembered with Andrea.

He'd wanted to tell Sophie how meaningless the Thanksgiving interlude was and assure her that one kiss from her meant far more than one bad screw with a former girlfriend. Sex with Andrea Kane had been a waste of even an archaic condom, but he hadn't wanted any part of himself to come in contact with Andrea. If memory served, he'd ultimately fantasized about a certain smart, beautiful junior executive he employed to finally get off. In his drunken state, he'd thought he was with Sophie. He'd pulled back to see Andrea's very angry face.

He'd been fairly inebriated that night. A regular occurrence back then to keep himself behind his self-imposed line and away from getting his arms wrapped around Sophie. If Andrea hadn't come to him in the first place and refused to take no for an answer, he would never have had sex with her. His cock had been hard from fantasizing about his untouchable employee. When Andrea had suggested they get naked and sweaty in his office, his first inclination had been to tell her "no thanks." He should have gone with his initial gut reaction, but his judgment had been impaired from too much scotch whiskey.

He'd just found out about the Tiberius Group's plan to take over. He knew then they'd probably succeed easily and everything would change within the next six months. He'd started scheming as he drank. He'd written the first draft of the Working Woman's Auction Memo that night along with notes on how he could save his business if half his executives were forced out.

Matt still hadn't found the courage to confess to Sophie about the memo he'd written. Or what he'd done in the name of saving his female employees. He knew in his heart that she wouldn't view it as he did--the only way he could conjure up quickly to save her.

Matt stumbled upon the true reason he'd done everything possible to put himself in a position to come to Sophie's rescue. The Working Woman's Auction Memo opened up the single opportunity he'd had to corner her and gain the chance to prove how good they'd be together. A piece of information he'd already tucked away in the recesses of his libido for many months. A fact he'd suspected from the first time he saw her angry determined face in Orin Prichard's office.

Sophie had acted like Matt saved her back then, too, but the truth was, he'd saved Orin from her. Matt had no doubt that, looking at her stubborn face, she could have kicked Orin's balls straight up his sorry ass and out his ears.

Matt hoped all his secrets remained secret at least until he could explain to her that his motives, while self-serving, had been to ensure their future and not for humiliation purposes.

He hoped she wouldn't kick *his* balls straight up his ass and out his ears when she found out everything he'd done in the name of saving her for himself.

* * * *

Sophie sat in front of her dressing table mirror putting on the new jewelry Matthew had graciously given her for tonight's dinner party. He told her to name her favorite precious stone. She looked into his deep blue eyes and made an easy choice. The elegant sapphire ear drops, necklace and bracelet set gracing her skin now looked perfect with the dress she wore tonight.

Her black silk, strapless cocktail dress had a slit up the side high enough for Matthew to have easy access to the jewel between her legs should he want to reach in for a quick stroke. The very thought of his hand up her dress combined with the word 'stroke' made her face warm and she saw the faint blush in the reflection before her. She shifted, wondering if she'd ever think of Matthew with out getting moist. She sincerely hoped not.

"You look good enough to eat." Matthew stepped into their huge bedroom and approached her slowly. "Are you excited about tonight, and do I need to relax you? Because I'd be happy to loosen you up a little, you know."

He was dressed in the sexiest power suit she'd ever seen. Even sexier than the one he'd been wearing today for court. And he'd looked fabulous in court.

"Oh, I don't know. Do you think we have enough time?" She stood up from the mirrored dressing table and turned to face him as he stepped close and dropped a kiss on one bare shoulder.

He laughed. "We always have enough time for relaxation." Kissing his way along her shoulder, he grabbed her waist with both hands and pulled her tight up against his toned, muscular body.

"But will your relaxation process destroy my hair and make up?"

"No promises," he whispered. His breath tickled her ear and sent a very warm electric pulse down to the dampened panties under her dress. She wore a scrap of lace, which barely qualified as an undergarment. The silk stockings she wore were held up with a sexy lace garter belt. She wore her 'fuck me' four-inch stiletto heeled shoes. Everything she wore with the exception of her jewelry was black. Sexy black and either silk or lace.

Matthew kissed her neck gently on the very sensitive place below her ear while his hand slid from her waist to her bottom. The thong panties, or perhaps better termed, scrap of under garment fabric she wore, didn't cover either cheek. His warm hand felt decadent through the silk of her dress.

His hand moved quickly once again sliding past her butt, down to the hem of her dress and up underneath before she took her next breath. The slit on the side gave him the ease of access he'd probably been thinking about when he bought it for her in the first place.

She moaned and let her head fall back when she felt his talented fingers already between her legs, stroking her through the now very damp lace of her panties.

"Want me to stop?" he whispered, his fingers pausing below momentarily for her to answer.

"Don't you dare," she panted and was rewarded as his finger niggled its way between the small scrap of lace to stroke her sensitized clit directly. She lifted her leg and wrapped it behind his calf to give him easier access.

Her knees wobbled slightly so she reached an arm up around his shoulder to hold on. She felt the ridge of his cock through layers of clothing press into her hip bone and wondered how she could get it inside her body quickly, but then lost the thought as he unzipped the back of her dress, loosening it enough at the top so he could kiss a path down to her now uncovered strapless black lace bra, which then magically popped open to reveal her bare breasts.

His mouth covered her peak in the next smoldering instant, sucking the hardened nipple between his teeth and tongue, the sensation of which drilled down to where his fingers strummed her to the edge.

"Matthew," she whimpered ready to blaze on into oblivion. But she didn't want to take the trip alone. She reached for his belt, trying to loosen it one handed, which she did as his fingers still circled and strummed her clit, building her imminent release closer and closer. She got him unbuttoned, unzipped, with her hand down his pants wrapped completely around his rock-hard, impressive cock, apparently before he realized what she was doing.

He moaned against her breast before releasing the suction of his mouth unexpectedly as his finger slid off her clit when his body convulsed once at her intimate touch.

"See how you like it," she said in a breathy voice and stroked him once, running her thumb across the spot she knew was most sensitive. His growl of pent-up passion also showed in his eyes when he suddenly stood up to his full towering height over her.

"No, I want to see how *you* like it," he whispered. His glance over her shoulder made her wonder what he was thinking, but a moment later she figured it out. He pulled her against his body, lifting her up and lightly slammed her against the closed closet door. It wasn't metal, but the warm wood against her partially bare back was unyielding all the same.

This put them in the same position from Christmas in the hallway against a door. All they needed was mistletoe to complete the scene. Or perhaps not. She felt his warm hands on either bare thigh, her legs were spread open, the skirt of her dress bunched around her hips. Her bare ass rested against the door. She was moments away from exploding in climax.

The color of his eyes had deepened to an even richer blue, piercing her soul in its intensity. The look registered as frightening, but she wasn't scared. She was instead very needy and wanted him with a single-minded ferociousness. The one she felt every time she came within pheromone range of her husband.

She felt his rigid cock slide between her legs and across the drenched black lace, stroking her clit through the thin material. Her legs clenched around his hips in reflex at the sensation. Matthew pulled the lace away from her sensitive nub, and she felt the tip of his impressive shaft enter ever so slowly inside, pressing her against the door. It felt as if he got halfway to her womb before he retreated and then thrust in again with more force. His growl of appreciation sent a flutter to her tummy. She caught a flash of black color across the room and realized she could see their reflections in her vanity mirror.

Matthew's face was buried against her throat, one of her breasts exposed with his fingers brushing across the nipple, his pants loose against his hips and he thrust rhythmically inside her as he held her against the closet door. The vision so powerfully erotic, she couldn't help but watch her face in the mirror. Her eyes closed halfway, just before she heard herself scream Matthew's name, finding oblivion and a body-clenching orgasm the likes of which she'd never felt before. Waves of pleasure rolled through her as every muscle in her body clenched in release.

Sophie opened her eyes again to that vision of Matthew pumping into her, his thrusts coming faster, now powering inside her slick, wet body, the feel of her lacy panties still providing a slight resistance, rubbing her with each withdrawal and pump forward.

"Harder," she heard herself whimper. "Oh, God, harder." She watched as he increased his pace as she'd requested. The thick feel of his cock inside stretching her as she watched him impale her was almost too much, but she couldn't close her eyes.

Matthew pulled back from kissing her neck to kiss her face and noticed her distraction. He turned slightly to see her focus at the mirror. Now they were both watching the action against the closet door in the vanity mirror.

A growl of pleasure issued from deep in his throat and his next endless thrust felt like it went to her ribs. He pulled out and powered in again as they both watched. A satisfied noise issued from his throat, and then his eyes closed. His movement stopped as he held her pinned against the door. His breathing came harshly against her bare shoulder for several long moments before he seemed to recover.

Ding dong.

The sound of the doorbell downstairs made Sophie jump. It was hours before the scheduled time for the party. She sincerely hoped it was the caterers and not their guests downstairs.

"At least whoever that is has better timing," Matthew said in a lazy, amused tone.

Ding dong.

"But they're impatient."

Chapter 9

Matt straightened his clothing as he flew down the stairs of their home. He left Sophie in her glazed over, recently satisfied state as she stood resting against the closet door. He went to answer the front door for the caterers who were there early to prepare for tonight's dinner.

He directed them to the kitchen and then held the door while several cooks and assorted other wait staff came in to set up. After a long while, he returned to the bedroom to see Sophie fresh from another shower. She was dressed like a fantasy from a lingerie catalog in a new black lacy ensemble. His dick twitched. He checked his watch again to see how much time was left before their guests were expected. He'd gladly relax her a second time.

She had moved from the door and stood in the black lace bra and barely there lace panties with the garters and stockings, trying her best to smooth the wrinkles out of her dress. Shaking her head, she darted into the closet door they'd just christened and came out with a mini iron.

"I should kick your ass, but your relaxation process was just so amazing." She smiled at him and started pressing the dress, now flattened out on the bed.

"I'm going to ask again. Are you excited about tonight with regard to seeing your sister?"

"Yes, I can't wait to see Hannah. I haven't laid eyes on her since Mom died. I hope my idiot father hasn't scared her, or worse, smacked her one."

"I hope not, either. Was he abusive to you?" Matt realized he probably should have asked sooner. He'd never found violent force a particularly good way to influence people. He tried to use his genetically engineered brain to work through the dilemma so he could take steps to solve the problem. But if he ever found out for certain Sophie's father had struck her, he was prepared to lay the bastard out on the dinner table tonight and stick forks in him until he was done.

She shrugged. "He threatened to smack me a couple of times, but I mostly did my best not to piss him off. Hannah, on the other hand, can be a little stubborn."

She finished touching the dress up and stepped into it, motioning him over to zip her up. He placed a kiss on her shoulder and fastened the dress.

"You're beautiful."

"Thank you." She turned in his arms. "So are you."

"I hope Hannah likes Paul."

"I'm sure she will. I know Paul, and in my opinion, he's perfect for her."

"He seemed reluctant to get married at first. I think it was because he didn't have lots of money to offer. I hope your father won't expect another hundred thousand dollars." The sour look she directed at him made him quietly apologize. "Sorry."

"Not your fault. He's the prick, not you. And he better be grateful to get anything, the louse."

"Well, after dinner I thought I'd call all the men into my study for brandy and cigars and contract signing. Tomorrow, we can go have the official ceremony and everything. Okay?"

"Thank you so much, Matthew. I can't tell you how much I appreciate all you've done." She hugged him and buried her face in his chest holding on as if for dear life.

Matt hoped Sophie never found out he'd supplied the money for Hannah's dowry to Paul. It made him feel like a pimp, but it wasn't the first time he'd taken money earmarked for investment into his company to use instead under the heading of good will spending.

It was the very same plan he'd come up with to ensure all his single female employees found good husbands. And more importantly, to save Sophie.

Good God, he *was* a pimp. He essentially got men to spend money to buy women.

Paul understood the dire circumstances and had been in Matt's private circle of understanding at Westland Industries. Matt figured it was the least he could do to make Sophie happy after all she'd put up with for him. She wanted her sister safe and close by. Besides, it was a small request in the great scheme of things He'd do everything he could to make it happen.

"I love you, Sophie. And everything will be fine tonight. Wait and see."

* * * *

The evening couldn't have gone worse if they'd planned it that way. By the time the dinner party was supposed to have started, it was already too late to save it anyway.

Sophie ushered in Paul Brody ten minutes before her sister and father were due to land at the local airport. Matt had invited him early to discuss some work-related things. Sophie spent the time alone arranging last minute details for her family's stay.

Matt had already sent a private car and driver to wait at the airport and bring her family directly to their home. The driver called about the time their guests were expected, to inform them that Hannah and her father hadn't been on the flight, which had already landed and deplaned completely.

After all the things Hannah had told her about the Las Vegas experience, she got a severe case of bad feeling in the pit of her stomach wondering what had gone wrong. She found out soon enough when the doorbell rang two hours after the guests of honor were supposed to have arrived.

Looking at the security camera feed, she saw her father standing alone, but then saw him motion to someone behind him. Hannah probably had to remain two steps back at all times.

The bastard.

Sophie answered the door to Dennis Hoskins standing alone on her doorstep. He looked like he'd been on a 'lost weekend' drinking binge of epic proportions. He wore dirty, smelly clothes and looked like he hadn't shaved or bathed for a week.

Matt stepped past him through the door to take care of the driver. He winked at her over his shoulder, behind her father's back, in seeming assurance. She was able to relax for about a nanosecond before all hell broke loose.

"So this is the fancy place you live now. Did good for you, didn't I, girly?" Dennis Hoskins said with misplaced pride and stepped across the threshold of their home. His greedy little eyes immediately sought out every item of value in the vestibule as if to assess the value for later theft. Sophie was appalled and glad Matthew wasn't there to witness his bad behavior.

"This is my home. Do not believe for one second you are welcome here beyond one night. Once we settle everything for Hannah, you will not be welcome here any longer. Do I make myself clear?" Sophie whispered angrily. He sneered as he passed by her, failing to wipe his shoes on the rug, thereby trailing mud and what looked like straw across the tile floor.

"Well, now, we only need one night here and then we'll take ourselves to greener pastures, girly."

"We? What do you mean?"

"There's been a slight change in plans. Now, all I need from you is a small stake for tonight and directions to the nearest lucky casino. Then I'll be out of your fancy-pants, hoity-toity residence."

"Sophie?" came her sister Hannah's anguished voice. She turned to greet her little sister, who threw her arms around her, sobbing in uncontrollable fits even as she started trying to talk, making no sense whatsoever.

"I...dog track...lost bet...stranger...I didn't say 'I do'..." Sophie wrapped her big sister arms around Hannah and shushed her sister's choking incomprehensible words, stroking her hair to calm her down.

Over Hannah's shoulder, Sophie saw a stranger enter her home followed closely by Matthew. At first, she thought the stranger was the driver carrying luggage but noticed Matthew had two bags he managed alone. Matthew wore the furious face he used when he spoke to his father.

If Matthew was that upset, something must be devastatingly wrong.

Good Lord, what could be amiss now?

Paul Brody entered the foyer from the library just then with a sincere smile, watching Sophie comfort her sister. He gave Hannah a concerned look from head to toe and smiled as if he already approved. Sophie was momentarily seduced into thinking things would be just fine, once Hannah settled down.

"I already found a husband for her," her father announced blithely. "This here is your sister's new husband, Reggie. We met at the dog track where I had a little streak of bad luck. After the wedding at the track ticket office, Reggie helped us with bus fare on the final leg of our journey.

"Otherwise we'd still be stuck at the track wondering how to get here." He laughed like Reggie had saved them from a lengthy, unavoidable delay. "Now, like I said before, all I need is a small stake to build up my miserable finances, and I'll be on my way. Do you have any cash handy here in the house?"

Only the sound of Hannah's occasional sniff echoed in the room. It was a foreign sound, which tore at Sophie's soul because her sister rarely cried about anything. It was a good thing she had a hold of Hannah or nothing would have stopped her from killing Dennis Hoskins with her bare hands in the silent-as-the-grave entryway to her house. The new information bombshell circulated around trying to find a place to land in Sophie's mind.

Had she just heard what she thought she had?

She opened her mouth to speak as the horror of the news registered in her brain and a multitude of questions choked her mind, rendering her speechless for a moment.

Her father had already married Hannah off? To a stranger at a dog track for what amounted to travel money here? Because he'd apparently already gambled away all the money he got for her? And the extra money she'd sent without Matthew's knowledge, as well? After all the trouble Matthew had gone to in preparation for tonight to hand over more money her wretched father didn't deserve in the least?

Sophie started shaking as the magnitude of her father's audacity sunk in fully. She separated herself from Hannah with only one clear thought.

Kill him. Kill that miserable excuse for a father of theirs.

Matthew's hands clamp onto her shoulders. She wrenched herself from him, throwing a dirty look over her shoulder that he would dare stop her justified murder, and took another step in her father's direction.

Matthew's snagged her around the waist and pulled her back against his chest. Perhaps he read her mind and didn't want to bail her out of jail tonight before the appetizers were served.

"Let me go!" she snarled.

"Not on your life. Take your sister up to her room so she can freshen up. Take a few deep breaths and calm down. When you return, we'll eat dinner. There's no need to let the food go to waste. It's done. Your sister needs you now." Matthew's civil voice of reason eventually permeated her vengeful intent.

Sophie looked at her sister. Hannah's red-rimmed eyes and general miserable countenance distracted her from her idiot father long enough to calm her down a notch or two.

"Thank you, Matthew." She took a deep breath and went into mother hen mode for the sake of her sister.

"Gentlemen, let me show you my library. We can have cocktails until the ladies are ready for dinner," Matthew suggested smoothly to the other men in the room. Sophie gave her husband a wan smile over one shoulder as she led Hannah to the staircase. He winked at her in response. Matthew *so* didn't deserve this tonight. He especially didn't deserve it after the day he'd had with the magistrate and his own miserable father.

"Well, now I guess I could stand to have a fancy cocktail and a bite or two of food before Reggie and me head out to try our luck at making our fortunes in this fine town of yours." Her father followed Matthew out of the foyer into the dining room down the hall, Reggie something directly on his heels.

Paul Brody gave Sophie an uncertain glance before looking down at the marble floor. He didn't say anything but turned and followed the other men down the hall. Poor Paul. This was the second wife he'd lost out on from the same family.

Sophie hoped Matthew never found out what she had done to try and save herself on the auspicious corporate auction day. With rumors of the Tiberius Group take over imminent, she'd withdrawn her life savings and the balance of the money from her mother's life insurance and given it all to Paul Brody with the intention of having him bid on her the day of the Westland corporate auction.

Paul had been the one in the audience that day with the final high bid, before Orin had said the words, fifty thousand dollars. That heart stopping moment had been followed quickly by Matthew's, save-her-life hundred thousand dollar bid. She didn't know how he'd feel about Paul if he knew the truth about that day. She certainly didn't want to ruin a good business relationship between them.

Paul had the most to lose, but she assured him she'd never tell. She met him on the sly at Westland Industries a week ago at night in her office and told him to use the money to buy her sister, but he refused. He gave her money back and told her he already had money for Hannah. But now, with her sister married off to a stranger, he'd have to go elsewhere if he wanted a wife.

"Let's go up and wash your face. You'll feel better. Okay?" Hannah nodded and they made their way arm in arm to the guest bedroom.

* * * *

Matt already had a pounding headache. He entered the library, which he also used as his office when he worked at home, to entertain tonight's special guests and to pretend her father wasn't the biggest prick who ever lived. He glanced at Paul who had a defeated look on his face.

Poor Paul.

He'd tried to recruit his lead accountant for the corporate auction, but at the time, Paul had acted as though he already had someone in mind he wanted to marry. Matt had seen him leaving the corporate amphitheater as his father the senator had entered but hadn't thought too much about his appearance. He wondered who Paul had wanted to bid on for a wife. At the time, he'd been focused on saving Sophie from Orin, but now something niggled at his memory. He cast it aside to offer his vile in-laws a drink.

"What'll you have, gentlemen?" Matt asked. He stepped up to the built in cabinet bar and poured a healthy tumbler full of whiskey for himself.

"Got any decent gin?" Sophie's father asked.

"Of course. Reggie?"

"Vodka, make it a double, no ice." Reggie's squeaky high nasal voice made Matt clench his teeth. The man had a voice like fingernails on a chalkboard.

Poor Hannah.

"Are there any good places for a man to try his luck close by?" Dennis asked, accepting the drink.

"Actually, my father is part owner in a riverboat casino called The Lucky Gentleman. It's docked at the river about a mile from here." Matt hoped Dennis would get the hell out as soon as possible and take Mr. Screechy with him. He took a big swig of whiskey and realized if his head pounded now, tomorrow morning would truly suck if he drank much more. But he figured, realistically, he needed to be slightly under the influence to face the rest of the evening still yet to come.

"About that stake I need for later on tonight," Dennis said. "You keep that extra cash in here?"

"I keep my money in a bank," Matt said, taking another deep drink to curb his tongue from saying what he really wanted to. He knew he'd pay the price in the morning.

"Well, what am I going to do for cash then?" Dennis Hoskins asked petulantly.

"If you'd made it here tonight without marrying Hannah off for bus fare, you could have had fifty thousand dollars." Matt felt the alcohol in his system loosen his tongue just slightly. "I find I'm not even remotely concerned where you get your next stake."

"Where's the money you had ready?" Sophie's father glanced around the room as if he'd find a stack of cash lying about for him grab and go.

"Paul over there was the one who had the money. But since you're all out of daughters to marry off, I guess you're out of luck."

"Surely a rich man like you has some extra cash he could afford to part with."

"I already gave you a hundred thousand dollars for Sophie two weeks ago. You won't get another penny from me."

Paul suddenly put his drink down on a side table and turned to the group. "Suddenly, I'm not feeling well. Since I'm not needed here any longer, I'd best be getting back home. Thanks for inviting me to dinner Mr. Westland. Give my regards and apologies to your lovely...wife." He turned and strode out of the library before Matt could stop him.

He took two steps towards the door and then decided to let Paul go on alone. What could he possible say to him to make up for tonight? Nothing that would matter. Besides, he didn't want to leave his father-in-law unattended, who would no doubt rob him blind. He'd speak to Paul at work. There would be time enough to re-hash tonight's debacle.

The lead caterer, who also acted as butler for tonight's ruined dinner party celebration, stepped up to the library door and asked, "Would you like me to begin serving, sir?"

"Yes, I would. Thank you. Let's go gentleman. Dinner is served."

Sophie and Hannah came down a few moments later to join them, but no one spoke a word. Everyone just ate their food in complete silence, the sound of silverware scraping against the china, the only sound in the room.

Dennis Hoskins managed to make it fifteen minutes before asking for money. "Sophie, are you going to tell your husband to give me a stake or—"

"Get out!" Sophie stood slowly, her face turning very red, the fury unmistakable.

"What—"

"I said get out." Sophie had her butter knife gripped in her hand threateningly. Matt had no doubt she's use it, given the least provocation...or request for money.

"I guess I know when I'm not wanted. Come on, Reggie. I'll just get a line of credit once I get to the casino. Let's go out and celebrate the nuptials by getting filthy rich."

Matt decided it was a good thing they didn't want to include Hannah in any nuptial celebration. He wouldn't have stopped Sophie and her weapon of choice, a butter knife. Her father and Reggie left, slamming the front door behind them.

An hour later, the night from hell was finally over, and Sophie had tucked Hannah in the guest bedroom to sleep. Unfortunately, early the next morning turned out to be even worse, and not just because Matt had the worst headache in the world history of pain.

Ring. Ring.

Matt grabbed the phone up before it had a chance to jangle mercilessly in his throbbing brain again. He'd been right the night before. He shouldn't have had anything to drink.

"Hello," he growled into the phone. Sophie didn't stir.

"I'm sorry to bother you so early, Mr. Westland," the caller said. "We have a Dennis Hoskins here at The Lucky Gentleman casino. He claims to be your father-in-law and is requesting you to cover his substantial losses for this evening. The amount is just over one hundred and fifty thousand dollars."

"Tell him he can go to hell. Don't call back here." Matt hung the phone up and promptly lapsed into a troubled, headache-ridden sleep.

Two hours later he got up to take some pain medication for the pounding headache that plagued him. He shut the light off in the kitchen, and the front door bell rang.

"Yes," he said to the two community lawmen standing ominously at his door. He assumed it had something to do with his father-in-law. Matt crossed his arms over his chest, preparing to be belligerent if they even mentioned the name Dennis Hoskins.

"We're looking for a woman named…Hannah." The taller of the two men said, checking an electronic device.

"She's asleep."

"I'm sorry, sir, but she needs to come with us."

"It's almost six o'clock in the morning."

"Her husband is in jail for unpaid gambling debts, and he's asking for her. Could you get her for us, please?"

"Wait here," Matt said and closed the door, leaving the lawmen to stand on his doorstep.

He passed his bedroom on the way to wake Hannah and glanced at the door to his bedroom where Sophie slept blissfully unaware of this latest twist. He should probably wake Sophie too, but she'd be upset. He felt his wife had suffered enough with the magistrate hearing and dinner with her father last night, so he let her sleep.

Hannah answered the guest bedroom door looking like she needed more sleep, too. He explained quickly about the lawmen at the door. She nodded, perked up, and met him downstairs ten minutes later dressed and ready to go.

"What's this about?" she asked the taller of the two lawmen.

"Your husband has requested your presence. He's been arrested for failure to pay a gambling debt. You've been named as collateral in his trial. He's asking for you, ma'am."

"I'll accompany her," Matt said and took Hannah's arm in his hand to escort her out the door.

"Are you a blood relative?" the shorter of the two officers asked.

"No, but—"

"That won't be necessary, sir. You aren't authorized to accompany a female who's not a direct blood relative."

Hannah turned to him and patted his hand. "Don't worry. I'll be okay. Tell Sophie not to worry, either." She then smiled at him warmly and departed.

Matt watched her step away with the two lawmen on either side of her. A hollow bad feeling stabbed his stomach to match the pounding in his self-abused head. He knew deep down in his soul that as Hannah departed with them, he should never have let her go. Then again, what choice did he have? None.

Fucking Tiberius Group.

Chapter 10

"What do you mean she's gone?" Sophie asked once seated at the kitchen table as Matthew poured her a cup of coffee. She'd slept late into the morning, unusual for her, but the nightmares she'd had all night had not given her restful sleep. She dreamed about that butter knife she'd wanted to plunge into her father and carve his heart out all night long.

She'd woken up with absolutely no clue as to how to help her sister. Matthew put a cup in front of her and dropped another bombshell.

Hannah was gone.

"Her new husband asked for her and two community lawmen came and escorted her to the jail where he was presumably locked up. I couldn't stop it. And before you ask, I tried to go along, but since I wasn't a blood relative, they wouldn't allow it."

"But when will she be back?"

"I can't answer that. I called a few minutes ago, and they refused to divulge any information to me as I'm still not a blood relative." His exasperation was evident, but she was too worried about Hannah to care.

"We need to go down to the jail and bring her back. Or better yet, we'll get my father to bring her here and—" She shot up out of the kitchen chair to run and do…something, anything.

"Sophie…" Matthew grabbed her shoulders and faced her towards him to gain her full attention before she exited the house on a mission.

"What?"

"Your father ran up a big debt last night at a casino using my name to get a line of credit. The casino called to collect at four in the morning and I declined to cover his very substantial debt."

"So?"

"I imagine your father is also in jail and unable to escort your sister anywhere. Have something to eat, get dressed, and then I'll take you there. Okay?"

Sophie gave him a nod then closed her eyes. When would the nightmare end? She took two steps forward and rested her weary head on Matthew's chest. She slipped her arms around his waist to feel the measure of assurance his proximity always gave her.

"Thank you." Sophie clung to him and refused to break down and cry an ocean full. She hated to be weak and girly but really wanted a single something to go right. She wouldn't stop worrying until her sister was safely back here with her.

Matthew didn't say anything. He just held her tight.

Two hours later, Sophie was assured only that her nightmare would be on going.

Hannah had been placed in the custody of a mail order bride company serving off world locations. Reggie something, her husband of less than one day, had annulled the marriage and signed her over as payment of his large gambling debt from the night before.

Hannah, they were informed by the mail order bride company, was already on a cryo-ship headed for a moon of Mars mining colony in space to marry a Thorium-Z miner. At Sophie's insistence, Matthew offered to pay the debt for Hannah upon her return but couldn't because he was already married. There were rules, apparently, regarding only single men being allowed to purchase mail order brides.

"How could her husband annul the marriage just like that?" Sophie asked.

"'Cause he hadn't popped her yet."

"Popped?" Sophie asked, hoping against hope the man didn't mean what she thought he did.

"I think he means they didn't consummate the marriage," Matt supplied smoothly.

Yep, that was what she thought it meant all right. Poor Hannah.

"And he was lucky, too," the mail order bride representative said confidentially. "That other fella he was with last night got popped outright for not paying his debt."

"Popped?" Sophie asked again, wondering how many more definitions of popped there were going to be forthcoming, hoping once again it didn't mean the same thing as the first one.

"You know, they gave him some cement over shoes if ya get my meanin'?" He gave them an exaggerated wink and then ran his thumb across his neck in the universal meaning of throat slitting death.

"They killed him?"

"Yep. Heard tell it was one of the owners himself that gave the order. Every gambler knows you don't run up a tab you can't pay, lest you want to get popped. "

* * * *

Matt had no doubt if he were to ask, he'd find out Senator Westland had been the 'owner' in question. Sophie slumped her shoulders and gave up right then. He could see the defeat in her posture. He'd already known he wouldn't be able to buy Hannah back. And the truth was he didn't have that kind of capital to spare to get her back anyway, at least not without being forced to sell his business, which was what he would have had to do to save her father.

They retreated in silence back to their home. Sophie said nothing on the trip back.

So Hannah was gone to parts unknown off world and Sophie was no longer speaking to him because of it. It wasn't fair, but Matt figured she deserved to burn some anger off in peaceable solitude, so he made himself scarce. He sat at his desk in the library, feet propped up, wondering how long before their tumultuous life would settle down.

Damn her father anyway. And goddamn his father, too.

Later in the day, he woke from dozing at his desk when the phone rang. He picked it up before the first ring finished sounding to keep Sophie from being further disturbed.

"I need to speak to Sophie Brent," said the strange male voice over the phone.

"Who is this?" Matt growled.

"This is Jonathan," the stranger growled back. "Put her on the phone."

"I don't let my wife speak to strange men." He hung up. But then his conscience started beating on him. Who was Jonathan? Should he know that name from somewhere? He couldn't think clearly from his hangover. The phone rang again and he and Sophie picked it up at the same time.

"Sophie! Are you okay?" came the voice of Jonathan the stranger once again.

"Jon? Is it you?" Sophie said with relief and delight evident in her voice, leaving Matt supremely jealous for which he had no right.

"I told you, asshole, I don't let my wife talk to strangers. Sophie, hang up right now."

"No, you hang up. This is a private conversation, one I'm sure you don't care about." Sophie promptly ignored his demand and began speaking to the other strange man on the line. "Jon, I need you to do something for me."

Matt ripped the phone out of the wall in his study and headed upstairs to force her compliance. If he had to, he'd rip that phone out of the wall as well. He wasn't allowing a strange man to speak to his wife. But by the time he'd barged into their bedroom, she was saying her farewells and telling the stranger Jon she loved him. A knife to his heart would be less painful than Sophie being in love with another man.

"I won't let him inside, Sophie."

"Really? What a surprise. Another member of my family barred from the residence."

"Family? Oh, shit, that was your brother, wasn't it?" Matt's ridiculous anger deflated immediately. He was being an ass.

"Yeah. He's a Federal Interstellar Lawman. I've sent him after Hannah. If that's all right with you."

"I'm sorry, Sophie. Please, let's not fight any more. The last two days have been difficult for both of us."

"I feel so completely hopeless, and I hate that feeling. I'm used to solving all the problems." Sophie sniffed and her face crumpled into tears. She sat down on the bed her hands over her face. He sat down next to her and pulled her into is arms.

"How could you not front the money for her, Matthew? How could you let them take her?"

"I was never offered the opportunity to buy Hannah back. I was only called on to pay your father's gambling debts. He ran up a hundred and fifty thousand dollars using my name to secure the line of credit.

"I refused to pay for your father, not your sister. Her husband Reggie had complete control over her destiny. He's the one who sold her to the mail order bride company. I knew I couldn't buy her, because I'm already married to you. I'm sorry. If I could have done something I would have, I promise you."

"I know. I'm sorry. It's just so unfair to Hannah." Sophie lifted her head from her hands and rested it against his shoulder "I'd like to kill my father all over again."

"You don't need to say sorry to me. And if I could, I'd help you kill him all over again."

Her head burrowed into his chest and she murmured, "Thanks."

"That gratitude again. Do you have enough to allow my return to our bed?"

"I didn't kick you out of our bed in the first place. I don't have the authority to. Besides this is your house, Matthew. I'm only the little woman. Should I endeavor to be barefoot and pregnant, too? Because all you have to do is order me around."

"Stop it. I wouldn't have the balls to order you around and you know it."

She smiled briefly then her face sobered. "The meeting with the Tiberius Group is in three days to determine whether you have to get rid of me. Perhaps we should spend what remaining time we have together wrapped around each other. You know, just in case the unthinkable happens and I end up on a cryo-ship on the way to a moon of Mars to marry a Thorium-Z miner."

"I won't marry you off to someone else," he said adamantly.

"I hope you get to make that decision."

He didn't say the words out loud, but he hoped so, too.

Matt pulled her into his arms suddenly and kissed her as if it would be the last time he would ever see her. He wrapped his tongue around hers, licking her, tasting her, and loving the way she fervently kissed him in return. He felt her unbutton his shirt quickly from the bottom to the top. Her hands spread over his chest, leaning in to kiss it once before she moved to divest him of his pants. He returned the favor and in minutes they were naked and rolling around the bed as if they hadn't seen each other in a month, having pulled each other's clothing off in record time.

Their legs tangled as groans of need bounced off the walls of the bedroom. Her hands alternated between grasping handfuls of his hair to pull his head closer, grinding her mouth harder against his and skating down his back scratching a path to his ass, pulling at him there, too.

Matt pumped forward when her fingertips pulled at his hips as if not caring if his cock was actually inserted inside her body at the time or not. The desperation he felt was unfounded, but he wanted her with an intensity he'd never known with another woman. Sophie was the only woman he'd ever craved. He was smart enough to know she was the only woman who would ever have this impact on him. He knew it the first time he'd laid eyes on her. Just as he knew he'd surly die inside, if she was ever taken from him.

Matt ran his hands down her soft undulating body, not stopping until he hooked a hand around one thigh. He pulled her legs open so he could bury his needy cock in her slick, wet pussy and pump inside of her until she screamed his name in pleasure. But before he could, she gained the upper hand and wrestled with him until he was on his back. His eyes opened in surprise at her aggressiveness. Not that she ever just lay there and let him do her, but she was about to fuck him like an animal in rabid heat if the noises coming from her throat were any indication. And he was going to let her with appreciative glee.

The ferocious make-up sex had just begun.

Sophie twisted herself on top of him, straddling his hips with her own. She leaned down as strands of her blonde hair tickled his chest. Her hands slid from his shoulders to his hands and pinned them to the bed. His cock snapped to attention between them and bobbed happily at Sophie's dominant position. She smiled as if she felt him get hard for her and gave him a positively scorching gaze. Her eyelids closed halfway and she promptly moved her hips back and forth, running her creamy wet hot pussy lips up and down his dick. She continued to watch his reaction while her gray eyes fairly smoldered and seductive moans escaped her lips. Sophie undulated as if in palpable pleasure with each stroke against the full length of his cock. Without warning, she slid forward allowing the head of his dick to slip between her warm lower lips and quickly shifted so that she impaled herself on his cock all the way to his balls.

The sudden vise grip of her warmth around his cock forced his hips to surge deeper, which spontaneously garnered an animalistic moan from Sophie. She leaned forward, her perspiration covered breasts and firmed nipples pressing into his chest. Her hands released his fingertips to grip his shoulders so she could leverage another withdrawal off his cock, only to slam down for yet another deep stroke.

Matt interrupted his panting to grunt at the sensation of pre-orgasmic bliss, trying to hold his climax back. He slipped his hands into her hair and brought her mouth down to his. Stabbing his tongue between her lips to the rhythm she set in her apparent goal to get him off quickly brought whimpering sounds from her. Matt stroked his tongue against hers wildly until he felt the clamp of her orgasm grip his cock at the same he released. A growl issued from him and she half whimpered half screamed into his mouth as he grabbed her close in simultaneous climax.

Matt wrapped his arms around her and lowered her, still pressed to his chest, down to the bed. He held her so tightly, she probably couldn't breath, but he found he couldn't loosen his hold.

"I love you, Sophie. I'll never let you go. I swear it," he said when he could speak.

* * * *

Matt hoped he'd assured his future with all the running around he'd done the past three days. He was feeling very confident. He'd done what he usually did when presented with a difficult problem. He let his genetically-engineered brain solve it for him. He was about to win this hearing and have the charged dismissed. He had the undeniable proof to do it, too. Then he planned to go about making things up to Sophie. They'd spent every moment possible together in each other's arms for the past three days, and he smiled in memory.

He was so deeply in love with her, he wasn't sure he'd want to continue on if he couldn't have her at his side.

The magistrate entered with the usual pomp and circumstance. He swept the room with a glance before he settled his sizable girth in his squeaky chair.

"Let's get started. What proof do you bring, Governor Kane?" He leaned back slightly as if to get comfortable for the story he was about to hear. Matt had no doubt it would be a nice fictional account of what *really* happened. He wished he could remember it for himself.

"I beg the Court's indulgence, Magistrate. You see, my daughter came to me only a couple of weeks ago with the news of her unfortunate status. In fact, she only came forward when the pregnancy could no longer be hidden. She was embarrassed, as you might imagine, by the deplorable incident. She is a shy girl and has been much taken advantage of by Matthew Westland, I'm afraid."

"Again, what proof do you have of this, Governor Kane?" the magistrate huffed in a tone which sounded like, 'Get on with it.'

"Well, my word as a gentleman and leader of this great state should have some weight, don't you think?"

The governor had adopted the same pompous, prick attitude that Senator Westland displayed regularly. Matt didn't think the magistrate looked in the mood for it. Perhaps this would go even better than he expected.

"Your word as a gentleman is not in question, sir. Do you have proof of this incident or not?" A murmur rose among the spectators and the magistrate leveled a stern look out at the court audience before turning his gaze back to the governor.

"Yes, Magistrate. I understand the rules you and I are both governed by. Therefore, I am reluctantly forced to submit a digital video of the incident in question. It has been generously provided by my good friend and father of the defendant, Senator John Westland. It was taken in his home during the holidays and caught Matthew and Andrea quite by accident on one of his intruder alert cameras. Also included is the separate second incident on the day of Matthew's current marriage."

"A digital video?" The magistrate looked intrigued by the possibility he'd get to view a video tape of Matt and Andrea screwing in the study. Matt would rather endure an all day caning than allow the tape to be seen in the courtroom today with Sophie watching. He'd completely forgotten his father had a security camera in his study.

"I'd like to take this opportunity to dispute the validity of the digital video they want to submit. How can I be assured the tape hasn't been tampered with? " Matt asked as he stood up to make his point.

The magistrate made a dubious face as if considering the possibility the tape was faked, but then he said, "I'll view the tape in my chambers during the recess and have my technical staff authenticate it."

"Magistrate, if I may approach?" Matt stood up, and at the man's nod he went to the bench. His father and the governor trotted up next to him, standing directly before the chin-level magistrate's desk.

"Yes, Mr. Westland?"

"Magistrate, I've not been allowed to see this tape..."

"It doesn't matter, Matthew. You have no right to dispute it," his father interrupted. "It's you on the tape. I think I know my own son when I see him fornicating with a poor innocent like Andrea—"

"Stop it, both of you," the magistrate interrupted when Matt opened his mouth to break in on his father's speech. "I'll give you a choice, Mr. Westland. Either I view the tape in private and then allow my technical staff to authenticate it, or we can set it up in the courtroom for all to see."

"Set it up for the courtroom then."

"Now see here, I will not allow my daughter to be publicly humiliated for the salacious press..."

The magistrate held up his hand to Andrea's father to stop his rant.

"In deference to Governor Kane's public persona and the embarrassment it would cause him, I will clear the courtroom of the media. However, the five you will be in attendance. Do you sincerely wish your wife to see this video, Mr. Westland?"

"Matthew, this is ridiculous. It is *you* on the tape!"

"Senator Westland, do not speak another word," the magistrate warned. "Mr. Westland, do you?"

"Of course I don't want my wife to see some doctored video of Andrea with some other guy fornicating in my father's study, especially if they created it to blame me for something I didn't do. But if it will serve justice, then go ahead. I know it isn't me. Will you still have your technical staff authenticate it? And furthermore, what qualifications do they have, if I might ask, since my entire future hangs on the balance of their expertise?"

"I have the finest staff in the state. Rest assured, if you are innocent, it will be proven." The magistrate looked past the three of them at Andrea who had lowered her head and started crying silent buckets of tears at the plaintiff's table.

"On second thought, I'll allow Mr. Westland to view the tape with me in the privacy of my chambers. Then I'll have my staff authenticate it."

He stood and dismissed the court until such time as he viewed the disc.

Matt explained briefly to Sophie, who nodded and sat back down at their table to wait. He patted her arm and followed the magistrate through the passage behind his large desk and into his private space behind the courtroom. The space was large and a nice-sized wall screen was centered to the left upon entering the office. Matt watched as the magistrate gave the package to another man with a few whispered instructions.

Five minutes later, they watched grainy black and white footage of Matt staggering into the study, obviously and totally shit-faced, directed by Andrea, who was looking around furtively and most especially right into the camera that was supposedly hidden.

In the suspect video, she managed to get him on the sofa, but he fell onto it face down, one arm dangling off, a hand resting on the floor. The clarity wasn't good and the camera was located at the end of the sofa where his head was, and not giving a very clear view of his face, but he thought he might be drooling.

Soon after, Andrea turned him over face up with much tugging and turning and apparently no help from him that night, but his eyes were closed and his face was barely visible to the camera's view. She ripped open his shirt and a couple buttons flew off, one landing in the black, decorative bowl on the table. She unbuckled his belt and opened the front of his slacks.

Andrea suddenly got up from the sofa, stepping out of the camera view a moment. On the film, he didn't move one drunken limb. The lights then dimmed to near darkness. Andrea returned to the sofa, and the show began. Andrea straddled him without removing her dress and immediately bounced like a pogo stick on top of the man below her, shrieking as if in a porno film that paid extra for noise. The man, almost impossible to see from the angle of the camera and the grainy texture of the film, made no noise whatsoever.

"That isn't me," Matt said.

"And what proof do you have of this? Do you deny it was you who staggered in at first?"

"No."

"Then why isn't it still you?"

"From the angle of the camera, and the sudden darkness in the room, it could be anyone."

"Anyone, including you."

"Explain to me how I morally corrupted the virtue of the governor's daughter by lying there and letting her fuck me. You can't even prove from this tape that I actually had my dick inside her."

"Don't be vulgar."

"This whole charade of a hearing is vulgar. After viewing this, you can't possibly still believe I did what I'm being accused of. If the person in that video *is* me, then I didn't say anything to coerce her. I didn't threaten her to fuck me or else. I didn't do anything except lay there in a dead unconscious drunk heap and fail to stop what she did to *me*."

"That remains to be seen. I'll render my judgment when all the evidence is in my possession."

Matt was incensed. Perhaps he'd do better if he filed a motion that Andrea had ruined *his* virtue. The monitor changed suddenly and Matt heard his father's voice. The magistrate looked back at the screen. It was footage from the night he'd married Sophie. It was from when he'd been called down by his father to listen to Andrea vent.

The camera angle was exactly the same as before. It was focused on the sofa area, pointing ostensibly to the safe his father kept behind his desk. Andrea was sitting on the sofa in this angle.

The scene started when he heard himself enter the room and then heard his own voice say, "What is so damn important to interrupt me from my wedding night?"

It didn't change from the original event until after his father left the room.

"I'll leave you two alone to talk." He heard his father say again and the sound of the doors closing.

"Come and sit with me, Matthew," Andrea said on the film as expected and patted the sofa next to her.

This is where the taped veered off of reality. The lights suddenly lowered and after a few moments there was undefined movement on the sofa. Then it seemed as if the lights magically increased enough to see a man with a similar hair cut as his, on top of Andrea who then began shrieking and wailing her love for him repeatedly while the man in the film lasted about five strokes before grunting and falling on her trapping Andrea underneath him against the sofa. Then the footage went blank.

"That was definitely not me." Matt felt suddenly very vindicated. He'd never only lasted five strokes and then collapsed on a woman...well, except for that one time in a semi-private limo with Sophie. Damn.

"It looked like you. It sounded like you when you entered the room. Do you deny being in the study that night?"

"No. I just deny everything that happened after my father left the room. I never crossed to where the sofa was. I stayed on my side of the room, then she screamed and vented about how she hated me and wouldn't marry me if I was the last man on earth."

"Well, someone turned the lights off and crossed the room. Did you see anyone else in the house?"

"There are lots of someone elses in my father's house. I'm telling you the video is a fake. I adamantly deny having sex with Andrea. And to tell you the truth, after watching the first part, I don't even believe I had sex with her at Christmas either.

"Being that sloppy drunk usually precludes *any* sexual activities, if you get my meaning." Matt lifted an eyebrow to convey his man-to-man meaning.

"You are dismissed, Mr. Westland. I'll be reconvening court in ten minutes." The magistrate remained seated.

Matt took his cue and exited the magistrate's private office. As it stood now, he didn't have a warm fuzzy feeling about the outcome of the hearing or any certainty the magistrate would rule in his favor.

But he sincerely hoped his own 'evidence' trumped the tape he'd just watched.

Chapter 11

"I have reviewed the submitted digital tape with Mr. Westland. Currently, my technical staff is studying it for authentication."

"I renew my strenuous objection as to the validity of the tape," Matt said standing up swiftly, to make his point.

"Noted, Mr. Westland. Please sit down. " The magistrate sounded gruff and irate. Not a great sign. "Governor Kane, do you have any further information to add?"

"I believe the tape speaks for itself. I have nothing further."

"Mr. Westland, what evidence have you brought today in defense of the charges brought against you?"

Matt stood up again, cleared his throat and started his defense. "I have been charged with corrupting Andrea Kane's virtue, impregnating her during the Christmas holidays, and finally of sleeping with her the night I married my wife, Sophie. I'd like to make it clear for the record that all three of these allegations are false.

"The first piece of evidence I have to prove my innocence is a digital video of Miss Kane." Matt nodded to a man in the audience who held the disc up. He was the top video tape technician employed at Westland Industries. The clerk collected it promptly delivering it to the magistrate.

"It's date and time stamped the fourteenth day of February showing Andrea Kane in my personal executive office after hours at Westland Industries with another man engaged in sexual activity…on my desk."

"He is a liar! He's doctored a fake disc, and I won't stand for this kind of slander against my daughter." The governor opened his mouth to shout again. Matt saw Andrea turn her head sharply and direct an angry look his way.

"Shut up, Governor! It's my turn to talk," Matt said and turned back to the magistrate. "I brought my personal technician with me today from

Westland Industries, who will swear that the video you just received was never in my possession. I gave him the date and time parameters, and he pulled and transferred a copy of the video to the disc you now hold in your hand."

"Noted, Mr. Westland. What else do you have?"

"I brought my personal physician with me." Matt turned back to the audience and nodded to his doctor, who stood up. "He will swear that during the six-month period from late August last year and until the end of February this year, I was under his exclusive care and more specifically, I was on a very carefully monitored medication regimen which made me temporarily sterile."

"Sterile!" Matt's father said incredulously. He and the governor then exchanged an uneasy glance between them. The magistrate gave them both a thunderously angry look, presumably because he interrupted.

"I cannot possibly be the father of Andrea's baby, as I was not producing sperm until at least March, if then." Matt wasn't going to mention that the medication was also for his biogenetic implants as a final regimen to assure continued genetically enhanced abilities.

"Is that all?" the magistrate asked. His surly tone was back, and it made Matt apprehensive.

"I couldn't possibly have gotten Andrea pregnant at Christmas. It was physically impossible. I am not the one who corrupted her. I have her on tape clearly being corrupted by another man after our experience, proving she also didn't consider our acquaintance exclusive.

"And I absolutely did not have sex with Andrea the night I married my wife. The tape you and I viewed was a fake. I know what happened in that room, and it is not represented on the tape the plaintiffs have submitted into evidence. If your technicians aren't able to determine that truth, then I figure my word as a gentleman should be worth something, too. With that said, I feel I have demonstrated my innocence very well as to the charges against me."

"We'll adjourn until one o'clock this afternoon so I may review all the evidence. When we return, you will each be allowed to make a final statement before I render my judgment." The magistrate banged his gavel once, raising his large frame from the seat behind the elevated bench and disappearing to his private chambers to watch more porn staring Andrea.

Sophie put a hand on his. He turned to see her speculative look. Her eyebrows went up in question. "Sterility as a defense?"

"Yeah," he admitted.

"Brilliant." She then gave him a radiant smile.

"Let's hope."

* * * *

Sophie and Matt retreated outside the justice center building and around the corner to a quiet exclusive restaurant where the media couldn't follow to enjoy their lunch break. Sophie sat against the ultra lush cushions of the small intimate secluded booth where they sat basking in the new-found thought that they might actually get to stay together. She thought Matt had proven beyond a shadow of a doubt his innocence.

The waiter took their order and retreated from the table as Matt turned toward her and wrapped an arm around her shoulder, pulling her close on the seat they shared. The forefinger and thumb of his other hand came up to stroke her chin. He held her face and kissed her passionately, his tongue teasing hers with careful deliberate strokes as if they were the only patrons of the restaurant. No one was in their direct view, but if she moaned in appreciation of his attention, others would certainly hear.

He paused his sensuous assault of her lips and murmured, "You're beautiful."

Sophie didn't respond because she tried to keep from moaning in public. Matt's hand suddenly slid down her body, pausing at her breast to squeeze tenderly and stroke her nipple. Seconds later, he promptly dropped his hand to her lap and under her skirt onto her bare thigh. Her sharp intake of breath produced that famous million-dollar smile. "Are you blushing?"

"I doubt it, but you tell me." Sophie palmed his cock which bobbed appreciably and grew in her hand the moment she touched him.

He jumped slightly as she squeezed his thickening cock through his slacks and chuckled. "Insatiable is what you are, Mrs. Westland. I love that about you."

"Kiss me, Matthew. I think it's all we'll have time for before our food comes."

His fingers under her skirt worked under her panties as if to contradict her comment. He gazed deeply into her eyes as he stroked her clit once before slipping a finger up inside of her body. Sophie failed to cover her moan at the sensation. His look of triumph made her glow inside as she inhaled those ever present pheromones he exuded in waves as usual wrapped around his delectable cologne. He removed his hand from her suddenly, but before she took her next breath he stuck that finger with her wetness covering it into his mouth while she watched.

"Yummy," he declared as the waiter stepped up with their drinks. Sophie felt a warm blush come up in her cheeks when it occurred to her she was becoming much too comfortable with sexual activities in public places.

She and Matt caressed each other throughout lunch despite three more interruptions from the wait staff. They ended up drooling over each other too long and had to fight through the throngs of media to get back inside the hearing room on time.

They came back into the magistrate's hearing room at about ten seconds before the one o'clock deadline. Trotting up to the defense box, they didn't have time to speak to some of the new faces now gracing the crowded audience.

The first odious person she recognized was Orin Prichard. He was over next to the plaintiff's table and conversed with Matt's father as if they were co-conspirators. Sophie watched Matt's head turn in their direction and he stared for a moment or two, but then turned away as if he weren't concerned. Sophie didn't like the idea of Orin Prichard contributing any information for the senator's side in this matter.

She then turned and glanced at Paul Brody. He sat in the very back and gave Sophie a positively grim expression as they passed before Matt pulled on her arm, propelling her the last few steps to their spot in front of the magistrate. As the clerk announced the magistrate's arrival back in the room, she noticed another familiar face from Westland Industries. She didn't know his name but knew he was a young intern still employed there.

The technician Matt had brought to authenticate the tape of Andrea was still in attendance. He also had a very dismal look on his face. She got the impression he'd wanted to speak to Matt as they'd hurried by, but there was no time.

Sophie put a hand on her middle to subdue the sudden bad feeling blazing its way across her insides. She got a chill just before she noted the row of spectators behind Matt's technician and found Orin Prichard seated comfortably now. She stifled the urge to shiver at the positively malevolent look he directed her way. Then just as suddenly, he smiled and winked at her. She knew that delighted look certainly didn't bode well.

She tugged on Matt's arm, but the magistrate entered the hearing room. Matt distractedly patted her arm but didn't look at her. His focus was between the magistrate and his father seated at the governor's plaintiff table. Everyone stood in deference and the proceedings began before she could mention all the visitors in the audience making her nervous.

"Are you ready to make your closing statements?" the magistrate asked.

The governor smugly turned to the audience. "I'd like to beg the court's indulgence, your Honor. I have new evidence to present. I only obtained this disc over the lunch break."

"What evidence is that?"

"I have a tape with some questionable activities of Mr. Westland's present wife."

"What relevance does a tape with my wife in it have on these proceedings?" Matt said angrily, standing up, releasing her arm.

"You are counter suing me for defamation of character." The governor smiled smugly once again. "I have a right to show how Sophie Brent Westland is undeserving of any protection for her character."

Sophie couldn't even imagine what tape they could have of her. She'd never even seen the inside of the senator's study. "Magistrate, I strenuously object to this 'new' evidence as being anything but more lies to perpetuate on this hearing," Matthew said.

"I have a tape showing Sophie Westland working in her former office, all alone, I might add, at Westland Industries. I believe the Tiberius Group law states explicitly she is not to be left alone in public, nor is she allowed to work without special permission."

"So what? Sophie used to work for me. And besides, my wife *can* work if she has my permission," Matt said in an even tone. Sophie could tell he was angry. But then a bigger problem became evident. How did they have a tape of her working in her office? Was there a camera in her office? And if so, how long had it been there? And why hadn't Matt told her?

"Matthew," she said in a loud whisper.

Matt looked down at her. His troubled eyes were apologetic and gave her the answer she dreaded. Oh God, there *was* a camera in her office. She could tell by the look in his eyes.

"I'd like to show the tape." The governor nodded to Matt's technician, who grudgingly handed over another disc.

"No!" Sophie stood up and shouted.

The magistrate banged his gavel. "Sit down, Mrs. Westland. You do not have a voice in these proceedings beyond that of your husband."

"You can *not* show that tape in here right now!" she stated emphatically.

Matt's eyes widened and she could tell he thought he knew what would be on the tape she so adamantly protested. He assumed she was upset about the sexual play acting they'd done on her desk, in what she previously expected was the privacy of her office, but he was wrong.

There was something else. Something worse.

"She's right. I protest another tape being shown. The others of me were obviously faked."

"We used the same technique and had Mr. Westland's own technician pull the company video within a certain time frame. Actually, the office Mrs. Westland used to work in has a motion sensor activation camera. Isn't that right?" The governor turned to Matt's technician who nodded morosely and sincerely looked like he wished to be anywhere but where he was right at this moment. He gave Matt an anguished look. More bad news for her.

"Sir, there may be private things on the tape that are of a confidential business nature. I must strenuously protest the viewing of this tape in open court."

"No one wants to steal your business secrets, Mr. Westland. I'll allow the tapes." The magistrate motioned for the tape to be brought forward.

"No!" Sophie raised her voice. "Please do not show that tape, I beg you."

"I will not tolerate another outburst from you, Mrs. Westland. Sit down and shut up this instant."

Sophie pressed her lips together and stared daggers at the magistrate, but she didn't sit down. It was a feeble protest, but she was screwed if they showed the tape.

Matthew put a hand on her arm in a comforting gesture and added, "Magistrate, my wife can't be condemned for the sexual things I require from her."

"You required your wife to have sex with you in her former office?" The magistrate's bushy eyebrows went up practically to his hairline.

"What I do with my wife is none of anyone else's damned business."

"The tape we have does not show sexual activity, just *her* working after it was clear by the date and time stamp…she shouldn't have been," the governor said casually, but from the smug tone of his voice, Sophie knew there was additional footage.

Sophie knew exactly what it was, too. Matt thought he knew, but he didn't.

"Set the screen up," the magistrate said. "Having your wife work for you is still punishable by a fine, Mr. Westland, with or without your permission. Do you know that?"

"Then I'll admit it and pay the fine. Why do you need to show the video?"

"Evidence, as rebuttal to the charges you yourself have brought forward."

Sophie was doomed. She turned to her husband and in a passionately quiet voice said, "Matthew, I can explain." His face showed his misunderstanding. He shook his head and winked at her. He sat down and pulled her down to her chair. Sophie sat on the very edge, her back ramrod straight.

A screen was lowered and the lights went off and the footage started. And she guessed it was too much for the hearing room, with all the salacious spectators, to be cleared before *her* humiliating video was shown.

The first part showed Sophie entering her office like she still worked there. She accessed her computer and began working away. They fast forwarded the tape to show how long she worked. Just as the hour marker showed on the footage, the magistrate grunted and made a notation. An hour was the punishable fine length of time for her working, apparently. Then the tape slowed back to normal speed and the door to her office opened.

Matthew squeezed her hand certainly thinking it was him about to enter her office, but it was Paul Brody instead. On the footage, she stood up from her chair and came around the desk. There was no sound on the tape, video only, and somehow that made it even worse. Matthew released her hand and twisted in his chair so he was no longer touching her.

Sophie watched in fascination like the others behind her in the audience, but soon felt tears spill over her lower lids and stream down her face. Matthew would leave her. Or he'd sell her.

In the film Paul pulled an envelope out and handed it to her. She opened it, and even the grainy texture of the video showed it was a stack of cash. She tried to give it back to him, but Paul refused. He then put his hand to her face in a loving gesture. He moved in close even as she backed into her office desk. It looked like a choreographed dance move from the point of view of the camera, although at the time, she backed away from him to distance herself.

Sophie knew Paul had a huge crush on her. He had for a long time, and while she hadn't returned his affection, she used him just the same. And now everyone would know it. She used him to save herself from marrying a stranger at the auction, or worse someone like Orin, and the money he was returning to her was her very own. It was a plan they hatched before the Working Woman's Auction Memo went in to effect. It was what Sophie had thought of to save herself and to solve her own problem. She certainly never expected Matthew Westland to rescue her.

Why would she?

Back to the footage, and the part where Paul told her he cared about her, and that he regretted not being the one to marry her. Sophie asked if he would be good to her sister, but on the tape it looked like she was returning his affection. Sophie had never felt so far away from Matthew even sitting so close to him.

Paul wanted to kiss her good bye and she'd let him...almost. She changed her mind at the very last second because she didn't want to lead him on. She didn't find him attractive in that way. Paul tried to kiss her on the lips. While she turned her head in deflection, it was hard to see anything on the video, with the exception of Paul Brody and her in a loving clench. It looked like she turned into him to accept the kiss, then both startled on the footage, obviously hearing someone in the hallway outside the room. As her final act of treachery in the video footage, Sophie shuffled Paul out of her office through the bathroom she shared with the office next door. Just in the nick of time.

Two seconds later, Matthew had come in. She wiped at her face next to her mouth where Paul's lips had touched her and turned to Matthew as if she hadn't just been in an embrace with another man. She then kissed Matthew passionately in the film. At the time, she knew Matthew was the only man she'd ever want. The only kiss she'd ever crave. But from the point of view of the film, that the entire hearing room now surveyed, it looked for all the world like she'd gotten caught about to get busy with another man, before her husband showed up to finish the job.

The tape went blank.

Matthew would of course remember exactly what happened next. They'd made love in her office...on *her* desk, and under it. And while at the time, she'd meant every kiss, touch, and murmur of love she'd expressed to him, basking in the glow of a relationship she didn't even know if she would get to keep, she knew how it looked right now in court.

Bad for her. Bad for Paul.

Bad for Matthew, too, since the room had just witnessed a video of which suggested she almost cheated on him. But she hadn't. Nor had she intended to. Given the same circumstances, she wouldn't believe her story, either.

Sophie chanced a look his way, but Matthew didn't look at her in return. His focus was on the table in front of him.

"Why did the man in the video give you money, Mrs. Westland?" the magistrate asked to the pin drop silent room. She couldn't even hear breathing.

"Don't answer that," Matthew said harshly. He'd turned only half way towards her, staring at her shoulder, and not at her face or into her eyes. Probably, she didn't want to look into his eyes just yet.

"I want an answer to my question," the Mmagistrate said in a peevish tone.

"She answers to me, not you." Matthew's anger was evident in the clipped voice he used.

"Well, then ask her what the money was for?"

"I already know what the money was for," Matthew said in the coldest tone she'd ever heard. It was the one he usually reserved for his father. She imagined she should get used to it.

"I directed that meeting to take place. I told Paul to give Sophie that money."

"Really," the magistrate's tone dripped distain and disbelief. "Why?"

"It's none of your business, and it has nothing to do with the proceedings here today."

Matthew didn't speak to her, or look at her, and he most certainly didn't touch her.

The magistrate looked very irate at first, then softened and said, "Very well. Is there anything else you wish to bring to my attention, Governor?"

"No. I'm ready to conclude my proof. I'd like my very good friend, former senator John James Westland to make my final statements, if it's allowed," The governor said with a self-satisfied smile.

"As long as he speaks to the case and charges at hand."

Sophie looked around the room at the others in attendance. The spectators all glanced at her as though she were the most horrible female ever born to this world. A fallen woman who'd successfully tricked her husband into his unflinching supporting of her wickedness.

A woman who didn't deserve a man such as Matthew.

"It isn't what you think," she whispered, leaning closer to him.

"Isn't it?" He still didn't look at her, but leaned as close as he could without touching her and began a low angry whisper. "Here's what I think. You never needed me to rescue you at all. You had a brilliant plan all of your own. You gave Paul the money to bid on you. I remember seeing him leave the auction directly after I bid. Did he have enough to cover Orin's bid?"

Sophie hesitated before answering a dismal sounding, "No."

"Then I guess I saved you after all. Too bad for me. I got a wife who wanted another man. He obviously loves you. No wonder he wanted to marry Hannah, easy access to you."

"That's not true. I never wanted him, but you're right, I used him. I used his feelings for me to save myself."

"Like you're using me?" Matthew suddenly withdrew from her without waiting for her answer.

She wasn't using him. She loved him, but he'd never believe it now. The sudden gut wrenching idea of losing Matthew engulfed her. Then a worse notion occurred to her. The horror of winning here today, and then having to spend her life with Matthew hating her for what she'd done.

Chapter 12

"My son, Matthew Westland, is a great man," the senator began, as if giving a stump speech. "He is a great leader of men. No father could be prouder of his son than I am. He runs a company he built up with his own two hands with no help from me. It's no secret I've wanted my son to have a career in politics, but more than that, I wanted him to succeed. And he has, even if it wasn't in the path I would have chosen for him.

"And much like me, he has loved unwisely. He has gone to great lengths for the woman he loves. He believes sincerely in a woman, who does not deserve his regard, as we have shown vividly here today.

"I have another piece of information only recently learned, that I'd like to share. It gave me great pride to know my son was a part of it. And it will show, without a doubt, his loyalty to the new world order. With his signature touch of compassion, my son made a significant contribution to the brilliant changes brought about by the Tiberius Group.

"I'd like to believe it will demonstrate and explain his determined character, but it will also show the creative lengths he'd be willing to go to in order to do what he believes in. This will serve us as a nation, regardless of how these proceedings turn out today.

"My son is the sole author of the very useful and effective Working Woman's Auction Memo which the Tiberius Group has used with very great success all across this great land of ours."

"Fuck!" Sophie heard Matthew say angrily under his breath. He turned to look her in the eye for the first time since the horrid tape of her with Paul. She felt her eyes widen in shock. Matthew had written the most hated memo in the history of the female working world?

She saw the truth of his father's words reflected in the expression on Matthew's face.

"You wrote that memo…" Sophie couldn't finish the sentence. There was no need. Her wounded tone and his guilty face said it all.

"I believe Matthew would do anything for his business to ensure its success. I believe he'd do the same for his spouse. However, I do not believe Sophie Brent deserves his continued unwavering support. Please find for Governor Kane in this action, if for no other reason than to save my son from his own honorable character."

Senator Westland sat down to hushed whispers all through the audience. Sophie tried to digest everything and then tried to keep her lunch down.

"Mr. Westland, are you ready to make your final statements?" the magistrate asked, his tone suggesting the most recent revelation was better entertainment than television.

"A minute please," Matthew said aloud, his gaze still transfixed on hers. So now they each had something to be angry about.

"If I decline to defend myself today, the magistrate will no doubt favor the other side. If that happens, I'll be forced to find another husband for you, quickly. I may not even get to choose. I see Orin Prichard in the audience as well as Paul Brody. I need to know if Paul is your choice…so I can make it a part of any agreement I make. Tell me now. Do you care for him? Did you want him, and I ruined all your plans by saying one hundred thousand dollars?"

"I did what I had to do to survive a certain egregious memo endorsed by the Tiberius Group for which I suffered the worst consequences. I dealt with it in the best way I could with very limited options." Sophie hated that tears welled in her eyes. She couldn't decide if she were more distraught at Matt being the author of the humiliating memo, or the stabbing pain of losing him.

"So do you want me to let you go? Do you want me to…sell you to him? Because I could try to do that…if you want."

She couldn't speak for a moment. Gathering her wits she asked, "Why did you write the memo? It was beyond humiliating."

"The simple answer is, so I could finish what we started in the hallway at Christmas. I wanted to save you. I wanted to have you for myself. I wanted you with an unquenchable desire, and like an idiot, I wanted to be your hero."

His eyes showed the despair she also felt. Did he believe she wanted Paul? How could he? Perhaps he'd had enough of her by now?

Sophie exaggerated a shrug her shoulders trembling in emotion. "But now you don't want me any more because your desire for me has been quenched? Or is it because you can't stand that you weren't the only hero that day?"

"I simply want a woman who isn't stuck with me because I bought her. I deluded myself into believing you cared for me from a certain incident during the holidays. That's why I went after you the only way I could, with the only tools available to me, in this fucked up new world order.

"But I'm not the only one who wants you, am I? Everything I did was with the single driving need to possess you. I thought you might return my affection. If you don't, well then, you're a fabulous actress, but tell me the truth. I need to know right now. Who do you love?"

For a moment, Matthew's face masked that of an angry spouse full of contained fury. Then his gaze became more tender, raking her face with a look she'd seen in his passionate eyes before and most recently at lunch. He loved her. But then it went back to anger again. Like he, too, was struggling with loving her, or being angry with the world at large, in which they now lived.

Sophie gathered her wits and went with her heart. If she was headed down and out, she intended to fight all the way. She didn't want Paul. Never had.

Sophie's voice quivered in a low passionate tone to make him truly understand. "I love you with all of my heart, Matthew. How can you not know that?" She threw her arms around him and put her lips to his ear so only he could hear her words. "Whatever else happens, whatever else you come to believe about me...I love *only you*. I want *only you*. I've wanted *only you* since the day I met you, too.

"I will remember every moment we shared with sincere love and gratitude for the rest of my life. Because your bidding on me was a wonderful thing I never in a million years expected you to do. I didn't even think you knew I was alive way back then. How could I have expected you to rescue me? I merely tried to find a way to survive, I swear. I never loved anyone but you, *only you*. Please, please, believe me, Matt. You have to believe me."

"More gratitude?" he whispered in her ear. His tone was playful and relieved.

"That's all you heard?" She pulled away to look into his eyes

"No. I heard it all. I love you, Sophie. You and me against the world, right?"

"Right."

"Mr. Westland, this is all very entertaining, but your minute is up," the magistrate said impatiently.

* * * *

"I'm ready, Magistrate. My final closing remarks are a plea. The only way I can truly win here today is if I get the charges against me dropped. Is that correct?"

The magistrate scrunched his substantial eyebrows in question but eventually nodded.

"I'm going to request my father ask his good friend the governor to drop these charges. If he is willing to do this, I will agree to drop my countersuit as well. I think we all know I'm guilty of only one thing here. I love my wife, Sophie. I love her with a determination that will last us no matter what happens here today. And I will never separate from her of my own free will. Never.

"So the only way I can win here today is to convince my opponents that the charges against me must be dropped. The true reason my father wants Andrea to be my wife instead of Sophie is because of that great leader speech he just gave you. He wants me to run for President of the United States. He believes sincerely that the only way a win is possible is for me to marry the governor's daughter.

"Unfortunately for him, I only want to run my business, a challenge since a significant portion of my employees aren't allowed to work for me. My wife was a former employee. A great one, I might add. I put her to work because she is completely capable and has the intelligence to perform even under the pressure of her enforced new strictures.

"She isn't even allowed to get credit for the procurement process she just authored for me. And it's brilliant. The Tiberius Group representative I showed it to yesterday is all excited to get a copy of it for nationwide dispersal. But if she is taken from me as my spouse, I will no longer have custody over that process. And if I don't have a business, that process will disappear completely. It will be unfortunate for the Tiberius Group who felt it was needed desperately for the betterment of the new world order.

"But my business aside, I have just had an epiphany today in court. Given the choice between the business I've sweated blood for or my wife, I'm always going to choose Sophie. She doesn't care about my money. I could be a beach bum and she'd love me anyway.

"So today in this very hearing room, I will ask my father to persuade the governor to drop his charges or I will tell a secret, too. This big secret will have a direct impact on both my business and my potential candidacy for president.

"But guess what? I still choose, Sophie. So I have a compromise. If you drop the charges, I will reconsider your wishes for a political career and pursue them with Sophie at my side. Or I will spill all and let the chips fall where they may."

Matt's father roared and stood abruptly, his chair wobbling to stay on all four legs. "You'll lose everything!"

"Matthew, no." Sophie looked up at him with big eyes. She'd never ask him to give up his business. He winked at her reassuringly.

"I don't care about everything. I only care about Sophie. Besides, have you considered what you will lose?" He held up another disc. "It's yet another video, can you believe it? I watched it, too. It's explicitly clear and details exactly what happened and who made all the decisions." He drilled his father a satisfied smug look in return when he said it.

"This cryptic summation is obviously a blackmail scheme to get what you want, Mr. Westland," the magistrate chimed in before Matt's father could speak.

"Well, isn't that why we're all here?" Matt raised his arms in a wide shrug as if calling the angels from heaven to hear his plea. "Each of us wants something and you are the arbitrator standing at the ready to decide who wins. Am I correct? My only recourse is to compel them to drop the charges against me. That is what I intend to do. Whatever it takes."

"Mr. Westland, if you have a disc with relevant information regarding these proceedings, you should turn it over to me as evidence."

"No, Your Honor, that won't be necessary," his father said. "Give me and the governor a minute to confer."

"Senator, Governor, what are you trying to accomplish here today?"

"Only what is best for all concerned." His father turned to the governor with a tense face. They began a whispering match between them.

Matt glanced at Andrea and noticed she wasn't paying attention to the men next to her arguing. He also noted she hadn't yet noticed the person he'd requested be in the hearing room today. Matt drilled a look her way, and after a moment or two, she turned her attention to him. Her eyes squinted in question until Matt directed his gaze to Bart, the young junior executive from his company.

The man he'd caught in his office with Andrea on Valentine's Day.

Andrea gave Matt a coldly sneering look, but soon followed his gaze to her lover. Her eyes widened and she stood up knocking her chair aside. The next look she sent to Matt was a guilty one and filled with confusion. Her eyes told him she'd been played by her father, too. Matt had spoken to Bart and forced the truth out of him. Andrea was truly a pawn, just as he was.

"Matthew, please don't jeopardize your business for me," Sophie said. Her eyes were still tear filled. He was about to tell her how relieved he was she didn't carry a torch for Brody, but raised angry voices from the plaintiff table distracted him.

"Your son will marry my daughter or else. He's the one who got her pregnant. I don't care what medication he was on," the governor shouted. "That is the way we planned it and that is the way it will be!"

Matt turned to make a rebuttal, but then Bart, Andrea's lover, stood up in the back of the courtroom. He gazed lovingly at Andrea as he spoke. "That's not true, sir. I was the one who got your daughter pregnant. And I want to marry her. I have since we knew she conceived. And Senator Westland, my mother died last night so you can't hold her medical care over my head any longer. I love Andrea. I came here to make sure she knows it."

"Oh, Bart, I love you, too," Andrea cried out as tears fell from her eyes.

The gavel started banging at the front of the hearing room as the speculation and noise in the room rose with the drama unfolding. The magistrate looked annoyed. Perhaps he saw that he was losing his voice in the proceedings.

"He told me they paid you off...that you didn't want me." Andrea started moving towards Bart even as her father tried to restrain her. "Get your hands off me," Andrea snarled over the din of the courtroom.

Bart and Andrea met at the open space between the audience and the plaintiff and defense boxes in a tender embrace. "Of course, I want you," Bart said passionately then locked lips with her in front of a very angry governor, a lively crowd, and a senator who looked very uncertain of the outcome of the pending hearing. Matt finally allowed himself to feel some smugness when he noticed Bart's hand lowered and rested on Andrea's swollen belly as if in protection of his child.

The noise level in the room reached a defining roar as the gavel banged on. The magistrate, with his ponderous and intimidating bulk, finally stood up. He was so tall that he looked like he might hit his head on the ceiling of the courtroom.

He bent over and hammered the gavel on his bench, shouting, "That is enough! Clear the hearing room this instant. I want every one gone except the principles in this case. Sir, you are out of order. Release the plaintiff or you will be asked to leave."

Bart released Andrea but entered the front section of the room to include himself in the proceedings. Several courthouse lawmen were brought in to clear the room. Once it was quiet again, the magistrate sat down in his squeaky chair and gave those left in the room a sour look.

"I'm ready to render my decision. Do you still wish to continue, Governor, or are the charges being dropped? Before you answer, keep in mind a stiff penalty will be forthcoming if you've wasted my time."

"I do not want to drop the charges."

"Tobias!" Matt's father gasped.

The governor silenced him with a hand in the air. "The charges stand."

"Very well," the magistrate visibly relaxed and proceeded with his decision. "In the matter of Governor Kane versus Matthew Westland, my decision is as follows. I do not believe Mr. Westland corrupted your daughter during the holidays, Governor—"

"He most certainly did!" The governor, who had not sat down to hear the decision, took an angry step forward, his countenance visibly livid.

"Governor, do not interrupt me again or I will have you forcibly removed from this room and my decision read to you by lawmen as you languish behind bars."

The governor pressed his lips together in a thin line, crossed his arms in defiance and huffed out a breath.

"I further do not believe he impregnated your daughter. I've read the report and my medical source informs me the drugs Mr. Westland took would indeed have rendered him temporarily sterile.

"Now as to the final matter regarding his DNA being present in your daughter after he married his current wife. That is a sticking point with me. How else could it be in her body unless he'd put it there himself in the obvious way?"

"I can tell you how," Andrea said suddenly.

The governor turned and slapped her viciously across the face. "Keep your mouth shut, you whore. You have no say here."

Bart reacted immediately, placing himself in front of Andrea. "Do not touch her again."

"Governor, I warned you," the magistrate said quietly and motioned a lawman forward.

"Magistrate, will you please finish your ruling so the marriage between Matt and that woman can be dissolved." Matt's father stood up to insert. "Perhaps Matthew can sell her to this young, passionate gentleman here, unless he wants to put her back up for auction at Westland Industries again. Perhaps then he could get some of his money back."

"Senator, you are out of order. Sit down or I'll have you removed as well."

"I apologize to you for my daughter's outburst," the governor said. "Please finish your ruling, Magistrate."

The magistrate took a deep breath and waved the lawman back to his post at the courtroom doors.

"I find there is no getting around Mr. Westland's DNA being in her body within the forty-eight hour period of time after his marriage to another woman. I find in favor of your third claim, Governor. My punishment decision will follow my ruling on Mr. Westland's countersuit against you. "

The governor and Matt's father turned and gave each other self-satisfied smiles. Andrea looked ill. Sophie squeezed Matt's fingers tightly.

"Now, Mr. Westland, on to your countersuit."

"Yes, Magistrate. I would like to submit this video to the court so that…"

"Wait," Matt's father stood angrily. "You can't give more evidence. The magistrate has ruled. You lost. You can't bring secret information into this courtroom which has no bearing on this case."

"Senator Westland, you have no voice here. I have ruled on the case you shared in. Sit down."

"Now, Mr. Westland, I will warn you. If the tape you possess is not relevant to this proceeding, I will fine you very heavily after I throw out your evidence."

"It is very relevant, sir. My technician got a copy of the video already submitted into evidence during these proceedings. I have the original, unaltered feed of the video pulled from my father's study, in my possession."

"And where did you get this tape?"

"From one of my father's guards who was forced to participate. He came to me himself after he heard about the charges against me. I believe it will explain the single remaining charge against me as trumped up and false, after which I want you to make my marriage to Sophie permanent and binding."

"Very well, Mr. Westland. You may show your video."

Matt sent a speculative look Andrea's way. This film was not going to make her look good. She returned his gaze and nodded once slightly. He took this to mean she gave her consent to it being shown.

The footage began with Matt entering his father's study on the night he married Sophie. After his father left the room and Andrea had invited him sit on the sofa, the rest of the tape played as it had actually happened. At the end of Andrea's vent session, repeating for the court how she wouldn't marry him if he were the last man on earth and that he was far too old for her, Matt left the room having never crossed to the sofa as he'd stated.

It was the next secret section of the taping that Matt wanted the magistrate to see.

"I see you failed to seduce my son yet again." The senator's voice registered from the direction of where Matt had exited a few minutes before.

"He's obviously in love with that woman he married," Andrea responded desolately in the tape.

"That's beside the point. You fucked things up at Christmas royally. You need to work harder or I'll tell your father the true identity of your baby's daddy."

"I'm familiar with your standard threat. Save it."

"It's a good thing you saved that condom he used with you at Thanksgiving or we'd be screwed."

"If he hadn't called out *her* name when he climaxed, I wouldn't have. You should have seen the drunken surprised look on his face when he pulled back and realized I wasn't his precious Sophie.

"I was so pissed at him back then, but you know...I'm not mad anymore. I should never have given that condom to you, Senator Westland. I don't want to marry Matthew."

"Shut up, Andrea. You'll do as you're told. Now, here's what we'll do. I'll get the condom from the freezer and you can stick the contents up your twat and let it melt, so it will look like Matthew fucked you tonight.

"Then after the body scan, I have a guard in my employ who resembles Matthew enough to pass in a grainy black and white video. But we'll have to wait until after the body scan to stage it so you'll have to come back here the day after. We'll fix up a very believable tape for the magistrate hearing this case."

"Whatever. I don't care."

"You'll care when you are the wife of the President."

"Maybe."

The study footage suddenly ended and the next segment starring the guard resumed. There was some discussion as they arranged everything to make it look like Matt had sex with Andrea in the study. The date stamp showed the day after the Tiberius body scan.

The lights came back up in the hearing room and the magistrate looked like he was about to have a stroke, his face almost purple with rage. He took several deep breaths. Matt sincerely hoped he wouldn't keel over and die before rendering his judgment.

"I have never seen two more scheming men in all my days. I find for Matthew Westland in all matters before me. And for starters, I'm fining both of you two million dollars each. You will be incarcerated until such time I can think of a punishment worthy of all the crimes you've committed here today.

"Mr. Westland, I'm granting you your permanent marriage papers." He took pen in hand and signed a document with great flourish. He had his clerk deliver it safely to Matthew.

"Thank you, Magistrate."

"I retract my judgment against you from the previous charges since I now know exactly how your DNA ended up inside Miss Kane. This court is sorry for any inconvenience to you.

"Furthermore, as a remuneration for the egregious charges against you in this court, I will also retract the fine I assessed you for allowing your wife to work alone in your company. In the future, Mr. Westland, make sure you are with her at all times when she accompanies you to your place of business regardless of what she does there."

"Yes, Magistrate, thank you." Matt would do what he wanted regardless of the edict from the magistrate and his first order of business was taking the video camera out of Sophie's office at Westland Industries.

"Orin, call my lawyer!" Matt's father shouted across the courtroom. Matt didn't wonder any longer about Orin Prichard's loyalty. He'd probably been working for his father all along. Matt continued surveying the room until his eyes found Paul Brody's mournful expression. Paul glanced at Sophie with a last longing look and exited the courtroom with his face pointed at the floor, plodding along.

"Fifty thousand will only buy you so much, Senator. I don't fetch and carry for anyone. Call your lawyer yourself," Matt heard Orin say to his father.

"Why, you ungrateful wretch! I gave you a job when you got fired.

Now, call my lawyer. Now!"

Matt's father and the governor were escorted from the hearing room by several lawmen. Senator Westland complained and threatened Orin all the way out. Orin snorted once and followed them, shaking his head until he caught sight of a redhead being escorted past the door in handcuffs and in the opposite direction of the senator and governor.

Orin followed the redhead.

Matt made a mental note to talk to Paul Brody the next day to straighten everything out.

Bart and Andrea followed arm in arm as if no one else existed for them in the world. Matt was glad for them. Andrea got the 'young' man she loved.

And Matt got Sophie. He turned to her with a grin shaping his mouth. They'd won.

Sophie threw her arms around him and squeezed him tight. "Now you've done it. You'll never be able to get rid of me now."

"Thank God. Let's get out of here. I need to take care of something at work, then I've got a surprise for you."

"Is it a surprise involving chocolate?"

"Not telling. It's a secret."

"I love secrets."

"I love you, Sophie."

She smiled and they exited the hearing room to throngs of media, but for the first time in a long while, Matt relaxed and enjoyed having won the battle and the war.

* * * *

"I guess you're wondering why I asked you here." Matt sat at his desk at Westland Industries. Paul Brody had just entered, quietly plopped down in the chair across from him, crossed his arms and shifted in his seat as if in extreme discomfort. Matt couldn't blame him.

"Not really. I know why you called me here, Mr. Westland."

"I believe you embezzled the fifty thousand dollars for the auction and then put it back."

"How did you find out?" Paul's sullen gaze lifted to meet Matt's patient one.

"I simply realized that Orin Prichard would never in a million years have put the money back once he stole it. He would have gambled it away. It's in his nature. I'm curious though…what were you going to do if you'd won the bid on Sophie?"

Paul's eyes broke the staring contest. "I have distant relatives overseas in Europe. I was planning to take her out of the country permanently."

"I appreciate what you were willing to do for her, but you do understand I'll have to let you go?"

Paul shrugged. "Are you going to press charges and send me to jail?"

"No. I don't think that would serve justice. I will give you a good reference though."

Matt had expected some sort of declaration regarding Sophie, but Paul only nodded without looking at him and left the office, shutting the door quietly behind him.

Sophie waited for him in her office, thumbing her nose at the women-can't-work policy. Matt disabled the camera permanently in her office. Now he could go begin his life with her. He couldn't wait.

They had some celebrating to do.

Epilogue

"Close your eyes," Matt said as they stepped on to the elevator to leave Westland Industries. Sophie snuggled up close to him and gave him a mischievous look.

"If you want to get busy with me in an elevator, I want to leave my eyes open."

"As enticing as getting busy with you on an elevator sounds, we're just here for the ride."

"Are there any cameras in here?"

"Yes, I believe there are."

"Too bad. If there weren't any cameras, then I would do wicked things to you."

"I have no doubt about that, but I have that surprise ready for you."

"What kind of surprise if not a chocolate one?" she asked, wanting his hands on her.

"Close your eyes."

She did with a sigh. She felt the smooth descent of the elevator car and felt a little weightless like she was on an amusement part ride from her childhood.

Ding. She heard the doors slide open and Matt led her out. She heard the clack of her shoes on the tile and laughed.

"I know exactly where we are, you know," she said.

"Keep your eyes shut, wife."

Her laughter rang echoing down the hallway she knew was the parking garage.

"I love the sound of your laughter, but do you know what I like better?"

"Um, let's see...my scream of pleasure echoing down the hallway, perhaps?"

"I knew you were brilliant."

He stopped her and turned her. She felt the metal door against her back and a thrill ran up her spine. Maybe they'd get to recreate their historical moment in the hallway.

"Did you remember to bring the mistletoe? I can't possibly scream without it."

"Open your eyes."

They were in exactly in the same spot as before. The mistletoe was above them. Matt leaned in and placed his lips an inch from hers and stopped.

"Let's make a new memory. What do you say?"

"Okay. And in the new memory, do you get to scream in the hallway, too?"

"No, in the new memory, we kiss here very chastely, and then I escort you outside to a non-public place."

"Okay. Kiss me."

"Only if you close your eyes again."

Her eyes slid shut in compliance.

His mouth swooped down on hers before she took her next breath. She closed her eyes as his tongue swirled with decadent surety between her lips.

He stopped before they had a historical re-creation of their first kiss in this hallway and led her outside, insisting she keep her eyes closed.

"Okay, open your eyes again," he said.

They stood before the limo they'd christened directly after they'd married. But this time they entered alone in the back.

"What, no one to watch us? I mean I was getting so used to sex tapes of the two of us, it's a little disappointing, Matthew."

"You're kidding, right?"

"Of course. I like it best when it's just the two of us." She snuggled close. "Where are we going anyway?"

"I got special permission to take you on a trip for the honeymoon we missed."

Sophie smiled. "Where are we going for this honeymoon?"

"I'd like you to meet my mom, and then I thought we'd go to Italy. I love you."

"Thank you, Matt. I love you, too."

* * * *

Shortly after they returned from their extended honeymoon, Sophie received a message from her brother Jonathan. He'd found Hannah. She was alive. Jon informed Sophie he'd be returning with Hannah on the next cryo-transport ship, right after he annulled her second marriage.

Thanks heavens, Hannah was safe.

Now, if only Jonathan could find a nice husband for her...

THE EXECUTIVE'S WIFE

The Wives Tales 2

THE END

WWW.LARASANTIAGO.COM

SIREN PUBLISHING

Lara Santiago

PROTECT

SERVE

THE LAWMAN'S WIFE

THE WIVES TALES

The Lawman's Wife

In 2078, two years after the Tiberius Group's take over, women are adjusting to the new laws that make them virtual property of the men who marry them.

Grace Maitland desperately needs to be bid on at the public auction to avoid losing her daughter Emma, the only thing that matters in her life.

Interstellar Federal Lawman Jonathan Brent never expected to marry. However, seeing the troubled young woman who has haunted his many dreams up for bid at an auction makes him overrule his common sense. He buys a wife for the pittance of ten dollars.

Having a ready-made family is surprisingly heartwarming after the life Jon has led, but Emma's biological father, a sexual vampire released from prison after the testimony of his only accuser Grace is overturned, now demands custody of a child he's never seen.

Jonathan puts his impeccable Lawman's career at stake and goes on the run to protect Emma and keep Grace safe.

The Lawman's Wife

The Wives Tales 3

By Lara Santiago

Copyright © 2006

Prologue

Earth, 2075
One year prior to the Tiberius Group takeover of the U.S.

Grace Maitland was petrified. She wondered if her heart would stop beating from sheer fright when she entered the tiny dark space...*if* she entered. That pivotal move remained in question as she stood before the brushed silver doors waiting the deathtrap's arrival.

She lingered in the first-floor lobby of the archaic justice building, having been denied the stairwell access due to a fifty-five gallon drum of wax on the landing between the first two floors. Stairs were her single means of travel in buildings taller than one story, particularly in tall buildings with ancient elevators.

What was the stupid wax barrel doing in the stairwell in the first place? This was the twenty-first century, for pity's sake. And furthermore, why did they still wax the floors by hand instead of installing maintenance-free synthetic shine tiles?

"I can tiptoe," she told the maintenance man, who looked at her as if she were off her medication.

"It's a safety risk," he insisted and directed her away, adding an exasperated "Just take the elevator!"

A riskier endeavor. She glanced one last time at the slick, wax-coated stairs. The janitor closed the door and locked it, shutting off the pungent turpentine scent of the wax.

"Why do justice buildings always have to be a hundred years old with rickety elevators?" she asked the empty lobby as she waited for the elevator she wasn't sure she possessed the courage to ride. She wasn't due in the courtroom for an hour, but she was expected to arrive early to go over her testimony. They all wanted to know what she would say, what truth she would reveal. Actually, she wondered too.

Lights on the display indicated the elevator was rising from the basement parking garage, which was another dark place she would just as soon avoid.

The district attorney knew she didn't want to testify. He'd threatened to send lawmen to ensure her attendance. She'd begged her way out of that inflammatory scenario. She had enough to worry about with the man she lived with, Danny, being perpetually pissed off and her sweet daughter, Emma, waking up so slowly in the mornings, without the added stress of lawmen to deal with too.

A sudden ping heralded the wretched elevator's arrival. The doors slid open in invitation. Grace's heart pounded. Dark wood paneling lined the car's interior like a casket. She tried to gather the courage to step forward. The space in the car wasn't deep, but looked fairly wide. Wasn't a wide, shallow elevator car safer to ride than a long, narrow one?

Her heart wasn't convinced.

She stuck her hand between the closing doors and they retreated.

"It's just an elevator, for pity's sake. People ride them successfully every single day. You can too, this one time," she said out loud and tried to build up some guts, but her bravery danced around her ankles, nowhere to be found.

The doors closed again, bouncing off her outstretched arms. They were waiting for her in the criminal division on the fifth floor. She closed her eyes, inhaled a deep breath, and squeezed her lids shut in primal fear.

Maybe, she thought, she could keep her eyes shut for the entire trip. Then she realized that was foolish since she'd yet to push the fifth-floor button. Admonishing herself for not having learned Braille, she stepped forward and winced as her foot landed on the metal rails, where the elevator doors threatened to crush her in their steely maw.

The gaping crevice between the landing and the claustrophobic interior of the elevator car glared at her. She scrunched her eyes shut again at the thought of slipping through the space her foot spanned.

"In or out!" said a deep, irate voice from the inside of the elevator car.

Grace shrieked and jumped at the sudden realization she was not alone.

"I beg your pardon." She opened her eyes to a tall, dangerous-looking lawman she hadn't noticed ensconced in the space she was valiantly trying to enter. He leaned forward from inside the car. Gorgeous. The warm, soft gray of his eyes almost drove away her fear.

All she could think of now was sharing the tight, dark space with a lawman. A big one. One she had already angered with her foolishness.

"Listen, lady, this isn't the morning to overcome your phobias. I need to go. So, in or out?" He gestured for her to make a decision.

"Of course you do. In. I choose in." She nodded, but still hesitated. She wondered if she might overcome her fear of small places by riding with a hulking, six-and-a-half-foot lawman. A quick study of his stern face negated the thought.

He huffed out a long sigh and offered his hand. "Allow me to help you aboard."

The look in his eyes said she should be grateful.

She put her hand in his, closed her eyes, and stepped onto the elevator. Once inside, she resisted the urge to pat herself on the back for the monumental task of getting on without screaming in tortured fear. The lawman's hand was not soft, of course, but not rough either. She liked the texture and held on. He didn't let go either, thankfully.

"What floor?" he asked. Her eyes popped open in time to see the doors close. She sucked in a breath as the elevator lurched upward and became momentarily distracted by the lawman's spicy scent.

"I...what?" A second inhalation came with the scent of his intoxicating cologne, and she was seriously unfocused by how attractive he was.

"I'm going to seventeen. If you want to stop before then, you'd better tell me now."

The mere thought of being suspended seventeen floors over a shaft of air made her queasy. "Five. I need five," she panted. Her courage darted back down to her toes.

The lawman stabbed the fifth-floor button with his thumb, and as he did, the elevator car shuddered to a screeching halt. Her eyes widened and she gasped.

"You've got to be kidding me," the lawman grunted, leaning forward to study the panel of buttons. "Damn ancient elevator."

"Why aren't we moving?" she wheezed and then realized she was still gripping his hand tenaciously.

"I pushed the button for your floor at a bad time. These old elevators are touchy."

"Touchy?"

"Yeah. I should have pushed the button before we were passing your floor."

"Now what?"

He exhaled. "We give it a minute and try again." He winked at her as if he went through this every day of his life. Perhaps he did.

She inhaled slowly and then let the breath out. "Maybe I can get a grip too," she whispered to herself. She silently thanked the lawman for not freeing his hand from her bone-crunching grasp.

A hollow, grinding noise rattled above them. Her stomach shot to the floor as she and the lawman both looked toward the ceiling.

"That can't be good," she squeaked. Her desperation sounded like nails on a chalkboard. She wanted out of here. Now. She heard a high-pitched, whistling noise and was embarrassed to realize it was coming from her. She clamped her free hand over her nose and mouth as if she could contain the panic by cutting off her own airflow.

The lawman looked bored or perhaps irritated that the elevator wasn't moving, at least until he heard her whimpering and glanced at her. He offered a comforting smile and then turned to the panel beside the door.

He punched a couple of numbers. Ten and twelve lit up, but the elevator didn't budge. He pushed the 'open doors' button a couple of times, which resulted in a new grinding noise that only unleashed more acid in her already nervous stomach.

She stepped closer to the lawman. Nothing short of a cattle prod to her wrist was going to make her release his fingers. Another ugly, protracted noise erupted, followed by loud thudding. She wished she could faint and end her misery.

Then the lights went out.

Grace released a prolonged, high-pitched scream and propelled herself into the lawman. She clawed at his chest one-handed until her free arm wound around his neck. Shaking, she buried her face into his throat.

The lawman bent slightly, pulled her against his chest, and whispered comforting words until the single tiny back-up light came on, barely qualifying as illumination. It sent spooky shadows around the small space.

"Are we going to fall?" She was crying now. "We're going to fall, aren't we?" Her voice sounded as hysterical as she felt.

"No," he said calmly, his voice muffled by her hair.

Ignoring the warm fuzzies his voice gave her, she wailed, "It really feels like we're about to drop!" She climbed up on him further and wound her legs around his hips. Several metal things on his belt shifted as she tightened her legs around him.

"We won't fall," he said calmly. His arm squeezed her waist and he lifted her off what she thought was his gun, but she was too preoccupied with her life flashing before her eyes to care.

"Please don't let go. Please don't let me fall." Grace clutched him as hard as she could one-handed. He curled their entwined fingers tightly and brought them into their embrace.

"We're not going to fall, and I won't let go of you." She let his deep, calm voice soothe her. She relaxed enough to release his hand from her death grip so she could promptly send it around his neck to squeeze him closer.

"We're going to die, aren't we? I'm going to die without ever getting a decent kiss!" She sobbed at the realization and buried her face in the lawman's neck, inhaling his mouth-watering scent.

Seeing her life's brief flashback had prompted her to remember the list of things she hadn't accomplished. She hadn't experienced a decent kiss. She hadn't had sex since her daughter's conception. And Emma was four. She lived like a monk with a man who pretended to care about her but was in fact mean, spiteful, and mired too deeply in his own self-worth to worry over her long list of things not yet done.

Grace worked three part-time jobs, kept Danny's house clean, took care of her daughter, and nursed her sickly aunt. She rarely had the time or the inclination to search out a worthy man for a decent kiss. Now, she was going to die having never known what one felt like.

The lawman, to whom she was suctioned like a vacuum cleaner to a throw rug, felt very nice under her grip. Good gracious, he smelled good enough to eat. With her mouth pressed under his jaw, she was tempted to lick his face and take a taste. Her fear morphed into a very salacious attitude. Before she plummeted to her death, she wanted one decent, soul-searching, tonsil-licking kiss.

She deserved it.

"Please. Please." She pulled back enough to place her lips on his cleanly shaven jaw. "Please." He cleared his throat, but didn't stop her when she kissed his chin.

She planted her lips on the corner of his mouth, and her tongue darted out for a little taste of him. Delicious.

"Listen, maybe we should…"

"Shh. Please. I only want one, before I die." Grace placed a hand on his face gently. She put her lips to his and counted silently to three. She risked rejection by parting her lips with utmost care and licking the seam of his scrumptious mouth. He didn't move, but a heartbeat later, he twisted and slid his mouth over hers. They were a natural fit. He swirled his tempting tongue into her mouth to delve and explore. He teased her tongue with his stroking until she couldn't resist, and soon they were wildly tangled together.

She inhaled him, tasted him, and as he fulfilled her wildest dream, craved more of him. They shared a wicked dance of lips and tongues and promises in the near dark. His hand traveled up her spine from her mid-back until his fingertips plunged into the hair at the nape of her neck.

She ran her fingers along the closely cropped hair near his collar, loving the neat, clean line of his regulation haircut. His hair was soft and silky beneath her exploring fingers.

During the lip-licking, exceptionally worthy kiss being delivered by the lawman, whose name she didn't even know, it occurred to her if she didn't die, this might be a little embarrassing. But that flash didn't last long. Lawmen had always fascinated her. She loved their uniforms and their swagger. Her anxiety level dropped at the realization that the lawman would naturally protect her. That was what lawmen did. They protected people.

She was also in the frighteningly inky darkness, kissing a stranger as if they were long-parted lovers about to be separated again by circumstances beyond their control. The next item on her list of things not accomplished surfaced like a blinking neon sign in her lust-filled mind. Sex. Sex. She wanted sex.

If she was hell-bound on this death car, she didn't want merely satisfactory sex—she wanted amazing sex. Unlike her first time. While her second experience had been ultimately horrendous in its aftermath, she had put the bad memory from her mind to focus on the good from it—conceiving Emma, and moved on.

However, she'd never felt the heights of ecstasy like the kind she read about in stories by her favorite author, Cinnamon O'Tingle. Her best friend, Marissa, told her over and over again that sex could be fabulous and amazing...with the right guy. She wanted fabulous and amazing sex. Just once, before she died.

If his kiss were any indication, the lawman attached to her knew about the heights of ecstasy. Her legs tightened. His tongue swirled decadently with hers and made her wet in places usually Sahara desert dry. Her new mission became getting the lawman to take her to fabulous heights so when they plunged to their deaths, she could go without regrets.

The lawman's other hand ran down her back to her butt, and another pulse of moisture shot between her legs. His warm fingers branded her skin through her slacks. She quivered with the anticipation of experiencing sexual delights with this man

If his kiss could make her lose her fear of tight spaces and the imminent plunge to her death, sex with him might cure all her foolish fears.

She loosened her legs from around his hips and lowered them to the floor, sliding her body seductively against his all the way until her toes touched the floor. She pulled his torso down with her until she was kneeling. He bent over in half before he released her mouth.

"What are you doing?" he asked, and she noted he sounded slightly out of breath.

"I thought perhaps since you kissed so well, you might be amazing at sex too. I haven't had any in almost five years, and since I'm about to die anyway..." She stopped talking and attached her lips to his once again, trying to express with her mouth what she was too nervous to say out loud. He squatted in front of her and braced a hand on the floor, and for a moment, she thought she had convinced him. Anticipation coiled around her spine and sent an electric charge to the space between her legs now ready, willing, and able to be pierced with the heights of ecstasy and pleasure.

He broke from her desperate take-me-now kiss and promptly doused her plans for sex in the deathtrap.

"I'm sorry, ma'am, but I'm not having sex with you in this elevator."

"But why not?" Grace was surprised. Her overriding urge to have sex with a gorgeous stranger evaporated quickly, replaced by anger. How dare he turn her down?

"This is a public elevator. I just hope the camera in the corner stopped recording when the lights went out."

She swiveled her head in the direction he was pointing. Then she stood up, squinting at the camera she could barely see. He straightened as well, towering behind her.

The lights came back on, and the elevator moved slowly for a moment or two before there was a ding and the doors opened on the fifth floor as if nothing interesting had transpired.

"Your stop, I believe," he said in a quietly amused tone.

Humiliation heated her cheeks. She was such a fool. A fraidy-cat fool who had accosted a lawman, no less, because of her fear of a stupid elevator. If it had been up to her, they'd be writhing on the floor half naked right now.

Thank heavens *he* had some control.

"Thanks," she said in a whisper and lowered her head to exit.

He stopped her with a hand to her shoulder. "My name is Jonathan

Brent," he offered, leaning in closer. "I hope you won't be afraid of elevators anymore."

She shook her head. "I'm not afraid of elevators. I just hate small, dark places."

He nodded and smiled. "Thanks for an interesting ride."

"Sure." She stepped off as supreme embarrassment engulfed her.

"What's your name?" he asked as the doors started to close. She turned her head, gave him a smile over one shoulder, and shook her head. He didn't need to know her name. He knew far too much already. He grinned boyishly as the doors closed. Jonathan Brent, the tall, gorgeous, dark-haired lawman with soft, gray eyes, fabulous kissing abilities, and a path she wished she could have followed.

"There you are! We've been waiting," said an impatient voice in the hallway. It was one of the men who worked for the district attorney.

"The elevator got stuck," she murmured and followed along behind his clipped stride, trying to keep up.

* * * *

"What took you so long?" David Elliott asked when Jonathan Brent made it to the courtroom on the seventeenth floor. Elliott was another lawman and Jon's immediate supervisor. An evil beast named Andrew Nelson was about to go free unless the D.A.'s surprise witness provided strong enough testimony to put him away.

"Elevator got stuck," he murmured as the salacious memory of the mystery girl licking his mouth slammed into his mind. "What's happening with the witness?"

"The D.A. has her in his office going over her testimony. If she testifies Nelson raped her five years ago and the judge believes her, then our old friend Andy will be going away for a long while."

Jon nodded. "Good."

"Sorry we couldn't get the evidence to put him away for Kevin and his wife."

Jon winced as the final image of his former partner covered in blood slid uncomfortably into his mind. Andy Nelson had raped and murdered Kevin's wife, and when Kevin had caught him in the act, Andy had butchered him. "As long as he rots in prison, I don't care what puts him there. Why didn't they have this witness during the earlier part of the trial?"

Elliott shrugged and sat behind his desk. "Didn't know about her. She brought the very first complaint against Andy, but her case got postponed and never brought back up. Plus the idiot D.A. back then decided it was a family court issue and dropped the case."

"Why?"

"She got pregnant from the incident."

Jon felt regret for the poor girl even this many years later. "Who was it?"

"A sixteen-year-old girl he knew from his high school. A member of her family found her handcuffed in a small basement room after he violated her and left her there. He only cut her once. He didn't have time to butcher her like the others.

"The parents brought him up on charges of aggravated statutory rape, but the case was postponed when the parents died in a car accident a year later," Elliott read from a file on his hand-held computer.

"Poor kid." Jon hated violence against women and instantly thought of his two older sisters. He made a mental note to call and make sure they were safe.

They discussed a few more details of the case until it was time to leave for the hearing down the hall. Jon sat at the very back of the courtroom. The defendant, Andy Nelson, was brought in with his sleazy lawyer. The D.A. stood opposite them at his table and shuffled papers until the judge entered.

"Have you brought your witness, Mr. Warren?" the judge asked the D.A.

"Yes, Your Honor."

"I renew my objection to this witness, Your Honor," the sleazy defense lawyer said. Jon didn't usually hate lawyers so adamantly, nor did he think of them all as sleazy, but Andy Nelson's lawyer was the very definition of sleazy and the very worst of ambulance-chasers.

"Noted," the judge replied curtly. He nodded to the D.A. "Call in your witness."

A bailiff opened a side door and called out, "Mrs. Grace Maitland

Cox."

Jon, glad this unseen witness had been able to overcome the horrible trauma of her youth enough to get married, silently applauded her resilience.

The witness entered the courtroom and Jon's breathing stopped. The mystery girl from the elevator took the witness stand, placed her hand on a bible, and swore to tell the truth, the whole truth, and nothing but the truth, so help her God.

He didn't hear her testimony, the weight of which actually swayed the judge enough to put Andy Nelson behind bars where he belonged for twenty-five years. The only fact reverberating in his head was that she was married and thus unavailable for him to pursue.

Which was a damn shame, since she was the first woman ever to have any impact on his usually dormant sexual desires.

Chapter 1

Earth, 2078
Tiberius Justice Center
Two years after the Tiberius Group takeover of the U.S.

"What's my first bid for this fine-looking little lady?" the auctioneer asked from the podium centered on the small stage.

"*What* fine-looking little lady?" someone called from the audience.

The auctioneer glanced at the empty spot where Grace was supposed to be standing, and frowned. She didn't want to go out to the stage. She didn't want to be bid on like last year's merchandise now on sale at bargain basement prices. She wanted her daughter back.

They'd taken Emma into custody yesterday morning pending the outcome of today's auction. Danny had promised he would be out in the audience to rescue her today, but she was afraid to step onstage and find him absent from the proceedings. It wouldn't be the first time he had let her down, but after today, it might be the last.

"Come on out so they can get a look at you." The auctioneer motioned her over again, and she reluctantly shuffled out to the big X marked on the stage. X marked the spot for her final destruction.

"Let's start the bidding at a hundred dollars," the auctioneer announced to the small room. The rows and rows of folding chairs were maybe a fifth full, Grace noted. Not a big turnout today. That wasn't necessarily bad; she didn't want her bidding price to be driven higher than they could afford.

Once positioned on the X, she searched the darkened room for Danny and breathed a sigh of relief when she saw him sitting next to his friend Walter in the last row. The stage lights above warmed her face. It made seeing the audience difficult, but at least she didn't have to worry any longer. Danny was here, just like he'd promised.

She would have to be especially nice to him tonight. He would certainly demand it after going out of his way to do this huge favor for her. A shiver of revulsion coursed through her at the thought of what he expected. He'd get his handcuffs out again. She put the ugly thought away for later. Instead, she concentrated on her only reason for continued existence: her daughter, Emma. Once Danny bid on her, she would get Emma back. Nothing else mattered.

Last night they had discussed how much money could be spent on her auction price, and Danny had calculated that a hundred dollars—the auctioneer's starting price—was the top end of what they could afford. She'd hesitated to tell him about the two hundred sixty-three dollars she had squirreled away for emergencies. She'd consoled herself with the knowledge that if the bidding went higher, she'd call out to Danny and tell him about the hidden money.

"Do I hear a hundred dollars for this fine young lady?"

The room was dead silent.

Grace knew that sometimes men simply raised a hand or finger or twitched their nose to bid. The auctioneer would then point into the audience, and the bidding would continue. Something was wrong, because the man at the podium stood silent. His finger remained still.

"Come on, men. A hundred dollars is the price of a fast food meal for four. Besides, we only have twelve women for auction today. I see more than thirty of you out there. Now, what's my bid for this lovely young girl?"

The silence in the room bore down on Grace. Why didn't Danny say something?

"All right then, maybe a hundred dollars is a bit rich for the first bid today. Does anyone have a bid? Any amount at all. Just call it out."

Some whispering ensued. She frowned as the sound of snickering laughter came from the direction of the man who was supposed to rescue her. She'd spent years supporting him. Danny had finally graduated from college only because she had killed herself to pay for it. Now he was supposed to return the favor and save her. What on earth was he up to? She'd been worried about him getting off his lazy butt to show up at all here today, but not that he would snicker and refuse to bid. He knew what was at stake: Emma.

The door at the back of the auction room banged opened, and a bright shaft of light from the outside hallway of the justice building silhouetted a tall form in the doorway before it shut, blocking her view. Grace couldn't see who'd come in, but she had deeper concerns anyway.

"Danny?" she called out in his direction. "Why won't you bid?"

"Hush now, little lady, you aren't allowed to speak during the auction."

"But…"

"But nothing. Quiet down now." The auctioneer turned back to the audience. "This is your last chance, gentlemen. So what's my first bid?"

Again the silence slammed into Grace, and she fought the urge to scream at the unfairness of it all.

The auctioneer heaved a long sigh and announced, "Well, I'm going to take a guess that you men out there want to see *all* the women before you start bidding. So I'll send this first little girl back now and bring her out again one last time after you've seen all the other women available. You'll see she's a rare find for a man."

The auctioneer motioned her back offstage. Grace heard more snickering and a bark of laughter in her wake. She paused and took one last look over her shoulder as she exited the stage. The next woman marched out to the big black X. Before the auction had started, Grace had heard the woman say there was someone out in the audience waiting to bid on her.

Grace had thought the very same thing, only she had been wrong.

She wanted to go out in the audience, punch Danny one, and demand to know what he was thinking. He could have bid twenty dollars so this humiliation would be over, and Emma would be saved. She closed her eyes, realizing for the umpteenth time that she wouldn't even be here if someone hadn't tattled on them.

Two days ago, a member of the Tiberius Group Family Planning Center had shown up demanding to see their marriage license and adoption paperwork. The representative informed them an anonymous call had been received about a bogus marriage arrangement. Unfortunately, the proper paperwork didn't exist because she and Danny hadn't ever been married.

Danny had told her years ago that they were technically married because they had shared the same address for more than a year. He'd quoted an archaic rule called common law marriage, which he had read about in one of his college classes. She'd believed him, like an idiot.

The Tiberius representative said common law was invalid and cited them for living in sin, outside the bonds of marriage. Danny promptly told them he and Grace had never participated in any sexual activity. This information made the representative even angrier, and he asked where her nearest male relative resided. When he found out she didn't have anyone, he filled out an electronic form on the clipboard he held. He informed Grace in no uncertain terms that she would be participating in an auction in two days' time as an unattached female charge of the state.

No amount of arguing or uncontrollable weeping had changed the pious bully's mind.

Thus, here she was, awaiting her fate and wondering what she had done to deserve this. Oh yes, she remembered. Once, a long time ago, she had made a terrible error in judgment. She'd been attracted to a good-looking boy from school who turned evil after she gave in to his advances. Grace realized once again the full extent of that blunder. Would she ever stop paying for that mistake?

She glanced at the auction house security guards. There were five of them to keep the twelve women up for auction subdued. If she made a run for it, they would shoot her like a rabid animal and deposit her in the nearest trash receptacle. Someone *had* to bid on her today. If she remained single after today's auction, her new home would be the Tiberius Institute for Orphaned Women. Worse, they'd take Emma away forever.

Once at the Institute, she'd be farmed off to a work camp to do menial tasks. Then, every three or four months, the Institute would put her up for auction to the poverty-stricken hoards of men looking for sex partners. The Institute paid men a stipend to take women off their hands and marry them. The longer a woman remained in custody, the more the stipend went up.

At her last job, Grace had seen a couple of women who'd been purchased at auction from the Institute. Hunched over in perpetual acquiescence, they'd had a haunted look. Perhaps they were grateful not to be at the Institute any longer, but Grace thought the circumstances of their daily lives were only a small step forward. Until yesterday, she'd never imagined facing the same dilemma.

When Grace went back out for her final chance at auction, she'd have to beg someone to bid on her. She wouldn't lose Emma only to face a fate worse than death directly afterwards.

* * * *

Jonathan Brent entered the auction room on a mission: to find a scam artist named Walter Dennis. As scam artists went, he was fairly low-rent, but a couple of days ago he'd conned a magistrate's elderly mother out of some money and had consequently elevated his arrest status.

Elliott had gotten the heads-up from an anonymous call that Walter would be present at today's auction at the Tiberius Justice Center, so he'd sent Jon to pick him up. If Walter was there and Jon made the arrest, the caller would get a reward sent to a private account. All snitches were graciously protected under Tiberius rule, especially the anonymous ones.

Jon signed the electronic registration sheet, and the clerk handed him a bid number. If he wanted to, he could kill two birds with one stone and acquire a wife today as he slapped handcuffs on Walter. He let out a disgusted breath at the way women were treated with regard to marriage. He had the utmost compassion for them, having grown up with a very loving mother and two tolerably pleasant older sisters. But even if he did find the perfect woman here today, he would never bid on her.

Career lawmen didn't have time for wives, in his opinion. He was away from home four to six months a year chasing scumbags across the galaxies, and being a lawman's wife was not the lonely life he wanted to subject a woman to.

Besides, he thought, he'd never found a woman who stirred him enough anyway. That wasn't entirely true, he knew. He still held a fond memory of a certain scorching kiss in a darkened elevator. He had been reminded of it earlier when he'd passed that very same elevator. As he entered the auction room, his mind filled with the memory of the dark space where she'd sizzled his lips with the most erotic and satisfying kiss Jon had ever shared.

He hadn't pursued her because he'd found out she was married. Plus she was the mother of a child sired by Andy Nelson. It was a hard fact to get past since the serial rapist had violated and murdered his partner's wife in cold blood right before murdering his partner, Kevin, for attempting to save her. It had been the single bloodiest night of his life and the worst case he'd endured to date.

He was interrupted from his morose reverie by a woman's voice echoing passionately from the stage. His eyes hadn't quite adjusted to the darkness in the room. For a moment, he thought he recognized the voice, but he was more intrigued by the fact that she'd spoken at all. Jon hadn't thought the women up for auction in this venue were allowed to speak. Then the auctioneer berated her. *Poor girl,* he thought, and then dismissed her from his mind to search the room for Walter.

"But nothing. Quiet down now." The auctioneer said to the woman, then turned back to the audience. "This is your last chance now. So what's my bid?"

Jon scanned the dimly lit room. Even with his secretly enhanced vision, he couldn't see a damn thing. He closed his eyes again momentarily in a meager attempt to help them correct.

The auctioneer spoke again. "Well, I'm going to take a guess that you men out there want to see all the women before you start bidding. So I'll send this first little girl back now and bring her out again one last time after you've seen all the other women available. You'll see she's a rare find for a man."

Jon felt immediate sympathy for the poor woman who hadn't been bid on. She was destined for a much worse fate if she ended up at the Tiberius Institute. He opened his eyes and saw the unauctioned female shuffle off stage. She looked vaguely familiar, and when she paused to turn her head to take a glance over her shoulder, he got an unexpected punch directly to his gut. The girl from the elevator. Grace Maitland Cox. What on earth was she doing here?

Shaken for a moment at seeing her again, Jon paused as his eyes fully adjusted to the absence of light in the room. Perhaps he'd stay and find out why Grace was up for auction. Or perhaps his genetically enhanced eyes were playing tricks on him. Maybe it wasn't Grace, but he was intrigued enough to stick around to find out for certain.

He spotted his target, Walter, in the back row of chairs and strolled over to stand behind him. Walter, a seriously skinny man with long, stringy hair in his mid-twenties, was currently engaged in a whispered conversation with another man seated next to him. Jon listened in easily, even standing several feet away.

"Did you see her face, Danny? You really made her mad," Walter was saying to his friend.

"She's going to be more than mad at the end of this auction. I can't wait to see the surprise on her face then." Walter's friend, Danny, looked like the Pillsbury Doughboy, only taller—but not by much. He was soft and out of shape and looked like a lazy couch potato.

"Are you sure this'll work?" Walter whispered as the next woman went up for bid.

"Of course. I researched it. When nobody bids on her today, she goes to the Tiberius Institute. At the end of a year, you can go and get her and they'll pay you three hundred dollars. It's a great deal. And the best part is you won't have to worry about raising her brat either. No one wants to raise a psycho prisoner's kid."

Jon straightened up. It was too much of a coincidence for the woman *not* to be Grace. The opportunity to see her once more became very appealing. At the very least, he could rescue her from the life of bondage she would endure at the Institute. He'd love to get her alone in a dark elevator one more time. All he had to do was make a single bid.

The memory of her sweet lips kissing him in the dark three years ago danced in his mind, forcing him to take a deep breath to calm down. He tried to keep in mind that he was in the room to catch and arrest a criminal, not to find a wife. No matter how luscious the thought of a wedding night with Grace might be, he was here on business.

"Well, what if somebody gets her before the year is up?" Walter whined. It shook Jon out of his lust-filled reverie of a honeymoon with Grace.

"Who's going to want a woman who can't have any more kids and is so terrified of sex she faints when it's suggested?"

"No one at this auction," Walter said, and together they snorted in laughter and did a quiet high-five.

Jon concluded the two idiots must have spread word about her past around the small auction so the others in attendance wouldn't bid either. Well, Jon would have to bid on her now. His new personal mission was to thwart these two morons. He couldn't wait to see their faces when he offered for Grace. He had several thousand dollars at his disposal should he need it. Now more than ever, he was determined to save her.

"But when she's mine to do with as I please, I'll do what you said. I'll tie her down and fuck her so she won't be afraid of sex or faint anymore." Walter looked a little too excited at the prospect of tying Grace down so he could 'fuck' her. Jon wanted to cuff him in the head for the foolish, vulgar remark, but didn't want to ruin the surprise.

First, he'd secure the high bid on Grace, and then he'd arrest Walter's sorry ass.

"No. You have to handcuff her and make sure the room is pitch-black. She needs to relive the experience from her past that terrifies her before she can move on to a better life. I'm a counselor with a college degree now, so I know," Mr. Playdough said pompously.

"How come you didn't handcuff her and fix her a long time ago?"

"I tried once, but she dropped like a rock when I snapped the first cuff shut. Besides, she never did anything for me sexually. My dick only gets hard for Sadie."

Jon fisted his hand to keep from punching the soft man Grace had counted on to rescue her. He wished he could let her know she wouldn't go to the Institute. She was probably in the back, worried sick about her fate.

"Are you going to marry Sadie now?" Walter asked.

"Probably. But first I have to make sure Grace and her brat are out of my place for good. I only kept her around because my parents said she needed a place to stay once her aunt got sick. She helped a little with finances too. Her old biddy of an aunt is dead three months now, and once Grace and her kid are gone, I'll be a totally free man."

"You sure were lucky. How did the Tiberius Group find out you and Grace weren't married all this time anyway?"

"They got an anonymous call." Danny snickered again. Jon had no doubt as to the identity of the 'anonymous' caller who had sealed

Grace's fate.

Jon seethed as he listened to their conversation. He figured Danny was probably making lots of anonymous phone calls. Wouldn't Walter be surprised to find himself in jail later today? What a bastard.

Grace hadn't been married three years ago when she'd kissed Jon. Interesting. It put a whole new spin on those few minutes he'd spent in the dark wrapped around a woman who made him forget who he was and where he was.

Back then he wondered why she'd been so forward since an hour later he'd found out she was Mrs. Grace Maitland Cox. He'd dismissed her as unavailable and very frightened of the dark, nothing more. He'd done his good deed and hadn't taken things too far, but it had been very difficult to turn her down. He'd cursed himself more than once for not having taken advantage of her intriguing offer.

"You're so smart, Danny," Walter whispered. "An anonymous phone call was a great idea."

Jon knew part of his motivation was curiosity about Grace, but he couldn't wait to put a big wrench in their plans. He'd wait to arrest Walter until after Grace came up for bid the second time. When they didn't bid on her, he would. Not to keep her, of course, but to rescue her from the Institute. He'd take Walter to jail and then help Grace relocate with her child. It was all in a day's work, and besides it would be great to see her again. He could kiss her once after the ceremony before he let her go. He closed his eyes in reverent contemplation. It probably wasn't a good idea to get his lips anywhere near hers if he planned to let her go. Did he want to let her get away?

The next woman out was quickly sold for a hundred and twenty-five dollars. The next four women also went quickly. If this pace kept up, he'd have a wife in less than twenty minutes. The thought of Grace being his wife, even for a short time, forced his libido into overdrive and spiked his lust. He'd thought about her many times in the past several years. Especially when he'd been lonely or whenever he entered an elevator. His unguarded thoughts would conjure up that first lick of her tongue across his lips. His cock stirred with this train of thought, surprising him.

Jon had controlled needs that he relieved infrequently, but couldn't remember the first name of any women in his sexual past, with the single exception of hers. Mostly, he used a synthetic injection to quench his desire, but he still needed an actual sexual experience once every year or so. The requirement angered him because it made him feel no better than Andy Nelson. Unlike the evil beast who'd killed his partner, Jon would never force a woman to assuage his needs.

He'd rather die.

Jon could be married to Grace for two days before they would have to consummate the marriage to be permanently wed. Forty-eight hours to think about all the sexual delights he *wouldn't* be participating in. His long dormant libido reared up suddenly to seduce him with a licentious visual of him and Grace and his oversized bed. It wouldn't be the first time he'd pictured her there. It wouldn't be the last either, especially not after seeing her today.

Jon inhaled deeply, knowing he would never have sex with Grace. His only intent was to save her from the Institute, then find her another husband. Someone who wasn't vile, like the man she lived with or his scam artist friend, Walter. The thought of finding a husband for Grace made his gut tighten for some unfathomable reason.

His communicator vibrated silently on his belt. A DC-5 message from Elliott, his boss. DC-5 was their personal code for red-hot emergency. Jon noted the time and exited the room quietly. Out in the hallway, he called headquarters to see what the Damned Chaos to the Fifth Power message was about.

"It's Brent. What's up?"

Jon heard an urgent, angry voice instead of Elliott's usual drawl. "I just got a notification bulletin for a new trial review on Andy Nelson. The Tiberius Group is reevaluating his case."

"You've got to be fucking kidding me. Why?"

"They're going through all old cases where the testimony of a woman was the predominant factor used to put a man in prison. Lots of cases have been overturned in the last few years. Perhaps you've heard mention of it?" Elliott was being sarcastic.

Jon knew several big-name cases had been overturned in which the word of only one woman had put a man away. Cases involving rape were particularly susceptible to this trend.

"Yeah, so what? They've only overturned cases with power names. Nelson isn't a prominent name."

"Well, they've been busy reviewing any and all cases with single female testimony convictions. It's just taken a couple of years to get to Nelson's. We knew this would come up, Jon."

"He's a sexual vampire. They have his paperwork."

"He's been using a synthetic medication called Zanthacorth to temper his sexual urges while he's in prison, where he's been a model inmate, by the way."

"You know as well as I do, if he gets out, he'll rape again. He likes it. No amount of medication will stop him once he's free."

"I know. That's why I used DC-5 to get your attention. Go dig up the old case file and find anything that will lead to evidence on any of the other victims. We need to find something and soon."

"We don't even know how many victims there are. We only identified two cases for sure, and both victims died from their injuries before they could testify."

"Do the best you can."

"How much time do I have?"

"Less than a week. You need to get moving on this now."

Jon closed his eyes and wondered how on earth he'd find any evidence on a cold case for which he'd looked at every conceivable angle the first futile time. Andy Nelson had been as good as released when the D.A. had stumbled across Grace Maitland Cox to testify.

Oh, no. Damn it. Grace. The auction.

Jon looked up at the closed-circuit camera feed on the monitor outside the auction room. It was showing the part of the auction he'd momentarily forgotten he'd planned to participate in. On the silent screen, he could see a tearful Grace onstage, crying out what looked like "Please, someone, bid on me!"

He snapped his phone shut in mid-conversation with Elliott and bolted toward the auction room, hoping he wasn't too late.

Chapter 2

Grace haltingly re-entered the stage. Every other woman ahead of her up for auction had fairly flown off the stage. She couldn't figure it out.

She was in serious trouble if she wasn't attractive enough to get a single desperate guy to bid. Even with her nearly non-existent pride, she had hoped for more than one offer besides Danny's today. But she hadn't even gotten *him* to bid. And he'd laughed when she'd exited the stage the first time. She'd know that whiney nasal snicker anywhere.

As each subsequent woman was snapped up, Grace formulated a plan to beg. She didn't care if she wasn't supposed to speak. She wanted her daughter back. Once they found out about the identity of Emma's father and her inability to have any more children, she'd have a hard enough time keeping any other man interested. She'd deal with that when the time came.

The auction was all she could manage for now.

"Here is the last female we have up for auction today. So you'd better get her while you can. Now, what's my bid for this lovely, young girl?"

Again, every man became mute. Grace couldn't help the angry tears tumbling over her lower lids. Emma's forlorn little face at yesterday's tearful separation swam in front of her eyes.

"Surely one man among you is willing to bid on this female. Look how pretty she is."

Tears fell copiously, and she sniffed loudly at the very moment everyone was supposed to see how pretty she was.

"Please," she whimpered. "Please."

"Little lady, you can't speak. I told you already. Now why won't anyone bid on this sweet little girl?"

"Because she's frigid and terrified of sex. Plus she's got another bastard's kid already, and she can't have any more children. She's completely worthless. Give it up. No one's bidding on her," said a callous voice from the audience Grace didn't recognize.

How did the man in the audience know all her secrets?

Grace squinted through her tears to search for Danny. He smiled in that superior way he had, making her feel small and valueless as a human. *He* apparently had made sure no one would bid on her today. She should have known. Now when she went to the Institution, they would pay him to marry her, but Emma would be gone to her forever. She fought the urge to run into the audience and strangle him.

"Please, someone, bid on me!" she screamed in anguish, not caring that she wasn't allowed to speak.

"Hush now. No more talking," the auctioneer admonished her again and then turned to the audience to seal her fate.

"No one willing to bid on this female? Not anyone in this room? You are all a bunch of damn fools." The auctioneer shook his head and raised his gavel to seal her fate as an institutionalized female. She covered her ears to muffle the sound of her doom.

The doors to the back of the room burst open and bounced off the interior walls. Grace lowered her hands. A huge lawman strode through the door and shouted, "I bid ten dollars over the standing floor bid for this woman."

"Sold to the lawman for ten dollars," the auctioneer said, not missing a beat, as if he'd expected the bid all along. He banged his gavel to complete the deal. Grace bent over in grateful disbelief. She was sold. Thank heavens. She didn't care if it was the devil himself who'd just bought her. She could have Emma back. She straightened quickly and looked to see who owned her. Her future husband would not be Danny. She found that a huge relief too. She didn't know what her future husband would want, but she knew exactly what Danny expected.

"Wait, I'll bid twenty dollars for her," Danny's friend Walter called out.

"Too late," the auctioneer said, "You gave up the right to bid when I asked the room."

"Well, the other guy was in the room earlier too, and he left. He shouldn't get special privileges."

"I'm a federal interstellar lawman. I was called away momentarily on official business. What's your excuse for not bidding the first time?"

Walter snapped his lips shut, pressing them flat, and gave the lawman a sullen look, as if he were the one being treated unfairly.

Grace listened to her savior speak, and a tingle of recognition brushed against her memory. She put a hand up to her brow to block the floodlights above her and to get a glimpse of the lawman soon to be her husband. He looked vaguely familiar.

"What's your name, Lawman?" the auctioneer asked.

"Jonathan Brent."

Grace sucked in a breath.

"Well then, this little lady is about to become a lawman's wife." He banged the gavel again. "Sold for ten dollars to the lawman, Jonathan Brent."

Walter started to protest again, but Grace ignored him, still stunned at the name of her intended husband. Jonathan Brent.

He was the lawman in the elevator from three years ago. Not a single day had gone by that she hadn't thought about his strong body hugged close to hers. The initial brush of his firm lips sliding over her mouth in the dark had crept into her dreams more than once.

She wiped the tears from her face and prepared to face him. Squinting into the dim light, she saw he was even more gorgeous than she had remembered. He exceeded six feet by several inches. His dark hair looked wiry and coarse, but she knew from personal experience it felt very soft sifting through her fingers. She couldn't see his eyes from this distance or in this light, but knew they were a comforting gray.

Grace waited onstage for him to come fetch her, but instead he crossed to where Danny and Walter were standing. She looked over at the auctioneer, who motioned for her to greet her soon-to-be husband. She wiped her face again, took a deep breath, and went to face her future. It was the first moment in a long while that she wasn't absolutely terrified. Grace's new-found courage lasted only until she saw her future lawman husband pull a set handcuffs off his belt.

She paused, waiting to see what he was going to do with them.

Was he about to handcuff her?

"Walter Dennis, I have an order from a magistrate to bring you in for criminal activity."

"What?" Walter looked at Jonathan as if he'd only just noticed he was a lawman and then turned to run. The tall, menacing, yet gorgeous Jonathan clamped a hand on Walter's arm and stopped him. He had the handcuffs around Walter's wrists in no time. She brushed away the dread that came with her fear of being handcuffed and started moving toward her now bright future.

"How did you find me?" Walter asked.

"Someone ratted you out and called in an 'anonymous' tip as to your whereabouts. I wonder who knew you'd be here today?" Jonathan asked.

Walter turned to Danny. His big, goofy face turned red. Grace wasn't the least bit surprised. She'd be willing to bet her last two hundred and sixty-three hidden dollars it was Danny who had ratted her out to the Tiberius Family Group too. She wanted to smack Danny, but decided she had already expended too much effort on him. It was time to move on to a better life as the wife of a federal interstellar lawman. She smiled for the first time in two days.

"Thank you. Thank you so much," Grace said to Jonathan, stepping close to him once she realized the handcuffs he brandished weren't for her.

"Sure. Listen, I hate to do this to you, but unfortunately, Walter will have to accompany us to the wedding ceremony."

"It doesn't matter. I'm so grateful you bid on me. You saved me— again."

Jonathan Brent tilted his head and gave her an engaging smile. "Come on. I need to get going." She wanted to throw her arms around him and bury her face into his throat. She knew she would be safe in his arms. He was a lawman. That was what lawmen did. They protected people.

"Wait a minute. Don't you want to know what you're getting for a wife? She has serious sexual problems, and she's got a kid too."

"Danny, shut up. You have no right to say a word." Grace operated under the hope that Jonathan didn't know all of her secrets. He hadn't entered the room until after the loudmouth in the audience had announced her life story. Perhaps she still had a chance to keep him.

The tempting and wicked thought of sex with him already danced around her brain. She remembered begging him for amazing sex in the elevator. He had turned her down then, but perhaps not because he wasn't interested. Perhaps her future husband had bid on her today so he could take her to some quiet place to make fabulous and amazing love to her. A buzzing sensation vibrated her long-buried sexual arousal wide-awake. It was about damn time for some amazing sex in her life.

Jonathan turned a ferociously lustful gaze toward her and winked. "Believe me, I know exactly who I'm getting for a wife." Grace smiled and held his stare. She relived the kiss in the elevator as if it had happened a minute ago. Her tongue slipped out to wet her lower lip. She couldn't wait to get him alone.

"But she's frigid." Danny insisted, as if Jonathan were too stupid to understand his brilliant analysis. Grace frowned at him, willing him to shut his fat face and leave her be.

"Not with me, she's not." Jonathan averted his gaze from her and scowled at Danny. "I know everything I need to know about her. You, on the other hand, are trying my patience. Get lost."

"Don't come crying to me when she won't have sex with you. I'm warning you, you'll have to handcuff her to a bed to cure her sexual deviance." Danny put his hand on his waist as if to suggest the lawman was the most obtuse human ever.

Jonathan frowned at him. "You're one sick bastard, you know that? Trust me, I won't cry to you for anything. She's not frigid. I suspect she told *you* that so she wouldn't have to endure your soft, clammy hands. Back up." Jonathan took a menacing step in Danny's direction, dragging Walter behind him. Danny frowned and took a shuffling step away.

Jonathan turned to her. "Ready to go?" She nodded and fell into step behind him. He had earned her eternal gratitude for telling Danny off the way she had wanted to for years, but couldn't. In her position as second-class citizen, she had put up with loads of crap and endured years of biting her tongue to keep silent. She enjoyed giving Danny a smug smile on her way past him as she followed her delicious future lawman husband.

They filled out the paperwork, and a few minutes later, for the pitiful price of ten dollars, she was married to a man who made her heart pound in her chest. A cheap hamburger at a fast food joint cost more. Ah well, it didn't matter.

Her new lawman husband held onto Walter during the ceremony, but she didn't care. She could get Emma back, which was the only important thing. She'd get a honeymoon, which was another thing gathering importance low in her belly. A heart-pounding vibrancy radiated through her at the thought of a real honeymoon night. Sex with Jonathan would certainly be the pinnacle of her sexual experience, as long as he didn't handcuff her or hold her arms down. She spoke her vows to love, honor, and—most importantly to the Tiberius Group—to obey her new husband. She wondered what he might require of her in the bedroom. They were pronounced man and wife. *Thank heavens.*

"How are you going to fulfill the forty-eight hour consummation dictate, Grace?" Danny asked.

Danny lingered several steps away, approaching her only after the marriage vows had been spoken. "You know the minute he snaps the handcuffs tight you'll faint. You should have let me cure you a long time ago…"

She didn't have time to answer. Jonathan pulled the regulation-issue weapon off of his belt, checked the load—presumably to make sure it was ready to fire—and gave Danny a positively satanic glare. His wicked-looking gun was pointed at the floor, but the threat was unmistakable. Grace wondered if Jonathan was going to shoot him.

"I've heard enough out of you. Grace and I will be at your residence later on to pick up her things. I don't need a reason to shoot you. Quit trying to give me one. Grace is my wife. She was never yours. I suggest you leave. Now." He tightened the grip on the gun's handle.

Jonathan radiated an aura of anger she could stick a fork through, and even she could tell he was trying to calm down and not kill her ex-roommate.

Danny gave them both a sour look and retreated, finally figuring out he shouldn't aggravate a grumpy lawman.

Jonathan promptly leveled the gun at Walter's chest. "Don't move, or I shoot to kill. Do you understand me?" At Walter's fearful nod, Jonathan wrapped his free arm around her waist and pulled her close before she realized his intent. His firm lips landed on hers in a passionate kiss. Even this early in the morning, he had a tantalizing five o'clock shadow on his face. His delicious scent wrapped around her with his sizzling, warm body pressed close.

Grace melted into him as her knees weakened. Her hands went to his chest first, then circled around his neck and anchored herself to his strong warrior body. She ran a hand up the back of his head, through his silky hair. Unlike the vigorous, eager kiss in the elevator, this one was lazy and thorough. He kissed her tenderly, stroking his tongue slowly and methodically against hers as if he had all the time in the world to make love to her mouth. She sagged in his arms, unable to hold herself upright any longer, and heard moaning.

Oh God, she was moaning!

He didn't stop his sultry assault of her lips, even at her noisy response. Several long moments later, he released her mouth, then kissed her chastely once or twice more before releasing the clench they shared, as if he hated to let her go. Grace didn't want to let him go either. She held onto his free arm while instructing her legs to work. Jonathan winked at her, turned his head, and gave Danny a satisfied smirk.

"Thank you so much," she whispered before peeling away.

"You're welcome. Come on, I need to go. We've got to drop off Walter at division headquarters, pick up your things, and then I imagine you'll want to get your child back."

Grace was so overcome by joy at his understanding of the situation, she couldn't speak. Mouth opened in shock, she recovered to throw her arms around his neck, pulled him back down, and buried her face in his throat. She trembled against him as silent tears of gratitude fell onto the sleeve of his gray and black uniform jacket. "Thank you so much," she said as another tremor of gratitude shook her voice. He patted her back as she got her emotions under control again.

Thank heaven's she was the lawman's wife. A nagging voice reminded her she wasn't his wife permanently until they consummated the union. Apprehension and longing vied for attention at the thought of the conjugal rights he could now demand.

She couldn't help the wicked smile that shaped her lips in contemplation.

* * * *

Jon held Grace's soft body and wondered what in the hell he was doing with a wife. But then, she had cried and thanked him after he'd mentioned picking up her kid. She wanted her child back, understandably enough. He didn't fool himself about her ultimate motives, but kissing her a moment ago had been very gratifying. When she'd moaned into his mouth, it was all he could do to stay vertical. He wanted her desperately, just as he had in the elevator during their first kiss.

The memory of her request for sex on the floor of the small, darkened space slid into his mind. He knew her demand was fear induced because she thought she was about to die. He'd almost done it too. His hand had gone to the fastener on his trousers, his libido ready, willing, and able to comply with her wishes. He imagined how exceptionally good it would feel to plunge his cock into her soft, grateful flesh. How volcanically amazing it would feel to take her with him to heights he'd only experienced a very few times in his own past. It would be paradise to share his life with a woman he wanted more than any other. He'd be able to forgo the injections and allow his sexual urges free rein.

Kissing Grace was inherently more satisfying than the whole of his past sexual encounters combined. The vision of her trusting face popped his bubble. He shook his head and told his libido to calm down. He wasn't having sex with Grace Maitland. He'd find a better man for her. Someone stable, who didn't jet off at a moment's notice to fight crime across the interstellar galaxy. He ignored the longing that erupted at the thought of losing her. Grace deserved a better life than he could provide.

He planned to discuss this issue with his eldest sister Sophie's husband, Matthew Westland. Matt ran his own import-export business and employed thousands of men. Surely he knew a stable junior executive who wanted a wife. He ignored the pain pinching his gut at the thought of Grace submitting herself sexually to a stable low-level businessman from Matt's company.

He hustled Walter out of the Justice Center with Grace following them. Jon shoved Walter into the back of his Interstellar Lawman's Thorium-Z cruiser, also known as his IL T-Z cruiser vehicle. Every lawman had one issued to him. It was a standard sedan with a clear, synthetic laser-resistant and bulletproof partition between the front and back seats. The outer windows were equipped with similar protective glass, and like all government vehicles, it ran on Thorium-Z, the clean-burning replacement for fossil fuels.

He opened the front door for Grace to get in and then circled to get in himself. By the time he slipped behind the wheel, she already had her seat restraint on. He regretted having to drag her along to the Law Enforcement Detention Center before they could proceed.

"Once we get to the LED Center, stay close to me."

She nodded and smiled warmly. He had no doubt she'd do anything he asked. He tried to tamp down his libido. He didn't get to keep her. A temporary marriage would not include imminent sexual activity. His lust, unfortunately, was not convinced, and he knew he'd have to find a way to inject himself with medication to control his now rampant urges. He would usher Grace and her child into his spare bedroom right before he locked himself securely in his own room.

Jon punched the vehicle start code on the numbered pad and pressed his thumb on the biometric print reader, turning the vehicle's engine over. He put his foot on the pedal and revved the engine a time or two, listening to the satisfying roar. Thorium-Z was a great replacement for gasoline vehicles from days long past.

Jon flipped the sirens on and sped toward the LED Center. He loved to drive fast and took every opportunity to do so. He loved being a lawman. It was all he'd ever wanted to do.

Twenty years before his birth, in the mid-2020s, the U.S. government had made a surprising yet decisive move and combined all law enforcement under a single command hierarchy. This served to eliminate with one fell swoop not only redundant efforts by law enforcement in general, but also all jurisdictional in-fighting among the different federal and state agencies. Thus, "the lawman," a single entity comprised of all police and law enforcement in the country, came to be.

Lawmen all wore the same black, charcoal gray, and red uniforms; the only distinction involved a delineation of experience and departmental level. A lawman could be at a local, state, federal, or interstellar department level. The patch his shoulder signified that he was at the top of the experience hierarchy. Jon had earned his stripes quickly before becoming a federal interstellar lawman five years ago. At this juncture in his career, he enjoyed the most flexibility of all his fellow law enforcement brotherhood and took pleasure in the freedom accorded to him. The downside was that he traveled—a lot. He was on the road more than at home.

The National Defense Bureau came about directly after the Tiberius Group took over and replaced the previous courtroom trials with a new arbitration system. Years later, everyone was still getting used to the new system. The Tiberius Group didn't like lawyers and were particularly intolerant of frivolous lawsuits. Ultimately, they denigrated much of the entire justice system, along with several parameters of his job.

The predominant outcome was a disintegration of women's rights. He and his fellow lawmen had spent the first several months trying to keep women from going out alone. Jon had kept his opinions to himself with regard to the new status of women. He knew several men who had spoken out and ended up in jail, missing, or worst of all, dead.

The ruling voice of the Tiberius Group would not be stifled or stopped. They told everyone the changes were necessary and promised a better system of justice in time as the laws were amended and rewritten. Jon only knew he had been very busy since the takeover.

In two short years, they had changed the greater part of judicial law to arbitration under the magistrate core. Defendants and plaintiffs stood alone against each other these days, which meant a significant reduction in work for lawyers. The district attorney's office was the last and best place left as a career option if a man wanted to be a lawyer. Otherwise, they were at the mercy of the dwindling private sector.

The private sector consisted of the rich who were still able to afford private lawyers, and many kept an attorney on retainer for consultations during significant magistrate hearings. However, those plum jobs were few and far between and the turnover rate was very high especially if a case was lost. There were still many hearings, but the frivolity of the past had given way to only serious offenses being heard by magistrates.

Technically, the charge against Walter Dennis was a minor one, but because his crime had been directed against the loved one of a magistrate, Jon didn't want to be in Walter's shoes for the upcoming hearing.

Grace remained silent and stayed on his heels as he processed Walter and turned him over to LED officials for his hearing.

"Where do you live?" he asked as they exited the center. She told him the address and grabbed his hand as they headed for his vehicle.

"After we pick up my things, are we going to go to your home before we get Emma?" she asked in a quiet voice as she stared at her feet.

"Emma?"

"My daughter."

Jon hadn't even known the gender of her child until this moment. He found a daughter inherently more palatable as the spawn of Andy Nelson than a son. Either way, it shouldn't matter. He would never blame the sins of the father on an innocent child. His own dad hadn't been much to brag about, but he and his sisters, Sophie and Hannah, had turned out just fine growing up without him.

"I thought you'd want to pick her up as soon as possible." Jon told her.

"I do, but..." Her cheeks turned a beautiful shade of pink.

"But?"

"But I know we need to consummate the marriage within forty-eight hours, and I'd feel more comfortable if Emma weren't..."

"We aren't going to consummate this marriage," he said curtly. His groin ached at the loss. His libido wasn't too happy either.

"Why not?" Grace turned to him, releasing his hand. Her face was no longer embarrassed, but surprised and fearful. Her clear, aqua-green eyes drilled down to his soul, asking him for a reason.

"I didn't bid to keep you, Grace. The Tiberius Institute is no place for a woman like you."

She stared at him as she digested his honorable intentions. After a moment, she stepped back. The hurt registering on her face confused him.

"Why don't you want me this time? It won't be on a camera," she said in a heartbreaking voice. Her eyes glistened, boring into his with unshed tears, waiting for him to answer.

"It's not personal. I just don't lead the kind of life favorable to permanent marriage." The truth sounded lame to his own ears. His libido told him he was an idiot and promptly sent a scandalous picture of what

Grace might look like in the throes of passion, back arched in ecstasy—
Stop it.

He wished they could go someplace private to discuss his true
motives, both personal and work-related. Unfortunately, he didn't trust
himself to be alone with her. With her current let's-hurry-and-
consummate-the-marriage attitude, they'd be rolling around on his living
room rug before the front door closed behind them. Convinced he
wouldn't be able to resist her if she instigated things the way she had in
the elevator, he took a mental step away.

"What does that mean?"

He sighed deeply. "Could we discuss this in the vehicle instead of in
front of the detention center?"

She looked around as if only just noticing they were still in public.
Her face softened and she nodded. Taking her hand, he led her to his
cruiser, opened the passenger door for her, and circled slowly to his side,
trying to think of something that might placate her, but his mind was
blank.

He slid inside and as soon as his door shut, she jumped on him. She
twisted her body to face him, pinned him to his seat, and planted her
warm lips on his before he took his first breath inside the vehicle.

God Almighty, she tasted good. He surrendered to her exuberant kiss
because he couldn't help himself. His libido told him he was a fool not to
take advantage of her offer. Her tongue slipped between his lips and he
sucked it further inside his mouth to tangle with his own. His arms
wound around her torso, crushing her closer before he devoured her
mouth the way he'd wanted to since he'd known it was her on the
auction stage.

She was so soft and she kissed like an angel. She was his own
personal angel. As if it had a mind of its own, one of his hands slipped
around to cup her breast and knead it, making his fingertips tingle in
delight. Her sultry response was a sweet moan of mirrored pleasure and
acceptance. He flicked his thumb over the peak of her nipple, which rose
under his palm. He slipped his hand underneath her shirt to test the
softness of her skin. His exploring fingers found it even more satiny than
he'd expected.

Stroking her breast, he inhaled deeply at the softness he told himself he couldn't really feel through her lacy bra. Her unique scent captured him as she pressed closer, giving his body no choice but to respond. His pants tightened painfully across his dick. His libido won as he realized he wanted her with a single-mindedness he could no longer subdue. Jon plucked her nipple once again, and the sound of her moan ripped through him. He would take her and make her his permanent wife. She could be his family, his partner in life. He'd finally have someone to welcome him home with enthusiasm from his exhausting trips.

A vehicle horn sounded on the street, breaking his lustful romp with her in the front seat of the cruiser. What was he doing? He pushed her away, breathing hard, and stared at her now very moist and swollen lips. His cock was fully erect and ready to go. If they'd been alone in any sort of private place, he had no doubt she would already be his wife in the most intimate sense.

His permanent bride.

Her hand slipped from his shoulder, trailing slowly to his lap. He jumped when her fingers slid over his throbbing cock, caressing it through his uniform.

"I think you want me after all," she said in that low, husky, passion-filled voice.

"I never said I didn't want you." Jon thought his voice sounded sort of satanic, it was so deep in tone.

"Then why won't you make me your wife"—she gripped his erection and stroked her hand down the length of it—"in the flesh?" The scent of her skin, laced with the musky undertone of her arousal, pounded his senses.

He couldn't stop the growl when he responded, "I'm a lawman. I travel. A lot. I leave the country regularly, and I go off-world even more. I wouldn't be here to take care of you or protect you." *But I want to.*

She smiled at his confession, as if relieved. "I can take care of myself. I have for years. I want to be your wife. Please, take me and make me yours permanently. I've wanted you for so long." Her hand squeezed him as if to punctuate her need.

Her aqua eyes mesmerized him. Her hand, stroking rhythmically up and down on his cock, ultimately convinced him. Or at least it won over his lust-filled libido, which then forced him to nod at her in complete acceptance of her plea. He needed to calm down before they got to his home…and the privacy it would offer him. Otherwise he'd have to think of a way to protect her whenever he was forced to leave to do his job.

And who did he trust to protect his unexpected new wife while he was away?

The short answer was no one.

Chapter 3

"Put your restraint on," he told her in a tight voice. His gray eyes had darkened a shade. His lids lowered halfway. Grace hoped it was from undeniable passion, but suspected not.

She nodded and removed her hand from his very impressive erection. She'd be lying to herself over the idea that she wasn't terrified of having sex. She'd egged him on more for her own sake than his, which was easy to do in the light of day. If she riled him up enough, he'd simply take her and she'd be powerless to stop him. The thought of him entering her with his very impressive cock excited her as much as it frightened her. She did want him. And besides, she needed sex to secure her future. She wanted a protected life with her daughter once and for all.

She migrated slowly to her side of the vehicle, avoiding his gaze. Whenever he looked deeply into her eyes, she got lost. Was she stupid to want him so desperately? He was a big, powerful lawman and he could demand she perform any number of sexual acts. Marissa had told her about quite a few of them.

If she had enough courage to endure a single sexual experience with him tonight, she'd be set. Even if he got rid of her later on, they'd have to let Emma stay with her. If he were gone a lot of the time in his job, that would be fine with her too. He seemed like a decent man, but she knew firsthand how men and their promises and attitudes could change. Danny had been a huge mistake and not even her worst one, but she'd made it through the gauntlet of horrible men littering her past.

One single sexual experience stood between a life of fear, with the constant threat of being ripped away from Emma, and one of security, married in the flesh to a lawman. A big, gorgeous, sexy one.

They were headed to her soon-to-be-former residence, and she needed to grow some courage. She knew Danny would be in attendance to watch every single thing she touched to make sure she didn't cheat him by taking something he considered his. Danny considered pretty much everything in the apartment his.

Jonathan drove toward the residence she had spent the better part of the last several years secluded inside, like a prisoner. The six apartments above the small grocery store where she worked had been her home and only refuge since the Tiberius Group takeover. She worked twelve hours a day, six days a week in the mini grocery store with the round-the-clock deli for the customers who frequented it. The only women she ever saw, besides the ones residing in the apartment complex, were the ones who had to be accompanied by the significant men in their lives. The word 'nuisance' came to mind whenever she thought of the Tiberius Group.

In addition to her meager salary, her boss, Alvin, had given Danny a break on his apartment rent as partial compensation for all her hard work. Alvin and his wife, Betty, had also thought she and Danny had been married all these years. After the anonymous phone call and the subsequent horror of the Tiberius Group representatives dragging Emma away through the grocery store for all to see, Alvin had promptly fired her.

Soon after the takeover had forbidden women to travel alone, she had applied for and received a special license to work. The license that had arrived by mail one day had been an oversight on the part of the new government. It had been issued to her as if she were married to Danny. It was very much to her advantage since she did not possess a male blood relative or a legal husband. With the citizen DNA database readily available to all lawmen, any man she traveled with could be tested with the wave of a wand to determine a blood relationship. Otherwise, she had to possess valid marriage papers.

She had given up her other two jobs across town once she wasn't allowed to travel alone. And because she didn't have authentic marriage paperwork to travel with Danny, he hadn't wanted to risk getting caught out in public. She knew she was fortunate to have the one job and had merely increased her hours there to make up for the loss of income at the other two places.

Grace worked a grueling seventy-two-hour week in her grocery store job before she spent her remaining waking hours working in the apartment like a slave. Danny made it clear she was lucky he allowed her to stay at all since she had so many faults, in his opinion.

She'd spent the majority of her time away from her job taking care of her keeper, lazy-ass Danny. She cooked, she cleaned, and she did mountains of laundry. She shopped downstairs for their food. She managed to get a whopping five or six hours of sleep each night, and she babysat for her best friend, Marissa.

Marissa worked the twelve-hour shift opposite to Grace's for her grueling seventy-two-hour work week to support *her* lazy husband. For years, they'd traded friendship and babysitting since the men in their lives didn't tolerate female children. There was her sweet Emma, who made being a mom easy. Up until six months ago, she'd also cared for her sickly Aunt Fiona, who'd been her refuge along with Emma after the death of her parents.

Danny could barely be bothered to be civil. Usually, the only words out of his mouth were to scold her because she wasn't working hard enough to put his dinner on the table on time. He went to school full-time and spent all of her hard-earned money on whatever he wanted. She couldn't say a word because he held her life in the palm of his hand. A hand which had promptly crushed her the minute he didn't need her.

Grace wondered what her new husband would expect—if he even kept her. She knew life as a lawman's wife would certainly be an improvement over the one she'd led these past years hiding out in the apartment like a criminal. She would simply seduce Jonathan and remain his wife. She relaxed into the thought of his arms around her. It had been easy to let herself go and kiss him passionately moments ago because they'd been in a bright, public place, but also because he warmed her insides whenever she touched him.

The minute she was in a dark room, she got nervous. She needed to speak to Marissa in private before leaving her former residence. Her best friend would know exactly what to do to seduce him quickly, so he'd be unable to stop himself from taking her and thus be forced to keep her.

Once her life with him was set, she'd do everything in her power to make him happy. She wasn't worried about him traveling. When he was present, she'd enjoy getting outside regularly again. Emma hadn't seen the light of day, except from their small balcony, since she'd been a baby.

Marissa would know what Grace could do to entice her new lawman husband into keeping her permanently.

"Are you ready to do this?" Jonathan's voice sent a vibrating electric pulse of desire through her. She looked up and realized they had arrived at her former apartment.

She stared at the ground floor grocery store dubiously and said, "I guess."

He exhaled deeply. "If Danny's inside, you don't have to speak to him. Gather your things. I'll be right there with you."

She nodded and gave him her best smile. Danny wasn't the only thing she was worried about. She also had to walk through her former place of employment to even get to the dreaded apartment waiting above the stairs. Letting her gaze linger on her husband a moment gave her strength. It would be okay. Jonathan would be there to protect her from Danny and whatever threats he thought up. He would walk beside her through the grocery store gauntlet too.

"Do you have any furniture?"

"No. It's just a few personal things. Not too much."

"I have some boxes in the trunk, if you need them."

"Do you think I could..." she stopped, shook her head, and decided not to finish her foolish question. It wasn't fair to ask for any further favors from the man who'd literally saved her life today. It especially wasn't fair to Jon since Grace wanted the time to glean from her friend the best way to seduce him into keeping her forever.

"What?"

"Never mind. It's foolish." She turned to open her door.

"Oh? What foolish thing do you want?"

She paused for a moment and then said, "I'd like to say goodbye to my friend Marissa. She and I worked in the grocery store together. She's my best and only friend. Her daughter, Lily, and my Emma are like sisters."

He made a face that suggested she shouldn't even have to ask, but then sobered. Perhaps he remembered the pressures she was forced to live under. Women had so few rights, and any simple request they made was often construed as shrewish and demanding.

"I'll make sure you have some time alone with her before we leave, to say good-bye." He gave her a compassionate glance.

She nodded and offered him a tight-lipped smile in return, too choked up to thank him yet again. He was being very kind, so she made it her new personal mission to make his life perfect. Grace would do anything to make him happy, right after she tricked him into having sex to trap him into a permanent marriage.

They exited the vehicle, crossed the sidewalk, and entered the grocery store. She made it two steps inside the place before Alvin, her former boss, blocked her way to the apartment stairwell. She tilted her head up at him. He was a big man and he'd been angry when he'd found out she wasn't married to Danny. He'd called her a liar...and worse.

Grace took a steadying breath, staring at his wiry, steel-gray hair. It always looked like an unruly steel wool pad perched on his head.

"What do you think you're doing?" he asked, crossing his arms over his white butcher's apron.

"I've come to get my things from the apartment."

"Are you lying again?"

"Please let me pass," she said, wishing for once she didn't have to fight for every step forward she took.

"You know what you've cost me by pretending to be married to Danny all that time? You know how hard it is to get help these days. How am I supposed to replace you? Huh?"

"Step out of her way," Jonathan said from behind her.

"Lawmen don't scare me, so save your breath. I already know she's headed for the Institution. Why are you here?"

Grace gave Alvin a curious stare, wondering why he thought she was headed for the Institution. Danny must have told him.

Jonathan stepped in front of Grace and leveled a grim look at her former boss. "She's my wife. Stand aside."

"You married her?" Alvin uncrossed his arms.

"Yes. And when we return from getting her belongings, I'll expect her final wages ready for me."

Alvin took a sharp deep breath and snarled, "I owe her nothing!"

"Then prepare the paperwork to show me you've paid her salary to date."

Alvin chomped his cheap dentures together and grimaced. Grace knew she was owed almost two weeks' worth of wages. If she'd gone to the Institute, her unpaid wages would have been forfeited, but now that she was married, her new husband could collect them.

Jonathan wrapped a protective arm around her shoulders and secured her to his warm body. They edged past a fuming Alvin to the stairwell leading to her former apartment. Jonathan motioned her to go first, glancing over his shoulder once before following her.

She entered the code in the keypad lock, hoping Danny hadn't had the foresight to change it. The door clicked open and she stepped inside warily, looking around for him. She hadn't seen his car parked outside in its regular place, but her anxiety level at being here was in the red zone.

"I don't think Danny's here," she said and breathed a sigh of relief. Tip-toeing across the room, Grace headed to her designated room. She opened the door to the small space she shared with Emma. It was stripped and empty.

"No! Where...? How...?" Grace was incensed at the violation of her bedroom. Jonathan joined her and stared into the empty room. The bed was stripped of linens. All of her own and Emma's meager belongings were gone, as if they had never existed. She flung the closet door open to find her clothing missing and only empty hangers dangling from the rod.

The front door banged open and Danny marched inside. He waddled over to her room and stood in the doorway with a smirk on his soft, fat face.

"I took the liberty of cleaning out your things, Grace," he said with far too much satisfaction. "I was certain you wouldn't be back for them since I wasn't planning to bid on you. I didn't expect anyone else would want you."

Grace tried to keep her voice under the level of a shriek. "Where are my things, Danny?"

He smirked. "I threw them out with the garbage this morning,"

"You had no right!"

"I had every right."

Grace put her hands to her face to stop the scream already forming in her throat. The money. Surely he hadn't found her hiding place. She strode to the cheap curtains sagging miserably at the single window in the room. She tore at the hem, and resting exactly where she had left it was her precious nest egg. The two hundred and sixty-three dollars she'd carefully squirreled away for emergencies was intact.

With shaking fingers, she pulled out the tattered bills from her hiding place in the curtain's hem and clutched the treasure to her chest. Cash was rarely used these days, but it was still available and could be spent.

"What do you have there?" Danny asked angrily.

"None of your business."

"Everything in this apartment is mine. Hand it over." He took a step in her direction, obviously forgetting in his zeal to steal her last few dollars that she wasn't alone. Jonathan blocked his path. Danny bounced off Jonathan's body.

"That money is mine!" Danny shouted into Jon's chest.

"Actually, it's mine," Jonathan uttered in a calm, rational voice. "If it had been yours, you would have already taken it when you cleaned out the room." Jon turned to her and held out his hand, indicating he wanted her money.

Grace gave him a petulant look until he winked at her. He snapped his fingers loudly, as if in irritation. She scrunched her eyes in confusion, but handed her precious savings over slowly. He crunched the prized dollars in his hand and slid the cash into his front trouser pocket. He grabbed her hand and pushed past Danny, seemingly on a trajectory to the front door.

"I'll bill you for the rest of her belongings you discarded without cause," Jonathan said to Danny over his shoulder as he opened the front door.

"It'll be a cold day in hell before you get a single dollar from me. No magistrate will hear the case. I know how things work."

"Then I'll make certain there is a stop payment put on the snitch money you got for all the anonymous phone calls you made."

"You can't do that!" Danny screamed, his doughy face turning bright red. Jonathan put a hand on his gun and gave him a glare. Danny retained his sullen expression, but stopped his approach toward them.

Jonathan hustled her out into the hallway, slamming the door on Danny's looming tantrum. Grace blinked a time or two, trying to take in her new spite-filled reality. The clothes she had on her back were the only ones she now owned.

"Where does your friend live?" Jonathan asked. She pointed down the hall to Marissa's door. The dejection on her face had to be apparent, but he put an arm around her waist, squeezing her once, and walked her to Marissa's door. She knocked quietly. The door opened after only a short pause.

"*Madre de Dios!* Grace," Marissa said with obvious relief. Her arms opened in greeting and Grace flew into them, unable to stop the tears.

"Come inside," Marissa said.

"I'll wait out here." Jonathan crossed his arms and leaned against the wall.

Grace pulled back in time to see Marissa giving the large lawman an appreciative once-over. She took a step back and ushered Grace into her apartment. The question in her eyes remained until the door closed.

"Is he the one taking you to the Institute?" Marissa asked, her face full of regret.

"No. He's my husband."

Marissa's eyes widened with a twinkle. Her suggestive smile was infectious.

"Lucky girl. I'm jealous."

"I need your help." Grace quickly explained the situation and her plan to seduce Jonathan Brent, her new lawman husband.

Marissa smiled even wider at the request for a step-by-step seduction plan. "I know exactly what you need to do!"

She whispered a plan describing every touch, kiss, and lick Grace should use to secure her husband permanently. Grace easily pictured every scandalous act with Jonathan.

"I guarantee he won't be able to resist you."

"Thanks, Marissa. I'll miss you so much." Grace threw her arms around Marissa one last time.

"Don't worry, my friend, we'll see each other again, you and I. And now you'll be able to get outside with Emma. I'm happy for you, Grace. You always deserved better than Danny.

"Oh, and speaking of that ass, I was able to retrieve some of your things from the trash this morning." She crossed the room and pulled a box out of the coat closet. It had many of Emma's favorite toys, a few pictures, and a several other personal belongings Grace held dear.

"Thank heavens." Grace smiled and grabbed the box.

After a loud wage dispute with Alvin on the way out, Grace's spirit lifted at the prospect of shedding her old life. Perhaps it was just as well Danny had thrown everything else out. She had nothing to remind her of the prison-like existence she'd endured these past few years.

"I need to stop at my home for a few minutes before we go to pick up Emma, okay?" Jonathan asked.

"Sure, whatever you want." *All the better to seduce you in private, my dear.*

"Oh, one more thing. This is yours." He leaned closer and extended a closed hand over hers. The tattered bills once hidden in her bedroom curtains fluttered into her palm.

Her eyes watered at the gesture. "Thank you," she said in a small voice and looked out the window so he wouldn't see her tears. He was probably sick of seeing her cry.

Grace settled into her seat and worried about what would happen when they were alone. She rode in silence, giving her willful fears a stern lecture. A sexual experience with Jonathan wouldn't be like the last time she'd had sex and even if it was, she only needed to stay conscious until he was done with her. She could do that. She wouldn't worry about the handcuffs if he required them.

"What are you thinking?" he asked.

"Nothing."

"Then why is your face ashen? Are you afraid of me?"

"No. Of course not." She turned to him and shot him a quick grin. *Buck up,* she told herself. *Time is running out, and this is the last chance to make certain Emma stays, so don't freak out.*

Jon laughed slightly and shook his head, as if he didn't believe her. She would have tried harder to convince him, but he pulled into the driveway of a small, well-kept house and parked the vehicle. He shot out of his door without saying a word and quickly came around to her side of the car. Her heart pounded in her chest. *This is it. Do or die.* She found she couldn't relax.

Her door opened. "Come on," he said tersely.

Had she made him angry already? She focused her attention on the belt of his uniform, specifically where his handcuffs hung at her eye level.

She stepped out of the vehicle. He put his arm around her and slammed the door shut. She stiffened at his touch, but he didn't seem to notice and marched her to the front door. The midday sun caressed the top of her head as they walked the short distance. Grace wanted to lift her arms and absorb the rays of warmth to gain strength for what she was about to do, but didn't want to anger him by pulling away. Jonathan unlocked the heavy, solid-looking door and pushed it open. She noticed the absence of light and stiffened in fear at her inability to see further than a few feet into the interior of his house.

"Go ahead," he said, motioning her to enter first.

Grace took a deep breath and took a small step forward, but not enough to cross the threshold. She stopped inches from the yawning darkness. Swallowing hard, she wondered how she could overcome an eight-year fear of dark spaces in the next few seconds.

"In or out." Jonathan's whispered words by her ear took her back to the first dark space she'd shared with him.

She jumped, startled at his words, before turning to see his easy smile. He leaned closer. She thought he might kiss her, but instead he snapped a switch right inside the door and turned the lights on. His living room was furnished with chrome and black furniture. Further in, she saw a small dining table.

Jonathan leaned close to her. "Nothing inside there will hurt you, including me."

"I know." She turned to gaze into his eyes, trying to sound light, but the words sounded muffled exiting around the cotton in her mouth. She was about to be all alone with her six-and-a-half-foot-tall lawman husband.

Grace took a breath and stepped all the way inside. Once she got through the small foyer and into the living room, she stopped dead a few steps away from another dark room to her left.

It was his bedroom. The bed was *in there*. The imminent sex, amazing or otherwise, would take place *in there*.

"Don't worry," he said mildly, as if reading her fearful mind. "You can have the guest room." He slid past her toward the dining room.

"No!" Grace reached out and grabbed his arm, stopping him.

"Please." She licked her lips and tried her best to relax. "I want to be with you. I do."

"But you're frigid and afraid of sex unless I handcuff you or some nonsense. Care to explain why your idiot ex-...whatever he was...felt you needed to be handcuffed down in a dark room to have sex?"

"Not really," she said regretfully. He nodded with an understanding look and turned to move away again. She couldn't allow him to leave. He was her last and only chance. "But I will. Please give me a chance to explain."

"You don't have to prove anything to me. I promise you, I only bid on you so you wouldn't have to go to the Tiberius Institute. No one deserves to go there."

She didn't try to hide the puzzlement in her tone. "What are you going to do with me?"

Jonathan looked her over from head to toe slowly before answering, "I'll find someone for you."

Grace crossed her arms. "Who?"

"Someone you'll like."

"I like you. Why won't you keep me?" The small, sullen voice that emerged was almost unrecognizable to her own ears.

"Because I don't want to be responsible for you when I'm gone for my job. It wouldn't be fair to you or your daughter." Jonathan's gaze traveled over her body again.

Grace gave an exaggerated shrug. "I don't understand."

"I don't have any direct male relatives to escort you about as Tiberius law requires. I only have a brother-in-law." He looked up at the ceiling a moment. "I have two of them, actually, but neither one is a blood relative. While I could get a special license if they were to agree, ultimately it's a big imposition on them whenever I leave at a moment's notice, which happens frequently."

Her head dropped in dismal failure. "I see." Grace stared at the space between their feet. He thought of her as a big problem. He'd only married her to do a good deed: rescuing her from a fate worse than death. She appreciated his selfless action but was disappointed at his lack of desire to teach her wild, amazing sexual things.

In retrospect, she was the one who had accosted him in the elevator.

While he hadn't fought her off, she had instigated it. The only kiss he had instigated with her was immediately after the wedding, but that could have been for show. She was such a dope. Grace's whole body sagged in frustration. Her wicked feelings were apparently one-sided.

Jon closed the distance between them in one half-step. His finger brushed her chin and lifted her face to gaze at his. "It's not because I don't ache for you, Grace. I do. But please understand, you deserve a better life than I can give you." His quiet, sincere tone seeped inside her muddled mind. His gorgeous gray eyes, with their piercing intensity, made her almost forget her fear of dark places.

Grace wanted him. They were alone. Nothing was stopping her from taking him…or persuading him, as Marissa has suggested. It was time to act and secure her future. She leaned into his personal space. He took a deep breath but didn't move away.

Grace drilled her best sultry look his way and whispered, "Prove it, Jonathan. Prove that you ache for me." Her arms wound unhampered around his neck. Having accomplished this much, she pulled his mouth to hers. She licked the seam of his lips, wanting desperately for him to desire her.

She wanted to taste him and love him and make a life with him. Everything about Jonathan Brent said he was safe and good and exactly what she had always dreamed of in a man. Grace desperately needed safe and good right now.

She deserved it. She wanted it. She needed him. She had earned at least a small taste.

As soon as his lips brushed hers, he lost whatever resistance he had exhibited before entering the house and melted into her completely. He slid his mouth sideways across hers and devoured her as if he'd been holding back for years and only now could kiss her as he wanted. It was so very easy to let him do as he pleased. The taste of him pervaded her already heightened senses and an electric charge stormed down her body, diving between her legs.

He grabbed her up in his arms, one beneath her back, the other under her knees. Two seconds later, he'd carried her over to sit on the soft sofa. Grace landed across his lap, never releasing his lips. One of his strong, muscular arms wrapped around her back, clenching her close to his frame. The other shifted from beneath her legs to stroke her thigh. The buzz from his touch sent warmth radiating across her limbs, making her relax. She leaned away, pulling him down to half-cover her. All the while, she kept the electric connection of his lips firmly attached to hers. A moment later, his fingers shifted from her thigh to brush across her breasts gently. She wanted to feel his hands on her bare skin.

As if reading her mind, he unbuttoned the top button of her pink blouse.

One button at a time came undone as more and more skin was revealed. His lips distracted her. She wasn't afraid, but rather, very aroused. He popped open the front closure of her bra, freeing her breasts and exposing her bare flesh. Warmth and a sexy vibration of sensation suffused her from head to toes, focusing between her legs. Increased moisture coated her core and made her wish his hand would travel lower. His lips and tongue mesmerized her with soft, coaxing licks. She heard herself whimpering in need.

Grace wanted Jonathan to teach her about amazing sex. He cupped one bare breast and her nipples reacted, hardening. He flicked one until she moaned, then plucked it, making her hips twist in desire. She felt the bulge of his erection dig into her hip. She wanted him to make love to her. Soon. Now. *I'm yours. Take me,* she wanted to scream.

His hand trailed from her breast to her belly and then lower to the pulse-pounding desire between her thighs. The knit skirt she wore already bunched above her knees. His fingers slipped below the hem, and the tingle of his touch on her quivering, bare thigh was exhilarating. Her legs fell open to accommodate him. She ground her mouth into his for encouragement, wanting him to stroke her on that one spot she'd never had a man touch before.

Please touch me, she silently begged him.

Chapter 4

Jon's libido had taken over his conscious mind. The glimmer of rational thought to keep Grace pure for her next husband had gone straight to hell the minute she stepped into his sensory range.

He'd stopped to pick up the Andy Nelson files and to somehow relieve his sexual desire for her. He'd planned to masturbate in his bathroom so he wouldn't be tempted to do exactly what he was doing right now: stroking her amazing body with the intent of fucking her. Administering the other alternative release for his rampant desires was not as appealing when his fingertips slid across satiny skin.

His new wife overwhelmed all his senses. Grace looked like all the sexual delights he had ever dreamed of in his perfect woman. Her dark, silky hair begged to be touched, her lips begged to be kissed, and her body begged to be stroked. But it was her unique fragrance that put him over the edge. A scent of pure, intoxicating sexual delight poured over his senses. His body refused to guard against her any longer. He relaxed and gave in to her sweet embrace, allowing Grace's seductive feminine power to override his foolish honor.

Jon would figure out a way to make this marriage work. Later. He wanted her. Now. He wanted to keep her. Forever. Taking her was inevitable. The urge to resist slipped away when he heard her sensual sighs as he touched her.

Grace kissed him as if she might devour him alive if he dared pull away. His cock had never been this marble-hard before. She moaned, and as if it had a mind of its own, his cock pressed against her soft body. He savored the anticipation of driving his shaft deeply. His desire wouldn't be quenched in any other way. Giving in to the inevitable was the first step, but he wanted to get Grace ready. He knew his cock was big, and he didn't want to hurt her.

His hand skimmed along her bare, smooth thigh on a path to her panties. He ran his thumb along her clit, which was already drenched through the fabric. She bucked once at his touch before sucking his tongue in her mouth, hard. Her sweet whimpers of arousal made him hurry along his seduction. Jon pulled her panties off and tossed them away. She didn't resist. He ran his hand up the inside of one thigh before inserting two fingers directly inside her creamy, wet pussy. He curled his fingers inside as his thumb stroked her clit with firm attention. He broke the seal of their kiss to trail his lips down to one smooth, creamy breast. Covering the center of it in one mouthful, he pulled back enough so that her stiff nipple was trapped between his teeth and tongue. He sucked to the same rhythm he used to stroke her clit below.

Grace's gasps and pants of pleasure egged him on. He released her peak and moved over to the other one. She tasted better than anything he'd ever had in his mouth. Her vocal cries of pleasure throbbed through his ardent body. Her hands pressed firmly on his head, pulling him closer to her breast as if he weren't sucking quite hard enough to please her. He closed his teeth around her peak in a gentle bite. She sucked in a deep breath the instant he bit down, and shuddered in his arms. Jon licked the tip of that nipple to soothe it. He shoved three fingers deeply into her wet, tight body, still stroking her clit with his thumb.

With her next inhalation, Grace arched back and a long, steady, breathy cry emitted from her lips. A wave of pleasure washed over him at her release. He felt her vaginal muscles clamp down on his fingers. He shoved them deeper inside and back out again several times as she climaxed. She shook as sultry moans of orgasm came from her lips.

Jon released her nipple and kissed his way to her face. With a look of supreme wonder in her shining eyes, she kissed him deeply, her tongue plunging inside his mouth as she convulsed on his fingertips, which were still buried. The pleasure radiating from her wrapped around his spine as she kissed and sucked on his mouth. Her climax had washed over him as if he'd experienced it with her. Afterwards, as she trembled in his arms, he knew it was her first climax ever. A climax virgin! It was as if he'd climaxed for the first time too—almost.

When she stopped shaking and released his mouth, he kissed a path to her breast, resting his face there. He wondered whether she was ready for his big, granite-hard cock to penetrate her.

Some part of him worried about her past experience. He didn't want to frighten her, but he needed to come. His impatient, regularly drugged-up libido had waited a long time for real live female flesh. He needed her and knew for certain that a shot of medication to settle his sexual urges wouldn't be nearly as satisfying. Nor would a self-induced hand job since her unique fragrance and the additional scent of her musky gratification wafted up to taunt him. He took a deep breath, and the scent of her arousal moved him to action.

Time to fuck, said his vulgar libido.

Kissing a path to her face, he glanced into her eyes to assess her fear level. Grace wore a satisfied look. She smiled at him and ran her fingertip across his lips. Jon decided she was ready. Or maybe it was his randy cock that made the decision. It didn't really matter. He needed to release. It was time. He straightened up to loosen his zipper. Grace scrambled close, surprising him by kissing his neck ardently as she reached for his pants. She brushed his hands away from the task, released her lips from his sensitive neck, and bent her head forward to reward his impatient cock.

He forced himself to relax and let her do what she was comfortable doing. His cock said she had better hurry up or Vlad the Impaler was going to rise up and conquer her cunt in a trice.

Grace kissed his jaw once and then trailed her lips to his collarbone. Her fingers brushed the closure to his pants. His cock sprang forward, ready to be pleasured when she unzipped him. He almost lost it when her fingertips touched his tip. Her soft hands stroked him tenderly. Jon did his best not to leap up, throw her down, legs open, and drive his cock directly to her womb. He should let her get accustomed to him. He forced his body to relax and enjoy her gentle caress. His cock told him he was a big pussy not to grab her by the hips to thrust deeply and repeatedly until…

"Is it okay if I put my mouth on you?" she whispered. He cleared his throat, realizing his eyes had closed in anticipation of her touching and stroking his cock. The seductive visual of her head in his lap, her tongue licking him while her lips surrounded and sucked on his dick, slammed into his sex-starved mind, nearly making her request redundant. His cock then informed him he'd made an excellent selection for a wife and bobbed once in hearty approval of her breathy suggestion.

"Sure," he managed to utter in a gravelly voice. He was proud of himself for not having climaxed in her hand as he spoke.

She smiled as if relieved and shifted to kneel between his legs, bending over his long-deprived and now insanely happy cock. She licked him first, and he couldn't stifle the hiss between his lips as he felt his cock bob again in utterly delightful anticipation. She closed her lips over his head, and he didn't care if he died right then. He'd die happy. She sucked him with her wide mouth, her sexy, bee-stung lips completely surrounding his cock. She slid him back out again slowly. And back in again. And back out again. He wasn't going to last four more seconds.

Jon brushed a hand down her dark, satiny locks to disrupt her before he embarrassed himself. She pulled almost all the way off, her lips resting on his very moist tip. She looked up at him from between his thighs. The sincerity of her expression made him pause. Removing his cock from the warm space between her lips, she promptly frowned. "Am I doing it wrong?"

Jon almost laughed at the insanity of her ability to blow him wrong. There was no wrong way. He tempered his mirth. "No. I just don't want you to get an unexpected surprise. It's been too long for me to...uh, last an extended time." He could hardly speak. He wanted her to continue. His raspy voice told him how close he was to exploding, whether or not she touched him again.

"I'd prefer it this way for this first time if it's okay with you."

Jon found he could no longer speak. He nodded. She held his gaze and inserted the over-swollen head of his cock in her luscious mouth again. Her tongue darted around to lick the sensitive spot underneath as her aqua gaze locked with his. She dropped her head down, breaking his gaze, suctioning tighter as she went to finish him. She sucked his cock deep. Her small hands slid over his uniform slacks, along the seam over his inner thighs, and the next rapturous suction she exerted on him was all it took to make him climax.

Grunting deeply in appreciation as he released, Jon lost awareness of his surroundings for a moment at the diabolically greatest oral experience he'd ever had. It was exponentially superior to what he'd intended when he came home. His head swam in the pleasurable climatic afterglow.

When he finally came back to reality several moments later, her face was resting on one of his thighs. Her hand stroked his other leg slowly.

He brushed a hand down her face and buried it in her hair. "Are you okay?"

"Yes. Are you?" she countered, her tone amused.

He chuckled, "Not sure yet, give me a minute."

"Okay. Thank you."

"You've got to be kidding. What are you thanking me for? If I'd known you could do that, I would have let you take me in the car."

The trill of her laughter caught him off guard.

"Well, I was frightened when I entered your home, but now I'm feeling much more secure. So thank you."

"I was impossibly horny, but trying to be honorable, when I entered my home. Now I'm supremely satisfied. So thank *you*," he replied, twirling a lock of her hair between her fingers.

"I guess the Tiberius representative won't scan my throat to see if I've been consummated," she said in a wistful tone.

He laughed at the comical visual. "No. Unfortunately, the scan equipment only looks below the belt."

"Guess I'll have to gain some courage then. I don't want to be afraid, but I confess I am...a little nervous."

"I promise to do whatever I can so you won't be afraid. I would never hurt you, Grace."

"I know." She took a deep breath and asked, "Can I handcuff you to the bed before we have sex?"

* * * *

"What?" His head shot up off the sofa. "Can you do *what* before we have sex?" His angry, surprised tone told her he hadn't counted on her requesting *he* be handcuffed down to tamp down her fears.

"Don't be mad at me." She used her pleading voice. She hated to be so needy. For heaven's sake, he was a lawman; of course he wouldn't consent to being handcuffed down to allay her foolish fears. She'd have to be strong. Maybe it would help to leave the lights on.

"I'm not mad, but I'm not handcuffing myself down either."

"Okay. I understand." She hoped she wouldn't faint or that if she did, he wouldn't stop until she was...a consummated wife. Marissa had told her a man would be hard-pressed to shy away from a woman who 'gave good head,' as she'd crudely put it.

"Do you understand?" He sat forward, piercing her with a sharp, stormy gray gaze. "I put handcuffs on other people—not on myself."

"Yes. I understand." Grace dropped her stare as a tear escaped and ran down her face.

He grunted, and she hoped she hadn't angered him. She needed his cooperation, but he deserved better than to be tricked.

"I should explain about my past before you're trapped with me. I don't want to lie to you. I need you to understand about my daughter. You see, the reason I don't like to be pinned down is..."

"I already know who you are. I know that Andy Nelson is your child's father and that he raped you. I was the lawman who finally brought him in, and I know you're the only reason he is incarcerated."

Her gaze shot to his weary expression. "How do you know about that?"

"I was in the courtroom when you testified at his trial. I recognized you from the elevator. I didn't identify myself or pursue you because I thought you were already married."

"Oh." A secret thrill rose inside. He remembered her. He might have been interested if she hadn't been wasting her time with Danny.

"Here's a question for you: if you are so traumatized by sex from your...violation, how come you were all over me in a public elevator years ago and then again in my car? And while we're on the subject, how were you able to then give me the best fucking blowjob I've ever had, before telling me I need to be restrained for further sexual encounters?"

"I gave you the best blowjob you've ever had?" Grace smiled at the compliment. "It was my first one."

Jonathan lifted one dark eyebrow into a perfect arch.

Her foolish question only delayed the memories and disgrace of her past. Humiliated by being dumped after her first sexual encounter with Andy, she'd confessed her sorrow to her mother. Her mother had told her father that Grace had lost her virginity. She'd been grounded. Two months later, after returning home early from her father's annual company Halloween party, her parents had discovered Grace naked and handcuffed in the basement.

The second encounter with Andy had resulted in Emma's birth.

Grace's parents, especially her father, had barely spoken to her during the last year of their lives before the accident that killed them. They died believing she had unnatural female urges. Her mother's head hung in perpetual shame whenever she looked at Grace, even after Emma was born, and this was worse than her father ranting all the time about her being a whore.

After they had died, she'd gone to live with her Aunt Fiona, and the subject of her 'urges' was never brought up again. Grace and Emma had lived peacefully until her aunt's illness forced their move. Fiona lost her job and couldn't keep up the payments on her large home any longer. Danny's parents lived next door to Aunt Fiona, and he reluctantly offered to let them stay at his apartment in the city...for a price. He wanted money to attend a school that his parents didn't think worthy.

Grace had worked three jobs to provide the funds for his counselor's degree. Danny knew about her past with Andy from the newspaper accounts and from his parents' gossip. Danny said she was a freak, but soon after, he wanted to 'cure' her. He agreed that she had unnatural female urges and as a counselor-in-training, he said he knew exactly what to do to cure her. He told her she should relive the experience and face it, or else it would haunt her forever. When he'd pulled out the handcuffs and clicked the first one shut, Grace had blacked out.

They never tried his *cure* ever again, thank goodness.

Marissa was the only friend who understood and had informed her she had very natural urges. Grace wondered if her new husband would understand, but was afraid to test him.

"Do you have some multiple personality disorder I should know about?" he asked in the wake of her silence.

"No."

"What then?"

"I'm not traumatized by sex, just by dark places. I don't like having my arms pinned. I never said I was violated. My parents did. They said it was statutory rape because of my age at the time and their supreme embarrassment over my being such a whore."

"You aren't a whore."

Grace nodded, eyes closed. She knew the truth. "I thought Andy was attractive. I chased after him. The first time I...we...you know..." *Had sex the first time,* she couldn't seem to say. "Andy told me...I was awful. He told me I was a terrible lay. I told him I'd do whatever he wanted, but he broke up with me and went back to his old girlfriend.

"The night my mother found me in the basement, Andy had come over to tell me what it would take to get him back. I agreed to do it because I desperately wanted to be his girlfriend."

Jon leaned back on the sofa and crossed his arms over his chest. "But he handcuffed you to a bed down in a dark basement room and raped you instead."

"No. He didn't rape me. Let me finish telling you what happened. I led him down there. I got on the bed. I...I asked for it." She lowered her head as tears slipped down her face.

"You did not ask for it! He's a monster. He would have taken you regardless." Jon leaned forward suddenly encircling her.

On some level, Grace knew Jon only meant to comfort her, but even the thought of being pinned down panicked her. She fought him off like a wild thing until her arms were free. The look of hurt in his eyes grieved her even more as she got up and stumbled away from him.

"I'm sorry. Please understand." She was fine if she could slide her arms around his neck so she could get them free. Otherwise, she freaked out. She took another step back and out of his reach, staring down in shame as Jonathan leaned forward on the sofa.

"I understand. He abused you."

"No. It wasn't bad the first time. I sort of liked it...a little." But not like she had enjoyed having Jonathan's hands stroking her and kissing her and nibbling on her. The memory of that blissful feeling of orgasm washed over again. She shivered and wondered if it would always be magical.

The thought of his very large cock shoved between her legs deeply inside made her perspire with sheer longing. She wished they could go have sex now. Gazing at Jonathan's troubled face brought the vile memory of the basement slamming into her mind. She would scream and fight him in utter panic if Jon got on top of her, even with the knowledge that he made her scream in pleasure. She took another step away from him.

He stood from his perch on the couch, suddenly towering over her. "Do not take another step away from me. I'm not him. I would never hurt you, or fuck you if you didn't want me to."

"I know. I get nervous in the dark, and the mere thought of you getting on top of me initiates a panic attack I can't control. The second time in the basement..." Grace trailed off, unable to articulate through her fear.

"Andy Nelson had genetic implants placed in his body. It made him a rapist. The second time, he raped you. Trust me. And if he didn't...well then, he would have."

Grace shook her head. "No. It was me. I led him into the basement for privacy. He told me to get undressed and get on the bed. He told me he wanted to handcuff me to the bed, and I said okay. He got on top of me and stuck...*it* inside of me. He told me to say how much I loved it. He made me repeat it over and over...so I told him how much I loved having..." She hesitated only a moment in embarrassment before finishing her thought. "Having him 'fuck me hard.' I screamed it."

"Stop. You don't have to..."

"Yes, I do. You need to understand. He didn't rape me that night. I wanted him to do what he did. I was desperate for him to..."

Grace halted her impassioned speech momentarily and decided she must be crazy. She couldn't stop herself from being a complete and utter moron by explaining a humiliating sexual encounter with a psycho ex-boyfriend in vivid detail to her new husband.

Moronic, because she and Jonathan hadn't consummated this marriage, and she might still lose everything. Instead of mouthing off, she should be bowing, scraping, and agreeing with every word he said in order to keep that which was most precious to her.

Emma had come from that sexual encounter in the basement and not from her first time seven weeks before in the back of Andy's car. She remembered seeing the spot of her own virginal blood on Andy's back seat after he'd removed himself from her and told her to hurry and get dressed. She hadn't pointed it out then, certain it would only anger him further. He was not impressed with her pitiful effort to have sex with him. He told her she had been a waste of his time and he was going back to his regular girlfriend, Cindy Wells.

Grace remembered crying bucketfuls at Andy's rejection, fearful she gotten pregnant. A humiliating trip to the doctor had relieved her mind. She wasn't pregnant, but by her parent's edict, she was forbidden from ever seeing Andy again. It wasn't as if it mattered—he thought she was worthless anyway. When he'd come to give her a second chance on the only night her parents were gone, she'd eagerly jumped at the opportunity, not noticing Andy's aggressive manner until it was too late. There were more than ghosts and goblins roaming around that Halloween night. Monsters were on the loose.

"I understand perfectly. You wanted a boyfriend, and he took advantage of your infatuation with him to violate you," Jon said, bringing her out of her trip down memory lane.

"No. It was my fault."

"You didn't climax with him." Jonathan's matter-of-fact tone made her look at him.

"What?"

"He never made you scream in pleasure." Jon closed the distance between them, giving her a lustful look. "You know, like I did a few minutes ago when I had my fingers deep inside you."

Grace, shocked at his words, could only stare at him and relive the vibrating sensation of release he'd brought her to. She shivered in memory.

"How did you know?"

"I felt the waves of pleasure radiate from you. That was your first orgasm, right?"

She squinted, wondering where this was leading. "Yes, but…"

"I'm the first man to stroke you until you screamed in climax. You can't ever take that away from me.

"I don't care what you did or didn't do with Andy Nelson when you were sixteen. He's a sexual vampire. If you had said no to him, the same thing would have happened. The illegal genetic implants he had installed don't work correctly after puberty. Now he requires sex, and he'll take it by force if it's not freely given. I'm actually surprised he only fucked you the one time."

She stopped to consider the events directly after she'd been 'fucked' by Andy in the basement. Grace vividly remembered the squeak of the mattress springs protesting as he got up, crossed the room and turned the lights off. She hadn't panicked until the door slammed shut cutting off the slim shaft of light from outer basement room.

When she saw his eerie, orange-rimmed, iridescent irises in the dark...coming for her, she'd started screaming. When she realized she couldn't move her arms, her agonized screams became shrill, but Andy only taunted her. When he told her in a hissing, slithery voice that he was going to make her bleed, she'd fought the handcuffs as her heart thundered in her chest. When the blade of his unseen knife cut an icy, wet path across her belly in the pitch-black room, she'd wondered how she was still conscious. All the while she struggled against the handcuffs, unable to free her arms and prayed for the pain to end quickly.

The maniacal laughter as that sinister voice told her all the other wicked things planned for her. "I'll cut you a pretty design." Those were the last words the monster spoke before the blessedly wonderful sound of her parents coming home unexpectedly. Those words also echoed in her mind for years to come and helped make her final decision to testify against Andy in court after her parents were gone.

Grace stifled a scream and shook her head to dispel the vivid memory. She knew why he had only taken her once. "My parents came home from the Halloween party early. He didn't have time."

"Andy Nelson needs sex," Jon repeated. "He will always take it by force because of the implants. On some level, I'm glad you agreed to the first encounter. I'm certain it was less traumatic for you, but make no mistake about what kind of animal he is. Besides, it'll always be a rape. You were sixteen." He paused and then whispered, "What happened wasn't your fault."

"I don't understand..." Her eyes narrowed. It was still her own fault, wasn't it? She'd always blamed herself for that night. Her parents, especially her father, had drilled that single truth into her head over and over as her belly had swelled in pregnancy.

"Sure you do. He's bad. You didn't do anything wrong. You didn't *ask* for what happened to you."

"I wish I could believe that," she whispered to herself.

He stepped into her personal space but didn't touch her and spoke in a low, sultry tone. "Believe this. The sound of your utterly delectable climax will forever make my cock rear to attention."

Grace heard Jon's passionate response, but still reeled from the possibility that the worst experience in her history wasn't her fault. She wanted to believe him. His seductive gaze meant to convince her of his belief made her consider the forceful way Andy had looked at her on that fateful Halloween night.

She remembered her first reaction had been to turn Andy down because of the fear her parents would find out. She also remembered that Andy didn't really ask her so much as told her what would happen between them, if she wanted to be his girlfriend. Had his persuasive attitude been because of the genetic implants?

"How do you know about his implants?" she asked. Grace was now recalling other differences between her two experiences with Andy.

In his car that first time, he'd been in a hurry and his attitude had been swaggering and conceited. In her basement the second time, he'd been different—more intense—and she'd admitted only to herself that she was frightened. Her only thought was of being Andy Nelson's girlfriend, whatever it took. She wanted to walk the halls of school on his arm and be accepted by all the popular kids. They were such childish desires in retrospect. She'd paid such a high price.

Jon cleared his throat. "There were several mutilated bodies discovered. The knife wounds were the same on each of the bodies. The victims had to be identified by dental records from the few teeth remaining. There was a phone call from a private medical center when a third victim fitting the description profile came in. The identity of key evidence led us to Andy Nelson. The woman died from her injuries before she woke, but they lifted some DNA that made Andy Nelson the primary suspect. Unfortunately, the evidence inexplicably disappeared during the trial. Andy was set free on bond.

"The lawman on the case tried to monitor him legally, but Andy was able to rape several other women while the court order was lost in red tape. These rapes were not allowed to be included in the case against him. Andy's defense attorney argued that the profile was different since the later victims weren't killed. It was assumed Andy had purposely refrained from killing them for that very reason. The raped women couldn't identify him or pick him out of a lineup. We didn't know the true victim count. The ones who came forward all had the same story—handcuffed to a bed, ugly knife wounds—but in the end, we couldn't get a positive ID. Andy was smart. Before the trial ended, the few women who came forward ended up dead from accidents. Andy was in custody, so he couldn't be charged. The D.A. argued he could have paid someone to kill his victims off, but the judge wasn't convinced."

"Were you the lawman on the case during his trial?"

"I was one of them. My former partner was one of his victims. He and I were state-level lawmen together when Andy Nelson broke into my partner's house and raped his wife.

"Kevin showed up unexpectedly and caught him, so Andy killed him. Then he finished raping Sarah and killed her too. I was waiting in the patrol vehicle during the murders."

The buzz of a communicator on his belt halted further discussion. He flipped open the device and said, "This is Brent," before he continued in a low voice. She couldn't hear what he said before he moved into the kitchen.

While he was distracted, Grace glanced at the clock on the wall. She caught his eye and motioned that she was going to the bathroom. He nodded and went back to his phone call. Her time was running out. She needed to submit to him. She knew she'd be nervous, but she should grow that elusive courage fast. At least he wouldn't handcuff her. Maybe he would let her get on top of him the first time. Marissa had suggested the sexual position as an icebreaker so she wouldn't be afraid. Would Jonathan let her get on top? Time to find out.

* * * *

"Another DC-5 message, Elliott? You keep using it and I won't think it's a red-hot emergency anymore."

"Where are you? We got cut off before."

Jon cleared his throat, nodded at Grace, and moved to the kitchen for privacy. He zipped his pants up, thinking about his suddenly complicated life. "I'm at home. I was about to dig out my personal files on Andy

Nelson's case. Why?"

"I just got some interesting information from a snitch. There is a woman who's fleeing the country tonight to escape Tiberius persecution and her sadistic husband. Her name is Cindy Wells. She was Andy Nelson's girlfriend in high school."

"What does she have on Andy?"

"Gee, I don't know. Maybe you could go to Eastlake City and find out for me," he said with characteristic sarcasm. "Get your ass going."

"You want me to leave right now—tonight?"

There was silence at the end of the line, and Jon knew he'd screwed himself. He never ever said anything to Elliott except "Where to?" If Elliott directed him to go somewhere, he went—no further discussion required. But now he had a wife to consider. Eastlake City would involve a flight. He couldn't take Grace with him. It was forbidden. Probably because it would make lawmen look like pussy-whipped cowards.

Leaving tonight would mean abandoning Grace. Jon wouldn't have time to secure a special license so that Matt Westland, his sister Sophie's husband, could be an escort for Grace. Jon wouldn't be granted a special license until he fucked her anyway, so it was a moot point. He didn't even have time to contact Matt and ask if he'd be willing to be Grace's escort.

Jon still needed to take Grace to pick up Emma at the Tiberius Family Center, unless she would be willing to wait for three more days to see her daughter. He imagined the answer to that was a resounding "No way in hell." What a royal mess he'd managed to land himself in for the sake of a wife. A wife whose wicked mouth made his cock rear in readiness even now.

"What in the blazes is wrong that you can't leave right now?" Elliott asked lethally. "And keep in mind the only acceptable answer has to do with your impending death."

"I got married today." Jon closed his eyes and waited for Elliott to explode.

"Married?"

"Yeah."

"That might actually qualify. Damn it, what were you thinking, Brent? You said you'd never get married. Did someone put a gun to your head or something?"

"No. I.… Listen. It doesn't matter. I got married less than two hours ago, and I have some things I need to take care of before I can resume my round-the-clock duties."

"Six days, Brent. We only have six days, and they review Andy Nelson's case before they let him go because a single female testified against him to put him away. You know ninety-five percent of the cases like it have been overturned."

"I know," he barked. No one needed to remind him of the stakes.

"You also need to track down that female witness, pronto."

"The female witness?" Jon asked as a grim feeling landed at the pit of his stomach. The witness in question was certainly very female and was currently freshening up in his bathroom.

"Yes, you remember the only witness in the case, don't you? Grace Maitland Cox. We need to get her in here. Let's hope she's strong enough to testify again. Since the case was pre-magistrate core, we'll have to get her husband's permission this time."

"That won't be a problem."

"Oh? And how do you know that? Did getting married make you clairvoyant?"

"No, I married her today."

There was silence for a moment, and Jon figured that either Elliott hadn't understood or he'd blown a vein out of his forehead in a stroke-induced fury.

"You married Grace Maitland Cox, the only witness in the Andy Nelson case? Are you fucking out of your mind?"

"Maybe. But she is alive and well. As her husband, I can give permission for her to testify."

"I don't even have words, Brent. Do you know how much fucking trouble you're in right now? The magistrate will throw the case out for any reason, and you just gave him a very prejudicial one wrapped in a bow."

"The fact that we're married doesn't mean she was lying. He still raped her, Elliott. She was barely sixteen." Saying the words out loud hurt him more than he'd imagined. Poor Grace. He glanced at the living room doorway to make sure she was still in the bathroom.

"And you married her! Have you screwed her yet? There still might be time to have her married off to someone not involved with the case."

Jon took a deep breath and resisted the urge to shout that he wasn't marrying Grace off to anyone.

The problem was he cared about her. He'd been lying to himself about finding her another man. He wanted her. After what had just happened in his living room, he wouldn't let her go. She touched a place in his core he'd never considered reachable before, the empty part of his soul. The lonely place where he wanted to find his soul mate...someone to love and care about. The sudden epiphany was not something a superior lawman's commanding officer would understand. Jon remained silent.

"I sense by this long silence that the deed is done and you've screwed not only her, but this case too."

"Shut up, Elliott. I hate to be the one to tell you, but it's none of your business what I do in my personal life. Let me take care of her. I'll leave first thing in the morning to talk to your witness."

"I have you booked on the seven o'clock flight tonight. It's the only IL flight headed to the east coast for the next five days. You'll have four hours to get any and all pertinent facts about Andy Nelson, high school prick, before Cindy is gone for good. Your return flight is at seven o'clock the next morning. You miss that flight tonight, and your ass is fired. Do you feel me?"

"Yes," Jon grated out, managing to sound almost sincere.

"Call me after you talk to Cindy Wells." Elliott hung up without saying another word.

Jon glanced at the clock and calculated he had less than an hour to find a place for Grace and pack before he'd have to leave to catch the domestic air shuttle flight. The return flight wouldn't arrive until twelve hours prior to Grace's scheduled Tiberius body scan...assuming it wasn't delayed. Air flight delays were common enough to be planned for.

What were his options? Do her, and take her someplace safe before the satisfaction melted from their faces. Leave her here, and hope he made it back in time to do her, so he could hear her climax again. His cock throbbed at the thought of seeing her face in the throes of gratification. If he didn't make it back in time, what was his backup plan? He'd take her to Matt and Sophie's and explain the situation to Matt. He could set up a husband for her…just in case.

"Grace?"

"I'm here. I'm ready. I'm sorry about all the things I said before. I shouldn't have told you…"

"I have to go."

"What? Right now?" Her tone sounded as incredulous as he felt.

"Yes. I told you. I'm a lawman. I believe I explained my obligations to you earlier. I'm leaving on a domestic shuttle for the east coast"—he glanced down at his watch—"and I need to leave soon to make the flight."

"What about Emma?" The color rose in her cheeks. "And what about…you know?"

"I'm sorry. Both will have to wait until I get back." He thought about delays and how long he could afford to be gone. He knew he couldn't just fuck her and leave. He didn't want their first time together to be hurried and frightening for her.

"Will you make it back here in time? Will you even try to?"

"Yes. Of course I'll try. I should be here by tomorrow night. There'll be plenty of time for us then."

"What happens to Emma and me if you don't make it back in time?"

"I don't know. I'll think of something. Perhaps I can get an extension due to my job obligations." Jon knew there was no way in hell Elliott would sign the paperwork to extend his forty-eight-hour consummation order. He'd married the only witness in the Andy Nelson case. Elliott was on the warpath. Given the chance, he'd shoot the plane down himself to keep Jon from making it back if he found out they hadn't consummated the marriage yet.

"Let's do it right now. Please. I won't faint, and I promise not to scream." She threw her arms around his neck, kissed his jaw, and pressed her curvy body into his.

"Grace, I don't want it to be rushed and scary for you." He peeled her away so he could think rationally and backed up a step.

"It won't be. Could I…um…"

Jon tamped down the visual of them copulating naked that danced in his mind. "Could you…what?"

"Get on top so I won't be pinned under you?"

* * * *

Jonathan's eyes closed halfway even as his pupils widened, darkening his expression. A sexy, dark, lust-filled look was what he gave her. Marissa was right. Some men apparently liked having women on top, if the volcanic look he now wore was any indication.

"If we do this...we won't have time to get your daughter before we leave."

"But when you get back, we can get her, right?"

"Yes." His eyes darted up and down her body with a sizzling, undeniably sexual gaze. Predatory.

Grace darted a look to the darkened bedroom doorway. Would he let her get on top *and* leave the lights on?

He strode closer and pulled her against his chest. Her arms wound around his neck. He twisted so his shoulders leaned against the wall as his hands slipped down to pull her hips into his groin. His fingers traced downward until he gripped her thighs, pulled her legs apart, and rubbed her sensitive clit against his very large cock through the material of his uniform.

Grace sucked in a deep, sharp breath as the quivery, needful arousal enveloped her. She wanted to feel that magical orgasm. He lifted her against him as moisture shot between her legs in gushing readiness. Her clit slid down his rock-hard cock again. The sensation was electric even through the layers of their clothing.

She had no doubt that once they were naked, she'd be shrieking and moaning in no time. Not all of this was about securing her future. Jonathan Brent had always intrigued her. He had since their first kiss in the justice center elevator. He was the only man to ever make her wet and tingly below with merely his delicious scent.

Grace kissed the spot on his chest where his uniform opened at the neck. He slid her crotch against his cock again, adding a little extra grind of pressure. She might climax before any clothing came off. Jon shifted and pushed into her clit again and again. The rhythm and pressure he exerted sped up. She was fast coming to a pleasurable pinnacle. A wave of delight pulsed across her body from the epicenter of her clitoris in unexpected orgasm.

"Ohmigod!" Grace climaxed and her legs clamped together reflexively against his hips. She fell limp for a moment but came to her senses quickly. Her legs dropped to the floor as her hands went to undo his pants. She had his cock in her hands in seconds. He groaned and closed his eyes as she stroked him. She released it to slide her panties off under her skirt. She placed her hands on his shoulders, ready to climb onto his huge cock.

Bang. Bang. Bang. Bang. Someone was pounding on the front door.

"Brent?" A muffled voice shouted.

"Fuck."

"Who is it?" Grace whispered, startled. She released her grip on Jon to grapple for her dropped underwear. She pulled her panties back on in a blind panic.

"My boss." Jonathan gave her a sorrowful look and fastened his pants as the pounding on the door continued.

Jonathan glanced over his shoulder at her once before he wrenched the door open to a tall man with pale blond hair and icy blue eyes. The stranger, who looked familiar, strode inside as if he'd been invited. Grace noticed he had a wicked scar running down one side of his face. The weapon used had barely missed his eye as the scar ended at the outer corner of his soulless baby blues.

"Sorry to interrupt your wedded bliss, but I decided to give you an escort."

"I'm fully capable."

"I wonder about that sometimes." The stranger eyed her a good long time. He looked up and down her body slowly, as if he found her lacking and unsuitable as a wife. "Get your stuff. Let's go."

"I've got to take her to my sister's house while I'm gone."

"Fine. I'll wait while you get ready." The blond stranger crossed his arms and rested his hip against the door he'd practically pounded down to enter.

"Wait outside." Jonathan huffed.

His eyes rounded, and so did his mouth, as if a sudden realization had hit him. "You haven't fucked her yet, have you?"

"That's none of your…"

"Good. Now we have a case again." The stranger stood. His face registered a stubborn mask she didn't mistake. Grace was screwed.

"The case isn't everything."

"Surely you know I'll do everything in my power to make sure our interests are maintained."

* * * *

"Jonathan. Please."

Grace's agonized voice registered in his mind, smothering the fury he felt from Elliott and his crass behavior. Jon turned away from Elliott to comfort her.

"Emma. What about Emma?" Grace put her hands to her face which mirrored her alarm.

"Grace, you'll always get to keep her. I promise you."

"Not if I end up with someone else who changes the rules. Men always change the rules." She glanced at the new stranger in the foyer. "I won't risk it. When you get back, promise me you won't do another thing until you come and make me your permanent wife. Promise me!"

"Grace. I…"

"Please." Her pleading voice registered deeply in his consciousness. How could he ever give her up? How could he ever sell her to someone else? "Okay. I'll keep you and make you my permanent bride…just as soon as I get back from this assignment."

"Not if I have anything to say about it." Elliott piped up.

Jonathan gave Elliott an evil look. Grace threw her arms around his neck and planted her mouth on his to seal the unholy bargain he'd agreed to. Elliott was going to kick his ass. Or fire him. Or both.

"I promise you'll never regret keeping me. I won't be a bother, and neither will Emma. She's used to being quiet. You'll see." Jon didn't tell her he already regretted it, not because of anything she had done, but because of his crappy life in general.

"I'm going to take you over to my sister's house for tonight. I only returned home last night. There's no food here, and I can't leave you alone, anyway. My sister Sophie is married to a rich executive with his own business. You'll be safe there." He released her reluctantly as Elliott watched and put in a call to Sophie.

The phone rang and rang. He got worried at the lack of response. Usually there was at least a maid or butler hanging around to take messages. If Sophie was out for the evening, where else could he take Grace tonight?

Elliott gave him a rude stare, tapped his watch with his forefinger, and motioned for him to hurry his ass up.

Jon grimaced as Sophie and Matt's phone continued to ring. A newly formed bad idea occurred to him as he listened to the endless ringing. He closed his eyes and cursed as the only other person available to him entered his mind.

Thomas "Brutal" Blackthorn, his *other* brother-in-law.

Chapter 5

Jon dialed the home of his other sister. Hannah and her husband, Brutal, had moved back to Earth from their off-world mining property less than six months ago. That was, after they'd finished mining the biggest Thorium-Z find in the history of the fuel discovery to date. He listened to the phone ring, praying silently that Hannah would answer rather than Brutal.

"Yes," growled a voice that was definitely not Hannah's. *Damn it.*

Jon didn't waste time on pleasantries or greetings. "Do you know where Matt and Sophie are?"

"Yep."

Since Brutal didn't offer the location, Jon gritted his teeth and asked, "Where are they?"

"Why do you need to know?"

"I'm a lawman. I don't explain my needs. Where are they?"

Brutal remained silent for a full fifteen seconds before answering, "Italy."

"What are they doing there?" He tried not to sound sulky, but probably didn't carry it off in his tone.

Another fifteen seconds went by, making Jon want to reach through the phone line and pistol-whip him, before Brutal sighed and answered, "Vacationing."

"When will they be back?" This time, Jon let the petulance in his voice have free reign. When Sophie and Matt traveled, they stayed gone for long periods of time.

"Why the fuck do you have a need to know, again? Or is this simply brotherly concern?"

"I need to speak with Matt on an urgent matter," he said and didn't know why he stopped without adding, "As if it's any of your fucking business." "Do you know when they're coming back or not?"

His black sheep brother-in-law sighed deeply and responded sarcastically, "Well, since they let me in on every intimate detail of their itinerary, I'd say they won't be returning until their travel visa expires in twenty-seven days. That's just a guess, though."

"Twenty-seven days? Fuck, are you sure?"

"Did I stutter?"

It was Jon's turn to sigh deeply. He closed his eyes and said, "Listen, Brutal, I need to ask for...a favor." Home surgery to remove his spleen with a rusty razor and his bare fingers would have been less painful than asking Brutal for a favor, but he didn't have a choice. With Matt and Sophie gone, he had to find a place to take Grace.

"Oh? I can't wait to hear this."

"I got married today, but I'm on a flight at seven tonight for the east coast until at least tomorrow night. I don't want to leave my new wife alone." Jon let out another deep breath to make his request. "May I bring her to your house for the evening and pick her up tomorrow?"

"You got married?" Jon had never heard Brutal laugh before. He had a deep, rich voice that women probably found intriguing, but Jon found it a gratingly annoying noise.

When he caught his breath, Brutal asked, "Was there a gun pointed at your head at the time of this wedding?"

"Save it. Yes or no, Brutal."

"Definitely yes. I want to meet the woman who intimidated the mighty lawman Jonathan Brent into marriage."

"Fuck you."

"No thanks. Besides, you should probably save yourself for the new little woman in your life. Wives can be very demanding in the bedroom, in case you didn't know."

Jon ignored the sexual reference, especially since it applied to his sister. "We'll see you in an hour," he said through gritted teeth.

"Can't wait. I'll leave a light burning for you, lover boy."

Jon ended the communication by hanging up without saying good-bye.

"Who was that?" Grace asked.

"No one important," he responded and wondered how he had gotten to this desperate place so quickly.

This exact same time yesterday, he'd been on a shuttle return flight back from Europe. When he'd entered his home last night, he'd gone straight to the bedroom and slept on top of the covers of his bed without changing clothes. This morning he'd showered, put on new clothes, and acquired a simple new assignment to pick up a common criminal named Walter.

Less than twenty-four hours later, he had a wife, a stepchild, a pissed-off boss hovering over him, and a brother-in-law whose existence he barely tolerated about to do him a huge favor. Not to mention a looming consummation he wasn't sure he should participate in upon his return with a new bride who was skittish about sex unless he was immobilized. He raised his eyes to the ceiling momentarily and wondered what celestial shit list he'd managed to land on and what he'd ever done to deserve being put there.

He knew he was crazy to think any of this would work out to his advantage, but then Grace put her arms around his neck and buried her face in his throat in gratitude. The scent of her never failed to arouse him or convince his logical mind he would be worse off without her.

He'd be damned, if it wouldn't be worth every excruciating moment if he could pull it off.

* * * *

"Jonathan, is it really you?" Hannah shrieked after answering the door. She launched at him in greeting. He caught her up in his arms and hugged her close as she wrapped her legs around his waist. Brutal hated when they did this, which was why Jon encouraged it.

"What are you doing here? I thought you were still out of the country," she said, her voice now muffled in his collar.

Jon looked up into Brutal's amused eyes. He stood just inside the door. Amused because he apparently hadn't mentioned Jon's call.

"I got back last night. I called a few minutes ago. Brutal didn't mention it to you?"

"I didn't want to ruin the surprise." Brutal arched an eyebrow up and smiled an evil smile.

"What surprise?" Hannah released him, slipped down back onto her feet, and finally noticed Grace standing behind him. "Who's this?"

"Your brother got married today. I think that's his new wife," Brutal informed her with a grin. He knew it would throw Hannah off guard and she'd take her reaction out on Jon.

Hannah punched Jon in the chest with her fist. "You got married? When were you going to tell me?" Then she ignored any response he might offer and pushed past him to greet Grace. "Hi, I'm Hannah. Don't mind them. They're men. They spend the bulk of their time marking their territory around each other, and still they barely get along. Come on into the house." Hannah grabbed Grace by her arm, led her toward the door, and asked, "What's your name?"

"Grace." She responded evenly, but perhaps slightly warily. Jon couldn't blame her.

"Grace. Nice name. Don't stand there, Jon, come inside." Hannah led Grace into the large foyer.

"Are you staying for awhile, Jon?"

"I'm leaving in ten minutes. I asked Brutal if Grace could spend the night here. I'll be back tomorrow night."

"Of course she can stay. Come on, I'll show you the guest room. You two be civil or face my wrath."

Hannah sucked in a deep breath—to berate him some more, Jon was certain—but then Brutal leaned down and whispered in her ear. She kissed his cheek and turned to escort Grace out of the foyer.

Grace smiled, glancing over her shoulder as she was led away by his sister, who was still yammering away. Jon watched Grace leave as if it would be the last time he ever saw her. He nearly gave in to his irrational fear. He wanted to stop them from walking away, but he didn't.

This left him alone with Brutal in the silent entryway. He came to his senses quickly, realizing Brutal was suddenly watching him like a hawk. Jon loved his sister. Hannah always cheered him up. She was a pistol and had met her match in her husband. Brutal, on the other hand, made him livid. It wasn't that Brutal was a bad husband. Jon simply hated the circumstances under which he and Hannah had met and married.

A couple of years back, immediately after the Tiberius Group took over, Hannah had been sold into mail order bride slavery by the moron in her first brief marriage. She had been shipped off to one of the moons of

Mars, where Brutal had bought her after fighting another miner.

Jon would never admit it, but after spending time with Brutal, he knew with utter assurance Hannah could have done worse. Especially after he'd met the man Brutal had fought to win her at the mining colony auction. The competitor for her hand in the mail order bride marriage had been Erik Vander, a sadist murderer currently in jail for killing another mail order bride. Jon had brought him back to Earth and put him away with no regrets.

Brutal gave him a smug smile and then motioned him to a door off the foyer. "Let's talk in here." Brutal motioned him into what Jon knew was the study. He followed behind, hating to not have Hannah available as a referee.

"What did you need with Matt?" Brutal asked. He crossed to the massive desk in the corner of the large room. The two connected walls framed behind his desk were filled floor-to-ceiling with enough paper books to make any modern-day librarian unquestionably giddy. The rare smell of wood pulp with ink assailed Jon as they got closer.

Wood pulp paper products were no longer allowed to be produced. Books published now were placed on computer disc or synthetic paper. Museum libraries were the only place you could see them on display anymore. And private collections like Brutal's.

"I wanted to ask him something about his business, but it doesn't matter," Jon said distractedly, looking at the books over Brutal's shoulder.

"I'm his chief security consultant. Maybe I could help."

"I'm shocked that Matt would stoop to nepotism. You must have begged."

Brutal stepped behind his desk and said, "Yeah, because I need the money so bad. Try me. Ask your question. I know things."

"Do you know anyone at Westland Industries I can get as a husband for Grace?"

Brutal stared at him a moment before arching one eyebrow up in obvious surprise. "No, my duties don't include pimping husbands for women, just straight security. Why did you marry her in the first place if you were going to find another husband for her?"

"Her kid. She was up for auction. No one bid. She would have gone to the Institute and lost her child. So I bid on her."

Brutal cocked his head to one side, smiled, and nodded, but Jon could tell he knew it wasn't the complete story. "That was certainly nice of you. You know, to go so far out of your way for a stranger. Or did you know her already?"

"Not exactly."

"Uh-huh. You're full of shit. Where did you meet her, and why get rid of her now?"

"None of your fucking business. How about that?"

Brutal sat down behind the desk and tipped back in the chair. He crossed his arms and said, "Since she's going to be living under my roof for the next twenty-four hours or so, I'd say it's my business."

Jon paced in front of the desk, trying to think of something to tell Brutal. He didn't want to get rid of Grace and definitely didn't want to explain his romantic feelings to his black sheep brother-in-law.

"I met her once a long time ago during the case involving the murder of my partner. She helped put the guy away. That's it. No big deal." He decided not to share the interlude in the elevator in deference to Grace. He convinced himself it was because he was the kind of guy that didn't kiss and tell. But truthfully, he didn't want Brutal, of all people, to know how deeply he cared for Grace, especially if he didn't get to keep her.

"She's kind of cute. Are you sure you want to find another guy for her?"

"If I stay married to her, I'll have to bring her and her kid either here or to Matt and Sophie's anytime I leave town, which is frequently. You don't want that responsibility, do you?"

Brutal shrugged. "No skin off my ass. This is a big house. It would give Hannah another female to talk to."

"I'd have to get a special license to assign you and Matt the permanent rights of a blood relative. I don't know that I want you as a blood relative. Did you want me as one?"

Brutal gave him a smirk before saying, "You could get yourself reassigned to a local law enforcement post instead of traipsing around the universe on someone else's whim."

"Purposely get demoted? There's no way in hell I'd ever do that, not for anyone."

"Marriage changes things, Jon."

"Not for me."

"You say that, but I don't buy it. You fairly radiate a lethal, protective aura around Grace. It made you uneasy to watch her walk away with your own sister. Imagine it's some strange guy from Matt's company leading her away to consummate her next marriage."

"Shut up." Jon lunged over the desk at him, but Brutal bounced out of the chair, well out of reach. Jon lost his balance and landed stomach-down on the desk. Unfortunately, he could picture that scenario all too well, and it infuriated him beyond all reason.

"You've already displayed one of the two signs of attachment."

"What sign?" Jon straightened up from the desk, brushing a piece of rumpled synthetic paper off his shirt.

"The first sign of attachment is the inability to allow even the thought of her to be with anyone else. The very idea of another man touching her crushes your soul because you know that no one will love her as much as you are trying not to. Plus you'd rather beat the crap out of someone than admit it."

"I'd rather beat the crap out of you."

"Yeah? Picture your life without her and say you aren't attached."

"Why?" But Jon knew why. He'd rather die than lose her. He knew it, and apparently Brutal was reading minds, because he had a smug expression.

"The second sign is the incapacity to imagine your future without them. In case you were wondering."

Jon straightened and drilled a smug look of his own at Brutal. "Remember back on the moon of Mars when you left to go back to your mine without Hannah?"

Brutal arched one eyebrow questioningly. "Yeah?"

"I *let* Hannah sneak out to meet you. Did you know that?" Jon had seen the look on Hannah's face when she'd come back down to dinner to find Brutal gone. Before he'd left, Jon had thought Brutal might shed a tear or two of his own at leaving Hannah behind.

"I figured as much." Brutal chuckled. "What kind of interstellar lawman lets his own sister escape so easily?"

"The kind who recognized you weren't what I thought you were at first glance—or punch, in our case."

"Genetically enhanced, you mean?" Brutal made a scoffing noise, "Well, it takes one to know one. That sucker-punch when we met clued me in immediately."

"No. I mean I knew you weren't a sexual vampire." Brutal stiffened as if Jon had clocked him one on the head at the mention of the word 'vampire.' But then Brutal's remark registered in Jon's mind, and he asked, "What do you mean, it takes one to know one?"

Brutal crossed his arms as if trying to keep his calm. "For starters, I'm *not* a sexual vampire, and I can tell you're enhanced because I am. I figure it's a big secret, you being a lawman and all, but don't worry. I probably won't rat you out."

Jon stared unbelievingly at one of only three people alive in the universe who even suspected he might be enhanced. One was his privately funded personal doctor, the man who'd been responsible for the very secret enhancements that had begun before he was eight years old and the current supplier of his sexual suppression medication.

The other was the man who'd paid for the enhancement all those years ago: a senile, ninety-one-year-old man who resided in a private nursing home. Jon's genetic abilities were courtesy of his mother's former boss. He didn't need Brutal to be the third charm in his super-secret, genetically enhanced life.

"I don't know what you're talking about. I'm not enhanced," Jon said with practiced lightness.

Brutal's gaze drilled into him. "Denial doesn't become you."

Jon shook his head and forced a benign smile. "I'm not in denial. I'm not enhanced. What makes you think I am?"

"Guys like you and me are rare. We were given our 'enhanced cocktail' before puberty. Many of the older test subjects…ended up vampires.

"You have the ability to sense the others too, like I do. That's why I'm the security officer for Matt. He had a vampire working for him and didn't know it. *Him* I ratted out. I sensed him easily when Hannah and I visited Matt's company. The degenerate vampire I encountered in the john had a wife, but had gotten tired of the same woman day after day and had begun to stray. I do what I can to help out when I find sexual predators loose.

"But I'm curious. If you require sex, as I suspect you must, how come you never seem to be looking for women? Ever! I almost convinced myself I was mistaken about your proclivities, but I got such a vibe off you tonight that I knew I was right. Grace walked past you and your pupils dilated until you had no color left. Then they snapped back as if nothing had happened. That's how I knew."

"Nice fiction, Brutal. But you're wrong. I'm a lawman. Lawmen aren't allowed to be genetically enhanced. They run endless and repeated tests to make sure." Jon leveled him with a look that said he never wanted the subject brought up again and made a mental note to speak to his doctor. He'd never noticed the pupils of his eyes changing for any reason, sexual or not. His eyesight had been imperfect of late. He'd noticed the problem at the auction while adjusting to the darkness. He'd never had more than a nanosecond of adjustment time in the past. Maybe he was sick.

Brutal tilted his head to one side as if he didn't quite understand, but then nodded and said, "My mistake. Grace will be safe here. I promise."

"Thank you. I'll be back late tomorrow night, but I'll need to pick her up no matter how late, okay?"

"Sure. Whatever." Brutal shrugged. "Have a safe trip."

* * * *

Grace entered the study at the direction of Hannah's huge husband, Brutal. "Are you leaving already?" Grace adored Jon's sister. She was a chatterbox, but she was friendly and completely accepting of a total stranger being in her home because her brother said it was okay.

"Yeah. I've got to go. My flight's in exactly an hour, which is how long it will take me to get to the airport. I'm running late, but I promise you'll be safe here."

"I know. I like your sister. She's funny."

"Yeah. Hannah's a good egg. Don't let Brutal scare you. He's big, but fairly harmless."

She shook her head to let him know she wasn't afraid of being here. She was more fearful Jon wouldn't make it back on time and then she'd be in trouble again. She shrugged and smiled at him. "Hannah doesn't seem to be afraid of him."

"No. He's good to her, but I'll never admit it to him." He winked and changed the subject. "I'm sorry we didn't have time to pick up your daughter."

"It's okay. Once you get back tomorrow night, we can...you know, consummate things...and then go get her, right?"

"Right."

Grace wished they'd 'consummated things' before leaving his home. Did they have time to accomplish the deed now? Elliott waited outside. She suspected that if Jonathan took too long, he'd simply come and beat the door down.

Then again, what did she have to lose? Grace threw her arms around Jonathan's neck and kissed him, sliding her tongue between his startled lips. He twisted her around and pressed her against the desk. The edge dug into her ass as he kissed her the way she wanted him to—as if he wanted her desperately.

Her arms were wrapped around his neck in a death grip. His hands burned through the fabric of her skirt. She felt his cock grow against her belly. He ground into her. She moaned, licking his mouth. She leaned back toward the surface of Brutal's desk, pulling him with her. He seemed to realize what she trying to do: allow him to take her on Brutal's desk. The rush of desire overwhelmed her.

She wondered briefly whether the library door was locked and decided she didn't care.

Jon broke the kiss and gasped, "Oh God, Grace, do you know what you do to me?" He clenched her tightly.

"Don't stop. Please, Jon." She clenched him tightly, too.

"I'm sorry. I can't..." He had to pry her off slowly. He checked his watch and cursed.

From the doorway of the study came an acerbic voice. "Do I need to turn a hose on you two?" Jon's creepy, angry boss stood at the now open door. "Let's go, Jon. We're late."

Jonathan steadied her against his body. "I'll meet you in the car."

"No. We should have left five minutes ago."

Jonathan separated from her, pulling away as if with great

reluctance. She knew he needed to leave. She knew he wanted her. He took several deep breaths and released her.

"I'll be back tomorrow night to continue this," he whispered.

"You'd better be."

Jonathan strode away from her, never looking back. Elliott gave her a dirty look, then a smug smile of victory. Grace understood that if he had anything to do with Jonathan's return, she'd be back up for auction before she could say, "Fucking Tiberius Group."

* * * *

Thoughts of Grace filled his mind constantly for the next several hours as Jon jetted his way to the east coast. As the flight soared eastward, he knew he wouldn't feel at ease until he had her in his arms again. He wouldn't find another man for her. Brutal was right about that too. He'd rather cut his beating heart out of his chest with a spoon than see her with anyone else.

The image of Grace came into his mind again—the one of her waving from the door of Hannah's house, and he smiled. Even when he slept, he dreamed about her. It was a wonder he didn't walk around with a perpetual hard-on. She seriously engaged his libido.

Jon hoped this meeting with Cindy Wells wouldn't turn out to be a big waste of his time.

"I don't know what I can tell you about Andy Nelson," Cindy began. "He was my high school boyfriend, but we didn't stay together after graduation. I heard he got implants, and I was already staying as far away as possible. He was an asshole."

"Did he ever threaten you?" She got a distant look in her eyes, and Jon knew she was holding something back.

"Tell me what he did."

"Why does it matter? I won't stay to testify. No matter what you do or say."

Jon gave her his most serious stare. "I want him to stay in prison."

"So do I, but nothing I say will help you. Trust me." She gave him an annoyed look, then softened. "He dumped me right after I had sex with him the first time, okay?"

"Was this before or after he had the implants?"

"Before the implants. He wasn't satisfied with my efforts. He was a shit-heel as a boyfriend, but he didn't do any freaky stuff to me like what I heard he did to that other girl."

"Grace?"

Cindy nodded. "He dumped me to go pop her cherry because I wouldn't have sex with him. He bragged about 'fucking' Grace in his car after he took me back, which pissed me off, but what could I do? Andy was a great catch back then, and I was a foolish high school girl."

"Did Andy ever try to contact you after he got the implants?"

"Not exactly."

Jon pushed out an exasperated breath. "What exactly?"

Cindy shrugged and replied, "I went to Europe for vacation, but one of the maids at our house said Andy showed up a week before I returned with a blood-red rose to give me."

"A rose?" Jon felt a familiar tickle of elusive memory scratched at his mind, but he couldn't grasp it.

"Yeah. She said he was pretty pissed because I wasn't home to receive his gift. Like a single rose would have made me spread my legs for him. What a jerk!"

"Do you remember when that might have been.?"

Cindy shrugged again. "I'm not sure. It might have been around Halloween. I got back to the states in early November. Listen, I wish you well, and I'm sorry I can't help you, but you wasted a trip. I need to get going."

"If you remember anything, will you send a message?"

"Sure. Whatever. But don't count on me coming back to this fucked-up country to testify. At least not until they get rid of the Tiberius sons of bitches. I'm sick and tired of being a second-class citizen. It sucks to be a woman here. My psycho husband would kill me if he ever found me, and the shame of it is that no one would care. You know?"

"Sorry, ma'am. The changes are definitely challenging."

"Challenging, my ass. They suck."

"I appreciate you meeting with me."

"Whatever. You wasted a trip. I told that Elliott guy everything I just said. I don't know why I needed to repeat it to you."

Jon knew why. If he hadn't been sure of it before, now he knew his boss had set him up.

* * * *

Jon headed back to the hotel and slept fitfully, dreaming of Grace until he awoke with an erection so painful he had to give himself an injection. The next morning, he arrived at the airport in plenty of time to catch his return flight home. Unfortunately, the delays he experienced were saved for his return flight. The aircraft sat on the tarmac for two hours while his nervous stomach ate at his patience.

"Ladies and gentlemen, sorry to have kept you waiting. Either we will be on our way in a few minutes, or we'll have to spend another night here and be on our way early tomorrow morning."

An hour later, he stood in the airport with a hotel voucher and a sincere urge to kill Elliott for sending him on this wild goose chase.

The scheduled return flight leaving the next day would arrive at the airport less than an hour before his forty-eight hours to consummate the marriage were up. Brutal's house was over an hour away, even if he drove his cruiser with the sirens blazing. He wasn't going to make it back to her.

He checked the possibility of taking a train, but they were less reliable than flying. Driving was out of the question due to the distance. Even if he could persuade Brutal to risk traveling with Grace across the country, it was too far, with too many checkpoints.

With a heavy heart, he called to let Grace know. The thought of losing her was almost more than he could stomach.

"Hey, Brutal. Let me talk to Grace."

"Where are you? I thought you'd be back by now. Grace is...well...to put it mildly, freaking out. Do I understand you haven't fulfilled the forty-eight-hour consummation requirement yet?"

"Yeah. And I'm not going to make it back in time either. I'm stranded."

There was a long silence on the phone. "Guess you should have done her in my office before you left. I would've tackled your boss in the foyer if you'd warned me."

"Yeah, hindsight's twenty-twenty, but I was always a fool for romance. The ambience in your office while you, Hannah, and Elliott listened out in the foyer wasn't conducive to my seduction plans."

"Yeah, 'cause I have nothing better to do than listen to your sexual proclivities. When does your flight come in, Romeo?"

"About ten minutes before time runs out, if I'm lucky. Unfortunately, you live an hour away, even if I use my sirens for the trip."

"Too bad we didn't take the time to become blood brothers before you jetted off. I could bring her to you."

"Yeah. I guess it wasn't meant to be. Fate, you know."

"Want me to break it to her?"

"No. I'll do it. Put her on the phone."

The sound of Grace's voice made him want to crawl through the lines and wrap himself around her. "Hi. Are you at the airport?"

"I'm stranded in Eastlake City. I already tried to get an extension from Elliott. It was denied, of course." Elliott had yelped in joy. The case was back on track, and Elliott had mentioned a promotion. Jon had told him to go fuck himself, but Elliott had been gleefully unmoved.

"What will happen now?" Grace asked in a dejected tone he echoed silently.

"I'll find someone for you so you can keep Emma."

"No. Please, I don't want anybody else. Why don't you want me?"

"I *do* want you, Grace. Believe me. I can't physically make it to you, not even if we met halfway in vehicles."

"But..."

"I'm sorry, Grace. I truly am."

"I should have made you do it before we left your house. I shouldn't have wasted my time spouting off about my past."

"Don't torture yourself. It's my fault. I'll find a good husband for you. I'll find someone who will let you keep Emma. I'll do a private sale, no auction, okay?"

"Fine." She slammed the phone down in his ear and broke his heart. He was a lawman. He was trained to kill without remorse if a criminal was in violation, and yet at this moment, he was surprised to learn he had another side.

He discovered a sentimental side long buried in his macho job. It was the emotional one he'd long since ignored in favor of his career, never believing there was a woman for him to love.

But there was. Her name was Grace and she was about to become his lost love.

* * * *

Jon spent a miserable night all alone in the hotel. He dreamt of Grace and thought about how stupid he was not to have done whatever it took to keep her. He should have left Elliott pounding at the door until he'd finished making her his wife. His foolish honor in trying to keep her fears at bay would cost him very dearly.

Jon boarded the first return flight the next morning. He drank about five cups of bitter, burnt-tasting airplane coffee on the flight to stay alert from his lack of rest the night before.

The pilot informed them they were ahead of schedule, and Jon stepped off the airplane and into the jet-way tunnel with thirty-seven minutes to spare on his forty-eight-hour time limit. The hour-long trip to Hannah's home was the only thing standing in the way of his continued marriage to Grace.

It seemed wickedly unfair to lose her because of only a few minutes. He thought once again about who he could sell her to, but he knew of no one. He was only acquainted with lawmen. If they weren't already married, they had the same life he did. His disturbing thoughts were interrupted by a commotion ahead of him as he exited the jet-way into the noisy airport. There were lots of people waiting on either side of two velvet roped areas for the plane passengers to disembark. Jon followed the marked trail which promptly opened into the main section of the terminal.

He couldn't believe his eyes when he saw Brutal with his big, meaty hand wrapped around Grace's forearm, dragging her along as he yelled at her over his shoulder on a direct path to him.

Chapter 6

Brutal gave Jon a quick smile of recognition and then his expression changed into a stern serious visage. He announced in an overloud voice, "Here's my sister. She's your problem now, Lawman."

He thrust Grace forward, whirling her to fall right into Jon's waiting arms. Jon held her to him as her delectable scent wafted around his unbelieving senses.

Grace turned her back to Brutal and said, "I hate you. I have since we were kids, you big bully."

"Back at you, princess. Good riddance. You're lucky I didn't whip you for your sassy mouth. I'll leave that to your husband because as a lawman, he's got better equipment for the job."

Jon forced his lips not to shape into a grin. The Tiberius-friendly men in the surrounding area smiled and nodded amongst themselves, obviously satisfied that yet another female was being put in her place.

"You've got your own transportation home, right?" Brutal asked quietly, leaning close.

Jon nodded and added sincerely, "Don't know how you did it, but thanks, Brutal."

"Uh-huh. Airport workers don't check licenses very closely if you give them a little drama for their ho-hum lives. I put my thumb over Hannah's picture and flashed her I.D. when I dragged Grace kicking and screaming through the first security point. Nobody even noticed." Brutal glanced down at Grace and then smirked. "Now, I expect you to treat my little sister with respect. Don't force her to do anything carnal, at least until you find a less public place." He winked once and then turned to walk away without saying another word.

Grace tightened her grip on his arms. "It's way past time to make me your wife, don't you think?"

"I do. Any thoughts on a private place for some carnal activity?" he asked jokingly. "Otherwise, we're going to my IL cruiser in the public sub-basement parking lot. The back seat is very small and uncomfortable. How can you resist?"

"The back seat of a car wouldn't be my first choice, as enticingly cozy as it sounds. Marissa told me about a broom closet by an old jet way that she and her husband used once. She said it's out of the way and no one can hear what's going on inside."

He laughed and glanced at his watch. "Okay. Let's go. We need to hurry."

They headed for the quiet space of the broom closet to consummate their marriage. Luckily, it was early in the morning and the airport was still fairly quiet. They arrived at the door to the janitor's closet...which was locked from the inside. Loud sexual noises already emanated from behind the closed closet door. Grace's disbelieving face spoke volumes as she blushed.

"Popular spot. Marissa was wrong. You can too hear what's going on inside." Jon tried not to laugh out loud and searched for the nearest bathroom to find some privacy.

"Now what?"

"Let's try the bathrooms. Maybe we'll get lucky and find one closed for cleaning."

Jon spotted an arrow directing them to the restrooms. Along the way, they passed a freight elevator. Jon stopped and pushed the down button. The doors popped open, as if waiting for them to come aboard.

"What do you think? And keep in mind we are seriously running out of time." Jon glanced at his watch for the umpteenth time.

"Okay. Let's do it."

Jon stepped into the elevator, turned, and noticed he was alone. Grace stood before the doors, and as they began to shut, she put her arm in and the doors bounced off. Jon stepped into the doorway again and held out his hand.

"In or out?" he asked, smiling.

"In. Definitely in." She hesitated. "I still don't like elevators though."

"I thought I cured you of that years ago with a kiss in the dark."

"Oh, you did. Unfortunately, the cure didn't last beyond that one time. If only you'd been available whenever I needed to ride an elevator."

Jon smiled and touched her shoulder. "I'll be right here. I promise not to let you fall."

"Okay." She closed her eyes and took a step. Jon wrapped his arm around her waist and led her inside. He turned to the panel and hit the down button for the sub-basement garage, where he'd parked his vehicle. He hit the stop button and waited for a blaring noise to ensue, but the elevator was silent. He took that to mean no one cared about the freight elevator, who was on it, or what anyone did inside it.

Grace opened her eyes and looked around at all four corners of the ceiling space.

"What are you looking for?"

"Cameras."

"If there are any, I don't see them. Come on. By my calculation, we have less than thirty minutes."

She turned back to him. She looked apprehensive, to say the least.

The reality of what they were about to do sunk into his conscious. Jon was delighted that fate had stepped in and allowed him to keep her. "Let me hold you a minute."

"Okay." Her voice trembled. She was frightened and hated small spaces, but they didn't have time to go anywhere else. He'd calm her down and coax her gently. Technically, this was their honeymoon. She deserved whatever tenderness he had time to offer. Jon pulled her close and brushed the knuckles of one hand along her jaw.

"Remember the first time we met?" he asked. The visual of them melded together in the near dark skated across his frontal lobe. He felt his dick thicken and lengthen, ready for the anticipated carnal action.

"Yes."

"I accept your offer to have amazing sex in the elevator."

Grace's hands lifted to rest on his chest. Her touch burned through his shirt. "Did you think I was a loose woman back then?"

"No, I thought you were frightened and beautiful. I cursed myself regularly afterwards for turning you down. I should have said to hell with the camera and gone for it. "

"But we would have gotten caught."

He shrugged. "Most things worth doing at all have some risk involved, especially sexual ones."

"I guess you're right."

"Are you going to be okay?"

Grace blushed. She then nodded and slid her arms up, hooking them behind his shoulders. This put her kissable, bee-stung lips right up next to his. His hands went to her waist. He needed to break the ice.

A lip-licking kiss was certainly in order. He kissed her hard, twisting his lips sideways as she breached his mouth with her tongue. She kissed him like she meant it. Lust surged through his body. He hadn't participated in lots of sex, settling instead for medication to take the edge off his ferocious sexual desires. He was anxious to have a willing partner for his sexual proclivities. Grace was the icon he based his fantasy woman on. She had been ever since he'd kissed her in the elevator.

It would be nice to have someone to come home to. Giving up his injector was yet another bonus of this marriage and yielded the eradication of monthly shots he endured to tame his libido.

Grace ground her lips and made a sexy, mewling noise, forcing his neglected cock to spring forth in his uniform trousers with an erection of epic proportions. He wanted to sink into her deeply and knew he'd come quickly, like the last time they were together. He vowed to make this up to her. Once they were done here, he would take her home and spend some time making sure she knew he could last longer than three strokes every time they were together.

She wore a skirt similar to the one she'd had on the day he married her. He reached underneath it, sliding his hand from her silky thigh up to the apex of her sex planning to remove her underwear. She wasn't wearing any. He rubbed her ass, shocked by her lack of under things. Grace moaned in his mouth as he stroked both bare cheeks.

He broke the seal of their lips. "I hope Brutal didn't know you were going commando."

"He scared the pants off me," she said in utter seriousness before smiling.

"Funny."

"Of course he didn't know. I was just glad there weren't any strip searches coming into the airport."

"Me too. Because I would hate to miss this." He slid his hand between her legs from behind and directly into her pussy to assess her readiness level for his epic cock. She was drenched. He stroked her clit a couple of times, letting her creamy moisture coat his fingertips. He inserted two fingers inside her pussy again as she sucked in a deep breath and squirmed. Jon watched her pupils widen as he circled her clit several more times until her eyelids dipped and she moaned.

"I've waited so long. Make me your wife, Jon. I promise you I'm more than ready." Her breathy, stilted voice caught every time he ran his finger across her small, sensitive flesh.

He kissed her again and loosened his pants and zipper, one-handed. He flipped her skirt up in front, lifting her thighs up and over his cock, which desperately strained to connect intimately. She climbed up on him, positioning herself. She reached a hand down to grab his cock and slide it into her wet opening. Jon shut his eyes at the contact of her soft hand on him. The head of his cock was now inserted and poised for his first thrust inside. He held her legs, shifting to make his move. She kissed his mouth as he lowered her onto his cock, feeling his way inside her very slick, warm pussy.

Paradise surely wouldn't be as good as this. She moaned, kissing him passionately as he thrust inside her slowly for this first time. She was tighter than he expected for having given birth.

Doing his best not to bruise her legs with his grip, he lowered and raised her several more times, his cock straining to pound inside. He broke from her insistent mouth to whisper, "Am I hurting you?" but didn't stop thrusting. He couldn't. His libido was on a mission now. She didn't answer, but moments later, she stiffened.

Grace's loud response to his question washed over him. She tilted her head back and climaxed, moaning. "Ohmigod. Ohmigod," she repeated over and over. He could feel her clamping on him, surprisingly enough. He gripped her legs and surged up inside, pumping as best he could for the awkward position he was in. She was tight and slick and Christ Almighty, he was ready to let loose his own orgasmic release. He thrust inside harder and deeper several more times as she clamped on him blissfully, finding his own volcanically fantastic fulfillment inside her tight slit moments later. He spewed forth his seed deeply inside her as his legs went weak from the aftermath. Braced against the wall, he pulled her close, his shoulders pressing back to keep him from falling on his ass.

Leaning against the elevator wall with Grace still wrapped around him in post-sexual bliss, he finally caught his breath and checked his watch.

They'd consummated the marriage with fifteen minutes to spare.

Now to race to his home to catch the Tiberius Representative so he could verify it. He felt like he was living his life on the run. Common criminals probably didn't have to sprint like he had to for the sake of amazing sex in an elevator.

"That was remarkable. I can't wait to finally get you into a bed." He felt her stiffen a moment before she melted back into him and sighed.

"It was amazing sex."

"When I can move my legs again, we need to get back to the house. We're late."

Grace leaned down and kissed him passionately and thoroughly, her soft tongue sliding lazily around his mouth. He felt his cock spring back to life, still embedded inside her. But they didn't have time for another round of amazing elevator sex.

She released his lips. "What happens when we're late for the body scan?"

"I don't know, maybe a fine. I'll use my out-of-town trip as an excuse. Don't think you get to escape me now." He laughed and hugged her, so grateful for the opportunity to share his life, such as it was, with her. Elliott would be only his first obstacle. The magistrate reviewing Andy Nelson's case would be next in line, but he didn't care. They could all go to hell. He got to keep Grace as his wife, and the rest would work out.

"Thank you, Jon."

"For the elevator sex or the permanent marriage status?"

"Both. Either. I feel secure for the first time in a long time." She gazed deeply into his eyes and said, "I promise you won't regret it."

"I already don't regret it. We'll figure everything out together, right?"

"Right."

They rushed back to meet the Tiberius representative, who promptly did the scan. He approved the permanent marriage papers, but not before giving them a disapproving look. He knew by the reading on his scanner that they had only recently completed the consummation.

Jon gave him a 'fuck off' look in return and pulled Grace inside to spend the day making it up to her. He'd been looking forward to the first taste of her for three long damn years. It was time. As soon as the door closed and locked, they slammed into each other, kissing and pulling pieces of clothing off while they shuffled their way in the direction of his bedroom.

They started in the shower because he wanted to wash his trip grime away. Also, he wanted to see her naked and soapy. He teased her by slathering soap all over the both of them, but didn't let her climax. He wanted her naked in his bed. He toweled them off and kissed her as he danced her into his bedroom.

By the time the reached the edge of his bed, he was glad they were already naked. He picked her up in his arms, trying not to throw her down and have his wicked way with her. Instead, he positioned her on the center of the huge bed and crawled on hands and knees over her. She reached up and grabbed two rungs of his slatted headboard as if to hang on for whatever he planned.

He leaned down and sucked leisurely on a nipple until it pebbled in his mouth. Her moans inflamed him. He released the one and then placed his mouth on the other. He snaked a hand down between her legs to play with her clit while he nibbled on her peak. His cock was presently rigid with pent-up desire, but he had plans to introduce her now creamy, moist slit to his tongue. He kissed a path from her breast to her belly and then ran his whiskered face even lower. When she realized his intent, she half sat up, but he buried his face in her curls and licked her lower lips appreciatively. She fell back to the bed, groaning in what sounded like pleasure, so he sucked her clit between his lips to further her satisfaction. The taste of her made his cock want to simply hump the bed and finish up.

Jon brought a hand up to tease her pussy with his fingers as he licked, sucked, and nibbled on her small, tasty flesh. He looked up to see her fingering her own nipples and had to clench all the way to his toes so as not to shoot off at the sight. He inserted two fingers inside her very juicy body and she rode them, grinding on him, still moaning. Her breathing came in harsh gasps now. He teased her clit with the tip of his tongue and inserted his fingers inside her as deeply as he could until she came in a screaming trembling rush.

He felt her orgasm wash over him and squeeze his fingers. She screamed his name over and over before collapsing in whimpering satisfaction. He couldn't wait any longer. He removed his hand from between her legs and grabbed his cock.

"Look at me," he demanded, releasing his cock to lift her hips into position for optimal thrust.

She opened her shining, satisfied eyes and smiled as he directed the swollen head inside her wet and still pulsing sex. He watched her as he drove his cock deeply inside her slick pussy.

He found he was trembling on the verge of his release, watching her while he pierced her body slowly and repeatedly. He glanced at her breasts and back to her eyes.

"Touch your nipples for me." Grace's fingertips slid over to caress her nipples and he growled in appreciation. She brought one forefinger up to her mouth, stuck it inside, and sucked on it until the tip was moistened. She placed it back on her nipple, swirling the moisture around the areola. Desire pounded through his veins.

He powered another thrust deeply and said, "Lick your finger.... Touch your clit."

She stuck the other finger between her lips, moistening it, and then slid it down until her finger reached the area where he plunged his cock over and over. She circled her clit as he thrust deeply. His eyes traveled to where she pinched a pebbled peak and back down to where she was pleasuring herself. Several strokes later, she arched in another climax. His eyes half closed when he powered his final stroke all the way inside and released a powerfully roaring orgasm.

His legs trembled in the aftermath of his climax. He fell forward, trapping her beneath him. She caressed his back with her fingernails, scratching a path to his soul.

When they had finally gathered their wits about them, Jon led her back to the shower. He touched her everywhere reverently, as if he still didn't believe he got to keep her. She clenched her arms around his neck and buried her face in his throat as warm water rained over them. He held her tight until the shower ran cool before releasing her. Grace. His wife. His future.

He was the luckiest man in the world.

Doubt about his actions wouldn't seep in until later.

Chapter 7

It took the rest of the day for the slow process of the Tiberius Group Family Center to bring Emma to the house. Grace made lunch, and after an hour, they'd finally eaten, still waiting for word of when Emma would arrive. Grace made her daughter a plate of food and cleaned up the kitchen to within an inch of its life. She then fidgeted around the house, cleaning here and there.

Jon pretended to read the files on Andy Nelson, toying with the uncomfortable sensation that he was playing with fire. He hadn't spoken to Elliott yet. He didn't know Grace was now Jon's permanent wife. It was a conversation he didn't want to have.

He shifted gears, wondering what he'd do with his regular cleaning service, a husband-and-wife team. Should he keep them on? Would Grace like to have a cleaning service? He didn't know how to live with someone. He hadn't shared a home with anyone since age eighteen, when he lived with his mother. Hannah and Sophie had left for college. He had spent his final year of high school with a mother who was never home because she worked like a slave even eighteen years after their selfish conman father had deserted them.

Jon glanced over at Grace and wondered if she would resent the time he devoted to his career. Amazing sex notwithstanding, he wondered what on earth had ever possessed him to marry her. She glanced over at him nervously, as if she could read his wayward thoughts, and frowned.

Grace paced the floor like a caged, angry panther ready to spring on the first person to startle her as she waited for her daughter. Jon tried not to be a sourpuss, but on some level knew the dynamic of his household would change dramatically with a child living in it. He barely knew Grace and hadn't lived with her as his wife for a full twenty-four hours yet. Adding another person would be a big change. Especially a small female child.

"I know what you're thinking," Grace said suddenly. He looked up and realized she had stopped pacing to stare at him daydreaming about the inherent life changes about to occur in his small house.

"What am I thinking?"

"You're kicking yourself for agreeing to keep me as your wife."

"No..."

"Yes, you are. Children change things. I know that. Children who don't belong to you change things in a big way."

"I'm sure it will be fine." Christ Almighty, she *could* read his mind.

"I promise Emma is very quiet. Danny wouldn't tolerate her speaking or making noise."

"Don't bring up that idiot's name again. It pisses me off. I'm not in any way like your ex-roommate."

"I know. I'm sorry."

He was being an ass. She was right: he was having second thoughts about turning his life upside down for a wife he barely knew and a child he'd never met.

Jon heard a vehicle enter the driveway to his property. He stood up and peeked out the window to see an official Tiberius Family Center vehicle pull into his circular driveway and park by the door. He got his first glance of Emma Maitland riding in the back seat. She was a beautiful child. Her coloring was exactly that of Grace's. She turned in her seat, and he saw that she was crying. Mouth open, tears streaming— she must be screaming. That didn't bode well for a peaceful drop-off. From experience with the Tiberius Family Center, Jon knew a pious crony with attitude would emerge from the vehicle. Clutched in his hands would be a copy of current Tiberius laws freshly printed on synthetic paper. If Jon were to exhibit any reluctance to Tiberius rule, the man would wave the laws in Jon's face to prove the righteousness of the new regime.

Jon could visualize the drama as is would unfold. Grace would kick the pious crony's ass for making her child cry, and Jon would spend the rest of the day making nice for the actions of his errant wife. He hated to make nice.

He dropped the curtain and turned to Grace. If her child was crying, she wouldn't want to deal rationally with the authorities. Jon didn't want to break up a fight if Emma had been mistreated. He decided to go without Grace to bring her inside.

"Stay here. I'll bring her to you. Do you understand me?" He sounded cross, when he only meant to sound firm. The minute she heard her child crying, she wouldn't listen to him anyway.

Grace gave him a hopeful look and stood straighter. "Is she here?"

"Yes. But I mean it. I don't care what you hear. You stay here. Do you understand me?"

"What's wrong?"

"Probably nothing. Do as I say. Wait inside."

"Okay." Grace crossed her arms and began pacing, as if ready to burst into a thousand pieces at the wait she'd already endured.

Jon knew he'd only have her quiet cooperation until she heard her child screaming. Then he hoped not to have to pull his gun to stop a murder. He stepped out of his house, closed the door behind him, and expected the worst: a bratty child about to be difficult to control. Jon smiled in reassurance so his wife, who had up to now had had the worst life in the history of human existence, could have her baby back.

He heard the unhappy shriek of the child just then. The sound drilled into his brain, but when he figured out what she was crying about, he immediately launched a defense for Emma.

"I...hic...don't want...hic...to live with...hic...Mrs. Brent. I want...hic...my mommy!" Emma Maitland wailed between hiccups.

"You are a spiteful little girl. You should consider yourself lucky the Brents want you at all. Girls like you should be put away." The matron turned, and Jon figured she was the ugliest woman he'd ever seen. The ponderous bulk of her frame didn't bother him as much as the uni-brow she sported. It startled him when she turned to face him, but not as much as the big, hairy, misshapen birthmark the size of Texas on one of her fat cheeks.

He tried not to stare, but damn, she was hideous.

"Perhaps if she knew Mrs. Brent was her mommy, she wouldn't be crying," Jon said in a raised voice as he approached the trio now out of the vehicle.

"Mrs. Brent is my mommy?" asked the forlorn little girl, looking up into his eyes with a hope he was pleased he'd provided. He squatted down to her level to speak to her again.

"Yes. She's waiting for you inside. If you let me escort you, she'll think I'm a hero for bringing her little girl back. Do you think you could wait for me to take you inside?"

She looked over at the front door first before looking back at him. She pierced him with her clear, alert eyes, which were the exact color of Andy Nelson's, and nodded once, wiping tears from her cheek with a small hand. She hiccupped twice after that, but was otherwise silent.

"What do you need for me to sign?" Jon stood again as he asked the two Tiberius Group Family Center members.

"Do you have the marriage documents?" the man asked, frowning. The TG hated when people got along with each other. They seemed, in Jon's opinion, very small-minded and only happiest when strife and fighting broke out in the course of their duties. Drama as entertainment.

"Yes, and I also have the adoption papers. I'd like to begin the process today."

"It's very civilized of you to offer to adopt the child. As a lawman, you probably see the worst of humanity. The Tiberius Group is making life better for everyone each and every day." The man puffed out his chest. Jon hoped he wasn't about to preach.

The woman with the uni-brow and birthmark nodded rigorously in agreement. Jon remained silent. He didn't think the world was a better place with Tiberius control. He was surprised they were still in power after two strife-filled, politically strong-armed years. It had been a difficult adjustment and one he hoped was short-lived.

"The child is an innocent. It's the least I can do," Jon said gruffly. Emma smiled up at him.

"Well, still it's good of you to accept into your household this child of Satan. She's the bastard child of a monstrous criminal, you know," the woman told him in an overloud 'confidential' voice. Spittle collected at the corner of her mouth as she spoke. Jon was repulsed by her attitude more than her appearance, but both were atrocious.

"I know she is innocent of any crime." Jon took and signed the electronic pad the man held out to him, thus taking custody of Emma. He then signed the application to petition the magistrate core that he might adopt one Emma Maitland. The fate of her life would become his ultimate decision someday, but her quiet countenance made him believe things might work out.

"How long until the papers are final and the adoption is complete?"

"Well, the prison warden will have to affirm her biological father is still incarcerated. Once that is determined, then the paperwork will go before a three-member panel of magistrates assigned to the Family Center's law section to determine whether you are worthy of fatherhood. They'll check to make certain you are an exemplary citizen in good standing in the community. I'm sure a lawman will have no problem."

"Fine." Jon returned the electronic clipboard and reached a hand out to Emma. "Are you ready to see your mom?"

"Yes, please," she responded and placed her hand in his. He hoped he would make a good father figure for her. He had to be better than Danny, the lazy bastard she'd lived with these past several years. With her small, soft hand trustingly wrapped in his, Jon knew if he ever found out Danny had mistreated Emma, he'd find a way to kill him.

Jon opened the door to Grace, who was still pacing at her post near the front door, and ushered Emma inside. When mother and daughter saw each other, both squealed in delight and hugged, crying and talking at the same time.

"I'll leave you two alone to settle in."

"Thank you so much, Jon. I mean it." Grace grabbed Emma up in her arms. Emma even pulled her little face away from her mother's to nod at him, smiling.

"You're welcome." Jon went back to his files, happy in the knowledge he'd done a good deed today. Perhaps being married with a child would agree with him.

* * * *

Grace clutched Emma to her as if she were dreaming. She had been worried about ever seeing her again. She owed Jon absolutely everything.

"Mommy, I'm so glad to see you."

"No one hurt you, did they, baby?"

"No. But they shook their heads and frowned a lot when I told them I wanted to see you."

"Well, we're together now, and nothing can separate us ever again."

"Where is our room, Mommy?"

Grace had dreaded this question. She had always slept in the same room as her daughter. Her aunt, who'd taken them in when her parents died, only had a two-room apartment. While living at Danny's, Emma, Grace and her aunt had shared a room until her aunt had died in a medical center last year. Now Emma would have the spare room all to herself. Grace would sleep with her delectable lawman husband. The thrill of this warmed her.

"You, my darling, will have a room all to yourself. Won't that be exciting?"

"But why, Mommy? I want to stay with you."

"Because the nice man in the next room is my new husband. Remember when we talked about my marrying Danny?" Emma nodded as uncertainty creased her features. "Jonathan is better for us, I promise. He's going to be your new dad. Mommies and daddies sleep in the same room, and children sleep in a different room."

"What if one of us gets scared?"

"If you get scared, you call for me and I'll come to you. But you need to get used to sleeping alone, Emma. It's the way it has to be. I love you more than anything. We are so lucky to be here. Please be a good girl about this."

"Okay…but can't you stay with me tonight, Mommy? Please? Just this first night." Emma's little, pleading face sent shards of guilt into her soul. How could she abandon her daughter tonight after all she'd been through?

* * * *

After seeing Emma securely in Grace's arms, Jon entered his bedroom and settled the idea in his mind that he would be sleeping alone. Grace wasn't going to abandon her daughter this first night in favor of his bed.

Damn, he wanted her again too. The interlude in the elevator had been a mere appetizer to the dinner portions of sex they had shared in his bed. Making love to her so many times earlier had only made Jon want her even more. He had a new outlet for his sexual proclivities, and her name was Grace.

He eyed the place in the bathroom wall where his secret panel of medicine resided. The place from which his customary sexual relief came. The Zanthacorth injection would be a poor substitute for sexual satisfaction after a flesh-and-blood woman. He wondered if he would ever be able to take a shot again as he relived the exquisite feeling of burying his cock into Grace and thrusting repeatedly.

The more he thought about it, the harder his dick got, until he started thinking of ways to lure her away from the guest bedroom for a quickie. Then he remembered Grace as she clutched her precious daughter, and banished any predatory sexual fantasies for tonight. He could wait. She and her daughter deserved to spend some quality time together after their separation. It wouldn't be forever.

He took a deep breath instead, trying to calm his libido with promises of future regular sexual activity. The door to his bedroom opened, and he wondered if his cock had psychic abilities when he heard Grace enter his bedroom, then close and lock the door behind her. A glance at her face made him think she was slightly pensive. When she turned from the door, Jon decided her expression was more wary. Once she saw him through the open bathroom door, startled fear shone on her features before a timid smile registered. His cock throbbed a greeting and bounced against the counter where he stood.

Jon turned without thinking of his ardent physical state. Grace's eyes fell to below his beltline, and she witnessed firsthand his lust for her.

Eyes widening, she glanced back up to his piercing stare.

"Did you need something?" he asked, surprised he had the wherewithal to merely speak and not growl or, worse, act on his rampant fantasies. He wouldn't win her over by leaping onto her right now like a feral dog after a bitch in heat.

"I need..." She stopped speaking and forced his rabid libido to fill in the blank. *She needs you to fuck her repeatedly,* it said. Almost without any thought, Jon advanced into the bedroom, his lusty cock leading the way for him.

"You need...what?" He was fast losing the battle with the reptilian part of his brain, which was pulsing with lust and about to override his single conscious gentlemanly thought of abstinence.

"I need a place to sleep," she said, smiling warmly, and glanced sideways at his bed before staring back to his surely lust-filled eyes . He cleared this throat to think.

"You aren't going to sleep with Emma?"

"No. My place is with you. I'm your wife, Jonathan. For better or worse and everything."

"Grace…" He wanted to tackle her to the bed and thrust deeply until they both screamed in release.

"Please." She stepped closer, and he smelled her. "I want to be your wife, in *every* sense. There hasn't been a night since I met you three years ago that I didn't relive that kiss in the elevator. I belong with you." Her lovely face seemed so determined to convince him she wanted him. Was it gratitude or desire?

"And if Emma wakes up…?" His eyes darted in the direction of the other bedroom.

"She won't. She sleeps soundly, like a rock, I promise. Please let me stay with you."

He took three steps closer without having remembered his legs moving. He was driven and controlled by his desire.

"I need you, Grace." He didn't explain the utter truth of that statement. "I'll always make a place for you in my bed."

Once she found out about his pervasive sexual needs, she might be frightened. He would do well to keep that tidbit close. He allowed one last momentary thought of his hidden medication. The original plan for his dismal satisfaction this evening, at least until his wife showed up looking for a place to sleep.

He smiled at the visual of his medication gathering dust in the secret compartment as he moved on to gain sexual satisfaction from an unexpected marriage. He approached her slowly.

"Good. I need you too," she said as he stepped closer still. The scent of her always knocked him on his ass. His impulse was to pounce on her, but instead he took a deep, cleansing breath and motioned her to come to him.

"I don't want to scare you, and if I make any further movement toward you, I may be too aggressive."

"I don't mind aggressive." She stepped closer, and the unique fragrance of her filled him. His cock pulsed with the desire to fuck blindly, but he strangled the thirst to take her.

He knew without a doubt she wouldn't stop him if he laid her down and slammed inside her until he was gratified. But she deserved to be gently wooed and tenderly made love to until she climaxed over and over before he should allow another orgasm for himself.

She had serviced him on the living room sofa for their first intimacy as man and wife. This was followed two days later by a quickly consummated union in an airport service elevator just so they could remain together, for Christ's sake.

This morning in his bed had been phenomenal but also frenzied. He had expected her to be less aggressive and mostly tolerant of his advances, but instead she was feisty and sensual in a vibrant way he hadn't expected from someone with limited experience.

While she had climaxed all the times they'd been together, Jon wanted this unexpected night to be unhurried. He wanted to show her tender love-making instead of rushed sex within a time frame to meet the initial dictates of a new frigid society.

Also, he wanted to taste her again. The vision of her legs spread before him, inviting him to taste her luscious, creamy pussy, lips, and clit forced his eyes closed in anticipation. That was what he was going to do first, once he got her undressed.

Her hands reached up to his chest, and she pulled his face to hers for a kiss. He put his hands to her hips as her tongue entered his mouth. He groaned in sexual delight. He pulled her hips forward to rub against her soft, willing body, nearly letting his lust loose at the sensation of warmth she radiated.

Grace's arms slid up until they hooked behind his neck. She stroked the back of his head, massaging his scalp and drawing him closer. Her breathing increased, her lips consumed his, and he decided he could climax without intercourse if she released another throaty moan.

Jon turned and danced them backwards, guiding her along with him until his thighs connected with the tall platform bed. He sat down hard on the bed, his face now level with her lovely breasts. Spreading his legs, he drew her between them, his hands now securely fastened to her ass and grinding her into his eager, insatiable cock. He let himself fall into the warm sensations of the new life he couldn't believe was his.

After pulling her shirt up to uncover her breasts, Grace broke the kiss only long enough to pull it off and fling it behind her. Jon bent to taste the tip of one peak that thrust forward. Her moan electrified him. She peeled her remaining clothes off, pushing her skirt slowly down her legs and kicking it aside. She was completely naked. He kissed her ardently and made a plan for her seduction. Slowly. He vowed to go slowly tonight. He tried to go slowly. Grace wasn't interested in slowly.

She pushed him back to the bed and climbed on top of him. Holding his arms down, she slid her soft body languorously over his until their hips were aligned and her breasts pressed against his chest. She shifted her hips and ran her slit along his cock until her clit rubbed against the sensitive tip. A flick of her hips, and his cock slipped inside her pussy an inch. Before he could take a breath, she impaled herself, slamming down until his balls rested between her thighs. Her tight grip wrenched a moan from his lips. Her hips lifted, releasing his cock from delicious confinement before she slammed down on him in the very opposite of slowly. She fucked him. Hard.

Jon slipped his hand between them to finger her clit as she rode him with ferocious intent. After several moments, Grace stiffened above him in mid-slam and whimpered. He felt her pussy clamp down on him and fought the urge to come. Her hands were on his shoulders. She slowed down, still whimpering her release.

Jon rolled them over, flipping her underneath him, and pounded inside her. He grasped both her hands in his, their fingers entwining. His forearms pressed and trapped hers to the bed as he powered inside of her body. Her legs soon wrapped around his hips like a vice, egging him on. Her eyes popped open, and the look of wonderment and love she gave him filled him with pleasure.

A smile played around her lips before she whispered, "You feel so good inside of me." He thrust once more, deeply, and the explosion of his climax made his heart skip a beat from sheer pleasure. Every time with her felt like his very first orgasm all over again, except that it got better each time. Every rapturous time he climaxed with her helped justify his choice to keep her.

He could love her. She was quite possibly the one. Perhaps they were meant to be together. Jon collapsed on her, clenching her fingers tightly. His breathing came in gasps hard enough that he couldn't speak. He had her pinned to the bed. She couldn't move her arms underneath his, but she didn't seem to notice. Or maybe she'd fainted in fear. He lifted his head and kissed her cheek. She kissed his in return.

"You're even better at this than Marissa said you might be," she said in a breathy whisper.

He laughed and kissed her throat. He was glad she was so distracted by his lovemaking that she didn't notice her arms were pinned down.

She turned her head and kissed his face again tenderly. He felt himself slipping into unconsciousness from the blissful gratification. They lay together with fingers entwined, both breathing deeply.

"I love you, Grace," he whispered sincerely and promptly dozed off, still pinning her arms down. She still didn't seem to notice.

Chapter 8

The next morning, Jon awoke early, wrapped around a warm Grace. His first thought was about sex, but his second thought was that his time was running out on the Andy Nelson case. Elliott was going to blow that ever-present vein out of his forehead when he learned Jon and Grace were permanently married. He glanced down at her sleeping form. The only witness keeping Andy Nelson in prison was peacefully trapped beneath him.

The recollection of the previous night forced him to take a deep breath to calm down. Grace was, quite simply, perfect for him.

He got up, quietly extracting himself from her—slowly, so as not to wake her—and then slipped some sweatpants and a t-shirt on and padded to the kitchen to make coffee. He decided pancakes were in order, since they were the only kid food he knew how to make. He made the batter and was flipping the first batch to cook on the second side when he heard the pitter-patter of little feet enter the room behind him.

"You can cook?" Emma's astonished voice came from the doorway of the kitchen. He turned away from the stove to see her clutching a battered, one-eyed, floppy-eared stuffed dog as she watched him.

"You bet. Have a seat. Do you want milk or orange juice?"

She shrugged and said, "Danny said I could only have water."

Jon made a mental note to go punish him for having been such a bastard to Emma and Grace while they had lived with him. "Well then, I say that you should have both this time. Then tomorrow you'll know which one you'd like better."

She nodded with a little smile and slid into a seat at his kitchen table. Her chin barely came up to the edge. He'd have to find something for her to sit on.

"Danny never cooked," she said in a solemn, awe-filled tone.

"He didn't, huh? What did he do?"

"He yelled at Mama to hurry her butt up and put food on the table or else." Suddenly Jon could see Danny's pudgy face turning red as he squeezed the bastard's throat between his hands. He needed to calm down.

"Maybe we should make some breakfast for your mom for a change. I think she's earned a break. Don't you?"

She nodded again, smiling her agreement. Her smile was so much like Grace's, it pulled his heart into a melted puddle. He knew he would do anything and everything in his power to keep this child safe, as if she were his own flesh and blood, no matter what.

"Danny didn't ever hurt you, did he?" Jon couldn't seem to help asking the question, although he was more afraid of her giving a positive answer. If Danny had so much as harmed a hair on her precious head, he'd be unable to control his anger. Emma and Grace had been treated abominably by the new Tiberius Group rules, and Danny had been a total bastard too.

"Well, he hurt my feelings. He told me I was ugly because my real father was a psycho. What's a psycho anyway?"

"A psycho is a bad man, but it doesn't matter who your father is. It still doesn't make you ugly. You are your own person." Jon flipped two pancakes on a plate for her and pulled the syrup out of a pantry next to the refrigerator. Then he brought her a glass of milk and another with orange juice in it. He grabbed a stack of kitchen towels for her to sit on and reach her food.

"I like both of them," she said after taking a sip of each beverage in front of her.

"I guess you'll have to have both each morning then. You have some catching up to do."

She giggled and started in on her pancakes. "These are the best pancakes I ever ate in my whole life," she said after one bite.

"Surely they aren't better than your mom's?"

Emma looked over her shoulder in the direction of the bedroom doors and back again quickly. "Let's not tell her, okay?"

"Okay." Jon watched her take another bite and poured more batter on the griddle.

"Do you like your room?"

"Yes. Mommy said I get to have it to myself. But if you don't want to share your room, I'll let her sleep with me."

"You deserve to have your own room. You've shared long enough. Besides, I'd be lonely without your Mom."

She shrugged and smiled, "Okay."

Jon heard Grace get out of bed. She stumbled by the kitchen doorway to enter Emma's room, then she shouted Emma's name and ran to the kitchen, then stopped abruptly, as if she had difficulty taking in the scene before her. She was half-dressed and looked half-asleep. Sexy as hell. Jon gave her a long, careful stare from head to toe and back again. He wanted *her* for breakfast.

"What are you doing? Why did you let me sleep? I would have made food."

"Mama, he made pancakes for you. Jon can cook! Can you believe it?"

Their utter surprise and shock at what were actually his meager cooking abilities brought a grin to his face. Having a ready-made family was kind of nice.

The phone rang, interrupting his happy family fantasy. He stepped away from the table, running a hand down the back of Grace's silky head and letting her hair slip through his fingers as he passed her.

Picking up the cordless phone, he answered, "Yes."

"Brent, it's Elliott. Are you still married?"

"Yes."

"I guess you made it back in time to consummate your ill-advised marriage. Damn your incredible luck."

"Yeah. No thanks to the wild goose chase you sent me on to talk to Cindy Wells."

Elliott didn't confirm or deny the trip as a ruse to thwart him. He just asked, "Why her? Out of all the women available in the world, why did it have to be the only witness in this case?"

"It must be fate. Get over it. It's a done deal now."

Elliott emitted a noise which sounded like a growl of frustration before he changed the subject and asked, "Why did you agree to adopt her kid?"

Jon frowned. "How do you know about that?"

"The paperwork you started yesterday to adopt one Emma Maitland, who also happens to be Andy Nelson's biological kid, made record progress in the cycles of government through the wee hours of the night. It is currently sitting on the desk of the magistrate who will be hearing Andy's case. Guess what?"

"What?" But Jon already knew what. He'd jumped from a flaming inferno into the molten lava of a volcano.

"Andy Nelson's hearing was just moved up to tomorrow morning, instead of the end of the week."

Jon tipped his head back closing his eyes. "Damn it."

"We meet bright and early with the D.A. Come prepared to sign a document giving your permission for Grace Maitland Brent to testify for the magistrate's review."

"What if I don't want her to testify?"

"Then I kill you with my bare hands, and Andy Nelson goes free immediately. You have twenty-four hours to find something—anything—that will keep Andy in prison. I'm not counting on your 'wife' being able to pull it off this time."

"There's nothing to find, short of convincing Andy to confess. Unfortunately, Grace is all we have."

"You do understand what will happen at the review, right? She has to face Andy Nelson alone. The D.A. won't be allowed to object to anything Andy asks her within the scope of the event which transpired, resulting in the birth of a child nine months later. You should prepare yourself to be silent or stay out of the courtroom."

"I'll be in the room, Elliott. I refuse to desert her because it might make the case look bad."

"You could appoint someone. You don't want to hear all the gory details, do you?"

"I won't abandon her. She's my responsibility."

"Yeah, I get that. I'm going on record as saying I think it's a colossal mistake. But you're already aware of my feelings. See you bright and early." Elliott hung the phone up.

Jon leaned his forehead against the wall and closed his eyes at the thought of Andy Nelson being let loose to do the evil things he knew how to do so well. For the present, he thought it might be prudent to have an ally in court tomorrow, especially if the worst happened and Andy was released.

He speed-dialed a number that he spent too much time calling lately.

Brutal picked up on the first ring and barked, "What?"

"I need another favor," Jon said without preamble.

"I told you I'd be your blood brother. Stop whining."

"Shit, I forgot about that. We need to do that today. But never mind that now. I need something else."

"What else do you want?" he growled, but Jon could tell he wasn't put out.

"I need you to do some investigative work for me on the sly. I don't want anyone to know what I'm up to." Jon was thinking of the worst-case scenario. If Andy was let loose, he wanted someone to help keep tabs on the monster.

Brutal chuckled mirthlessly. "Does it involve the slime you put away for your partner's murder?"

"I won't ask how you know that, but yes. Andy Nelson needs to be watched." Jon was surprised he knew details.

"Like I told you, I know things. I'm in. Andy Nelson is purported to be in a class by himself where sexual vampires are concerned. "

"He is...and Grace has to go head-to-head with him in court tomorrow morning after the D.A. presents the original case to the magistrate. I'd also like for you to be in court with us. I can't testify as to his depraved sexual nature, but you can since your genetic enhancement isn't a secret."

Brutal sighed. "I'll be there. Anything else?"

"I'll pick you up and drop Emma off. Hannah will watch over her, won't she? It'll just be while we're in court."

Brutal laughed. "Of course. I'm certain she'd love to meet her new niece."

Jon forced himself to utter, "Thanks, Brutal."

"Uh-huh." Brutal snorted. "Whatever. Try not to break down into tears."

"I'll pick you up this afternoon to get the license."

"Right." Brutal laughed again. "You're so whipped."

* * * *

"I can't believe I agreed to let you testify," Jon told Grace the next morning as they waited outside the courtroom for Andy Nelson's release review to begin. They'd left Emma and Hannah together for the day. Elliott hadn't even wanted Jon to be in the same five-mile radius as Grace, let alone the same building.

The magistrate was the one who required his presence even over Elliott's veto. Jon was listed as the arresting officer.

Jon had arrested Andy Nelson on a charge of aggravated rape resulting in death. Before the Tiberius Group takeover, that charge had been considered murder. Their initial case was based on DNA evidence and his being found in the immediate proximity of the victim. At the time of his arrest, Andy had told Jon he'd simply found the woman battered and tried to help her. He was naked and his whole body was covered in her blood, including his dick. He laughed maniacally when Jon pointed out the obvious. Andy was out of control and had become high on his own power in the wake of evading the law.

The rose on the ground next to the victim had convinced Jon that Andy was the serial rapist killer, but he had also sensed something evil emanating from Andy. Jon had to concentrate completely so as not to be detected by others who were genetically enhanced if he didn't move physically away. He had the early radar warning system, as he called it, but it only worked in close proximity. It hadn't helped him as he'd sat outside while Andy had murdered Kevin and his wife.

He'd always blamed himself for not accompanying his former partner into his home that fateful night. He'd have known about Andy as he entered the house. His guilt had eaten at him for years after. He hadn't been close enough to sense Andy the night of Kevin's murder. There had been two roses in the house when Jon entered, the length of Kevin's absence finally sending him inside. One rose lay on the bed next to Sarah's bloody body, and the other was still clutched in Kevin's hand.

Andy Nelson was pure evil. He craved the screams of his victims. He loved to hear them plead for mercy while he tortured them until they wanted to die. Then he would oblige them.

Grace had helped put Andy away long ago. However, Jon didn't think today would be a justice-rich day. He dreaded so many things he couldn't begin to count them.

At the first trial years before, the defense attorney hadn't been allowed to ask whether Grace had asked to be tied down by Andy Nelson. Grace had been told it didn't matter whether she had consented or begged for him to do what he did; it was still rape because she was only sixteen. The age of consent had been unilaterally changed to age eighteen across the States back in 2027.

Things were dramatically different today before a member of the magistrate core in the pre-trial review for Andy Nelson's release. This time, instead of lawyers debating the facts, the only two people allowed to give testimony would be Andy and Grace. The magistrate would be the one to discern the truth and react accordingly.

Jon didn't hold faith that Grace's testimony would keep Andy in prison this time. The magistrate for today's trial was exceptionally unsympathetic to women. Magistrate Silas was notorious for overturning rape cases in which the testimony of the victim had been the only factor in conviction. It would be disastrous if Andy were let free.

Of the ninety-one percent of previously convicted rapists Magistrate Silas let go annually, eighty-five percent committed crimes again against the convicting witness within the first twenty-four hours of release and were put back in prison. No one was allowed to bring this fact up to the magistrate core, though.

Brutal had agreed to sit in the audience and wait for Andy's arrival.

The magistrate entered the room even before Andy made it to court. Bill Warren, the district attorney who had tried the case the first time, when Grace's testimony had been critical, was still the D.A. Warren called Brutal in officially to verify that Andy Nelson was a sexual vampire who required medication to temper his urges. Warren tried valiantly to explain to the magistrate that Brutal had the ability to recognize sexual vampires due to his genetic engineering. Magistrate Silas was so far unimpressed with his statement that Andy was dangerous to society.

The magistrate looked down his nose at Brutal and said, "You also are a sexual vampire, as I understand the definition."

"No, sir." Brutal barked, "I most certainly am not."

"Don't you take medication to alleviate your sexual needs?" the magistrate asked absently, not looking up from whatever he was reading.

"No, sir. I do not require medication. It doesn't work for me," Brutal grated out.

"Then how do you keep from sexually accosting women?"

"I imagine the same way you do, Magistrate," he said and smiled as laughter broke out in the room.

The magistrate looked up, red-faced and angry at being made the butt of a joke. "My personal life is not in question here!"

"Neither is mine. I don't understand how my sex life is any of your business, Magistrate, for the purposes of this trial. I'm here only to testify as to whether Andy Nelson is a sexual vampire and how deep his sexual proclivities run. You wouldn't want to unleash a sexual vampire into society, would you?"

"How will you know whether he's a sexual vampire or not, if you aren't one too?"

A clerk of some sort leaned in at that opportune time and started speaking earnestly to the magistrate, so Brutal didn't have to answer.

"The prisoner is being brought in now. You may be seated, Mr. Blackthorn." Brutal remained standing. He was waiting to sit until Andy Nelson was brought into the room. Jon knew he wanted to get a sense of how deeply disturbed the prisoner was as he walked by. When Andy got within six feet of where Brutal stood, they both flinched as if in recognition.

Andy Nelson hissed in a deep breath that whistled between his teeth, stopping in his tracks three feet away from Brutal. He brought his handcuffed hands up as if in defense, but they rattled and caught against the chain that was attached to his leg shackles.

Jon watched Brutal clench and unclench his hands a time or two. Jon remembered the utter blackness that oozed from Andy's soul as it encountered his, back when he'd arrested him. Andy was the worst and vilest rapist he'd ever encountered. Thankfully, Brutal was here to voice this for him so that he could keep his career as a lawman.

"Mr. Blackthorn, sit down or you will be held in contempt."

Brutal turned to face Magistrate Silas. "This man is a sexual vampire, Magistrate. It's deep-seated."

"You, sir, still haven't explained to my satisfaction how you are not one of these predators. I don't like genetically altered men." He wrinkled his nose. "It's unnatural."

Brutal opened his mouth to respond, but was cut off with the rap of the magistrate's gavel and a distasteful glare. He gave the magistrate a dirty look in return, then seated himself. Jon noticed he held himself rigidly. Jon caught his eye, and Brutal nodded slowly, grimacing.

The clerk recited in a clear if monotone voice, "The parents of Grace Maitland filed a complaint against Andy Nelson after they came home early from a company Halloween party. They had tried to call home, but Grace had not answered. They became concerned and returned home unexpectedly. Grace was discovered nude and handcuffed to a bed in the basement guestroom. They discovered a bag in the room left behind with Andy Nelson's prints on the contents. The list of items found in the bag includes surgeon's knives and several other torture devices."

The clerk continued reading from the previous court trial transcripts. "Grace, under pressure, had told her parents what happened. The boy they'd forbidden her to see because of a previous sexual encounter nearly two months before had come over unannounced and invited himself in.

"According to Miss Maitland's statement, at Mr. Nelson's insistent request, she led him to a more private room in the basement of her home, where he handcuffed her to a bed and had sex with her. Shortly thereafter, her parents came home unexpectedly and found her naked and bleeding from a knife wound to her lower abdomen. The D.A. at the time was convinced Miss Maitland would have been disfigured in the same way other victims had been."

Andy stood, rattling his chains. "Objection. What other victims? There is only one person who ever testified against me. The slut is sitting over there."

"Because you killed all the others," countered the D.A. "We have testimony from several medical examiners that several victims had the same cuts inflicted."

"That information is irrelevant, Mr. Warren." The magistrate broke in and gave both stern looks. "There is only one witness account on record."

"Be that as it may, we still have the bag and contents. I'd like to re-enter them into evidence today to show what Miss Maitland was saved from by the early return of her parents that night."

"I object to that." Andy stood again. "I found that bag on my way to Grace's house. I looked through it, and so of course my prints were on the items inside. Just because I looked doesn't mean I used them. Did you find any blood in there?"

"You know we didn't because you bleached them and degraded any blood samples. Why did you bring the bag into Grace's house if you didn't intend to use the contents?"

Andy smiled and shrugged. "I planned to sell the items and didn't want to leave them for someone to steal."

"Like you stole them?" D.A. Warren smirked. "Isn't that funny—"

"Stop, both of you. I'm not inclined to allow this evidence, Mr. Warren."

"Magistrate Silas, sir. I must strenuously object. You are required to consider the original evidence. Mr. Nelson denied having been at Miss Maitland's house upon first questioning." He turned a nasty glance at Andy, adding, "Which was a lie."

"I had recently turned eighteen," Andy countered, shrugging again. "I was considered an adult even though I hadn't graduated from high school yet. I admit I didn't want her parents to find out about us. They called and threatened me the day after they discovered I'd popped her cherry."

"That is vulgar, Mr. Nelson," the magistrate huffed.

"But it's the truth. Vulgar or not, she wanted me to fuck her, and I did. So what? Doesn't mean I'd want to do it again. If you asked me, would I do it today? My answer would be of course not. I was a boy then."

"And now you are a man? Is that it?" The D.A.'s tone was sarcastic.

"I'm a man who has spent years incarcerated because of the testimony of one woman. I didn't do the things I was accused of. I shouldn't be in jail for doing what *she* asked me to do."

"So you want this court to believe that a sixteen-year-old whose 'cherry' you admittedly popped only weeks before suddenly found an interest in bondage and dominance. That you inherently sensed this newfound sexual awareness and happened to stop by when Grace's parents were gone. She was alone for the first time since you were allowed to rape her..."

"Objection..." Andy cut in.

"I'm sorry," Warren continued. "I meant to say, to 'comply with her wishes.' You are insane if you expect anyone to believe this fiction."

"I can only tell the truth. That's exactly what happened."

"Why did you get genetically enhanced? You knew it was against the law."

"I did it on a dare. You know, boys will be boys."

Warren huffed out a disgusted breath and turned to Magistrate Silas. "I contend the same things I did before, Magistrate. Nothing has changed. He raped her. He denied being at her house until nine months later, when a child with half his DNA was born. He admitted he lied. We can't believe he isn't lying about everything."

"Why was the original suit dropped?" The magistrate asked, shuffling some papers in front of him.

"My predecessor felt that because our courts were so overworked, it would serve justice to send it to family court. It was dropped into the family court judicial level so the DA could pursue child support."

"And why was it not followed up at that level?"

"I can only surmise, Magistrate."

"Surmise then."

"Miss Maitland's parents were killed in a tragic accident right before the family court hearing. She was still a minor, but living out of state with a relative. When the action was rescheduled, I can only conclude that the family courts allowed the case to fall through the cracks of the system. I found her case quite by accident when I cross-referenced all cases with Andy Nelson's name."

"I will hear testimony from this witness now," the magistrate said haughtily.

Jon didn't want Grace to testify. Why had he signed the consent form? Andy was evil. He would be evil to Grace...again.

Grace stood. Jon rose with her and shot his best demonic stare at Andy over Grace's head.

"Hello, Lawman," Andy said, smiling. The bastard would enjoy telling the world about all the sadistic things he'd done to Grace.

"You will not address anyone in this room but me or your accuser, Mr. Nelson," the magistrate cautioned.

"Sorry, Magistrate."

"Hello, Grace. How's my bastard child?"

"Magistrate!" The D.A. shot to his feet.

"Mr. Nelson, you will restrain your vulgar comments, or I will send you back to prison without further review. Is that what you want?"

"Of course not, Magistrate. I fear the long false imprisonment has damaged my manners. I'll make a concerted effort." He bowed once to the magistrate.

"See that you do. Sit down, Mr. Warren. You may ask your first question, Mr. Nelson."

"Grace, did I *really* violate you all those years ago?"

Grace stiffened, responding in a monotone. "Yes." Her gaze remained on the space of floor between them.

"How did I do this?"

She glanced up momentarily. "I don't understand the question."

"Then let me be specific. Did I force you to go down to the basement? By that I mean, did I drag you down there?"

Grace shrugged. "No, not exactly."

"Once we got down there because you led us, did I force you to lie on the bed?"

"No. But…"

"Did I ask you whether you wanted to be handcuffed?"

"Yes." Grace glared at him.

"And what did you say?"

"You told me I had to."

Andy signed disgustedly and turned toward Magistrate Silas. "Magistrate, she's not answering my question."

"Mrs. Brent, answer the question asked."

Grace took a deep breath and answered quickly, "I told you to go ahead and put the handcuffs on me, but…"

"Did you ever even make any negative response the entire time we were in bed together?" Andy cut in with his next question.

"No, but it doesn't matter because…"

Andy broke in again. "So let me get this straight. You led me to your basement. I didn't force you to get on the bed, nor did I force you to be handcuffed. And you never said the word 'no' the entire time we were together. How did I manage to rape you?"

"I was sixteen. It'll always be statutory rape, Andy. My child is proof that we had sex that night. Besides, I did say no to you, later on."

"I don't know what you are talking about. I left you directly after your second pitiful effort at sexual enticement. You're a lousy lay, Grace."

"That's a lie. You turned the lights off and—"

The D.A. stood and spoke at the same time as Grace, "Magistrate!"

"Never mind that. Are you trying to tell this court, young lady, that Andy Nelson didn't force you to have sex that night?" The magistrate sounded dangerously angry. His rage was directed at Grace and not Andy this time.

"I was sixteen…"

"It doesn't matter. In the testimony before this court, it clearly states you fornicated with him several weeks before the night in question. Is that what I understand from your testimony?"

"Stop talking, Grace." Jon stood up next to the D.A. to face the magistrate.

"Mr. Brent, you gave your consent for her to testify. You are not at liberty to stop her."

"I didn't give consent for her to be abused."

"'Abused' is a harsh term. I believe it's more important to ensure an innocent man doesn't spend time in prison because of a promiscuous sixteen-year-old who admittedly agreed to the sexual contact. Sit, Mr. Brent, and do not disrupt this court further." He turned back to Andy. "Do you have further questions, Mr. Nelson?"

"Yes. I have a couple more questions." Andy turned back to Grace.

"You wanted me to be tricked into being your boyfriend, didn't you, Grace? You got pregnant on purpose to try and trap me into marriage."

"No!" Grace cried out. "I never wanted to trap you. I never wanted to be married to you."

"You're a liar!"

"Magistrate…" The D.A. leapt to his feet in protest.

The magistrate banged his gavel and stood up behind his desk with a thunderous look. The room silenced. "I'm through with all the discourtesy. Everyone be silent!

"I will ask the questions in this matter." Magistrate Silas turned his glare to Grace. "In your previous testimony at the pre-magistrate court trial, you testified under oath that Andy Nelson raped you, but that isn't true, is it?"

"Yes. It's true. It was statutory rape. My parents said it didn't matter whether I agreed."

The magistrate sat back down and heaved a deep sigh, as if perturbed beyond his capacity for reason. "Did you ever tell Mr. Nelson to stop during the time you fornicated with him?"

Grace raised her head as tears streamed down her face and answered, "Yes. When he was through with me, he got off the bed and turned the lights off. Then he cut me with a knife in the dark while I was still handcuffed to the bed. I screamed for him to stop, but he didn't."

"But did you ever tell him to stop the sexual intercourse before the lights went out?"

"No."

"Did you ever make any negative response during the time of the sexual contact whatsoever?"

"No."

"Mr. Nelson, did this witness ever tell you to stop having sexual contact with her?"

"Not once, Magistrate. She said some very wicked things to keep me going. Want me to tell you what she said?"

"That won't be necessary. Did you turn the lights off in the room after the encounter?"

"Yes, but I only shut them off on the way out of the room afterwards. I heard her parents and decided not to stick around and get caught with my pants down, if you get my meaning."

"And did you cut her with a knife?"

"How could I? I left directly afterwards."

"Mrs. Brent, did you or did you not see Mr. Nelson after the lights went out in that basement room? Did you see his face?"

"It was him."

"How do you know if you didn't see his face?"

"I saw his eyes in the dark. The irises were rimmed in flaming orange as he taunted me...with a knife. I still carry scars."

"Yes, well, that's unfortunate, but what makes you think it was Andy Nelson and not someone else?"

"It was him."

The magistrate took another deep breath. "This court is adjourned while I ponder the facts of this case."

Grace hung her head.

Chapter 9

Jon knew as well as everyone in the room that the magistrate would rule in Andy's favor. Brutal had asked to see him after he adjourned to express his sincere warning that Andy not be let loose in society. Now he marched out of the magistrate's chambers with a solemn expression. "The magistrate is a complete and utter moron. We should make preparations."

Less than an hour later, Brutal was proven right.

The magistrate entered the courtroom from his chambers, his robes billowing out behind him like smoke, as if the stick shoved up his ass and rubbing against his bony butt had caused a fire.

"I have come to a decision." The magistrate spoke ominously after he sat, made himself comfortable, and looked down on the assembled crowd waiting for his decision. His bifocal glasses, so old-fashioned as to be antique, sat on the end of his nose. He adjusted them repeatedly as he studied the papers before him. He placed the fingers from each hand together, as if making a steeple, and began exercising them before speaking again. "The preponderance of evidence before me is compelling. However, I do not feel that the word of one single woman supports the district attorney's contention that this man should be in jail."

"Magistrate!" The D.A., red-face and angry, stood up to protest.

The finger pushups stopped abruptly, and the magistrate's face suddenly turned a particularly vivid shade of crimson.

"Do not interrupt me!" he thundered at the D.A.

"My apologies." The D.A. folded the flap of his tie back down and straightened the lapels of his jacket. He cleared his throat, sat down, and focused his eyes on the table in front of him.

"I cannot in good conscience allow Mr. Nelson to remain in prison as I do not believe he raped this…woman." His lip curled as if in disgust. "I firmly believe sixteen is not too young for a girl to entice a man into sexual activity.

"In my opinion, the statutory rape laws were far too lenient prior to the establishment of the magistrate core. I believe the laws were established for girls raped at a much younger age. This woman has admitted the act wasn't against her will. The testimony from her own lips is that she directed him to fornicate with her so she could garner favor with him. This indicates to me she was stretching the truth regarding an actual rape taking place, statutory or not."

There was a lot of rustling and agitation in the audience, and an expectant vibe could be felt in the room as if it were a presence all its own.

Jon stood up. All eyes in the room were on him. "She isn't a liar."

"Yes, she is. She lied about being married to one Daniel Cox. I have his voluntary testimony in front of me."

The D.A. stood again. "Magistrate, I was not informed of any additional testimony."

"I'm not required to inform you, Mr. Warren. Sit down."

The district attorney did not seat himself right away. He took a deep breath first, shook his head, and plopped down in his chair as if he were a marionette with severed strings.

"I find I must grant Mr. Nelson his freedom today with this court's sincere apology for his confinement. Mr. Nelson, you are free to go. Do you have any questions?" Magistrate Silas asked.

"I have one. How can I sign up for my parental rights? I'd like to petition for custody of my kid."

"Over my dead body!" Grace screamed. "Emma is mine. You never wanted her. Never!"

"Oh, so it's a girl," Andy said with amused contempt. "Well, in that case, I want to sign her up for the Tiberius Young Girls' School. I get money to send her there, right? Then she can marry some Tiberius official someday."

The magistrate gave Andy a warm smile. "Why, yes, it's a fine program for young ladies to learn how to cook, to keep a fine, clean home for their husbands, and be good wives for our important future leaders. I think that is a fine idea, Mr. Nelson."

"No! I won't allow it." Grace shot out of her chair. Jon stood too.

"Mrs. Brent, you have little say here."

"I'm her mother. I'm the only parent she's ever known and *I* have little say?" Grace asked with disbelief.

"What about my adoption papers?" Jon asked.

Magistrate Silas furrowed his eyebrows as if in confusion. "Now that Mr. Nelson is free, you do not have the authority to adopt your wife's child."

"I have another question, Mr. Magistrate," Andy piped up to steal the magistrate's attention. "What if I wanted to marry the mother of my kid?"

"That would be over *my* dead body," Jon said, turning an incredulous look his way. "Not ever going to happen, Nelson."

Magistrate Silas gave Andy a sympathetic look. "I'm sorry, Mr. Nelson, she's already permanently bound to her lawman husband. And even if he wanted to get rid of her…"

"Which I don't," Jon broke in.

"…a period of a year must elapse before an offer to buy is allowed."

"As I said, that is never going to happen."

"I guess it's just my sorry luck then," Andy said. "I want you to know, Mr. Magistrate, I would have done right by Grace and married her if things hadn't happened the way they did."

"You are such a fucking liar!" Grace shrieked and took a threatening step toward Andy's table. "You denied even knowing me when my parents tried to make you responsible. You hired private detectives and lawyers out your ass so you wouldn't have to do the right thing." Jon put his arms around her to calm her down. The magistrate was not on their side. Grace was making it worse.

"Mrs. Brent, you will refrain from any further outbursts. You are vulgar, and I wouldn't be referring to Mr. Nelson as a liar if I were you since you seem to have the same propensity. Mr. Brent, you're a lawman. I know you possess the skills necessary to keep her in line. I suggest you start using them and keep a rein on your foulmouthed wife."

Jon took a deep breath and responded, "Yes, Magistrate." Those two words of acquiescence earned him a livid look from the spitfire in his arms. But Grace's child was in more jeopardy than she understood; it was not a good idea to provoke this magistrate.

"Is there no option for me, Magistrate, not anything I can do to bring my family together now that I'm vindicated and free to live my life? I mean, I never should have been put away in the first place. Must I continue to suffer?" Andy was playing the martyr.

Jon placed his hand over Grace's mouth. She growled into his hand. He whispered for her to stop before she said anything further. This earned him another feral look.

"Well, the only thing at all—and it's a long shot, mind you—is to appeal to a higher member of the magistrate core if you truly want to marry her."

"She's mine in the flesh, Magistrate," said Jon. "Permanently bound to me as my bride as per the laws and dictates of the Tiberius Group."

"I don't mean to be vulgar, Magistrate, but she was mine in the flesh long before she was his." Andy gave them a sidelong glance with a placating evil grin on his face. "Besides, it's my understanding that after giving birth to my child, Grace became unable to have any further children. She'll never produce any children for the lawman. Shouldn't I get some sort of priority over him? I'm only asking for clarification."

"It is a possibility." The magistrate put a hand on his chin as if to think the idea through.

"Magistrate, I won't allow my wife to be taken from me," Jon said, his voice threatening to become a shout. "Mr. Nelson knew of Grace's pregnancy years ago. He lied about having been with her until the DNA from the baby proved him to be a liar. After the test, he fought against taking any responsibility for his child and hid behind his expensive lawyer to escape paying child support. When her parents were killed no one picked up the gauntlet, including Mr. Nelson, to ensure the welfare of the child or the mother. Mr. Nelson didn't even know the gender of his own child until today. His passionate speech over bringing his 'family' together now is suspect."

"I was a young, foolish boy. Now I'm older, and I've spent years in prison thinking that if I only had a chance, I'd make Grace my wife and raise my child the right way…"

"Save the fake speech. I don't buy it for a minute. You will never have Grace. Don't test me on this."

Andy's smile faltered a bit as Jon stared at him, but he perked up again and said, "Magistrate, can I least meet my child? Perhaps I could take her out to a park and we could get to know each other."

Grace launched out of Jon's arms and took a step in Andy's direction. "No! You may not take her anywhere! You may not be alone with her. You are a monster!" Jon grabbed her.

"Yes." Magistrate Silas pointedly ignored Grace and answered Andy's question. "I order you to make the child ready for an unsupervised visit tomorrow. Mr. Nelson, here is the Brent's address..."

"Do not give my address out," Jon snarled at the magistrate.

"Mr. Brent," the magistrate said in a tone that suggested forced civility. "Mr. Nelson deserves the right to meet his child without the shrieking harpy mother standing over him. There is obvious ill will on her part." The magistrate handed a small electronic programmable map device to a court clerk, who promptly took it to an eager Andy. He smiled and licked his lips as he pocketed the device.

Grace stopped fighting Jon's hold on her. She put her hands to her face, bent at the waist, and sobbed with heart-wrenching clarity, as if the tears came from her frightened soul. She shook off Jon's attempt to comfort her as drops fell from her eyes and landed on the table. He could read her mind. Men always changed the rules, and now her precious Emma was in danger.

"My ruling is final. You will have the girl child ready at noon tomorrow at your home, or I will throw you both in prison."

"Magistrate, surely you do not mean to let the prisoner loose on our citizens. Could we at least release a caution bulletin and warn them?" D.A. Warren asked.

"Warn them of what?"

Warren huffed incredulously. "It is a stated fact, as even Mr. Nelson will attest, that his sexual proclivities require him to self-medicate in order to keep his sexual demons at bay. We wouldn't want him forcing women because of the enhancements he received illegally years ago."

"Mr. Blackthorn seems to have a handle on his sexual proclivities. I order Mr. Nelson to continue to medicate himself with the drug Zanthacorth as a condition of his discharge. In addition, there will be the monitoring device on his ankle for the first thirty days of his release. I'm satisfied he will take this chance he is being offered to be a true and righteous citizen of this great country of ours. Won't you, Mr. Nelson?"

"Of course I will. Thank you, Magistrate." Andy stood and bowed slightly in deference to the court.

Magistrate Silas banged his gavel, stood, and strode out of the room. A roar of whispers erupted in the audience, and the clicking of PDAs recording the news could be heard in the background.

Andy turned to Jon and approached with a cocky swagger in his step. "How do you like the way I broke her in for you, Lawman? Is her pussy still tight after shooting out that brat?"

Jon smiled at him. "Do yourself a favor, Nelson, and don't show up at my house tomorrow. I don't care what the magistrate says. You're not welcome."

"But I so want to meet my little bitch so I can get her ready to sell to the Tiberius Young Girls' School."

Jon had to restrain Grace again. He had no doubt she'd kill him with her bare hands before he could pull his weapon.

Andy Nelson gave Brutal a wary look as he passed him, and went back to speak to the lawmen who'd escorted him from prison. They still had to remove his shackles.

* * * *

"I'll keep Emma with Hannah and me. If they come after her, then Emma will run far, far away to a very secret place I have on my property where she won't be found until Andy Nelson is in custody or dead," Brutal whispered to them once the magistrate had banged his gavel after delivering his supremely foolish ruling.

"Good. Grace and I will collect a few things and take a trip. I won't endanger her. Since the prick magistrate just gave out our address, we need to leave immediately," Jon whispered back. "I don't trust Andy to wait until tomorrow.

"Wait." Grace clutched his arm. "We have to leave Emma? Can't we take her with us?"

"If we get caught with her, any lawman in any state, country, or off-world planet will be able to legally take her from us—by force if need be—to hand her over to Andy. If we leave her with Brutal and Hannah, you can truthfully say you have no idea where she is, not exactly."

"Can I stop and say good-bye to her? Please? She's been through so much, Jon. I hate to abandon her without a word."

"I won't promise. It's best if we just leave."

Andy looked over at them and smiled sadistically.

Grace stepped closer to Jon. "Never mind. You're right. Let's just go. "Will Elliott give you time off?" Grace asked.

"I'll ask forgiveness later, when we return, instead of permission now. I think it would be the best course of action."

"Won't that fuck up your career?" Brutal asked in a surprised tone.

"Probably, but what else can I do?"

Brutal shrugged and removed himself from their circle to block Andy Nelson before he left the magistrate's courtroom a totally free man.

"I'll be watching you, Nelson. Don't fuck up, because I'll be there to catch you." Brutal slapped him on the arm and then pinched his cheek like an old woman greeting her nephew during the holidays.

"Don't touch me, you heathen. I know what you are. You're no better than me. At least I can go forth to taste a variety of women. I can tell you've attached yourself to one female. I can smell her on you too. She smells delicious."

Brutal laughed and said, "The last man to make a pass at my wife is now doing twenty-five to life. The next one won't live to have any regrets for his stupidity, and that's a promise, dickweed."

"You don't scare me."

"Then you're overconfident, and it will contribute to your demise."

Chapter 10

Grace and Jon hurried home to prepare for a sudden vacation. Jon wanted her ready to leave in ten minutes or less. Her only regret was that she wouldn't be able to warn Emma.

She knew Hannah and Brutal would take good care of her daughter, but she hated the life she was about to embark on. Once again, her past had reared up to spoil the happiness she'd found with Jon. It broke her heart to drag him down with her. He didn't deserve to lose his career. Both he and Brutal had assured her repeatedly it wouldn't matter since Andy Nelson was a threat to others, but guilt ate at her acid-filled stomach while she packed her meager belongings.

Grace moved into the bathroom to grab everything she'd only put in place the day before, grateful to finally have a home to call her own. As she stuffed toiletries into a bag, her elbow connected with the tile wall. When she pulled back to rub the sore spot, she saw the hidden compartment.

Using her toothbrush handle, she pulled open one corner of the small door below the medicine cabinet. The space contained something shiny and silver-white. Tentative fingers reached into the small, dark space as a tingle of apprehension clawed at her nerves. She pulled out the medical mist injector and a bottle with clear liquid. Slowly, she turned the small vial over in her hand to read the label.

Zanthacorth. She recognized the name. It was the medication Andy was required to take for his sexual proclivities. She remembered the magistrate ordering him to continue administering it. What was Zanthacorth doing hidden here?

The lights went out in the house before she could reason out her discovery. Darkness consumed her. She couldn't see her hand in front of her face. Grace sucked in a deep breath to keep from screaming in tortured agony.

Her fears of Andy and what he had turned into slammed into her memory as she clutched the glass vile and metal mist injector to her chest. Those orange-rimmed, iridescent irises glowing in the dark like mutant cat's eyes coming for her. A noise from the bedroom forced the air from her lungs in a rush. Clamping down on the urge to scream, Grace turned toward where she thought the door was and recognized a new sound of someone approaching.

"Shit," she heard someone whisper into the pitch-black darkness. It should be Jon. He was the only one here with her, right? She wasn't sure, her terror conjuring all sorts of beasts real and imagined from her subconscious to frighten the bejesus out of her.

She stared, seeing nothing but black nothingness all around her.. Then she saw light blue, rimmed, iridescent irises glowing in the dark and coming toward her. She unleashed the scream she'd held back.

"Grace?" Jon's concerned voice came from the direction of the glowing blue eyes.

The lights blinked on once or twice, as if trying to decide whether to return or not. Jon framed the doorway to the bathroom. His eyes were not glowing and blue, but their normal soft gray. He zeroed in on the contents of her still shaking fingers. She looked down in puzzlement, having momentarily forgotten her discovery of the hidden compartment.

"Where did you get that?" he asked chillingly, his gray eyes now stormy.

"I accidentally...I mean..." Grace stopped stuttering, fixed her gaze on his, and asked, "Why do you have this, Jonathan?"

He glanced down at her hands and then back into her certainly fear-filled eyes and sighed. "I used to use it." The quiet tone of his voice still carried all the way to her trembling self.

"But I thought it was only for..." Her worst fear materialized before her.

Jon lowered his gaze to the floor between them. He took another deep breath. She watched his chest expand and retract with air. He didn't answer.

"Are you like him?"

"No. But I am genetically engineered." His confession wrapped around her terror. He *was* like Andy. His eyes glowed in the dark. She was married to…

"Oh, God! It can't be true." Grace retreated a step backward. She had nowhere to go and was unsure of what to do next.

"Please don't back away from me. You must know me well enough by now to know I'd never hurt you."

"I…" Her eyes found his harsh, angry features and she wavered.

"Grace…" he dropped his head as if in despair and turned his defeated countenance away from her. He deserted her to the other room. She didn't know what to do. The fears she'd held buried all this time rose to the surface of her mind.

How could the man she loved beyond all reason be like Andy Nelson?

The fearful, orange-glowing eyes that had taunted her in her nightmares were no longer a threat. Andy wouldn't get her because she had a husband who loved her. Jon was a lawman who would protect her and Emma from the evil of her past. She knew on some basic level Jon would never hurt her. He had saved her from losing Emma. He had tried to let her go, but she was the one who had hounded him, seduced him, and forced him to keep her.

He had willingly agreed to adopt her daughter without her even asking him. He cooked for her, he treated her like she was the most fragile of princesses, and he loved her—of that she had no doubt.

It was the shock of discovery. The fact that he had used this medication did not make him a monster. She knew Jonathan Brent, heart and soul. Grace took a deep breath and steadied herself to call out and sincerely apologize to him.

"Jonathan?" He didn't respond, but she heard a noise like something had dropped in the living room. Perhaps he had dropped the luggage.

"Jonathan," she called out again tentatively, "I'm so sorry." There was no answer from him. Now she'd done it. She had made him angry—or worse, hurt his feelings.

"Please…I know you aren't like…him. I know you would never hurt me." He didn't answer, and a thin line of apprehension slid down her spine. It wasn't like him to pout. She had fully expected him to have his lips planted on hers and kissing her once she said his name the first time. Her sixth sense sent up a big warning flare, but unfortunately it was already too late to help her.

"He can't hear you, Grace," said Andy. He came out from behind the door in the bedroom, carrying a thick metal pipe in one gloved hand.

Grace froze at the sound of his voice. Her limbs refused to move from sheer terror. That slithery voice from her past penetrated and held her in fear. She remembered the pitch-black room and the orange glow of taunting eyes threatening to cut her until no other man would ever want her.

"Jonathan!" she screamed. Andy laughed in the same voice she'd heard in her lifetime of nightmares. He dangled what she recognized as Jon's handcuffs in the other gloved hand.

"Now it's your turn. Why don't you save me the trouble, Grace? Spread your legs open for me so I can fuck you until I'm satisfied. You know the last time we were together, our little sex party was so rudely interrupted."

"You should be locked up."

"No. I will go forth and love women as God intended, starting with you. As I was saying, the last time your parents interrupted us before I could do all the things I promised you. I took great pleasure in killing them, you know."

"You killed my parents?" She didn't know why she was so shocked. Andy was crazy and fully capable of murder.

"Of course. You were knocked up, and they were screaming for my blood. Once you gave birth and the DNA was found to be mine, I was watched very closely. I couldn't go out and spread the joy of my cock as I wanted, so I arranged a terrible accident for the four of you. Mommy, Daddy, She-whore, and Baby. But you didn't go out with them as you were supposed to did you, Grace?"

"The baby was sick, and I stayed home." The pervasive guilt of surviving after her parents hadn't, assailed her momentarily. Her father had been nearly apoplectic when she hadn't accompanied them that day. They'd been on the way to a party at her father's place of employment. He'd wanted to embarrass her by parading her in front of everyone they knew as a stupid unwed teenage mother. Emma, so tiny, was vomiting, and Grace begged her mother to let her stay home. It was the last time she had ever seen her mom alive. The lawmen came hours later to inform her of her parents' death in a tragic vehicular accident.

Andy moved a step closer. "You promptly left the state to live with some relative, and the charges were buried in family court. It was relegated to an unseen file under the heading of 'Verify Child Support', thanks to my expensive attorney hiding it there.

"So I reluctantly let you alone since I was busy discovering my prowess and spreading my passion for women. They all want me, you know. All of them. They want to feel my cock buried all the way from their cunts to their throats. They like the feel of my blade too, just like you will."

Grace had been inching her way to the bedroom door, as they spoke. She was halfway across the room. She chanced a glance and saw Jon's crumpled form outside the bedroom doorway. He wasn't moving.

"Thanks for distracting your lawman for me, Grace. I never could have gotten the drop on him if you hadn't devastated him by outing his secret condition."

"You're vile," Grace spat out and took another step toward Jon.

"Sticks and stones." He took a deep breath, closing his eyes as if in appreciation of the very air around him. "I can smell the delectable scent of your fear. Do me a favor. When I fuck you, then cut you, please scream as loud as you can. It makes for a richer experience. Or is that the scent of your arousal begging me to penetrate your cunt deep and hard?"

Grace edged her way past the corner of the bed, intent on dashing through the doorway to Jonathan. He was wearing his gun. She couldn't believe Andy hadn't relieved him of it when he'd grabbed the handcuffs.

"Was the lawman's cock as satisfying as mine, Grace?" he taunted and caught her eye. She remained silent, but laughed uproariously to herself. Men, even in the most psychotic of moments, still needed the assurance their dick was the biggest in the room.

The blatant insanity he displayed gave her strength. For all his crazy talk, she was more furious than scared. She wasn't going to lie down in fear tonight. Andy was about to find out how hard she was willing to fight for the life she and Emma had stumbled onto with Jonathan Brent.

"No response?"

"Yes, Andy, you are the biggest dick in the room. Is that what your ego needs to hear?" she asked with a smile purposely curving her mouth.

She watched as he hesitated a moment. Did he register her anger and appreciate that she wasn't going to be threatened one single moment longer? Did he understand her sudden resilience to survive?

Something in Grace's psyche snapped right then. She was furious. She was around-the-bend livid at being endangered yet again.

Grace was fucking sick and tired of being talked down to, and she was not going to feel small and scared a moment longer. Andy was about to find her a force to be reckoned with, or at least not a Casper-Milquetoast-wannabe victim any longer.

She tensed her body in readiness for the fight of her life. She glanced down at Jon's motionless body, and it fortified her anger. She seethed. The mother bear-like fanatic protection gene she'd always held for Emma sprouted expanding to include her husband.

Andy had struck down the finest man she'd had ever known. If she could only get to Jon's gun, she would fight to the death, regardless of how slim a chance she faced.

"Don't think you can best me! You will lose. Accept your fate."

Grace took two steps forward closer to Andy. The surprise on his face was immediate because he didn't expect a fight from her. His next mistake was sneering at her. His expression said he didn't take her brave approach seriously.

When she planted one foot down and powered the other into the spot directly between his legs with all the force she possessed, the scorn dissolved from his face. Andy went to his knees as a roar erupted from him, sounding like it came from the dark dimensions of hell. The shock on his face, while satisfying, didn't hold her attention. She turned and dove through the bedroom door, sliding down next to Jonathan in a crouch.

Grace ran her hands down his back lightly and called his name softly a couple of times. He was breathing, but there was blood dripping off his forehead in a line from an ugly wound on his temple to a small puddle collecting and drying on the floor. She traced her fingers over the gun holster.

Wrapping a hand around the grip of the pistol, she pulled as hard as she could, but it didn't budge. She chanced a look, but didn't see any obvious snap or other device to release Jonathan's weapon. Andy screamed in agony from the floor of the bedroom. She ran her hand down the holster and tried to pull up on the handle again, but it wouldn't budge, frustratingly enough. She didn't even know how to use it once she got it out. What was she doing wrong? Cowering next to a gun wasn't the same as pointing it at an attacker as a threat.

"Jonathan, please wake up. How do I get your gun out? Please, Jonathan. Please help me. I love you. I'm so sorry about before. Please, baby. Of course I know you would never hurt me. You're the best thing in my life. Emma and I love you. Please wake up."

"I'm going to kill you!" Andy growled from the bedroom doorway. She turned to look over her shoulder, and he was there, looming, about to strike.

She screamed and tried to slip out of his reach, but she felt his hand clamp on her ankle. She was dragged three feet away from Jonathan in one pull and back into the bedroom. Flipping over, to Andy's obvious surprise, Grace kicked him in the head twice rapidly and screamed like a banshee. He let go of her ankle and put his hands to his head. He rested on his knees, and she hoped his balls were throbbing all the way into his chest.

"You bitch! Don't you know it's useless to fight me!"

"I'm not the stupid weak teenage girl this time, asshole!"

"I'll kill you slowly for this when I get you."

"Bring it on, you bastard. I've waited a long time to take out my frustrations on a worthy opponent." Grace stood up, hands out to her sides, ready to react. She backed through the door back into the living room glancing at a still unmoving Jonathan on her way by.

Andy managed to get to his feet, swaying. He came through the bedroom door with a murderous look. She hoped it paled in comparison to the one she sent him in return.

"I'll kill our brat next. With my unwanted progeny out of the way, the DNA evidence will be useless. I'll be free to spread my passion to all women."

Grace rushed him. It was stupid, she realized. She should have found a large, heavy object to bash him with, but he threatened Emma and she lost control. She placed her hands to his throat squeezing with all her might in an effort to grab his windpipe and yank it out of his neck. He wrapped his hand around her hair and jerked. He wrapped his hand around her throat and flicked her away from his body as if she were no more threatening than a fly. She still scratched at his neck.

"Prepared to be fucked..."

Boom! The sound made Grace release her finger hold and fall to the floor. Andy retreated a step.

Boom, boom, boom. The sound of a wickedly powerful gun fired and Andy fell to the ground at her feet. She scooted backwards away from him before turning to see Jon, smoking gun in hand.

"Grace," he croaked out once, before his arm dropped and he passed out again.

Bang! Grace turned to the new loud noise bursting in the direction of the front door. Brutal and several lawmen barged through the entrance. Tears of surprise sprang forth.

"He's hurt," she said simply and lay down on Jonathan's back sobbing. Grateful for being rescued, her tear wouldn't stop.

"Damn it. We need a medic in here," she heard from above her. It was Elliott, Jon's boss.

"Are you hurt, Grace?" Brutal said in a low voice, trying to extract her from her husband's prone form so the medic could work on him.

"I'm fine," she said, even as tears of relief slipped down her face. Lawmen streamed inside, trampling through the center of the house.

Grace looked through the bedroom door and saw the medication and injector on the floor at the edge of the bed, where she had dropped it sometime during the fray with Andy. No one else tromping around seemed to notice, but she couldn't take her eyes off it.

"Brutal?"

"Yeah."

"Look." She directed her gaze to the problem she knew no one else present should know about. She kept staring at it until she heard him say, "I see it. I'll take care of it."

"Thank you."

Brutal sauntered into the bedroom and, out of sight of any of the lawmen milling around the house, pocketed the medication and injector. He grabbed her purse, which still rested on the bed, and returned to her side.

"Why don't I take you to my house for tonight? Maybe Emma will turn up soon."

"What?" She turned questioningly, then got his reference to Emma 'supposedly' being missing. "Oh, right. Emma will turn up. I'm sure she wouldn't go far."

"Are you ready to make a statement, Mrs. Brent?" Elliott asked, standing up from examining Andy Nelson's dead body.

"Can't it wait until later? Jesus, hasn't she gone through enough?" Brutal asked angrily.

Elliott ignored him focusing on Grace. "We already know Andy cut the power to the house before he broke in through the back door to the kitchen." Elliott paused and stared at Grace with raised eyebrows as if he expected her to continue the story.

"He knocked out Jonathan and attacked me. I fought him off until Jonathan woke up and shot him."

Brutal flashed his new license to escort Grace around as Jon's blood relative. "Home invasion gone bad. I like it. Can I take Grace away from this now?"

"No." Elliott crossed his arms and shot Brutal a look of attitude. "I need details. What happened after the lights went out, Mrs. Brent?"

Grace took a deep breath and the coppery smell of blood came with it. She shuddered at the scent, but responded in a trembling voice, "The power came back on suddenly. Jon and I were in the bathroom...um...talking...and, um...getting ready to go look for Emma."

"How did the lights come back on?" Elliott's eyes squinted in puzzlement. Grace shrugged.

"Jon has a backup generator system built into his house. It kicks on in a matter of seconds after the power is cut." Brutal supplied this since Grace had no idea why the lights came back on. She'd been distracted by her husband's eyes glowing in the dark.

"Right," Elliott said and then added, "Did you witness Andy bashing your husband in the head?"

"No. But I didn't see anyone else in the house, and Andy was carrying the pipe, which was dripping with blood. Plus he admitted it right before he told me his plans to rape me and kill my daughter."

"He threatened you?"

"He wanted to pick up where we left off the night Emma was conceived. He said my parents interrupted our 'fuck party.' He told me he planned to find Emma and get rid of her so his DNA would no longer be evidence of his crime."

Elliott grunted quietly at her profanity while she spoke. She wasn't sure whether he was offended or not, but she silently dared him to call her on it. The Tiberius Group felt it wasn't ladylike for a woman to curse, and so there was a law in place against the offense.

Brutal smiled when she said it. She guessed he didn't care if she used foul language.

"Surely you don't need any more than that," Brutal said to Elliott and then grabbed Grace's upper arm as if he were beyond ready to guide her away from the carnage around them. Elliott didn't stop him.

"How did you know to come here?" Grace asked Brutal.

"Jon asked me to follow Andy after he was released. He visited Magistrate Silas at his home first in order to get his ankle monitor removed. According to the magistrate's mother, who witnessed the entire thing, Magistrate Silas refused his demand and Andy pulled out a knife and killed him. By the time I arrived and got out of my car, Andy ran out of the Magistrate's house covered in blood dragging an elderly woman in his wake.

"When I ran towards him he let her go and hopped in a waiting vehicle. I called Elliott who checked the ankle monitor location as being on it's way to Jon's home address. I came here as fast as I could."

The medics had transferred Jonathan to a mobile carrier ready for transport to the nearest medical facility.

"Grace." She heard the weak voice of her husband as he passed by on the stretcher. She turned to walk alongside the carrier, dismissing everyone but Jonathan. She made the medics halt the carrier, she then bent over and kissed Jon on the mouth. He moaned against her lips and cracked a smile.

"I love you and I already miss you. So hurry up and get better. Emma and I will be waiting for you at your sister's house."

"I love you too. Where did you learn the throat grip you had Andy in before I shot him?

"Brutal taught me a couple of self-defense moves while you were away the last time. Your sister taught me the infamous groin kick she learned from you, as well."

"Good for her. I'll see you soon."

Elliott stood behind her shamelessly listening in on their private chat.

"There will be an inquiry once you're well enough to face it, but the preliminary is fairly routine. Did you see him?" Elliott asked Jon.

"Yep, just in time to get bashed in the head. When I woke up, he had his hands around Grace's throat. I drew on him and fired once in the air. When he released her and she fell out of the target zone, I fired three more times into his chest."

"Clearly this tragedy was the result of a home invasion and was a clean kill since you were protecting your loved one. It should be an open-and-shut case." Elliott snapped his small hand-held computer notebook shut and pocketed it. Smiling, he finally walked away.

Brutal approached the two of them and flashed Jon a grin. "God, you're such a big baby. I can tell from here it's just a scratch."

"Thanks," was all Jon said before the two medics started moving the carrier again.

* * * *

"...So anyway, when I couldn't get your gun out easily, he managed to grab my ankle and pull me back. I kicked him in the head until he released me. When he threatened Emma, I lost it and grabbed his throat. It was stupid, I know, but I was mad." Grace sat next to Jon's bed at the hospital, explaining what had happened after he'd gotten clocked. Once the doctor arrived, he would be released. He couldn't wait to get home.

"You don't have a strap lock on your holster, do you?" Brutal asked. He'd accompanied Grace to the medical center while Hannah watched over Emma, who'd been 'miraculously discovered' in their attic crawl space the day before.

Jon smiled. "No, I have a biometric handle. It won't come out of the holster unless it's my palm on the handle. It also applies to the firing mechanism. I'm the only one who can shoot it. I had that installed after my return from your mining colony a couple years back. I hate when unauthorized people grab my gun."

"You are such a sissy. I only grabbed your damned gun one time, years ago on a moon of Mars, in order to threaten another prick, Eric Vander. Remember how he was threatening Hannah? I was completely justified."

"Maybe, but I hate grabby criminals. My biometric handle is a safety device. You should get one."

Brutal laughed heartily. "I already have one. And before you ask...yes, it was already on the gun you pressed to my head back at the mining room bar. I was never in any danger."

"You mean your life wasn't threatened back then? Damn it."

"Is your manly lawman pride wounded?" Brutal smirked.

"No." Jon glanced at Grace once. "And even if it were, I have a wife to soothe me."

The doctor arrived to do Jon's final medical check for release. Grace excused herself to wait outside the hospital room. Brutal edged away from his bed, but Jon noticed he was milling around the door, waiting until the doctor finished. He looked as if he had something on his mind.

When the doctor exited the hospital room to the hallway to speak to Grace about his care, Brutal crossed his arms and sidled up close to Jon's hospital bed. He glanced at the open door and lowered his voice. "Something's in the wind. It's something you should know about."

"What?" Jon also glanced at the open door, scrunching his eyes in puzzlement.

Brutal pierced Jon with a riveting gaze. "Rebellion."

"You have my undivided attention. What are you talking about?"

Brutal lowered his voice further. "There is a rumor going around in certain secret circles that there's a contract murder out targeting top officials in the Tiberius Group. I usually ignore gossip, but the Tiberius Group is taking it seriously. They're scared shitless."

"Who set it up?"

Brutal shrugged. "I don't know. They don't know either, which is why they're worried."

"It's got to be someone with money. There are lots of folks hiding around the world waiting for an opportunity to come back if the Tiberius

Group is overthrown. It's bound to happen sooner or later."

"Killing key leaders would certainly weaken their regime." Brutal smiled without mirth and added, "I find it ironic since that's what the Tiberius Group did for years before they took over."

"What's that?"

Brutal sighed as if he should already understand the world at large. Jon wanted to hear him say out loud what he knew, or what he thought he knew.

"The Tiberius Group, formerly Tiberius Security, spent a decade strategizing their take over. It seemed fast, but it wasn't. For years they carefully eliminated people they knew would oppose them even as they set up good-ole-boys in key power positions across the nation. After a decade of lining up their ducks, they swooped in and took over with little opposition."

"I never knew you were such a political analyst, Brutal."

"I wasn't until I made lots of money in mining."

Jon lifted his brows in surprise as he stared Brutal down. "Why are you telling me this?"

Again Brutal broke his intense gaze to check the door. The doctor and Grace still talked, not paying them any attention. Brutal's paranoia was palpable and starting to rub off on Jon.

Leaning closer, Brutal said, "You need to pick a side. One you plan to defend. If this comes to pass, it'll mean out-and-out war."

Jon had also heard rumors, but Brutal's inside knowledge surprised him. "Maybe I already have."

"What side, Jon? I want to know."

"You should already know."

"Enlighten me. I don't want to assume."

Jon sighed deeply. "I'm a lawman. I live my life protecting people under the law. If the laws change, I'll defend the new laws put in place even if they fail to include the Tiberius way of life."

"What if the Tiberius Group sends you into war? What side will you be on then? Will you fight for them?"

"You know better. I'll choose my family, of course, even if it includes my grumpy blood brother."

Brutal smiled and nodded. "Good. I'd hate for us to be on opposing sides."

"Why? Because you know I'd kick your ass?"

"No, because I don't have any siblings of my own, and I'd hate to permanently injure *my* shiny new blood brother."

Jon rolled his eyes but smiled. "Thanks for the warning. I'll keep my eyes and ears open for developments."

"I have travel contingencies in place for all of us if it becomes unsafe. So do Matt and Sophie."

Jon's mind raced at the possibilities. "Good. Thanks for the information."

Brutal nodded. "One other thing."

"Now what?"

"I got your sister pregnant." Brutal took a large step back from his bed and grinned. "She's due in six months."

Jon inhaled a deep breath as if trying to find strength. "Good thing you already married her, or I'd be testing my biometric-handled gun on you again."

Brutal rolled his eyes. "Whatever."

Grace walked into the room, interrupting any further posturing between them. He would never admit it out loud, but he was happy for Hannah and Brutal.

Besides, Uncle Jon had a nice ring to it.

Epilogue

One year later

"How can you be pregnant?" Jon tried to digest the visual evidence of the positive home pregnancy test he held. The idea of a child had never occurred to him.

"I don't know. The doctor who delivered Emma said I was messed up from giving birth so young. He told my parents Emma was the only child I would ever have. That's the only reason they let me keep her instead of giving her up for adoption." She glanced back at the test and squinted her eyes as if puzzled.

"Sterility is a temporary side effect of Zanthacorth, you know?"

"But you don't take it any more." Grace smiled, as if remembering why he didn't take it any longer. They had a phenomenal sex life instead.

"Which is probably why you're pregnant. We don't often miss any opportunities, do we?"

Grace giggled. "No, we don't." The smile slid from her face and she asked, "Are you upset?"

"Of course not. Do you feel okay?" Jon placed the test stick on the bathroom counter and took Grace into his arms for a hug.

"So far." Her muffled voice came from the area of his chest.

The recent addition of Jon's nephew and nieces drifted into his mind. "Emma will have a new baby in her own house to play with instead of visiting Hannah's baby boy or Sophie's twin girls."

"What do you think Elliott will say?"

"Threats will ensue as usual, but I don't care. It might be all right anyway. His new girlfriend is calming him down some."

Grace giggled again. "Hard to believe Elliott would ever be calm."

"It's a miracle among anyone who knows him." Jon squeezed her again. His life was damn near perfect.

"Maybe we'll have a boy. Would that make you happy?"

"I don't care if it's a boy or girl. I just want us to be safe and happy." Jon squeezed her tighter. "I love you, Grace."

"I love you, too, Jon."

THE LAWMAN'S WIFE

The Wives Tales 3

THE END

WWW.LARASANTIAGO.COM

Other books by Lara Santiago at

www.sirenpublishing.com/larasantiago

ELECTRONIC FORMAT

What would a woman do, and how far would she willingly travel, to love a man who made her climax with his chocolate-flavored kiss?

In *Just a Kiss*, Gabrielle travels to Tiburon unwillingly with Keller after an improper kiss. Will she be forced to reside on a planet of warrior aliens who hate her?

In *Just One Embrace*, Ellie travels to Tiburon willingly to be with Crag. When another female claims their top military commander, will Ellie be considered a worthy life-partner or will she lose Crag forever?

PRINT COLLECTION NOW AVAILABLE

The Tiburon Duet
Just a Kiss : Just One Embrace

"Santiago blends sci-fi and steamy erotica in this two-book collection. The stories will captivate readers looking for something imaginative and different. Cleverly written dialogue brings the characters to life in this entertaining read, and the alpha aliens are out of this world.

4 Stars—Romantic Times BOOKreviews Magazine

Siren Publishing, Inc.
www.SirenPublishing.com

Printed in the United States
149996LV00001BA/47/A

9 781933 563282